BRIDAL JEOPARDY

BY
REBECCA YORK

(RUTH GLICK WRITING AS REBECCA YORK)

MILLS & BOON

Published in Great Britain 2014
by Mills & Boon, an imprint of Harlequin (UK) Limited,
Eton House, 18-24 Paradise Road, Richmond, Surrey, TW9 1SR

© 2014 Ruth Glick

ISBN: 978 0 263 91353 8

46-0314

Harlequin (UK) Limited's policy is to use papers that are natural, renewable and recyclable products and made from wood grown in sustainable forests. The logging and manufacturing processes conform to the legal environmental regulations of the country of origin.

Printed and bound in Spain
by Blackprint CPI, Barcelona

Award-winning, *USA TODAY* bestselling novelist Ruth Glick, who writes as **Rebecca York**, is the author of more than one hundred books, including her popular 43 Light Street series for the Mills & Boon® Intrigue line. Ruth says she has the best job in the world. Not only does she get paid for telling stories, she's also an author of twelve cookbooks. Ruth and her husband, Norman, travel frequently, researching locales for her novels and searching out new dishes for her cookbooks.

Norman, who's always there for me

Prologue

The horror of that day had replayed over and over in Craig Branson's mind. What if he, Mom, Dad and Sam had gone to a different restaurant? What if they'd stayed home and ordered in? Life as he knew it would have continued on the same happy track.

But Dad had just brought in a big ad buy at the local TV station where he was promotions manager, and he'd been in the mood to celebrate his hard work.

"Where should we go to dinner?" he'd asked his twin sons, two dark-haired, dark-eyed boys only a few people could tell apart.

Craig and Sam were identical twins, born when a single egg had split in their mother's womb. Twins were supposed to be close, but there was more between these two eight-year-olds than anyone else knew. There was a hidden bond and a fierce love born of the connection they could never explain to anyone else.

They'd looked at each other and begun a silent conversation about the merits of various choices.

Then Sam had spoken for the two of them. He'd asked to go to Venario's, an Italian restaurant. If they ate at Venario's, they could order an extra pizza and have it for breakfast the next morning.

Mom had protested that pizza was no kind of breakfast,

but Dad let the boys have their way. If it made his twins happy to bring home pizza, he was all for it, as long as they had a nice portion of chicken or veal for dinner.

That evening they'd sat across from each other at the square table topped by a snowy cloth, silently debating the merits of ground beef or ham on their take-home pizza. Almost as soon as they'd come home from the hospital, they'd been able to read each other's thoughts, a skill they instinctively kept hidden from the world. Mom suspected, but she had never asked them about it because the idea was too outlandish for her to wrap her brain around. She was a down-to-earth woman who wanted her sons to be strong and independent, even when their inclination was to present a united front.

At the next table, a group of men was talking loudly; their voices annoyed Mom and Dad, but they didn't interfere with the Branson boys' happy conversation.

That was another what-if that had tortured Craig for the twenty-two years since that night when his whole world had been shattered.

What if he and Sam hadn't been so focused on each other? What if they'd been paying more attention to their surroundings?

Could Craig have saved Sam's life?

He didn't know because it all had happened so fast.

The door burst open, and two men had charged into the restaurant with guns drawn, already shooting as they ran. The guys at the next table hardly had time to react. One of them tried to stand and went down in a hail of bullets. Another one collapsed in his chair. And the third fell to the side, hitting Mom as she screamed in horror.

People all over the confined space were crying out and hitting the floor. But the chaos around Craig had hardly registered. His total attention was focused on Sam, who had been sitting closer to the scene of disaster.

He'd made a strangled sound and had fallen forward, his head hitting the table as blood spread across the crisp white cloth. His chest had been a mass of pain that Craig felt as though it were his own body on fire.

He'd leaped out of his seat, charging around the table to his brother's side, slipping from his father's grasp as he reached for Sam, struggling to maintain the fading connection between them. Panic rose inside him, and he'd clutched at his brother with his hand and with his mind.

Sam, don't leave me.

Craig?

Sam. I can't hear you, Sam.

I...can't...

Those were his last memories of his brother. He had started screaming then, his cries drowning out the sound of a siren approaching.

His father's arms had folded him close, protecting him from harm. But the harm was already done.

Sam was gone, vanished as though he had never been—leaving an aching gap in Craig's soul.

Despair and anger raged inside the boy who lived. But even at the age of eight, Craig knew that he would find out who had killed his brother and avenge his death.

Chapter One

The light from the computer screen gave a harsh cast to Craig Branson's angular features, yet he couldn't conceal the feeling of elation surging inside himself.

He'd only been eight when his twin brother had been cruelly ripped away from him, but on that terrible day, he'd vowed that he would find the killers and bring them to justice. Now, finally, he had a lead on one of the shooters in a gangland assassination twenty-two years ago.

The restaurant where crime boss Jackie Montana and two of his men had been gunned down had been full of witnesses. Many of the patrons had identified the killers from their mug shots. They were two hired hit men named Joe Lipton and Arthur Polaski who had taken jobs all over the U.S.

Although the cops knew the assassins' names, the men fled the scene and disappeared from the face of the earth. Now Craig knew why.

Unable to sit still, he stood and strode out of his office, then paced into the hall of the brick ranch house where he'd lived in Bethesda, Maryland, for the past few years.

It was in an upscale neighborhood just outside the nation's capital, the perfect place for the career he'd started planning even before Sam's funeral. He would make sure he was tough enough, smart enough and well trained enough to find his brother's killers. To that end he'd graduated from college at George Washington University, then enlisted in the army and gone to officer-candidate school right after basic training. From there he got his first choice of assignments, the military intelligence service. After learning everything he could about investigative techniques, he returned to civilian life and started his own detective agency.

When his dad died nine months after Mom, he inherited all the money he'd ever need—if you considered his unassuming lifestyle. He had no family. No wife and children, because he knew he was lacking something that most people took for granted—the ability to connect with others on a deep, personal level. He craved those things with a fierce sense of loss because he'd had them with Sam. When his brother had been ripped from him, his anchor to the human race had been severed.

Although that was a pretty dramatic way to put it, he understood the concept perfectly. Other people formed close friendships and loving relationships. He'd never been able to manage either, although he thought he faked it pretty well. He had friends. He'd had physically satisfying affairs with women, but he had always known that marrying one of them would mean cheating her out of the warmth and closeness she deserved.

Failing that, he'd focused on his work, partly because it was intensely rewarding to put bad guys away and partly because it was a means to an end.

He *would* find who had killed his brother, and he *would* make sure they would pay for what they had done.

He'd traveled around the U.S., and he maintained contacts with police departments all over the country. One of those contacts had just paid off big-time.

He walked back to his desk, activated the printer and

made a copy of the report that had come in from a lieutenant named Ike Broussard in the New Orleans P.D. According to the detective, the body of one of the men who
had shot up that restaurant, Arthur Polaski, had just turned
up dead on private property outside the city. The local police had identified him by dental records, and the murder
weapon was with him.

A very neat package. Maybe too neat.

Craig skimmed the report again. Polaski was beyond his
reach, but that didn't mean there would be no justice for
Sam. The hit man hadn't been operating on his own. Every
indication was that he'd been working for a local New Orleans bigwig named John Reynard.

As a boy, Craig had focused on bringing Polaski and
Lipton to justice. But as he'd matured, he'd come to understand that the shooters were just hired thugs working for
someone who wanted a rival crime boss dead. Now Polaski
had led Craig to John Reynard.

Craig worked into the evening, collecting information on
his quarry. Finally, when he saw that it was almost ten, he
got up and stretched, then fixed himself a ham-and-cheese
sandwich, which he took back to the computer, along with
a bottle of beer. One advantage of living alone was that he
didn't have to stick to regular meal times, eat at the table or
stop work while he fueled up. Once he knew about Reynard,
it was easy to find a boatload of information on the man. He
was in his early sixties and owned an import-export business in New Orleans, probably a front for drug smuggling.
But the cops apparently didn't look into his company too
carefully, undoubtedly because Reynard was very generous
with his bribes and also contributed significant amounts to
local charities. Public record presented him as an upstanding citizen, although it was interesting that two of his former wives had died while married to him.

Craig took a swallow of beer as he came to an intriguing piece of information. Reynard was about to tie the knot again. In the society pages of the *Times-Picayune,* there were pictures of him with his bride-to-be at several charity events. She was a very lovely blonde woman named Stephanie Swift who looked to be half the age of the man she was going to marry.

Craig shook his head. He could see why Reynard was attracted to the woman. But what did she see in him?

As Craig studied her wide-set eyes, her narrow nose, her nicely shaped lips and the blond hair that fell in waves to her shoulders, he felt an unexpected jolt of awareness. Something about her drew him, and he struggled to dismiss the feeling of attraction to her. He didn't want to like her. What kind of a woman would marry a lowlife like Reynard? Could it be that she was too stupid or unaware to understand what kind of man her fiancé was? Or maybe she was attracted to his money, and she didn't care what the man was really like.

He made a snorting sound, then warned himself to stay objective. That usually wasn't a problem for him, but apparently it was with Ms. Swift, and letting himself feel anything for her would be a big mistake.

With another shake of his head, he clicked away from a smiling picture of her with Reynard and went back to her dossier. Apparently she came from a family that had been prominent in the city. But the Swifts must have fallen on hard times because now she spent her days in the dress shop that she owned in the French Quarter.

Well, she'd be able to give up that business and get back to her society lifestyle once she married Reynard.

But maybe in the meantime she'd be useful to Craig. What if he got to know her before he made a move on Reynard? Yes, that might be the way to go.

THE BELL OVER the shop door jingled, and Stephanie Swift looked up. It was a delivery man, carrying a long cardboard box. When she saw the logo on the package, she stiffened, but she kept her voice pleasant as she spoke to the deliveryman.

"Thanks so much."

He nodded to her as he set the package down on the counter and left her Royal Street shop.

Before the bell stopped jingling again, her assistant, Claire Dupree, came out of the back room, where she'd been unpacking merchandise that had arrived from New York that morning. Claire was a pretty, dark-haired young woman who wanted to get into fashion, and she'd offered to work for Stephanie at minimum wage for the chance to learn the business. She was a quick study, and Stephanie had come to rely on her.

"You've been expecting your wedding dress. Is that it?" she asked.

"Yes."

Claire eyed the box. "I'm dying to see it."

"We'll open it in the back room," Stephanie answered, struggling to sound enthusiastic. She'd known all along that John Reynard was the wrong man for her. Or she'd known that perhaps there *was* no right man, given the way she failed to connect with anyone on a truly intimate level. But she'd held out hope for…something more.

Then fate had overtaken her hopes.

Still, she wasn't going to let on to her assistant that she had doubts about her upcoming wedding. She was too private a person to talk about her secret worries. And she couldn't shake the nagging impression that it might be dangerous to reveal her state of mind to anyone. Besides, even if she weren't marrying John Reynard out of love, maybe it would turn out okay.

That was what she told herself, even when she feared she was heading for disaster. Too bad she was stuck with the bargain she'd made.

"Should I open the box?" Claire called from the next room.

"I'll be right there," she answered, then took a couple of deep breaths as she looked around the shop that had been the major focus of her life for the past two years. It was feminine and nicely decorated, a showplace where women could relax while they browsed the dresses and evening outfits that Stephanie imported from designers on the East Coast and Europe.

She'd always dressed well and loved fashion, but her interest morphed from an avocation into a business when her father had given her the bad news about his gambling debts.

She'd wanted to scream at him, but she hadn't bothered raging about his lack of regard for anyone but himself. The criticism would just roll off his back like rain off a yellow slicker.

Instead, she'd taken her sense of style and the money that her mother had left her and bought a small shop in the French Quarter, a shop that had done well until a downturn in the city's business cycle had put her in jeopardy.

She stepped into the back room and found Claire talking on her cell phone. When she saw Stephanie, she clicked off at once.

"Sorry. I was just checking in with Mom."

"Sure," Stephanie answered, distracted. She knew that Claire's mother was living in a nursing home and that her daughter spoke to her frequently.

Taking a pair of scissors, she began to carefully open the dress box. The top came off, revealing layers of tissue paper. Beneath them was an ivory-colored sleeveless gown decorated with seed pearls and delicate lace. She'd seen it at a wedding outlet in New York and had used her professional capacity to order it at the wholesale price.

"Beautiful," Claire breathed as she touched the delicate silk fabric.

"Yes."

"Why don't you try it on? I can help you with the buttons up the back."

"Not now."

Stephanie slipped the dress onto a hanger, then turned away to put it on the rack in back of her, where it dangled like a headless hanging victim.

She winced, wishing she hadn't thought of that image.

Of course, that wasn't the only thing she wished. What if she'd never met John Reynard? What if her shop hadn't taken that downturn? What if she met a man who could connect with her in ways that she could only imagine?

She made a disgusted sound. As if that was going to happen.

"What?" Claire asked.

"Nothing. I'm not really feeling well. Do you mind if I get out of here for a few hours?"

Claire gave her a sympathetic look. "Oh, no. You've got that reception with John this evening."

Stephanie felt a wave of anxiety sweep over her. She'd put the reception out of her mind, but now she knew what had been making her feel unsettled—even before the dress had arrived. "Lord, I forgot all about that."

"You'd better go home and rest. You don't want to disappoint him."

"Right." Once again, she wished that she'd never met John Reynard. Wished that he hadn't listened to her dad's sob story, then stepped in to pay her debts—and Dad's. But she'd taken his money because her father had begged her to let John Reynard handle their problems. And at the time, it had seemed the only way out. She'd been willing to let her shop go under. She could always find a job with someone else, but that wouldn't work out so well for Dad. He'd lose the house—his last tie to the luxurious past that the family had enjoyed. And she'd known deep down that would kill him.

If she were the cause of that, her guilt would be too great for her to bear. Which was the irony of this situation. She'd never really felt close to her parents, yet she was compelled to make sure her father ended his days in the manner to which he was accustomed. Probably because she'd never felt like a dutiful daughter—and Dad had made sure she understood that.

Claire's voice broke into her troubled thoughts.

"Don't worry about a thing. I'll take care of it."

"Thanks." She thought for a moment. "If Mrs. Arlington calls to ask about her ball gown, tell her it hasn't come in yet."

"Of course. Don't trouble yourself about it," Claire repeated.

Stephanie nodded, wishing she could really relax and stop worrying about her future.

Chapter Two

After three days in New Orleans, Craig was getting a feel for the city and the power base that ran it. The Big Easy was so different from any other American urban area that it might as well have been in a foreign country. The atmosphere was hot and sultry. The houses were painted bright colors. The landscape was almost tropical, and the people exuded a laid-back attitude that belied the hard times that Hurricane Katrina had caused.

He'd avoided his contact with the police department because he was in the city under an assumed name—Craig Brady. Unlike Craig Branson, Brady had inherited considerable wealth and lived off his investments. The persona was one he'd established several years ago when he'd been hired to take down a finance guy who was using a Ponzi scheme to line his own pockets. Craig had posed as an investor ripe for the picking and nailed the guy.

The Brady persona made a good cover for investigating John Reynard. But so far Craig had stayed away from the man. He wanted to establish himself as being in the city for profit and fun. To that end he'd gone prowling around, sampling the food, the jazz and the strip clubs along Bourbon Street.

He'd also found a high-stakes poker game at a private gentleman's club, where he could pick up some money and also some information. The minimum bet was fifty dollars, but that had been of little risk to Craig. He might not be good at intimate relationships, but he was excellent at reading people, and he used that skill to win a couple of sizable pots.

Then he'd allowed himself to lose half of it back, which put the men around the table in a friendlier mood than when he'd been raking in the chips.

"So where do you meet high-class women?" he'd asked as he and his new friends helped themselves to the club's bourbon.

"The United Hospital Fund is holding a charity event at Oak Lane Plantation, out along the river."

"Sounds interesting," he answered

"Tickets are a thousand clams a pop."

"Well, it's for a good cause," Craig allowed. "And you're saying that some of the ladies are single?"

"The young gals looking for husbands come out in droves."

He'd found out where to buy a ticket and purchased one, pretty sure from his research that John Reynard would be there.

After buying the ticket, he'd gone to one of the rental shops in town and gotten a tuxedo. Not his usual attire, he thought as he stood in front of the mirror, adjusting his bow tie. But he guessed he'd do.

His hand shook for a moment, and he pressed his palm against his thigh, annoyed at his unusual reaction. It came from being so close to Sam's killer, he told himself, but he wasn't entirely sure he believed it.

He couldn't contain the mixture of anticipation and nerves racing through him. He'd been waiting a long time to confront the man who had been responsible for his brother's death, and now the meeting was almost here.

Well, *confrontation* wasn't exactly the right word. He was going to have a look at John Reynard and start planning his attack on the man. After all these years, there was no rush. Reynard wasn't going anywhere. And neither was his beautiful fiancée. As Craig thought of Stephanie Swift, anticipation tightened his gut.

Stephanie Swift was not the main event, but she could be a means to an end, he told himself.

Craig walked to the parking lot and picked up his rental car, then headed out of town to Oak Lane Plantation.

The mansion house was ablaze with lights when he arrived, and he found a space among the Cadillacs, BMWs and Mercedes that dominated the parking area.

Inside he accepted a flute of champagne from a waiter hovering near the door because he didn't want to look out of place among the men and women enjoying themselves at this upscale gathering.

The mansion, which was often rented out for private functions, was lavishly furnished with period tables and chests interspersed with more modern chairs and sofas and Oriental rugs on the polished pine floorboards.

He wandered from the front hall to the other rooms on the main floor, watching the guests talking, drinking and eating. As promised, some of the ladies were young, and many gave him speculative looks, although he didn't stop to talk to any of them.

But he had his story ready if needed.

He was from out of town and considering settling in the city, and he thought this gathering would be an excellent introduction to the local social life. He'd act as if he was looking for new investments—and open to suggestions from the New Orleans financial elite.

He made his way slowly through the crowd and finally spotted John Reynard on the veranda. He was talking with a group of men and women who all seemed to know one another. And Stephanie Swift was at his side.

Craig had been taken with her picture. He hadn't been prepared for the reality of the woman. His breath caught as he looked at her from the doorway leading outside. She was stunning in an emerald-green gown that perfectly set off her blond beauty.

She must have known he was staring at her because she looked up, and he would have sworn she had the same reaction to him that he was having to her. Her breath hitched, and she went absolutely still.

Apparently Reynard sensed something. Bending close to her, he spoke in a low voice. From twenty feet away, Craig couldn't catch the words, but he understood the proprietary way the man spoke. This woman was his property.

She must have said something reassuring, because Reynard went back to his previous conversation. But the moment had been telling. From Stephanie's reaction, Craig knew that she understood her place in her fiancé's world.

He lingered in the doorway and took a small sip of his champagne, thinking that he'd like to approach the couple, but he wasn't going to press his luck. After a long moment, he turned away and went in search of the buffet table. He'd paid a lot of money to enjoy this reception, and he might as well get a decent meal out of it.

STEPHANIE WATCHED the broad shoulders of the man who had been staring at John—and her. She'd noticed him right away, noticed how his tuxedo accentuated his rugged good looks. She knew she had never seen him before. Who was he, and what was he doing here? For a moment he'd looked interested in John, then he'd switched his attention to her, and she'd felt as if there was an invisible wire connecting the two of them, drawing them to each other.

She hoped John hadn't caught the intensity of her interest in the man because she knew he was jealous of any interactions she had with other guys. John had staked his claim on her, and she fully understood that playing any role but the one she'd been assigned was dangerous. Before she'd agreed to the marriage, her suitor had done his best to charm her, and she'd tried to convince herself that marriage to him wouldn't be so bad. But once he'd known she was his, there had been subtle changes. He didn't outright say that he owned her, but she got that message.

"Excuse me for a moment," she murmured.

"Where are you going?" her companion asked.

"To powder my nose."

He nodded, and she moved back through the mansion toward the grand staircase. The ladies' room was on the second floor, and she was glad to escape from John and the society types who populated the party.

As she walked through the main floor, she scanned the crowd and was relieved and disappointed not to see the mysterious stranger. He couldn't have just come in for a few minutes and left. Not at the price he'd paid for the ticket to this event.

Then she felt the hairs on the back of her neck prickle and she turned quickly. There he was, in the corner, his gaze fixed on her again.

In that instant, the other people in the room seemed to vanish. Or maybe it was more accurate to say that they had turned into shadows, because the man in the corner was the only distinct thing she could see. She fought for breath, fought for sanity if she was honest about it.

What are you doing to me? she asked, the question never leaving her lips because she spoke only in her mind. Still, she had the weird feeling that he could hear her, although he gave her no answer.

She thought of crossing the room and...touching him. That idea leaped into her mind, and she wondered where it had come from. Touch a stranger? Why?

Yet the compulsion was so strong that she started toward him. Then she stopped after two steps and clenched her fists.

He was standing with the same rigidity, and she knew that at any moment he would come striding toward her. He would reach out and put his hand on her arm, and then what?

Everything would change.

She didn't know what that meant, and she didn't want to find out. No, that was a lie. She couldn't afford the luxury of finding out.

The temptation was so overwhelming that she had to force herself to turn away and hurry up the stairs. With a sigh of relief, she closed the ladies' room door behind her, putting a barrier between herself and the man who had drawn her like no other.

Marge LaFort glanced up from where she sat at one of the dressing-table stools. "Is something wrong?"

"No," she lied.

"You look like..."

"Like what?" she demanded as the other woman's voice trailed off.

Marge shrugged. "I'm not sure. Is that handsome fiancé of yours giving you a hard time?"

"No. Of course not," Stephanie denied. In fact, she had forgotten all about John Reynard when she'd been caught in the stranger's web. Or was he caught in hers? She didn't know which.

She walked through the dressing area and into the bathroom, where she used the facilities, not because she needed to but because it would seem strange to simply come here and take refuge.

To her relief, when she emerged, Marge was gone. Or was that good? What if Marge went straight down to talk to John?

Stephanie dragged in a breath and let it out, wishing that she didn't imagine every person in the mansion as a spy for John Reynard, yet she knew that he did have a network of informants—or at least people who were anxious to stay on the good side of such a powerful man by feeding him information about people and events he might think important.

For example, she knew there were some new customers who had come to her shop to check out John Reynard's fiancée. And some of them were probably reporting back to him, much as she hated to think it. But she supposed she'd have to live with that, and maybe he'd trust her more when they were married.

She stayed at the dressing table for several more minutes, fussing with her hair, wondering whom she was hiding from—the dark-haired man or her intended. When she finally emerged and came downstairs, she didn't see the stranger. That was a relief. Now she only had to deal with John.

MEN WERE WATCHING HIM, Craig realized as he filled a plate with boudin balls, Cajun rice and crawfish étouffée. Tough-looking types who didn't exactly fit in with the other guests at this fancy event. Since they were dividing their attention between Reynard and Craig, he had to assume that they were the other man's bodyguards. Apparently Craig had caught Reynard's attention. Or perhaps Reynard had noticed the silent exchange when Craig and Stephanie had made eye contact. At any event, he decided it would be best to leave.

After taking a few bites, he put down his plate on one of the trays set around the room for dirty dishes and made his way out of the house and into the parking area, half-expecting somebody to try to jump him. But apparently his leaving had the desired effect. He drove away and back to his upscale New Orleans B and B without incident.

But what was his next move?

He'd focused his research on John Reynard. Now he was going to find out everything he could about Stephanie Swift. He told himself he was doing his job. He told himself that digging into the woman's life would be the key to taking down Reynard, but he wasn't sure he was being honest about his motives. If he admitted he was obsessed with her, that would be more like the truth.

The feeling was a novelty for Craig. He'd enjoyed the company of women. He'd learned the art of pleasing them in bed. But none of them had drawn his interest the way Stephanie Swift had.

He had looked up details about her on the web, but that was too impersonal an approach. Switching his tactics, he decided to get a firsthand picture of her life.

The morning after the charity reception, he waited in his car outside her apartment on Decatur Street and discreetly followed her Honda sedan to a sprawling mansion in the Garden District. It was her father's house, he knew, and he drove around the corner and waited until she emerged about a half hour after she'd entered, a frown on her pretty features. Apparently her meeting with Dad hadn't gone so well.

Her next stop was her shop on Royal. When she went in, he walked past and took up a discreet position around the corner.

He thought of himself as good at surveillance, but he wondered if she knew he was following her. Not because a normal person would have caught on, but because there was something between them that he couldn't explain. He'd been prepared to dislike her. Instead, he'd been drawn to her when they'd seen each other at that charity reception, and she'd been as aware of him as he was of her.

That knowledge set up an unaccustomed buzzing inside him. He hadn't felt this way since…

Well, since he and Sam had played hide-and-seek. Only back then it had been a different kind of game. Most kids hid and hoped that the other person couldn't figure out where they had gone. With him and Sam, there was an extra element. One of them would hide, then try to break the connection between them—try to be as quiet as possible in his mind so that his brother would have no idea where he was.

Sam had been better at it than Craig, who hadn't been able to turn off his thoughts, and Sam had always found him. But why was he thinking of that *now?*

Two days after the charity reception, Stephanie was still feeling unsettled as she went through the rack of clothing on the left side of the shop, buttoning blouses, straightening straps and generally making the merchandise look tidy. She struggled to stay calm, but her heart was pounding. She couldn't shake the feeling that something was going to happen, and every so often, she glanced toward the window, wondering if she was going to see the dark-haired man with the broad shoulders who had stared at her in the plantation house. Well, it hadn't been just him. She'd stared back because there had been something about him that had compelled her interest. It wasn't simply the way his formal attire had set off his dark good looks. She'd felt a pull toward him that she couldn't explain, even to herself. A pull that excited her and made her nerves jump at the same time.

The bell over the door jingled, and she went rigid. As she turned, she thought she would see the man from the reception. Instead, two rough-looking guys came striding in as though they owned the place.

Both of them were wearing light-colored business suits that seemed out of place on anyone so tough-looking. One was short and completely bald—or he'd shaved off any remaining hair on his head. He was trying for a Yul Brynner effect, although his face was too ugly for a movie star—unless he was playing a Mafia heavy. The other guy was a couple of inches taller, with a wide mouth, bushy eyebrows and thick, wavy hair.

They both had big hands and beady, assessing eyes. Or perhaps the better word was *hungry*.

Neither one of them would inspire confidence in a dark alley at night. But here they were in her shop, and she was pretty sure that neither one of them had come to buy a dress for his girlfriend.

"Nice place you have here," the taller one said.

As they stood looking her over, her mouth turned so dry that she could barely speak, but she managed to say, "Can I help you?"

The spokesman answered. "That depends, sweetheart."

"On what?"

"On what you have to offer."

"Nothing," she heard herself say.

"We'll see."

She took a step back, wishing that Claire wasn't out on her lunch break. But what good would Claire do against these guys?

Maybe call 911 from the back room, if she'd been here.

But Stephanie was on her own, and she was sure that they already knew it. Wishing the counter were between her and the men, she took a step to the side. One of them kept pace with her while the other one stood by the door. She saw him turn, and she had the awful feeling that he was planning to lock the three of them in there.

Chapter Three

Before the thug could accomplish his purpose, the door burst open, and another man charged into the shop. She had a split second to see who it was. The darkly handsome stranger from the charity reception. The other night, he'd been in a tuxedo. Today he had on jeans and a dark T-shirt.

The man in the doorway reacted to the interruption by reaching into his coat, perhaps for a gun, but he never connected with whatever he was going to pull out. The stranger cracked him in the jaw with a large fist, then pushed him backward into the other man. They both went down in a tangle of arms and legs, pulling some of the clothing from the rack with them, but it wasn't going to be that easy to get rid of them.

The one on the bottom threw his partner to the side and pulled an automatic from his pocket. Stephanie reacted instinctively. She kicked out with her high-heeled shoe, catching the guy in his gun hand, making him howl in pain. She followed the kick by stamping down on the back of his hand, drawing a scream and sending the gun flying.

The bald one had scrambled up and launched himself at the stranger, who was prepared for the move. He stepped aside, letting baldy crash into the glass of the door. He made a strangled sound as he bounced back, then reached for the knob and flung the door open. He was outside and running down the block before Stephanie realized that the other man was on his feet and trying to get away as the rescuer made a grab for him. But the thug had the strength of desperation. He pushed the stranger against the wall, then leaped around him, charging out the door, following his partner down the block.

The man who had come to Stephanie's rescue pushed himself upright, determination in his eyes, and she was afraid he was going after the two men. She grabbed his hand to stop him, and everything changed.

In that moment of contact, the breath whooshed from her lungs, and she stood staring at him—as she had stared when they'd been standing across the room from each other at the plantation house. Only this was different. Last time there had been twenty feet of space between them. Now her hand gripped his, and somehow the physical connection had opened a gateway between them.

Images flooded into her mind. She saw a long-ago scene. Two little boys in a restaurant. She knew one of them was… Craig. His name was Craig. And the other one was Sam. And their minds were open to each other the way his mind was open to her at this moment.

The other boy was his mirror image. He must be his twin brother. There was a completeness to the two of them, a bond that made her sharply aware of all the unfulfilled longings that permeated her life.

She was just sinking into the long-ago scene when the door of the restaurant where the boys were sitting flew open, and gunmen charged in—like the men who had charged into her shop. Only these guys had assault rifles, and they started shooting.

She felt the seconds of fear. She felt the pain as Sam was hit. She felt Craig's utter desolation as his brother slipped away from him.

Gasping, she tried to pull back, but his hold only tightened on her, and she knew he was pulling memories from her mind as she was from his.

More recent memories. The talk with her father where he'd told her that he couldn't pay off his gambling debts. And then the look in his eyes when he explained that there was a solution to all their problems. A rich man was interested in marrying her. A rich man who would take care of their debts and take care of her for the rest of her life.

"He spoke to you first?" she asked her father.

"Yes."

"Why?"

"He thought that was more appropriate."

Was that the real reason, or had he known that he had an advantage with the father that he didn't have with the daughter?

She found out her suitor was John Reynard, a man she had met at the country club out by Lake Pontchartrain, where she'd gone for a friend's birthday celebration. He was another guest at the party, and he'd sat at her table and talked to her. They'd danced, and she'd known he was interested in her. He'd asked her out several times, and she'd accepted because she saw no harm in it. But the idea of his wanting to marry her came as a shock.

"I'm not ready for marriage," she blurted.

"You're going to have to change your mind about that."

"No."

"I'm in financial trouble."

"Whose fault is that?"

"You could say it's my own fault, but I'm not going to go down in disgrace if someone is willing to help me. Besides, John Reynard will make a good husband. He's rich and well connected. You'll never want for anything."

She felt as though she were living in the Middle Ages.

Women in the twenty-first century married for love, not for the right connections.

Yet she'd long ago secretly given up on love, and maybe that was why she had finally agreed.

She didn't want to be revealing any of that to Craig Branson. Or was it Craig Brady? She couldn't be sure, because both names came to her strongly.

But the exchange of information was only part of what was happening between them. She felt his emotions. The emptiness that had consumed him since his brother's death. It was like the emptiness she had always felt, only she'd had nothing to compare it to.

And below the mental connection was a sexual pull that she had never experienced before in her life.

It was as though she must make love with this man—or die. Or perhaps she *would* die if she made love with him.

That thought was so outrageous that she pushed it from her thoughts. Which wasn't difficult, because sexual desire was limiting her ability to think.

Craig Branson or Brady pulled her into his arms and lowered his mouth to hers.

She wanted to push him away. No, that was a lie. She wanted him to show her the pleasure of making love—pleasure that she knew would never be hers with John Reynard.

She tried to drive that last thought from her mind as his lips moved over hers, hungry and insistent. It was too private to share with anyone, least of all the man who held her in his arms. But she knew he had picked it up and knew he was glad she understood what a mistake it would be to marry Reynard. Not just because…

Branson cut the thought off before it could fully form. She was sure that he and Reynard had never met each other before the night of the charity reception, yet he seemed to know a lot about her fiancé.

She tried to hang on to that observation, but her mind was no longer operating in any rational manner.

Feelings had become more important than thoughts. The feel of Craig Branson's lips against hers. The feel of his hands as they stroked up and down her back, then cupped her bottom, pulling her more tightly against the erection straining at the front of his jeans.

He was ready to make love with her. And she was just as ready, yet she knew in some part of her mind that this was going too fast. They had to stop, and she was the one who had to do it.

She wrenched her mouth away from his and pushed at his shoulders.

The move caught him by surprise, because in his mind he was already taking the heated contact to its logical conclusion.

She slipped out of his grasp and put several feet of space between them as she stood panting.

When he reached for her, she shook her head. "Not now."

He was breathing hard, and his face looked as if he'd just touched a live electric wire, but he said only, "Why not?"

Now she couldn't meet his heated gaze. "Is this usually the way you act with a woman you don't know?"

"You know it isn't."

"What happened between us just now?"

"I felt the connection to you. Like the connection to Sam." He laughed. "Well, I never felt the sexual part with my brother."

She nodded slowly.

"But you've never felt anything like that?" he asked.

"No. What does it mean?"

"You weren't a twin?"

"No."

"Then what in the hell just happened?" he asked, revealing he was as perplexed as she was.

"I don't know," she answered.

It seemed he was still trying to come to a logical conclusion when she was sure there was no logic to what had happened. Or, at least, no logic that she had ever encountered.

"I..."

Before she could explain that to him, the bell over the shop door jingled, and her head jerked up. Claire stepped into the shop and gave the two of them an appraising look.

"What's going on?" she asked, her voice going high and sharp.

"Two men came in here. I don't know what they wanted, except that they were going to hurt me. Then Mr...."

"Brady," he supplied, and she knew when he said it that it wasn't his real name. But for some reason he had decided to use it.

"Mr. Brady came in and fought with them. Then they ran away."

Claire's gaze swung to him, her eyes assessing. "That was lucky—your being here. But how did you know what was happening?"

"I was on my way to the po'boy shop down the block," the man who had rescued her said. "I noticed them on the street, and they looked out of place. When I saw them come in here, I didn't think they were planning to buy dresses."

Claire was still staring at Stephanie and Craig as though she didn't believe a word of what they were saying. And Stephanie silently acknowledged that they were lying—by implication, at least, about what had happened after the men had left.

Craig turned away and came down on his knees under the rack of dresses. When he stood again, he was holding a gun. "They left this," he said to Claire.

She sucked in a sharp breath as she saw the weapon. If Claire hadn't believed them in the first place, she would now.

"What should I do with it?" Stephanie asked.

"I'll take it," Craig said.

"Shouldn't we call the police?"

"Do you want to?"

She thought about it before shaking her head, then wondered if he would accept the decision.

As she looked at him, her gaze zeroed in on the bruise that was discoloring his forehead.

"You got hurt in the fight," she said.

"Did I?"

"Yes. Your forehead is bruised. You need ice on that."

Glad to escape, she slipped into the back room, where she paused to run a shaky hand through her hair, thanking her lucky stars that she and Craig hadn't been in each other's arms when Claire had come in. That was all she needed, for someone to report back to John that she was kissing another man. Would Claire have ratted on her? She didn't know, but she still understood that she had to be careful.

She got several ice cubes from the refrigerator, wrapped them in a paper towel, then put them into a plastic bag. She wished she didn't have to go out there and face Craig again, but she was pretty sure he was still waiting for her in the front of the shop.

He and Claire were talking when she returned and handed him the ice pack, being careful not to touch his hand.

Something had happened between them when they touched, and she didn't want it to happen again. At least not now.

He took the ice and pressed the package against his forehead.

"Thanks."

"No problem."

"Mr. Brady and I were talking. He's in the city to get some investment advice," Claire said.

Stephanie nodded. She hadn't picked that up from him, but she supposed it could be true. She canceled the last silent observation. He wasn't in town for investment advice. He was here to investigate John Reynard.

That realization made her suck in a sharp breath.

"Are you all right?" Claire asked, her gaze anxious.

"I'm…I'm just reliving the moments before Mr. Brady came in," she answered. "It was pretty scary with those men coming after me."

"What happened, exactly?" Claire asked.

"Not too much. They came in, and I could tell they—" she gulped "—wanted to harm me."

"Why?" Claire pressed.

"I don't know," she answered, flapping her arm in frustration and wondering if it had something to do with her father. What if he'd let his gambling get out of hand again and they were here to make sure he paid up?

Nothing like that had happened to her before. Nobody had come after her because of her father's debts, but maybe she'd been lucky in the past.

Craig was also staring at her. Afraid he might try to touch her, she took a quick step back.

"Are you all right?" he asked.

"Yes."

"I'd better go."

She felt relief. She needed some distance from him. But the relief was tinged with disappointment. They had made some kind of weird mental connection, and she couldn't simply let that go. She wanted to ask if she would see him again, but she couldn't start a conversation like that in front of Claire. And she already knew the answer, because she understood that she and Craig Brady couldn't keep away from each other.

She shivered, drawing a reaction from Claire again.

"You should go home and rest."

"I can't keep bugging out on you."

"You've just had a pretty bad experience."

She might have argued except that she wanted to be alone with her thoughts—and her reactions.

OUTSIDE ON THE STREET, Craig took a deep breath, then looked around, making sure that the two men who had attacked Stephanie weren't lurking.

Perhaps if the other woman hadn't come in, Craig would have stayed in the shop. But their privacy had been compromised. Which was lucky, because following through on his impulses would have been dangerous for Stephanie.

He thought about her reaction to his question about calling the cops. A regular, upstanding citizen would have wanted to report the incident, but she'd decided not to do it. Which was good for him, he supposed. If he got dragged into making a police report, he'd have to give his real name.

He wasn't quite steady on his feet as he walked down the sidewalk, not sure where he was going.

His head was spinning as he tried to take in everything that had happened in the past hour. Starting with the attack and ending with the intimacy of his contact with Stephanie. He was still reeling from that. Probably she was, too, although he knew her reaction wasn't exactly the same as his.

From the contact with her, he knew that she had never experienced anything like what had happened when they'd touched. She'd been totally unprepared for the way their minds had connected.

To be honest, he hadn't been prepared, either. But it was

different for him. He had known that kind of mind-to-mind contact before—with his brother. He'd mourned Sam's loss and mourned the loss of that perfect communication. He'd thought he would never experience it again. Then he had— with Stephanie Swift. A woman who was engaged to marry the man who had caused Sam's death.

He swore under his breath, trying to wrap his mind around all the implications. If she married Reynard, she'd be lost to him. And lost to herself, too, because she'd be committing herself to a man who didn't understand her and couldn't give her the intimate contact she needed.

Craig huffed out a breath. And he could?

Yes, of course. He'd proved it when he'd touched her, kissed her. Their minds had opened to each other, but there was an added component he'd never experienced with his brother. He and Sam had been twin brothers, sharing the intimacy of siblings. He and Stephanie were adults—and intimate on a whole new level. Not only could they communicate mind to mind, they were drawn to each other with a sexual pull that was startling in its intensity.

He wanted to make love with her. Desperately. Yet below the surface of that need was a hint of warning. The sexual contact was dangerous if they didn't handle it right. He wasn't sure why he realized that truth. He only knew that he wasn't making it up.

Something else he knew. He couldn't allow Stephanie Swift to marry John Reynard for a whole lot of reasons. Yet he knew that was another thing he'd have to handle carefully if he didn't want Stephanie to end up dead.

He winced. That was putting it pretty strongly, but he couldn't discount that truth. John Reynard would fight for what he thought was his. And if he couldn't have it, nobody could.

And what about Craig's original purpose—to avenge

his brother's death? He hadn't forgotten about that, but he knew he couldn't simply go blasting into Reynard's life. All along he'd known he had to be careful about his approach to the man. That was true in spades now.

Chapter Four

"You don't mind staying here by yourself?" Stephanie asked her assistant again.

"I think I'll be okay."

"I'd hate for anything to happen to you."

Claire gave her a direct look. "The way it sounded, they were after you—not me."

She answered with a tight nod.

"Go on, then." Claire looked around. "And maybe you want to take the back way."

Stephanie hated the idea of sneaking out of her own shop, but she knew that Claire was probably right. She slipped through the back door and stood looking around before heading down the alley and over a few blocks to the house she'd bought. She kept herself from running, but she walked quickly along the afternoon streets. When she stepped inside her living room, she breathed a sigh before locking the door firmly behind her, then looking around at the room she had so lovingly furnished—with some pieces from the Garden District mansion and others that she'd picked up at flea markets and garage sales.

The house itself was old but charming, and she'd gotten it at a very good price after Katrina, from a couple who had decided to leave the city for a safer environment.

The down payment had taken a chunk of the money she'd inherited from her mother. But she hadn't wanted to live with her father in the Garden District mansion. She'd been happy here—well, as happy as she could be. And now her life had turned itself upside down *again*.

The first time had been a few months ago, when John Reynard had asked for her hand in marriage, and she'd known she had to accept. Then an hour ago, Craig Branson had touched her, and the world had flipped over again.

Her mind had opened to Craig's. And his to hers. He'd tried to hide it from her, but she knew he had come to New Orleans because he thought John Reynard had something to do with the death of his twin brother. That was why he'd been at the charity reception the other night. He'd been stalking Reynard—and he'd locked eyes with her.

She thought about that and about what else she'd discovered. Since birth and perhaps before, Craig had been tied to his brother, Sam, in a way that he had taken for granted. That connection had been ripped away by a stray bullet, leaving him hardly able to cope with his life. But he had coped. And he'd vowed to avenge his brother's death.

She shuddered as she thought about the rest of what had been in his mind. He'd never expected to experience that intimacy with anyone again—but he had. With her.

What did it mean? How was it possible?

She was trying to work her way through the encounter with him when a knock on the door made her whole body jerk.

Was that Craig? Coming after her.

"Who's there?" she called out.

"John."

Oh, Lord, John. The man she was going to marry. One of the last people she wanted to see now.

She got up on shaky legs and crossed to the door. From the front window, she saw John standing on her doorstep, his arms folded tightly across his chest. He dropped them to his sides when he saw her staring at him.

Quickly she unlocked the door and stepped aside. He came in and closed the door behind him, then turned to her.

"What are you doing here?" she asked.

"You were attacked."

"How do you know?"

He hesitated for just a second before saying, "I was calling to say hello, and Claire answered the phone. She sounded upset, so I asked her some questions. Are you all right?"

"Yes."

"She says two men came into the shop and threatened you. Then a stranger came to your rescue."

"Yes."

"I assume you got his name."

"He's Craig Brady," she said, using the false name that he'd given to Claire.

"And you never met him before?"

She wondered what the right answer was, then decided and said, "I didn't meet him, but he was at that charity reception the other night."

"The guy who was watching you?"

She winced. "I guess. I didn't really pay much attention," she lied.

John kept his gaze on her, and she worked to keep her expression neutral. She knew he'd noticed Craig at the plantation house. And done what? Maybe had his guys make a move on him?

"So what about the men who attacked you?" John asked. "Had you ever seen *them* before?"

"No."

John continued his interrogation. "And what did they want?"

"I never found out."

His eyes narrowed. "But I suspect you think it has something to do with your father."

Her mouth had gone dry, but she managed to answer, "Yes."

"He's gambling again?"

"I...don't know for sure."

"You'd better tell him to behave himself. I'm not a bottomless well of money."

"I understand."

"I hate it that he's responsible for bad stuff happening to you," he said, the tone of his voice changing. She knew that change. He was feeling tender toward her, and amorous.

He reached out and took her in his arms, cradling her against himself, and she fought to keep the stiffness out of her body. She didn't want him to hold her, but she could hardly object to her fiancé comforting her after a frightening experience.

He crooked one hand under her chin and tipped her face up as he lowered his mouth. His lips touched down on hers, settled, then began to move with the skill of a man who had made love to many women.

Stephanie tried to relax and kiss him back, when all she wanted to do was duck out of his arms and flee the room.

He was an experienced lover, and she'd convinced herself that marrying him wouldn't be a personal disaster for her, yet, as he kissed her, she couldn't stop herself from comparing her feelings now to the sensations and emotions that had threatened to swamp her when Craig had held her in his arms.

Then she'd been aroused. Hot and pliable and ready for sex. Now she was only tolerating the attentions of the man whose bed she would share in a few months.

She hoped he didn't realize what she was really feeling. And when he drew back, she felt relief and shame warring inside her. If she were honest, she would tell John Reynard that she couldn't marry him, but she knew that was as impossible as her flying off to Oz in a hot-air balloon.

At least he hadn't forced her to make love with him. She'd told him that she couldn't do that until they were married, and he'd grumbled about the edict. But he'd respected her wishes. She wondered if he thought she was a virgin. Probably not. Probably he'd investigated her background enough to know that she'd been intimate with a few men, but the relationships had never gone very far. Maybe he was thinking that he'd wait until marriage so she didn't have a chance to walk away when she was disappointed.

He looked down at her. "I guess you're still upset by what happened."

"Yes. I'm sorry."

"I should let you rest." The edge in his voice made her grasp his arm. "I'm sorry. I just can't…" She let her voice trail off rather than try to explain any further.

"I'm going to have some of my men protect you," he said.

Her gaze shot to his face. "What do you mean?"

"They'll be watching over you."

"You mean they're coming here?"

"They won't bother you, but they'll be around."

"Yes, thank you," she managed to say, when she really wanted to scream at him to leave her alone.

He left the house then, and she collapsed into a chair, glad to be alone. Yet at the same time she was terrified by what had just happened. She'd never wanted to marry this man. Now she understood just how bad a decision it would be.

Would be? Was she still thinking that she had a choice?

FOR THE PAST FEW DAYS, Craig had been following Stephanie around. Now it was more important than ever for him to keep up the surveillance—not just for himself but for her. But as he rounded the corner at the end of her block, he saw John Reynard leaving her house.

He stopped short, ducking back around the corner, fighting a spurt of jealousy that stabbed through him. That bastard had access to Stephanie, and Craig did not. She was engaged to the man, but she was never going to marry him. Craig would make sure of that. The depth of his emotions shocked him. He hadn't felt this strongly about *anything* since Sam's death. Then he'd been filled with despair. But also determination, he acknowledged.

The determination was just as strong now, along with an excitement that coursed through his veins and made his heart pound.

He had to pry Stephanie away from John Reynard, but he couldn't exactly pull out a gun and shoot the man. He had to get something on him—something that would stop him in his tracks. Evidence from Sam's murder? He'd been prepared to play a long game getting that kind of information. But now the time frame had changed. It would be much better if it was something more recent that they could take to the cops.

They? Was he already thinking Stephanie was on his side?

He pulled himself up short. *Take it a step at a time,* he warned himself. *You just met her. You can't change her world in a couple of hours.*

Still, he did feel a small measure of victory. Reynard had

come running over to Stephanie's house after the incident. Probably he'd thought he could comfort her—like in the bedroom. But now he was on his way out the front door. Hopefully because Stephanie hadn't wanted him there.

How could she, after the connection she and Craig had made in the shop?

John left the house, but before he drove away, he glanced toward two men sitting in a car across the street from her house.

The men who had attacked her in the shop?

What would it mean that Reynard knew they were here?

Craig waited with his heart pounding until Reynard had finished his conversation with Stephanie and driven away. He ached to stride down the block and confront the watchers, but caution made him walk back in the other direction, then take the alley in back of the houses across the street from Stephanie's. They were typical French Quarter dwellings, many of them built butting up against one another or with enclosed courtyards, but there were passageways between some, and he took one that would bring him almost up to the car where the men were sitting.

He stayed in the shadows, noting that they were both turned toward Stephanie's house. He recognized them. They weren't the thugs who had come into her shop. They were the men who had followed him around at the charity reception. John Reynard's bodyguards. Apparently, after the disturbing incident in the shop, he'd assigned them to watch over his fiancée.

In a way, that was a good move on Reynard's part. And it argued that Reynard had nothing to do with the attack at the dress shop, but it created a problem for Craig. He needed to get close to her again, and he'd have to make sure the men didn't spot him. For a couple of reasons—chief of which was that it would put Stephanie at risk.

He cursed under his breath, feeling as if Reynard was beating him in a chess game. Craig was going to have to rethink his strategy.

STEPHANIE STOOD, too restless to simply sit and do nothing. Instead she went to the window and lifted one of the venetian-blind slats. She spotted the men in the car across the street immediately. As promised, they were keeping watch on her house. But she saw something else, as well. A flicker of movement drew her attention to a passageway between two houses near the bodyguards' car. A man was standing in the shadows, watching the watchers. For a moment she thought it might be one of the men who had come to the shop. But that was only until she saw his face.

It was Craig Branson. He must have followed her home, and now he was watching the two men in the car.

Were there more of John's men guarding the rear of her house? She'd have to assume that was true, since she could leave that way and not be spotted from the street.

Feeling like a prisoner in her own home, she gritted her teeth. But maybe that was the way John wanted her to feel. He'd said he'd arranged protection, but knowing him, that probably wasn't his only reason. He wanted her to understand that if she stepped out of line, he would know it.

She let the slat slip back into place, glad that the men out there couldn't see through the walls of her house. Crossing to the kitchen, she got out a box of English breakfast tea. After filling a mug with water, she set it in the microwave and pressed the beverage button.

When the water was hot, she added a tea bag and let it steep while she paced back and forth along the length of the kitchen, waiting for the tea to be ready. After removing the tea bag, she carried the mug to the office, where she sat down at the computer and thought back over the details of her encounter with Craig Branson. From the mind-to-mind contact, she knew a lot about him already. Or maybe none of that was true.

She made a dismissive sound. How would it be possible to lie when you communicated mind to mind with someone? Maybe if you rehearsed a story and fixed it firmly in your thoughts. But if you weren't expecting the contact, you'd be taken by surprise. That had been true of her and true of Branson, as well. But there was one more possibility she had to consider. What if he was a lunatic who believed the story he'd given her?

She clenched her fists so hard that her nails dug into her palms. Deliberately, she relaxed. The encounter had knocked her off-kilter, but if she was trying to say he was insane, she was grasping at straws, probably because she didn't want to deal with the shock of what happened when they'd touched each other.

That observation gave her pause. She'd been alone all her life, and wasn't this what she'd been longing for—a soul mate?

But just at the wrong time. She had already committed herself to another man—a man who considered her his property. What could she hope for with Craig Branson? Was this going to be like that old movie, *The Graduate*, where the guy comes charging down from San Francisco to stop the woman he loves from marrying the wrong guy? He's too late to prevent the ceremony, but he takes the bride away anyway.

Was that the fantasy she was hoping for?

Unable to cope with her own muddled thoughts, she put the name Craig Branson into Google and got several hits. There was more than one man by that name, but she quickly zeroed in on the right one.

He owned a private security company, which meant he

thought he could go up against John Reynard. But he didn't know Reynard.

She'd assumed she knew the man, but she was becoming more and more shocked by the things she found out. Not dark facts, but his attitude of owning her—and having her father enslaved to his will.

With a shudder, she put Reynard out of her mind and went back to the information on Craig Branson.

Searching back, she found a newspaper article that made her chest go tight. It was an account of the incident that had killed Craig's brother. There was a picture of a smiling little boy, obviously a school portrait. He was what she'd imagine Craig would have looked like at the age of eight.

So it was true. He hadn't made up the story. Her heart was pounding as she scanned the text, reading about the murder of a mob boss in a restaurant and how some of the innocent diners had gotten shot. Most had been wounded. The only fatality was Sam Branson.

The article told her something else. The target in the restaurant had been a mob boss. If John Reynard had something to do with his death, what did that make him? She pushed that question out of her mind because it was more than she could cope with. Which left her contemplating the tragedy.

She sat for a moment, imagining Craig's reaction to the loss of his brother—and imagining what it must have been like for him to touch her and get back that kind of closeness. Lord, what would her life have been like if she'd had a brother or a sister she could communicate with that way? And what if she'd lost them?

But she'd never had a brother or a sister. She'd once heard her parents talking in whispers about her mom having trouble getting pregnant. She'd gathered that they'd gone to a fertility clinic, but she'd never directly asked about it, because it had seemed like something they wanted to keep quiet.

As she thought about it, long-ago memories came back to her. She remembered being in a waiting room with a lot of other children. Could that have had something to do with the clinic?

It didn't seem likely because she hadn't been a baby. Maybe she'd had some illness and her parents had taken her to a specialist?

She wasn't sure, and probably it wasn't important. Or maybe it was. She was getting married. Would she have trouble getting pregnant?

A shudder went through her. She wanted children. Maybe she could be close to her own children, the way she'd never been close to her parents. But did she want to have children with John Reynard?

The idea sent another frisson through her. She'd felt trapped the moment she'd agreed to the marriage with Reynard, but meeting Craig Branson had made it worse. Unfortunately, she was drawn to him as she'd never been to her fiancé.

She closed her eyes, willing those thoughts out of her mind. Thoughts of Reynard and of Branson. She had a more immediate problem. Men had come to her shop and threatened her, and she'd better talk to her father about it.

She turned off her computer and looked out the window, seeing the men in the car across the street. They were supposed to be protecting her, but her impulse was to slip away without their knowing it. Because she didn't trust John? Or because she didn't like the idea of his having her followed? And she had the feeling that would only get worse if they married.

Chapter Five

Instead of walking out the front door, Stephanie slipped into the courtyard at the side of her house. From there, she went into the alley where her car was parked. Before she'd gotten two blocks from home, she looked in the rearview mirror and saw that she was being followed—by the men who had been sitting out front.

How did they even know she'd left the house? Apparently there was some mechanism for spying on her that she didn't know about and didn't understand.

As she drove to her father's Garden District mansion, she kept glancing in the rearview mirror, checking the men behind her who were making no attempt to hide the fact that they were following. She drove around the block, partly to make the men wonder what she was doing and partly to have a look at the house. Once it had been painted in shades of cream, purple and green to create the classic "painted lady" effect that was so popular in the Garden District, with different colors used to accent different parts of the trim. But the paint had faded, making the house look sad instead of distinctive.

And the shrubbery was overgrown, contributing to the general air of neglect. She hadn't really looked at the exterior in ages, and it was a shock to see how much the property had gone downhill in the past few years.

When she finally pulled into the driveway, the men stopped on the street in front of the house, watching her through the screen of shrubbery as she walked to the wide front porch. She knocked to let her father know that she was there, then used her key to let herself in.

Once again, she stopped to notice details that she hadn't paid much attention to in years because they were simply part of the environment. Now she looked around at the familiar furnishings, many of which had been handed down through several generations.

The front hall boasted a long, antique marble-topped chest, centered under an elaborate gilded mirror. Both of them needed dusting. And in the sitting room to her right, she saw the old sofas and chairs that had been in the house since before she was born.

"Dad?"

"Out here," he called.

She walked through the kitchen that hadn't been updated since the seventies and into the sunroom that spanned the back of the house. It had always been her favorite room, filled with blooming plants and wrought iron and wicker furniture. And she noted that her father must be keeping it up because the plants all looked healthy.

He was in his favorite wicker chair, where he could look into the room or out at the formal garden. Although the plants in the sunroom were well tended, the back garden was more bedraggled than the front. When she was little, they'd had a crew come by several times a week. Now it was probably once a month, and the neglect showed. Really, she should come over here to trim some of the bushes.

In her spare time, she thought. She was plenty busy with her shop and with the wedding preparations.

She had given the house and garden a critical inspection. Now she did the same thing with her father, who was in his early seventies. Once he'd been a vigorous man. Now his broad shoulders were stooped, and his white hair was thinning on top. His complexion had always been ruddy. The color hadn't faded, but the lines in his face were more prominent.

He was dressed in a crisp white shirt, a blue-and-red-striped tie, a navy sports jacket and gray slacks as though he might be ready to receive company. The sartorial statement was a holdover from the old days. The world might have switched to casual dress, but her father had stayed with his traditions.

He looked up to meet her gaze.

"You were just here a couple of days ago. Now what?"

It wasn't a very warm welcome. No "Hello" or "How are you?" But she was used to that kind of reaction from him. She and her father had never had that great a relationship, and it had deteriorated after her mother had died five years ago of ovarian cancer. It had been a quick death because her mother had kept her symptoms to herself until it was too late to do anything about the cancer.

When Stephanie had been a kid, Mom had tried to keep up the appearance of a warm, close family, and maybe she fooled some people who didn't know them all that well. Dad had always done his own thing. He'd had a sales job that had taken him out of town frequently. Being away from his family had given him the opportunity to gamble. He'd retired several years ago, but since his wife's death, there had been no one to pull him back from his gambling obsession. Which was how he'd gotten into debt and almost lost the house—until John Reynard had approached him about marrying his daughter.

Dad had always been a pretty decent poker player. In fact, there were many times when he'd won instead of lost. In her more cynical moments, Stephanie wondered if John had somehow arranged for her father to lose—so he could approach him with the offer of financial salvation.

"You know I like to stop by and see how you're doing," she answered.

"I'm doing fine," he said, his brittle voice a counterpoint to the claim.

"That's good."

"What's bothering you?" he asked bluntly.

She might have taken the time to work up to her question, but since he was forcing the issue, she asked, "Are you gambling again?"

He sat up straighter in his chair when he answered, "I agreed not to."

"That wasn't the question," she said, determined to meet his words with equal force.

"I've abided by my agreement. Is there some reason why you're asking?"

"Two men came to my shop and threatened me," she said.

"What men?"

"They looked like they could be connected with the mob or something."

"They weren't there on my account."

"Are you sure?"

He glared at her. "Maybe you ought to think about what you might have done to attract their attention."

"I have."

He kept his gaze on her. "And you can't think of anything?"

"No."

"You always did keep your own secrets."

"I'm not keeping secrets," she answered, but as soon as the words were out of her mouth, she knew they were a lie. She was keeping the secret of Craig Branson from her father. For several reasons. She knew he wouldn't approve, and she also knew that he wouldn't understand about what had happened between her and Branson. Nobody would understand.

Still, she managed to say, "Do you think I'd come over here and ask if you might be the cause of the problem if I already knew what was going on?"

He shrugged. "I never know what to think about you. You were usually off in your own little world—where nobody could reach you. Good luck to John Reynard. He thinks he's getting what he wants, but he's in for a surprise."

She stared at her father, hardly able to believe his words. She'd sacrificed her future to save him, and he was acting as if he didn't give a damn about her. Had his attitude toward her changed when she'd agreed to marry Reynard? Or had he seen a chance for her to do something useful for the family? And why had she agreed if this was the kind of thanks she got?

"Did I do something particular to upset you?" she asked.

"No." The word was clipped and she wondered if he was lying.

"All right," she said, then turned on her heel and left, thinking that this visit had been a waste of time.

Well, not entirely, she corrected herself. She was pretty sure that her father had nothing to do with the men who had threatened her. Which left her—where?

She shivered. She was in danger, and she could let John's men deal with the threat. Or…

Another idea was forming in her head. Craig Branson had a detective agency. Didn't that make him equipped to find out what was going on in her life that she didn't know about?

It was a logical conclusion, but she knew it was also a rationalization. She had pulled away from Branson because she'd been afraid, but now that she had some distance from him, she wanted to repeat the experience.

Which meant she had another problem. John's men were following her around. If she approached Craig Branson, they'd know it.

TOMMY LADREAU MOVED restlessly in his seat.

"You gotta pee?" his partner, Marv Strickland, asked.

"Yeah." Tommy was thinking he'd ask Marv to make a quick stop in an alley when his cell phone rang. He looked at the number, then pressed the answer button.

Marv looked at him questioningly.

Reynard, Tommy mouthed

"Report" was the crisp command from the other end of the line.

It was the man who paid him a good salary to do a wide variety of jobs—from messenger duty to surveillance to murder. Murder got his adrenaline going. Sitting around in a car keeping track of Stephanie Swift was another matter. But he always carried out his assignments to the best of his ability. He'd known all along that he was working for a dangerous man. Then Arthur Polaski had washed out of the ground in the bayou country.

It was well-known that he'd been an employee of John Reynard when he'd disappeared twenty years ago.

Reynard had been upset about the man's reappearance as a fleshless skeleton. He'd tried to keep the information quiet among the guys currently working for him, but the word had gotten around—eliciting quite a bit of speculation.

Was it the boss who'd put Polaski in the ground? Or was it someone else? Nobody knew. Nobody was happy about the discovery. And everyone was wondering—why now?

Tommy cleared his throat. "Ms. Swift left the house and went over to her father's place."

"And?"

"She stayed for about a half hour. Then she came back home, and she's been there ever since."

"And you had no problem following her?"

"No problem."

"Okay. Good. Stay on it. If anything unusual happens, I want to know about it immediately." He hesitated for a moment. "And I want to know immediately if that guy shows up. Brady. The one she claimed rescued her at the dress shop."

"Will do."

Reynard clicked off, and Tommy looked at his partner. "You hear that?"

"Yeah."

"He didn't like Brady sniffing around his honey the other night. Now he's upset about the guy showing up again at the dress shop."

"Want to bet that Brady ends up dead?" Marv asked.

Tommy shook his head. "I'm sure as Shinola not going to bet against it."

STEPHANIE SAT in her car for a few moments, trying to calm down after her meeting with her father. It was hard to believe they were related to each other. Sometimes she had fantasies about being someone else's child—and that was the reason she could never connect with him on any meaningful level.

She switched her thoughts back to Craig Branson and felt a rush of emotions—only some of them pleasant.

With a sigh, she climbed out of her car and headed for her back door. When she stepped inside, she gasped as she took in the shadowy figure sitting in the easy chair across from the door.

Chapter Six

Craig Branson watched Stephanie's security detail take off. When the car was out of sight, he crossed to the alley in back of her house and found her car missing.

They were tailing her, and either they had X-ray vision, or they had some other way to know which way she was going.

He clenched his teeth. There was no way to find out about *that* for sure until she came back.

Instead, he used his lock picks and went inside, then focused on the interior of the house, liking the mixture of antiques, comfortable chairs and sofas, and whimsical decorations.

She must like animals, because she had a lot of little ceramic, glass, wood and metal figures on the shelves among her books. He picked up a cat that looked as if it came from Mexico, stroking his fingers over the smooth, painted surface, half hoping that he'd pick up some impression of the woman herself. But he got no mental connection to her by touching any of her things.

He walked upstairs to her bedroom and stepped inside the room, loving the cool blue-and-white color scheme that reminded him of a beach cottage. His eyes zeroed in on the neatly made bed. Had John Reynard slept there with Stephanie? The thought of them naked in bed together made his throat close, and he fought to banish the image from his mind.

He wanted to linger in the bedroom, but he knew that was an invasion of her privacy.

A laugh bubbled inside him. An invasion of her privacy? Like getting into her mind? Well, that contact had invaded his privacy, too. A fair and equal invasion. He wouldn't start off their relationship by looking through her underwear drawer.

The word *relationship* stopped him. He was making assumptions. But he knew they were valid. They were going to mean something to each other. Really, they already did.

Forcing himself to turn away from the bed, he went back to the living room and sat down in one of the easy chairs to wait for her return.

Forty minutes later, he heard a car pull up outside. When he heard the lock click, his whole body tensed, and he focused like a laser on the door.

Some part of him wondered if he had imagined the intimacy between them in the dress shop. The minute she stepped into the room, he could feel the air crackling between them. If she crossed to him…if he got up and crossed to her…

He ordered himself to put away that thought.

"How did you get in here?" she demanded.

"It was easy."

He saw her lick her lips and knew that her mouth must be as dry as his.

The words she spoke weren't the ones he wanted to hear. "Don't touch me."

He felt his gaze sharpen. "Afraid?"

"Yes. You should be, too."

"Why?"

"Because…" She lifted one shoulder, apparently unwilling to put a warning into words.

He stayed where he was, but he knew that at any second he could change the rules between them by crossing the room to her, and there would be nothing she could do about it.

He felt tension course through him as he asked, "Where were you?"

"Like that's any of your business," she shot back.

When he kept his gaze fixed on her, she answered, "Visiting my father."

"To ask if he was gambling again?"

She answered with a small nod.

"What did he say?"

"He denied it."

"Which leaves you in an interesting position."

Probably she'd been considering the same thing. Instead of pursuing that line of thought, she said, "I don't appreciate finding you in here. Is this how you operate as a detective?"

"You've done some research on me?"

"Yes. I suppose you know that John Reynard has men following me around."

"Yes. I came in here after they took off after you."

She looked toward the closed venetian blinds. "They're outside now. How are you going to get out of here?"

"I'll worry about that when the time comes." He cleared his throat. "Did they show up at your father's?"

"Yes."

"Did you wonder how they knew where to pick you up?"

She swallowed. "I thought they might have some idea where I was going."

When he stood, she tensed, obviously bracing for him to come to her and put his hands on her, which was what he'd longed to do since she walked into her house. But he was going to restrain himself, at least for now.

"Maybe we'd better have a look at your car."

"My car?" she asked, obviously struggling to refocus.

"Yeah." He stood up and crossed to the door from where she'd just entered. Looking back over his shoulder, he said, "Are you coming?"

Her face was grim as she followed him, staying a few paces back when he crossed the courtyard.

At the alley, he paused and looked around. They seemed to be alone. Quickly he approached her vehicle, stooped down and felt along the edge of the bumper, then continued around the side of the car. When he found what he'd been looking for, he felt a mixture of satisfaction and annoyance.

Turning, he held out a small plastic rectangle.

She took an involuntary step closer. "What is it?"

"A GPS tracking device."

Her breath caught.

"They used that to follow you. That's why they could sit out front and wait for you to drive somewhere."

She shuddered. "What are you going to do with it?"

"Put it back."

She swallowed hard. "Why?"

"So they'll think you're still here, even if you're not."

"But…"

He shook his head. "Let's go back inside."

She stepped away, giving him room as he entered the courtyard again, then the house.

Inside, they stood in the darkened room, a feeling of anticipation zinging between them.

"Sit down," she said.

Fine, he thought. If she wanted to postpone the touching part, he'd give her some space—for now. But he could feel the need building inside him and knew that he couldn't let it go forever. He needed to find out if he'd had some kind of psychotic episode back in her shop.

He canceled that thought. He wasn't going to try to fool himself. He wasn't leaving this house without touching her.

But for the moment he lowered himself into the chair where he'd been sitting when she arrived.

She took the sofa, her wary gaze on him.

"Do you believe your father about the gambling?"

"I think so."

"Which leaves us with the question, why do you think those men showed up at your shop?"

"Do you think you can find out?"

"Yes."

"Thanks." She dragged in a breath and let it out. "You think the man I'm going to marry is responsible for your brother's death."

"You're not going to marry him," he answered, punching out the words.

She reared back. "Why not?"

"You know why not."

He'd issued a challenge. Before she could react, he was out of his chair and across the room. Pulling her to her feet, he wrapped his arms around her.

The shock of the contact made them both gasp. It was like the first time, only more intense. He knew she'd been going to ask him for information about John Reynard. Now she didn't have to ask. It was in his mind for the taking. His import-export business was a front for bringing illegal goods into the country. He had insinuated himself into New Orleans society to make his place in the city invulnerable. He had men murdered when he thought that was the best course of action.

She moaned when she saw the pictures he'd seen of the man who had been buried in the swamp for twenty years.

"Sorry," he said when words were almost impossible.

She'd told him she'd visited her father. He hadn't known how the meeting had affected her. Now he felt her pain and her bewilderment at the way her parent had just treated her.

Was it always like that? he asked.

Not as bad when my mom was alive.

I'd like to strangle him.

He's a sad old man.

That's charitable of you.

The conversation cut off as physical sensations made it difficult to focus on anything besides the two of them, the feel of his body pressed to hers and hers to his. Because both sets of sensations played through each of them.

She felt the insistence of his erection pressing against her middle, and at the same time he felt the way that part of him swelled with blood, making it difficult to form coherent thoughts.

He reached between them, cupping her breast, stroking his thumb across the hardened tip. The feel of her made him ache more painfully, and at the same time he felt her reaction, the pleasure of his cupping and stroking her and the way the sensations shot downward through her body to her center.

She gasped, rocking against him.

That's the way it is for a woman.

Yes. And for a man.

The overlay of sensations—feeling his own arousal and hers—made it almost impossible to stand as they swayed together, clinging to each other for support.

Somewhere in the back of his mind, he felt a headache building, but he ignored it. The only thing he wanted to focus on was the woman in his arms.

He wrapped her more tightly in his embrace, closing his eyes and absorbing every sensation that they shared.

He breathed in her delicious feminine scent and knew she was tuning herself to him with all her senses. Each thing they shared was magnified by the intensity of the doubled experience.

They were both breathing hard, and when she rocked her hips against his, he knew that they were heading for the bedroom. Or the sofa, because the bedroom was upstairs—too far away.

He had never felt this open to another human being.

That realization took him totally by surprise, shocking him to the marrow of his bones. All his life he had craved the closeness he had shared with his brother—searched for it—but what he felt now was more than he had experienced with Sam.

The enormity of that recognition was like a blow to his solar plexus. He dropped his hands, staggering away from Stephanie.

"Craig?"

He couldn't answer her. Not in words and not with his mind. His head was spinning as he backed up, bumping into the wall and pressing his shoulders against the vertical surface to keep his balance.

She took a step toward him, but he managed to raise one hand to ward her away.

"Don't." His voice was a harsh croak.

Her face had turned pale. Another woman would have asked what had gone wrong. But she didn't have to ask because she knew what had happened.

"I'm sorry," she whispered.

"Not your fault." He might have shaken his head, but the pain in his skull had flared to killer proportions.

Killer?

The thought had formed unbidden, but he knew it was close to the truth.

"You should sit down," she murmured.

He staggered back to the chair and flopped into the seat, throwing his head back and closing his eyes. For long moments, he struggled for equilibrium.

When he opened his eyes, he saw that she was watching him.

"You came here thinking you knew what to expect," she whispered.

"Yeah."

"You were always looking for what you had with Sam."

Again he answered in the affirmative.

"You and Sam were young." She paused, then went on, "And there was no sexual pull between you."

The statement hung in the air.

"Is it the sexual pull that brought us together?" she asked.

"It's obviously part of it," he answered, struggling to think clearly in the aftermath of the emotions that had churned through him.

"What was different about you and Sam?"

He fought to ground himself, to think about his relationship with his brother in a new way. It was a long time ago. Maybe he didn't remember it exactly as it had been.

Slowly, thinking as he spoke, he said, "We talked with thoughts, but there were other things we could do. Like if we worked together, we could move things with our minds."

"What do you mean?"

He glanced around the room and settled on the shelves along the opposite wall. "If we wanted to, we could pull a book off a shelf and drop it onto the floor without touching it."

"You and I could try that," she said, and he wondered if she was trying to get them on a different track.

"We just met today."

"No—a couple of days ago at the reception," she reminded him.

He made a huffing sound. "Yeah. There's that. But we just danced around each other there."

"Even so, we knew…something."

"True. But I don't think we're…bonded tightly enough to do any…tricks."

"I want to try," she insisted, determination in her voice.

He shrugged. "Okay, you focus on a book you want to pull off the shelf, and I'll try to help you."

He watched her turn toward the shelves and look at the titles. "There's a paperback of *The Wonderful Wizard of Oz*. That would be appropriate."

"You liked it when you were a kid?" he asked.

"Yes. Did you?"

"I liked any books that took me away from the real world."

"Well, that's something we have in common."

She walked to the shelves, found the book and pulled it a little way from the line of other books so they could both see it. Then she returned to her seat on the sofa and focused on the book. He could see the deep concentration on her face as she struggled to make something happen, and he tried to help her, giving her what he thought of as extra power. But there was no effect.

He saw sweat break out on her forehead and knew she was working as hard as she could, even though she wasn't exactly sure what she was doing. He kept up the effort to help her, but the effect was the same. Nothing.

She dragged in several breaths and sharpened her features, looking defiantly at him before turning back to the bookshelf.

Again he tried to help her, but it was clear she was only exhausting herself.

"Sorry," he murmured. "We might be able to do it if we were touching. That was the way Sam and I started out."

"If we touch, we won't end up focused on books."

He sighed. "You're probably right."

She took her lower lip between her teeth and then released it. "So why did we…open up to each other when we touched?"

"I don't know."

"What about you and Sam?"

"We always had it—whatever it is."

"I didn't. I didn't have anyone."

He heard the pain in her voice and asked the question that had been in his mind since he'd first seen her at the reception. "Did you always feel alone—like other people could connect with each other, but you couldn't?"

Her face contorted. "Yes," she whispered, and he knew it wasn't something she was sharing easily.

"I'm sorry."

"You knew there was something better."

He nodded.

"Did you have it with anyone besides Sam?"

"No."

"Then the big question is— why us?"

Chapter Seven

Stephanie waited for Craig's answer.

"There must be something we have in common." He shifted in his seat. "We might find out what it is if we touch each other again."

She stared at him, tempted by the suggestion, heat shooting through her as she remembered where they'd been a few minutes ago. He'd pulled away from her when he realized that what they were building between them was more intense than what he'd had with his brother. Now he was ready to try again, and she was the one who was feeling cautious.

"I think it would be better to do it the old-fashioned way. I mean talking. You researched me. Did you find anything that was similar?"

He shrugged. "Okay, if you want to play Twenty Questions. We're about the same age. But what else do we have in common?"

"Not our location. You grew up in the D.C. area, and I always lived down here."

He nodded. "What we're looking for could be anything. From chemicals in the air to the treatments we got on our teeth, to the medicines we took, to the food we ate."

She made a low sound. "I suppose neither one of us was near a nuclear test site."

"I guess not. And it was early for oil spills to contaminate Gulf seafood."

"Nice of you to think of that, but that wouldn't have applied to you, anyway. Anything strange about the food you ate? I mean, were your parents on any kind of health-food kick?"

"Actually, they were on a low-carb kick for a long time."

"But you had gone out for Italian food and take-home pizza," she said, then regretted the reference to his brother's murder.

His face clouded. "That was a special treat."

"I'm sorry."

He lifted one shoulder. "It will keep coming up."

She focused on the original question. "Well, it's definitely not from low carbs. I ate a pretty normal American diet—with Cajun touches because we lived down here. So that's not it."

"What about mental illness in your family?"

"What's that got to do with it?"

"This has something to do with our brains. Maybe you can only do it if you're schizophrenic," he muttered.

"You really think that?"

"No. But something else, maybe."

"If you dig around enough, you find out that everyone has a relative that was 'off.' You have an uncle Charlie who was committed?" she asked.

"When he came back from Vietnam and was never quite right again. What about you?"

"I guess my mother's sister suffered from depression. They didn't talk about it much."

"Okay, what about physical illnesses? Anything unusual?"

"No, what about you?" she asked.

"I had all the vaccinations."

"I did, too. But people have suspected vaccinations of causing various problems—like autism."

"I suppose," he allowed. "I wonder what our moms ate when they were pregnant with us."

The question made her mind zing back to something she remembered, and she cleared her throat. "There is something else. I once heard my parents talking about how hard it was for my mom to get pregnant."

He went very still. "And she had some kind of treatment?"

"I think she went to a fertility clinic."

"That's interesting. Mine did, too," he said slowly. "A friend of hers who lived in New Orleans told her about a doctor who was supposed to be very good, and she traveled to Louisiana to see him."

They stared at each other. "To New Orleans?"

"I don't know. Do you think that could be it?"

"It's something unusual," he conceded.

"What clinic?"

"I don't know."

"Would your father know the name of the place?"

A MAN NAMED Harold Goddard could have given them the answer—if he'd been so inclined.

But he wasn't the kind of man who did things simply because they were in the best interests of others. His moves were always careful and calculated. He was cautious when it came to his own welfare, yet the quest for knowledge was a powerful motivator. Not just knowledge for its own sake. He wanted information he could use to his advantage.

This afternoon he was waiting for a report from New Orleans regarding a scenario that he'd set in motion a couple of months ago.

He turned from the window and walked to his desk,

where he scrolled through the messages in his email. Unfortunately, there was nothing he hadn't known a few hours ago.

With a sigh, he got up and left the office, heading for his home gym, which was equipped with a treadmill, a recumbent bike and a universal weight machine. This afternoon he stepped onto the treadmill and slowly raised the speed to three miles per hour.

He was in his sixties, and he hated to exercise, but he knew that it was supposed to keep his body fit and his mind sharp, so he made himself do it.

He was retired now, but he kept up his interest in the projects that he'd handled for the Howell Institute, working under the direction of a man named Bill Wellington, who'd operated with funds hidden in a variety of budget entries. Wellington had been interested in advancing America through the application of science. Everything from new ways to fertilize crops to schemes for improving the human race.

Some of the experiments were well thought out, others bordered on lunatic fringe. And all of them had been shut down years ago. Or at least Goddard had thought so—until a few months ago when the news from Houma, Louisiana, had been filled with reports of an explosion in a private research laboratory. The local fire marshal had ruled that the explosion was due to a gas leak, but Goddard had sent his own team down to investigate, and he suspected there might be another explanation—because the clinic had been owned by a Dr. Douglas Solomon. He'd been one of Wellington's fair-haired boys, until his experiments had failed to pan out.

Solomon had operated a fertility clinic in Houma, Louisiana, where he'd been highly successful in using in vitro fertilization techniques. It was what he'd tried with the embryos that had not been a roaring success. Solomon's experiments had been designed to produce children with superintelligence, but when his testing of the subjects had not shown they had higher IQs than would be expected in a normal bell curve, the Howell Institute had terminated the funding.

But now the children had reached adulthood, and there might be something important the doctor and Wellington had both missed—as demonstrated by the mysterious explosion in Houma.

Goddard had partial records from the Solomon Clinic, and he'd followed up on some of the children. A number of them had disappeared. Others had died under mysterious circumstances—often in bed together—around the country.

But had Solomon unwittingly created men and women with something special that had previously been latent—until they made contact with each other?

Because he wanted to know the answer to that question, he'd decided to try an experiment. After scrolling through the list of names, he'd found two that looked as if they were perfect for his purposes. Stephanie Swift and Craig Branson.

He'd set in motion a scenario that had propelled them together. Now he was waiting to find out the effects. But he couldn't afford to leave them on the loose for long. And what he did when he captured them was still up for consideration. He'd like to know what they could do together, but it might also be important to examine their brain tissues.

STEPHANIE LOOKED DOWN at her hands. "I don't know if my dad remembers the name of the clinic, and I don't know if he'd tell me if he did. He wasn't too friendly when I went over there this afternoon."

"Why not?"

"Maybe he's feeling guilty about my agreeing to marry John to pay his gambling debts—and he's showing it by acting angry with me."

"That doesn't make perfect sense."

She sighed. "And I did accuse him of gambling again, which didn't go over too well."

"Yeah, right."

"How did you get along with your parents?" she asked.

"They knew I was devastated by Sam's death. They tried to make it up to me. I let them think they were succeeding."

"But it didn't really work?"

"It couldn't. The other half of me was…gone."

When her face contorted, he said, "Let's not focus on that."

"Okay, are your parents both still alive?"

His features tightened. "Neither of them is alive. Sam's death did a number on our family. My mom was depressed— like your aunt. But it didn't develop until after Sam died. She died of a heart attack. And my dad started drinking a lot. He died of cirrhosis of the liver."

"I'm sorry."

He shrugged. "I felt like I was on my own a long time before they were actually gone."

She nodded.

"I didn't keep much of their stuff. If there's information about the clinic, the information is back in Bethesda. Do you think your father will tell you what clinic?"

"I don't know. There are probably some old records we could find if he doesn't want to talk to me."

"We should go over there."

She glanced toward the window, then got up and lifted one of the slats. "My bodyguards are still here."

"They can sit there all night. We'll leave your car in the

parking space out back, walk to my bed-and-breakfast and get my rental."

"Okay."

It was strange to be sneaking away from her own house, but she followed Craig out the door, across the patio and into the back alley. Bypassing the car, they headed for his B and B. He checked to make sure they weren't being followed and kept to the shadows of the wrought-iron balconies that sheltered the sidewalk.

He stopped down the block and across the street, still in the shadows. "The parking lot is around back. You wait here. I don't want anyone to see you with me when I get the car."

She quickly agreed, pressing back against the building as she watched him cross the street and disappear into the B and B.

In a few minutes, a late-model Impala pulled up at the curb, and she climbed in, shutting the door quickly behind her.

"I suppose you know where my dad lives," she said as he pulled back into the traffic lane.

"Yeah."

As they drove out of the French Quarter, then to St. Charles Avenue, Craig kept glancing in his rearview mirror, making sure that nobody was following them.

"I guess you're used to this cloak-and-dagger stuff," Stephanie murmured.

"Part of my job description."

As he headed up St. Charles, then turned onto St. Andrew Street, her heart started to pound. She hadn't exactly had a pleasant encounter with her father, and she hadn't expected to meet up with him again so soon.

"You get out. I'm going to leave the car around the corner," he said as he pulled up in front of the house.

"I'll wait for you outside."

He gave her a critical look. "You really don't want to be here, do you?"

"No. And I'm thinking that it's not so great for you."

"Because?"

"Because he's given me to John Reynard, and he's not going to be happy to see me with another man."

"*Given* is a pretty strong word."

She shot him a fierce look. "You don't think I agreed to marry Reynard because I was madly in love, do you?"

"No. I thought you were interested in his money."

She dragged in a sharp breath. "Thanks."

"I didn't know you then."

"And now you do?"

"You can't lie with your thoughts."

"At least that's something."

He turned his head toward her, then looked back to the road. "I'm working my way through this situation—just the way you are."

"You've had some experience with it."

"This is different." He waited a beat before saying, "To get back to the current problem, tell your father I'm a detective you've hired to find out who the men were."

"He'll think John could handle that on his own."

Craig shrugged. "Do you have a better idea?"

"No."

Stephanie climbed out of the car and walked up the driveway toward the detached garage. When she looked inside and saw that her father's car was missing, she breathed a little sigh of relief, then started wondering where he was.

Because she said she'd be outside, she waited for Craig on the wide front porch.

"It looks like my dad isn't home," she said.

"Good."

"I hope so. He doesn't like…" She stopped.

"What."

"…me sneaking around."

"What the hell does that mean? This is your house."

"Not anymore. I moved out."

"Your father sounds like a real winner."

"He's had…a hard life."

"Oh, come on."

"He was used to wealth and privilege, and he lost that."

"His own fault," Craig pointed out.

"Maybe that makes it worse."

"Do you always make excuses for him?"

"Let's not go on about him," she snapped, and he pressed his lips together, maybe because he realized he would gain nothing by continuing to focus on her father's failings.

After she unlocked the door, she turned to him. "Come inside, but wait in the front hall."

"I should check out the house."

"For what?"

"Intruders."

"Unlikely."

To her relief, he stayed in the hall while she darted into the living room, then circled through the rest of the downstairs before climbing quickly up the stairs.

Leaning over the balcony, she beckoned to him. "Come on."

"WHAT ARE WE looking for?" he asked when he reached the top of the stairs.

"I'm not sure. It was almost thirty years ago, so it's not going to be on the computer, but Mom kept some boxes with papers and pictures in the top of her closet."

Craig followed her into a bedroom where the furnishings

were antique and the once-expensive fabrics were dusty and faded.

"Your dad sleeps here?" he asked.

"This was Mom's room."

"They had separate rooms?"

"She told him about fifteen years ago that she needed her own space," Stephanie answered, embarrassed to be revealing private family matters.

The room had two large closets, both full of women's clothes.

When Stephanie saw them, she caught her breath.

"Everything's still right where she left it," she murmured.

"I guess he misses her. Or he didn't feel like making the effort to get rid of her stuff. All he had to do was shut the door."

She dragged in a breath and let it out. "I feel funny about poking around in their lives."

"Yeah, but we need to do it," Craig answered. "Are those what you're looking for?" He pointed to the cardboard boxes neatly stacked on the top shelf. They were old department-store boxes, the kind nobody made anymore.

"Yes."

He lifted several down and set them on the bed.

Instead of reaching for them, Stephanie stood unmoving.

Craig turned his head toward her. "I know this is making you feel…unsettled."

She nodded. "And Dad is going to be mad if he comes back and finds me snooping."

"I guess that's tough. But maybe we can get out of here before he comes back. Do you want me to help you look?"

"Yes. Thanks."

They each opened a box and began checking through

the contents. Inside were old photographs of Stephanie and her parents, plus other memorabilia.

Craig held up a childish crayoned picture of a house surrounded by a flower garden. "You did good work."

"I must have been pretty young. It's a drawing of this house."

"I actually can tell."

She found a pile of essays she'd written.

"It's strange to find this stuff. I wouldn't have thought she'd kept it."

Craig said nothing, only continued searching through papers. When he pulled out a thick folder, she looked at him. "What's that?"

He thumbed through the contents.

"Do you remember anything about a place called the Solomon Clinic?"

"What is it?"

"Maybe this is what we've been looking for. It was a fertility clinic in Houma. There's a copy of an application, then instruction sheets for what your mother was supposed to do before going there."

He handed her some of the papers, and she went through them. "I guess this is it."

"Well, we found out about me. Does the Solomon name mean anything to you?" she asked.

Craig considered the question. "As a matter of fact, it does."

"How?"

His stomach tightened as he said, "Like you, I used to listen in on conversations. Probably all kids do."

"And what did you hear?"

"It was after Sam died, and my mother was pretty upset. I think I heard her on the phone trying to get some information about the Solomon Clinic."

"You really remember that?"

"Yes, because of the way she was reacting. In her grief, I think she might have been considering trying to get pregnant again, but she found out that the clinic had burned down."

"She could have gone to someone in the D.C. area."

"Maybe she thought Dr. Solomon was God—and he was the only one who could help her. For all I know, he could have acted that way with his patients." He dragged in a breath and let it out. "Anyway, she apparently gave up on the idea."

"But it sounds like your mother and mine went to the same place," Stephanie said. "Only she didn't take you back there for checkups, did she?"

"You went for checkups?" he asked.

"Yes. I remembered going *somewhere* with a waiting room full of kids my age. Now I think it must have been part of the deal—that the parents would bring the kids back to be examined."

"And my mom was back in D.C., so she couldn't do it." He thought for a minute. "I wonder if she agreed to take me and Sam there for checkups, but then didn't comply," Craig said.

"Was she that kind of woman?"

He lifted one shoulder. "She was always willing to bend the rules when it suited her."

"Can you give me an example?"

"I was supposed to have Ms. Franklin for my sixth-grade homeroom teacher. Mom got me into a different class because she thought Ms. Franklin was too lenient with the kids. Another time we moved into an apartment building where you weren't supposed to have pets, but she brought our cat anyway. Lucky for her it was a well-behaved animal and didn't mess up the place."

They gathered up the papers and put them back into the boxes, then returned the containers to the top of the closet.

"Your mom found out the clinic closed," she said.

"But maybe we can find out something online—or if we go to Houma."

Stephanie turned to straighten out the bedspread, where they'd laid the boxes, and he took the other side, pulling to remove the wrinkles.

"If we get out of here before your dad comes back, he'll never even know we were here."

They hadn't finished smoothing out the bed when they heard the front door open.

"What do you want to do?" Craig asked in a harsh whisper.

"Climb out the window," Stephanie answered in the same tone.

"You're kidding."

She shook her head. "I don't want Dad to find me upstairs with you, and I don't want to get into an argument about what we were doing—not if I can help it. And I sure as heck don't want him telling John about it."

"We're on the second floor."

"But there's an easy way to get down. We can climb onto the sunroom roof and go down that way." She hurried toward the window, opened the sash and stepped out. Craig looked around to make sure nothing was out of place in the room, then he followed her onto the roof. When he was outside, he closed the window behind them.

They moved along the wall toward the edge of the sunroom, and Stephanie pointed to the trellises that were fixed to the walls of the sunroom.

"Let me go first," he said.

"No, I've done this before."

"You snuck out of the house?"

"When I was grounded, yeah. The trellis is as good as a ladder."

"But you haven't used it in years, right?"

She shrugged. Before he could stop her, she stepped over the side, holding on to the weathered wood as she began to lower herself. He watched her going down, thinking that the wood might not be as solid as when she'd tried this last.

His speculation was confirmed when he heard a cracking sound and she fell several feet before catching herself.

"Are you all right?" he called.

"Yes."

When she'd made it to the ground, he followed, testing the rungs as he went. The rest seemed solid, and he reached the lawn right after Stephanie.

They stared at each other. He would have hugged her in relief that they'd made it, but he knew that touching her now was a bad idea. They'd forget what they were supposed to be doing—which was getting away from her father's house before he discovered them.

She must have been thinking the same thing. After long seconds, she walked rapidly across the back of the house and turned the corner.

As soon as she disappeared from sight, he heard her make a strangled sound.

"Stephanie?" he called in a hoarse whisper.

She didn't answer, and he hurried to catch up, then stopped short when he rounded the corner.

Stephanie was standing rigidly in front of a man who was holding a gun to her head.

Chapter Eight

The man was one of the thugs who had threatened Stephanie in her shop. The bald one.

"If you don't want me to shoot your girlfriend, do exactly what I say."

Craig went still as he looked from the man to Stephanie's terrified face.

"Don't hurt her."

"That's up to you. Play this smart, and everything will be okay."

He doubted it, but he asked, "What do you want?"

Without answering the question, the man said, "Walk ahead of us down the driveway, then turn right."

Craig's heart was pounding as he followed directions. He walked carefully, knowing that any false step could get Stephanie killed.

As they headed down the sidewalk, he kept searching for a way out. What if a neighbor suddenly appeared? What if someone called the police? Craig prayed that *something* would happen. The big problem for him was that Stephanie and the guy were behind him, and he couldn't see what was going on back there. If he moved on his own, she'd get shot.

Desperately he tried to reach out to her with his mind, but he couldn't make the contact across the space that separated them.

"Stop here," the guy ordered as they drew up beside a van that could have been a delivery truck. The only windows were in the front and in the back door. The rest of the rear compartment had solid walls.

The other man, the one with the wavy hair, opened the door at the back of the vehicle. "Get inside," he ordered.

Craig hesitated, thinking that if he followed directions, he'd never gain control of the situation.

"I said get in." The man behind him gave him a shove, and he flew forward, striking his head against the bare metal floor of the interior compartment.

His head hit the floor so hard that he saw stars. Behind him, he heard Stephanie cry out.

"Shut up," the man with the gun growled.

Craig fought to stay conscious as the man flipped him onto his back and pulled his hands behind him, quickly securing them with tape. He did the same with his legs, then rolled him back over and banged his head again, sending a wave of pain through his skull.

"Easy," the other guy complained. "We're supposed to deliver them in good shape."

"Yeah, well, that's for mauling me this afternoon," the curly-haired one answered while he tore off more tape and slapped it over Craig's mouth.

He was still trying to clear his mind as the bald-headed man shoved Stephanie into the van.

She gasped as he pushed her to the floor, then began taping her the way Craig was already taped.

He was silently screaming, racking his brain for some way out of this, but he could come up with nothing.

When both of them were secured, the men climbed out of the van and slammed the door closed, leaving their prisoners in the dark.

Craig struggled to think clearly, struggled to send Stephanie a silent message, but he couldn't reach her mind.

As the vehicle lurched away from the curb, he sensed Stephanie moving beside him. Through the fog in his brain, he realized that she was wiggling her body closer to his. Finally her right shoulder and arm were pressed to his left.

He felt her fear and also a spurt of hope as his thoughts collided with hers.

Are you all right? she asked urgently.

Yeah, he answered, knowing that she immediately picked up on the lie.

She rolled so that her body was half on top of his, and they pressed more tightly together. When she moved her cheek against his, he longed to raise his arms and fold her close. But the tape prevented that.

Still, as he absorbed the physical and the mental contact with her, he felt a profound sense of relief.

I'm sorry, she whispered in his mind.

For what?

For rushing out the window.

You thought your father was coming in.

Now I don't even know. Was it him—or them?

He had no answer, but he was thankful for the strong mental link that was letting them speak directly to each other.

What matters now is escape.

Who are these men?

No idea. But we have to get away from them, he repeated, trying not to think of horrible possibilities. Unfortunately, he knew Stephanie was picking them up from his mind.

We have to get this tape off.

How?

Remember when you were trying to move that book?

It didn't work.

Because we weren't touching. We are now.

He tried to send reassurances along with the silent words. It would have worked better if his head wasn't throbbing from the banging against the floor of the van.

I'm going to work on the tape on my hands.

How?

I'm going to stretch it. You send me energy. I can't explain exactly what that means. Just...maybe focus on what I'm doing.

He hadn't done anything like this in years, and with Sam, it had always been for fun. Now his and Stephanie's lives might depend on it.

When he heard her wince, he wished he had kept away from that last thought.

The van lurched, and he lost his concentration for a moment. He gritted his teeth as he struggled to focus. He had met Stephanie Swift only a few days ago, and he expected her to help him with a mental task that seemed impossible on the face of it.

We can do it. She answered the unspoken thought.

He made a sound of agreement, not because he was entirely confident but because they had no choice. They had to get out of this mess.

The pounding in his head made focusing difficult, but he kept at it. For minutes, nothing seemed to happen. Finally he felt some small measure of success—a tiny loosening of the bindings on his wrists.

Stephanie must have noticed it, too, because he felt her spurt of hope.

He worked at the tape. It seemed to take centuries, but finally he could part his wrists a little.

He was almost too mentally exhausted to continue, but

he kept at it, feeling the tape loosen more and more, and finally he was able to wiggle his hands free.

He glanced toward the front of the van and was relieved to see that the two men were both facing forward.

Reaching for Stephanie, he began to slowly pull the tape off her wrists. It was easier to work manually, and he quickly got her hands free. She breathed out a small sigh and pulled her legs up so that she could remove the tape from her ankles. He did the same.

When his hands and legs were free, he eased the tape off his mouth, seeing that she was doing that, too.

Thank God, she whispered into his mind.

He thought about their next move. They were free of the tape, but they were still in a moving van. He looked around for something he could use as a weapon and saw nothing. Too bad he'd gotten rid of the gun that he'd taken from these guys.

We can't fight them.

What are we going to do?

Hope they have to stop at a light.

He glanced at the men in front who were paying no attention to the prisoners. Obviously they thought that the man and woman they'd restrained were no threat.

Praying that neither of their kidnappers decided to check on them, Craig inched his way toward the back of the vehicle. Pausing again, he checked on the gunmen. When he saw they were still facing forward, he pulled down on the handle, easing the door open a crack so that he could see out. He was relieved to find they were still in the city—but not a part he recognized.

Stephanie picked up her purse, which had been lying beside her, and slung the strap across her chest before moving to the back of the van with him, her shoulder pressed to his.

Get ready.

Their chance came when the van lurched to a stop again. He pushed the door open and leaped out, then reached to help Stephanie down. They were on a city street with cars immediately behind them.

"Where are we?"

"The financial district."

They heard an angry shout and turned to see Curly, the one in the van's passenger seat, jump out with his gun drawn.

"Come on," Craig said to Stephanie, taking her hand. They wove through the traffic, the maneuver creating a blast of honking horns. As a car came around the corner and almost plowed into them, the driver slammed on the brakes, then lowered his window and started cursing at them.

Ignoring the chaos, they kept running for their lives through the darkened streets as pedestrians stared at the scene. And the car that had almost hit them gave them cover for a moment.

As they ran, Craig looked around wildly, trying to figure out the best escape route.

It was Stephanie who took the lead. "This way," she shouted, darting down a dark passageway between two tall buildings.

Craig followed. He wanted to look behind him to see if the guy with the gun knew where they'd gone, but turning would slow them down.

Stephanie pulled on a side door. It opened and they stepped into a hallway.

They ran down to the first turn and dodged around the corner. Finally, risking a quick look back, Craig saw the gunman charging after them.

Instead of continuing the evasive action, Craig waited for the man to come barreling down the hall, then stuck out his foot, tripping the guy and sending him sprawling. Craig was on him in an instant, grabbing his hair and slamming his face against the tile floor, thinking that turnabout was fair play. The man gasped and went still.

Craig lifted the gun from the man's limp hand and shoved it into the waistband of his jeans, then covered it with his knit shirt. When he searched the man's pockets, he found no identification.

"We'd better get out of here."

"Don't you want to ask him why they're after us?"

"Yeah, but his partner could show up at any moment. We have to put distance between us and them."

She answered with a tight nod and followed him to a glass-enclosed lobby.

They stepped out into a plaza surrounded by office buildings.

Walking rapidly, they crossed to the opposite side, then back to the street. When Craig saw a taxi heading their way in the curb lane, he hailed it.

"Where to?" the cabbie asked.

Craig gave the address where he'd left his car.

As the vehicle took off, he scanned the street for the van and the men who had taken them prisoner, but neither was in sight.

When Stephanie started to speak, Craig squeezed her hand.

Not here.

She clamped her lips together and knit her fingers with his.

They were both breathing hard from the chase and the narrow escape. And now that the crisis was over, he could feel the sexual pull starting to surge between them.

Touching her made him want her, but the physical connection also seemed to strengthen the silent communication they'd first discovered in the dress shop. If they had been in a hotel instead of a cab, he would have taken her directly to the check-in desk and booked a room.

She caught the thought and glanced at him, then away.

"Sorry," he muttered. "It's a guy thing."

Not just a guy thing, apparently.

We have to find a safe place where we can figure out what's going on.

You think we can do it?

I hope so.

The cab pulled onto the street near her father's house where he'd left his car, but he asked the driver to stop halfway down the block.

The guy pulled to the curb, and they got out.

After paying the man, Craig motioned Stephanie into the shadows of an overhanging pepper tree. "Wait here."

"Why?"

"They could have staked out my car."

"If they know where it is."

"We can't assume we're in the clear."

She waited while he walked swiftly down the block, all his senses on alert, but nobody approached the car. It could be that the men didn't even know this was his rental. When he gestured for Stephanie to follow, she hurried down the block and climbed into the passenger seat.

He'd kept their physical contact to a minimum. But now they were off the street, and when she turned to him, he reached for her, feeling emotions flowing between them. Relief that they had made their escape, coupled with the sexual need intensifying between them. And, under that, the uncertainty about their situation—on so many levels.

He lowered his mouth to hers for a kiss that left them both gasping. He knew they should drive away because their attackers could come back. But he couldn't turn her loose, not yet. Everything inside him had gone cold when he'd seen that gun pressed to her head. He'd been scared spitless—for her. And he'd realized in that moment that he couldn't lose her.

He knew she took in his thoughts. Wrenching her mouth from his, she stared at him.

Yes, she whispered in his mind, telling him the same thing. She couldn't lose him.

How could I have gotten engaged to John Reynard?

You didn't know what he was.

It's more than that. If I'd married him, I would have tried to make the best of it. But that was before I knew you.

He tightened his arms around her. A while ago, he had been unable to comprehend a relationship stronger than the one he'd had with Sam. Now he was starting to understand the depths of what he had found with Stephanie. The link between them had gotten them out of that van—maybe saved their lives.

But we need...

To be closer.

Just allowing that thought sent a surge of arousal through him, yet he eased his body away from her.

We have to find a safe place where we can...

Make love, she finished for him.

"Yeah," he said aloud.

"My family has a cabin out in bayou country, near New Iberia. We can go there."

He let the picture of the isolated cabin fill his mind. They'd be alone, uninterrupted.

"Does Reynard know about it?"

"I don't think so."

He nodded, deciding he'd make a judgment about the hideout later. "Right now, I need to get my laptop from my bed-and-breakfast."

She tightened her hand on his. "Isn't that dangerous?"

"It's dangerous for my hard drive to fall into enemy hands."

"Enemy hands. You mean Reynard—or whoever those men are working for?"

"Right. Either one."

"What do they want with us?" she asked in a strained voice.

"I don't know, but we'd better find out."

"I know it's a stretch, but do you think it has something to do with…that clinic?"

"Someone who wants to hurt John could be after you."

"He didn't share that with me if it's true. And they came after both of us."

"Well, they could be mad that I rescued you."

"Okay. Right."

"On the other hand, they could have just killed me and left me there—then taken you in the van. But they took both of us."

She sucked in a sharp breath.

"But back to your question about that clinic. You have to wonder why they wanted to keep testing the children." Deliberately he took his hand away from hers.

She leaned back against the seat with her eyes closed.

Hell of a day, he said.

Hard to imagine, she answered.

His head jerked toward her. "We weren't touching."

Her eyes widened. "That's right."

"But we spoke mind to mind."

Yes.

"We have to strengthen that skill."

"Yes," she answered again. "We have to see how far apart we can get and still do it." She turned her head toward him. "Did you and Sam have to be touching to speak mind to mind?"

"At first we did. Then later we could do it farther and farther apart."

Excitement bubbled inside him as he contemplated the possibilities, but he ruthlessly cut off those thoughts. The first thing he had to do was make sure they were safe. From Reynard and from whoever else was after them.

"WHY HAVEN'T YOU reported in?" John Reynard asked the men he had stationed outside Stephanie's house.

"Nothing to report," Tommy Ladreau replied. "She's still home."

"How do you know?"

"Her car is still where she left it when she came home from her father's."

John considered that assessment. He would have called the shop if it had still been open. Was she still holed up in her house?

The tracking device he'd had the men put on her car showed the vehicle hadn't moved. But what if she'd left on foot. Or—in another car?

That question brought to mind the man who'd been stalking her. Craig Brady. There was no information about him, which probably meant that Craig Brady wasn't his real name.

"Give her another hour," he said, "then go knock on the door and tell her you're just checking in."

He got off the phone and called a man in the police force who often did some work for him.

"This is John Reynard," he said when his contact picked up.

"Yes?" came the cautious reply.

"There was an incident at Stephanie Swift's clothing boutique earlier today."

"Like what?"

"Two men came in and threatened her, and another guy charged in afterward and fought them off."

"Okay."

"I want you to go over there and dust for fingerprints. I want to know who those men were."

"I can't do it right away."

"I think you'd better drop what you're doing and get busy," he said, then hung up.

CRAIG DROVE BACK to the French Quarter and found a parking space around the corner from his bed-and-breakfast. He would have told Stephanie to wait in the car, but he knew from her thoughts that she wasn't going to let him go back there alone.

They held hands, trying to look casual as they kept to the sides of the buildings, heading back toward the antebellum mansion where he was staying. But all his senses were on alert as he scanned the area around them. Before they reached the mansion, he spotted one of the men who had kidnapped them, waiting in the shadows across the street. It was the bald guy.

Stephanie caught Craig's thought and went still, then followed his gaze.

The man was looking toward the house, and they were able to back up and around the corner.

"We have to get out of here."

"I need my computer."

"That's too dangerous."

"Let me think." He laughed softly. "Too bad we can't convince him we're invisible."

"Oh, sure."

He shrugged. "It's worth considering."

She stared at him. "You think we could do something like that?"

"I think we may have a lot of possibilities we can explore. But not until we can get out of the city."

He knew she wanted to ask him to give up on his computer, but he wasn't willing to do it—not with so much data in it. Of course, it was password-protected, but an expert could probably hack his way in.

"If this guy is out front, you can assume the other one is at the back."

"Yeah."

"Let's check that out."

They reversed their steps, heading back to the alley on the perpendicular street. Staying close to the buildings, they walked quietly toward the mansion. They spotted the curly-haired man in the yard across the street before he spotted them. As Stephanie stared at him, she took Craig's hand.

He caught his breath when he saw what she had in mind. "No."

Chapter Nine

"No," Craig repeated.

"You have a better idea?" Stephanie asked as she scanned the alley, which was empty of people.

When he couldn't come up with one, she said, "There's a drugstore in the block back there. Let's go get some duct tape."

"You like the idea of poetic justice?"

"You know I do."

They went back for the tape, then separated. Stephanie walked to the end of the alley where they'd entered before, and Craig went the other way. When they had visual contact with each other, she started walking down the alley as though she wasn't aware that she was in any danger. Craig hurried to get into position.

As she'd predicted, the man saw her and stepped out of the backyard where he'd been hiding, his gun in his hand.

Stephanie stopped and gasped.

As the man closed in on her, Craig rushed behind him. The thug must have heard him, because he whirled. Before he could fire, Stephanie pushed him to the side, throwing him off balance. Craig brought the butt of his gun down on the man's head, and he collapsed.

After looking around to make sure nobody was watching, they pulled his limp body into the backyard where he'd been hiding and quickly taped his hands and feet, the way they'd been taped in the van. His face was already battered and bruised from when Craig had slammed his head against the floor.

He groaned, and Craig shook him. His eyes blinked open. For seconds they were clouded with confusion before he focused on his captors.

"Who are you working for?" Craig asked as he crouched over the captive.

Curly's only answer was a feral glare.

Craig slapped him across his bruised face, and he gasped. "Who?"

The man looked desperate, but he answered, "I don't know."

"Nice try."

"It's the truth. We was hired by phone."

"How did they know to contact you?"

"I guess we got a reputation."

Craig snorted. "Okay, I can buy that. Where were you supposed to take us?"

"To the parking lot of a shopping center in Thibodaux."

Craig sighed. If it was true, it was an arrangement designed to reveal the least possible information if this guy was apprehended.

"We got away from you. Did you tell your client?"

"Yeah."

Craig fired more questions at their captive. "And what did he say?"

"He sent us here."

"It's a man?"

"Yes. At least I think so, unless it's a woman using one of those fancy things that distort your voice."

Craig sighed. "Why did he want us?"

"He didn't say."

"So you have a number to call. What is it?"

"I can't tell you."

Craig raised his hand, and the man cringed, then spit out a number. Stephanie pulled a pen and paper from her purse and wrote it down.

Figuring he'd gotten what he could, Craig slapped a piece of tape over the man's mouth, then handed the captured gun to Stephanie. "Keep him covered."

While she held the gun in a two-handed grip, Craig went through the man's pockets. This time he found a wallet and a cell phone, which he took.

The man made an angry sound as Craig took the money from the wallet. There were no credit cards or identification.

"I'll be back in a couple of minutes. Keep him covered."

He knew she didn't want to be left alone with the guy, but she didn't voice the complaint as he hurried to the back door of the bed-and-breakfast.

Was he making a mistake coming back here?

He hoped not.

Cautiously he opened the door and scanned the back hall, but it was empty. Still ready for trouble, he climbed to the second floor and tested the knob on his door. It was still locked, and he inserted the key.

To his relief, it looked as if nobody had been in the room since he'd left it that morning. He threw his computer into a carry bag and grabbed the suitcase that he'd left packed. Two minutes after he'd entered the room, he was on his way out.

As he ran back down the alley, he cast his mind ahead of him. At first he heard nothing mental, then about twenty yards from where he'd left Stephanie with the thug, his thoughts suddenly collided with hers.

Thank God.

Everything's fine.

She answered with a silent laugh. *I guess that's relative.*

The guy glared at them as Craig stepped into the backyard. "Let's get the hell out of here."

The man on the ground stared bullets at their back as Craig hurried Stephanie away.

"Can we stop at my house?" she asked.

TOMMY LADREAU HEAVED himself out of the car and stretched.

He'd been watching Stephanie Swift's house for hours, and he was sure he wasn't going to find out anything new by knocking on her door.

But those were his orders, so he ambled across the street and knocked.

When there was no answer, he looked back toward his partner.

Marv Strickland got out of the car and joined him.

"Now what?"

"Let's see if her car's really there."

They walked around to the back of the house. The vehicle was still sitting where Stephanie had left it when she'd come home.

They exchanged glances, then crossed the enclosed patio and knocked on the side door. Still no response.

Marv pulled out his cell phone and called their boss.

"Stephanie Swift's car is here, but she's not answering her door. What do you want us to do?"

There was a long silence before Reynard answered.

CRAIG SIGHED. "We're already pressing our luck. You can pick up some clothes at a discount department store outside of town."

"It would be a lot more efficient for me to just take some stuff from my house."

He thought about it, knowing that she'd be more comfortable with her own things. "If you're quick," he finally said.

They drove toward her house, and he slowed as he came to the cross street. The car where the two men had been watching the house was still there, but he couldn't see anyone inside.

"Duck down," he said to Stephanie.

She slid lower in her seat as he turned the corner and drove by the car. It was empty, but as he drew abreast of her front door, it opened, and one of the men who had been in the vehicle stepped out. He saw Craig, and their eyes met.

Craig swore under his breath and stamped on the accelerator. The man shouted to his partner, who also dashed out of the house. Both of them ran for their vehicle as Craig sped away.

Stephanie popped up in her seat, trying to see what was going on.

"Stay down," he shouted, but he had the feeling the damage was already done.

He wove through the French Quarter, trying to avoid pedestrians. A truck pulled in front of them, blocking their way.

Craig leaned on the horn. Stephanie looked in back of them and dragged in a strangled breath. When he looked in the rearview mirror, he could see the car gaining on them. It pulled up behind them, and one of the bodyguards jumped out.

"Make sure your door is locked," Craig shouted.

Stephanie pressed the button seconds before the man reached her side of the vehicle and yanked on the door handle.

Just then the truck moved a couple of feet, giving Craig

room to maneuver around it by putting his left wheels on the sidewalk.

"Turn down the alley," Stephanie told him.

He took her advice, turning right and heading for the next street. They came out on Esplanade, and he turned right again. Although the bodyguards were no longer in back of them, he kept up a circuitous route through the city, thankful that there was no tracking device on his rental.

"They saw me with you," Stephanie whispered. "They'll tell John."

"You can say I kidnapped you."

"Oh, sure."

"It could be true."

"That guy saw me lock my door."

"Maybe I was holding a gun on you."

She clenched her hands into fists.

"Sorry," he murmured.

"What do you want to do?" he asked, his breath frozen in his chest.

She swung her head toward him. "I don't want to go back to John Reynard, if that's what you're asking."

He managed to breathe.

She reached for his hand, and he felt the mental connection they'd established—and sensed her thoughts. Her fear of John Reynard. Her relief that she'd escaped. Her fear that perhaps she'd jumped from the frying pan into the fire.

Yeah, he silently answered.

So now what?

I think we'd better not go to your cabin. Give me some other suggestions.

Houma?

The other guys could be looking for us there.

She named another town. "It's about twenty miles from Houma."

"That should work."

As they drove away from the city, he felt a mixture of emotions. He'd found a woman who shared a bond with him that was stronger than anything he'd ever experienced, but that might be the reason someone was trying to capture them.

She caught the thought. *Sorry.*

We'll deal with it.

How?

It depends on what we're up against.

He put thirty miles between them and the city before stopping at a shopping center.

"Just pick up a few things," he said. "You can use my toothpaste."

"I'm very particular about toothpaste. What brand?"

When he told her, she laughed. "I guess we were on the same wavelength there."

He knew she was trying for a light tone as she exited the car. He hesitated for a moment, then climbed out.

She looked at him.

"I don't want to leave you alone."

He pushed the shopping cart while she made some quick selections of T-shirts and jeans, then headed for the health section, where she picked up deodorant and moisturizer.

In some ways, it was such an ordinary domestic shopping trip. A man and his girlfriend getting a few things for a weekend getaway.

When she glanced at him, he knew she'd caught the thought.

But it's something I never expected to share.

Yes, she answered.

When she pulled out her credit card at the cash register, he shook his head.

"I'd better pay cash."

Right. I wasn't thinking.

I can use the money I took from baldy.

She laughed. *Perfect. And your gambling winnings.*

Yeah, there's that.

They finished up quickly, then headed for the town she'd mentioned. On the outskirts, she pointed to a bed-and-breakfast called Morning Glory that advertised cottages.

"What about there?"

He slowed and looked at the place, knowing it appealed to her.

"How are we going to pay," she asked, "if we can't use a credit card?"

"I still have money from that thug. He had a lot of cash on him."

"Yes. Good."

"Stay in the car while I register."

When she gave him a questioning look, he explained, "I don't want us seen together, if possible."

When he stepped into the office, he saw a middle-aged woman sitting at the desk. Her name tag read Helen Marcos.

"Can I help you?" she asked.

"My wife and I have been traveling around the area, and we'd like a nice room. In a private cottage, if possible."

"Magnolia Cottage is one of my best. It's got a bedroom and a sitting room and a large bathroom with a separate tub and shower."

"That sounds perfect."

He took the key and went back to the car. "I have a room I think you'll like," he said, feeling the tightness in his chest.

They'd both heard the phrase "get a room." They both knew why they were getting this room.

The cottage was white clapboard, with green shutters and a couple of wicker rocking chairs on the porch.

"Nice," Stephanie murmured as she inspected the exterior.

They were careful not to touch each other as they gathered their things.

Craig unlocked the door, and they stepped into a sitting room furnished with antique chests and tables and what looked like a comfortable chair and couch.

"Let me check it out," he said, taking a quick look at the bedroom and then the large bathroom. He came back to the bedroom and drew the drapes over the window, darkening the room.

When he turned around, he saw Stephanie was standing a few feet away.

The mixture of anticipation and uncertainty on her face made his mouth go dry. He hoped his expression was more certain. He had longed for this kind of connection since he'd lost Sam. They'd grown up together and forged a bond as naturally as breathing. And now he felt even closer to Stephanie. It must have something to do with the clinic, but he didn't know what that was yet. He knew he and Stephanie were on the verge of something astonishing. If they dared to take the next step.

"Are you afraid of this?" he managed to ask.

"You know I am."

"You think it would be possible to walk away from each other now?"

The question brought a spurt of panic. "No."

He saw her swallow.

"I never made love with John Reynard," she said.

"Thank God," he heard himself say.

"I came up with excuses."

As she spoke, she took a step forward, and he did the same. They reached for each other, swaying as they clung together.

It's going to be okay, he said.

We don't know that.

Do you want to...stop?

I don't think we can. Not now.

He absorbed the truth of her silent words as he lowered his mouth to hers for a long, hungry kiss.

When they'd gotten close before, they'd picked up thoughts from the other's past. Now there was nothing between them but this moment in time.

They were alone with each other. And this time nothing was going to stop them. And yet they both understood that they were taking a risk that neither of them fully understood.

Chapter Ten

Craig kissed her again, his hands moving over her back, down to her hips, pressing her middle to his erection, knowing they were about to change everything.

Everything already changed the first time we touched.

That was true, too.

His head was pounding, a counterpoint that he wished he could banish. But it seemed to come with the arousal.

Maybe this is like the first time a woman makes love—there's pain, she suggested.

Not a headache. That's a different cliché. But we should go back to what you said first. What if we have to break through a barrier between us?

How?

He sent her a very graphic picture. When she moved her body against his, he knew they were on the same wavelength.

He slipped his hands under the edge of her knit top, sighing as he stroked the soft skin of her back.

Then he reached up to unhook her bra so that he could slide his hands to her front and cup her breasts, gliding his thumbs across the hardened crests.

"Oh."

He bent to kiss her again, his goal to make her so hot that she couldn't think about anything besides what they were doing together. Maybe that was the way to wipe out the pain building inside his skull.

He knew she'd captured that thought when she slid her hand down the front of his body, cupping his erection, rocking her palm against him.

Not too much of that. I want this to last.

She raised her hands, doing what he had done, slipping her fingers under his T-shirt so that she could stroke his back before pushing the fabric up.

He stepped away from her and pulled the shirt over his head.

By the time he'd tossed the shirt away, he saw that she was standing in front of him naked to the waist.

He stared at her in the dim light coming through the crack at the edge of the curtains. "You are so beautiful."

She grinned. "Your chest isn't bad, either."

He crossed to the bathroom, turning on the light and leaving the door a little ajar. When he looked back to her, he saw that she had turned down the covers and was reaching for the button at the top of her slacks.

"Let me."

She went still as he crossed to her, worked the button, then slowly lowered the zipper so that he could shuck her pants down her legs, taking her panties with them.

He felt so much. Too much. Sexual arousal, the thoughts leaping toward him—and the pounding in his head that might wipe out everything else.

He strove to put that worry out of his mind. It wouldn't happen if they did this right.

Which was what, exactly?

As he caressed her, he moved his lips against hers, stroking then nibbling with his teeth. He knew the exact amount of pressure that would bring her pleasure instead of pain, because he felt her reactions as well as his own.

She was busy, too, removing his pants and briefs.

Finally they were naked in each other's arms, and his need for her threatened to overwhelm him.

If he didn't make love with her...

He couldn't finish the thought because he knew that neither one of them could stop. If he pulled away from her now, his brain would explode. And if he didn't pull away, the same thing might happen.

She understood all that, and he sensed her fear. But they clung together, never breaking the contact as they staggered to the bed and fell onto the mattress. He rolled toward her, gathering her close, his body rocking against hers, both of them gasping at the sensation of skin against skin.

They were both trembling, coping with more than it seemed possible to bear. His head throbbed, and he knew that he might stroke out from the intensity.

He heard her gasp. Not just the sound, but in his mind—generated by the same pain he felt.

But he couldn't let her go.

Maybe that was the key to survival. The courage to see this through—no matter where it led.

Remembering his vow to arouse her to fever pitch, he slid his hand down her body again, dipping into the folds high up between her legs. She was wet and molten for him, and he didn't have to ask if she was ready to take the final step. He knew.

And she didn't have to use her hand to guide him into her. They simply did it, moving from separate individuals to one being in a smooth, sure motion.

He was inside her. Or was she inside him? He didn't know anymore where he ended and she began. He only knew that every sense was tuned to her. Every thought. And she to him.

One of them began to move. No, it was both of them, because the pressure in their brains was too great and the only way to relieve it was through sexual climax.

That didn't make sense. Yet he thought it was true, at least with the part of his mind that could still function coherently.

Or was it simply instinct that had him grasping for orgasm and bringing her along with him, because if it didn't end soon, he knew he would die.

He couldn't make absolute sense of that, but he was far beyond trying to understand what was happening. He was captive to the fiery sensations—his and hers—that were rushing them toward ecstasy…or death.

He couldn't have stopped now if the door had burst open and men with guns had come charging in, firing at point-blank range.

He clung to Stephanie and she to him. Not just with his hands but with his mind. He had thought he was searching for remembered intimacy. This was so much more that he was at a loss to comprehend it. Yet as he hovered on the edge of a blinding explosion inside his brain, he wasn't sure he would survive.

Only the woman who held him in her arms saved him from destruction.

And because every barrier between them had vanished, he knew it was the same for her. They would die together—or pull each other into a new life.

They crashed through an invisible barrier that separated them from everything they had always known. Climax shook them, blinding them to everything but what they had forged. They clung tightly to each other as they came down to earth, each of them panting, each of them marveling at what they had done together.

In that moment, there was nothing he could hide from

her. Nothing she could hide from him. He didn't even try, just drifted on the perfect oneness of their shared consciousness.

Since his brother's death, he had felt cut off from humanity. This woman had filled the empty void within himself. More than filled it. She had given him a perfect union that he never could have imagined.

I always felt alone, she whispered in his mind. *Not now.*

He held her and stroked her, so grateful that she was in his arms.

But I still don't understand it, she silently added.

I thought I did. This is more than I ever imagined, he answered.

She clasped his hand and held on tight. *Making love gave us everything we wanted, but it could have killed us. If...*

If we had a failure of nerve.

You knew what we could gain.

I only thought I knew.

Neither one of us was going to give up.

Rolling to his side, he took her with him, feeling more peaceful than he had since the terrible day Sam had died.

Emotionally exhausted, he felt sleep wafting over him and tried to fight it off.

Yes, I don't want to lose a moment of this, she whispered in his mind.

I'll be here when you wake up. I'll always be here, he answered. But for the moment, it was impossible not to drift off after the energy they had expended.

BACK IN NEW ORLEANS, a woman named Rachel Harper went very still. She was alone in her shop in the French Quarter where she did tarot-card readings and sold psychic paraphernalia. Once she had been alone and isolated, and she'd used her ability with the cards to connect with people on a level that would have been impossible otherwise. But last year she had met a man who had changed her life. Jake Harper.

The two of them had bonded in a way she had never dared imagine. And being with him had changed her life in ways she was still trying to understand.

As she sat alone in her darkened reading room, a burst of mental energy came to her from miles away. It startled her, and she knew she wouldn't be alone here for long. Only a few minutes passed before the door to her shop burst open, and her husband, Jake, rushed in, out of breath from running.

He'd been in his office at one of the restaurants he owned in the city.

Something happened. Are you all right? he asked.

Yes.

Are we in danger?

I don't know, she answered honestly.

Jake crossed to her side, reaching for her hand and folding her fingers around his. For long moments, neither of them moved or spoke, although speech was no longer necessary for the two of them to communicate.

You sensed another couple bonding, he finally said.

I think so.

Are they going to attack us?

Someone who didn't know their history might have thought the question paranoid, but the first couple like them that they'd encountered, Tanya and Mickey, had tried to kill them. The fight for their lives had made them cautious.

They were thinking the same thing now.

We have to wait and see what happens.

Are they in trouble?

Probably.

Does that mean we *have a new enemy? I don't mean them. I mean...someone connected with the Solomon Clinic.*

I guess we'll find out.

SOMETIME DURING THE NIGHT, Stephanie woke. Beside her, so did Craig.

He eased far enough away to switch on the bedside lamp, and they both blinked in the sudden glow.

When he raised himself on his elbow and smiled down at her, she felt her own smile starting with her mouth and spreading through her whole body.

"Would you have believed that could happen—if anyone had told you?"

"No."

"We've found something nobody else has."

"Maybe somebody," she answered.

"Who?"

"You think there's nobody like us? I mean, you and Sam had it."

"Close. But not exactly."

"Before we had to leave my dad's house, we were talking about the Solomon Clinic. About maybe it having something to do with…" She raised one shoulder. "I don't know how to put it, exactly. With children who had special abilities. Maybe we should look up the place."

"Nice that I was able to get my computer from the bed-and-breakfast."

As he went to retrieve his laptop, she admired his broad shoulders and tight butt.

I heard that.

She flushed. *I guess there are some disadvantages to... being so...open to each other.*

Sam and I used to practice closing off our minds from each other. We could try that.

And that other thing—that you didn't mention.

He went still, then turned around. *You mean putting thoughts into people's minds.*

Yes, that. Why didn't you say something about it?

Even as she asked the question, she knew that he'd considered it a questionable skill. Like stealing.

I understand, she answered. *But it might come in handy when someone is trying to kidnap you—or kill you.*

Yeah.

When he returned with the laptop, she had an opportunity to admire him from the front. And although she did her best to keep her thoughts to herself, she knew he'd picked them up again.

As he slipped into bed beside her, she asked, "How *do* you keep from having everything in your mind like an open book?"

"You build a wall."

"Like how?"

"With Sam, I used to picture a wall made out of metal plates. Let me show you."

She saw the concentration on his face as he made the wall. Reaching for his hand, she held on tight as she tried to get into his mind and came up against the barrier. Maybe there was a way around it, but she didn't find it as she searched.

You try it, he suggested.

She tried to do the same thing he had done, make a wall that would block out her thoughts. It was easy to picture the wall but not so easy to keep it in place.

I'd spend a lot of energy keeping it intact, she said, struggling with a sense of defeat.

Keep practicing, and you'll get better. I hadn't done it in years, and it came back to me.

She built fortresses in her head while he booted up his computer.

"You think there's anything on the web after all these years?"

"We'll find out."

She moved beside him where she could see the screen, pulling the sheet up over her breasts.

He glanced at her and grinned. "I've seen them."

She flushed. "I know, but I'm not as casual about walking around naked as you are."

She knew from his thoughts that he planned to desensitize her—in the shower.

I should practice that wall thing, he answered.

She smiled and moved her shoulder against his. It would have been impossible for her to imagine this wonderful closeness with anyone. But Craig had changed her world.

Mine, too. When the computer finished its start-up routine, he went to Google, looking for information about the Solomon Clinic. At first they found nothing. Then he added Houma, and a startling newspaper entry came up.

"The explosion at a research laboratory owned by Dr. Douglas Solomon is under investigation. The facility was being used by Dr. Solomon for medical research. His body was found in the wreckage of the lab, along with Violet Goodell, who was the head nurse at the doctor's former fertility clinic and also a close personal friend. She was active in charity work in Houma. Another body found in the wreckage was that of William Wellington, former head of the Howell Institute, a Washington think tank. According to anonymous sources in Houma, Wellington may have had a financial interest in the Solomon fertility clinic, but it is not known why he was at the research facility when it exploded.

The Solomon Clinic was in operation until the early nineties, when it burned to the ground in a fire that was believed to be the result of arson. There were no casualties.

Dr. Solomon was a native of Houma. His clinic drew patients from all over the U.S., but principally from Louisiana and neighboring states, and was instrumental in helping over two hundred women conceive. Although the clinic was known for charging high fees to wealthy clients, it also took less-well-off patients at greatly reduced fees. After the facility burned down, the doctor maintained a low profile, but his research facility is believed to have developed vaccines for several nationally prominent drug companies."

Stephanie looked at Craig. "That article is interesting, as much for what it doesn't say as for what it does."

"Yeah."

Craig went back to the search panel and looked up the doctor's biography. He was a Yale graduate who had gone on to Harvard Medical School, then returned to his hometown to open his fertility clinic.

"I guess he was pretty smart," Stephanie murmured. "I'd like to see his records from the fertility clinic, but they probably burned."

"That may be the reason for the earlier fire—to get rid of the records."

"Why?"

"It sounds like he was doing more than fertility treatments." She looked from the computer screen to Craig. "We should go there."

"Not until our skills are more solid."

"Why?"

"I'm thinking we're going to need them to defend ourselves."

Stephanie shuddered, and she knew Craig had picked up on her thoughts as she felt him stroke his hand down her arm.

We just found each other—why can't whoever it is just leave us alone?

Because there's something important about the children from the clinic. And someone's interested in what it is.

When Stephanie jolted, Craig didn't have to ask what had leaped into her mind.

We both forgot we got that phone number.

You want to call it? He asked.

She considered the question. *I don't think that's going to get us any information. And we'd just be revealing something about us.*

Yeah. Forget calling.

Chapter Eleven

Harold Goddard slapped his fist against his left palm, but the physical gesture did nothing to relieve his anger.

He was used to working with professionals, and now he was finding out the pitfalls of relying on local talent.

The men he'd hired had had Stephanie Swift and Craig Branson in custody—and the incompetent asses had let the couple get away.

They'd compounded the mistake by waiting a couple of hours before reporting their failure.

"Tell me again what happened," he said to Wayne Channing, the bald-headed man who had been recommended to him as the best there was if you needed an undercover job done in the Big Easy.

"Like you said, we looked for them at her father's place and found them there. They were climbing out an upstairs window, and they dropped right into our laps. We took them to the van, with our holding her at gunpoint and his cooperating so she wouldn't get hurt. We loaded them in the van and taped their hands and feet."

"And then what?"

"Something happened. We was in the middle of traffic, and they got loose and got out the back door."

"How did they get loose?"

"We don't know."

"Didn't you restrain them securely?"

"We thought we did."

"You thought?" Harold said in a calm voice when he wanted to scream.

"Somehow they got away."

"Did you look at the tape?"

"No."

"Bring me the tape. Well, leave it in a plastic bag next to the Dumpster at that shopping center where I wanted you to bring them."

There was a moment's hesitation before Channing said, "Yes, sir."

"And how did they get the better of you at the B and B?" Harold asked.

"They spotted us, then made a tricky move. She acted like she didn't see me, and he snuck up behind and brained me."

Harold thought for a few minutes. He could yell at this guy. He could bring him in and kill him. But that would be counterproductive because he'd just have to find someone else to do the work.

"After you drop off the tape, I want you to go to Houma, Louisiana, and stake out a building in the business district." He gave the address. "I expect they are going to show up there."

He thought about what had apparently happened in the van and what he thought might be going on with the children who had been born as a result of their mothers' treatments at the Solomon Clinic.

"When you catch them, make sure you separate them. I don't want them touching each other. Understood?"

"Yes, sir," Channing answered.

WE HAVE TO STRENGTHEN our powers, Craig said when they woke up the next morning, too late for breakfast.

How?

When Stephanie caught the suggestion forming in Craig's mind, she gave him a doubtful look.

You don't think that will be effective? Even if we've never done it before? he asked.

Before she could make any decisions on her own, he had her out of the bed and into the bathroom. He turned on the shower and let the water run hot before helping her into the tile enclosure where a rain shower sent a torrent down on her.

The heated water turned her skin slick and sensitive, and her whole body tightened as he pulled her close.

For long moments, he simply held her, the two of them standing together under the pounding spray.

From behind her, he began to run soap-slick hands over her back and shoulders. As they glided with a total absence of resistance, they sent heat vibrating through her body.

He turned her in his arms and brought his mouth to hers for a heated kiss while he angled her upper body away from his so that he could stroke his hands over her breasts, turning her nipples into taut peaks of sensation.

She squeezed her eyes closed, focused only on Craig Branson and the sensations he was creating—and the thoughts pouring off him as he told her how much it meant to him to have found her, how much he wanted her, how much he loved her.

Love.

The word stunned her. She had never expected to love anyone. She hadn't even loved her parents, she silently acknowledged, which was probably why she had let her father persuade her to marry the wrong man.

But everything had changed.

I love you, she answered him, sure it was true, even though she had known him such a short time. But what had happened between them had changed her life. Had changed everything.

He lowered his mouth to hers for a long, hungry kiss as his hand stroked down the length of her bare back, sending heat shooting through her as he caressed her bare bottom.

As his hands slid over her, wet heat pooled between her legs. She knew he felt it, felt it in his own body. And she felt the fullness of his erection, felt his need to join with her.

The need built, pulsing through her and through him in time to the wild beating of their hearts.

And she knew what he wanted her to do. Following his lead, she slicked her hand with soap and wrapped her fingers around his jutting erection, starting with a teasing stroke that drew a strangled breath from him. When she closed her fingers tightly around him, the breath turned into a moan.

Looking down, she grinned at the effect she had created. He'd been fully aroused when she'd started. Now he was impossibly hard.

She caught what he had in mind, and tried to do what he'd suggested before.

And suddenly the water stopped, leaving them standing in the shower, dripping.

You did that.

Yeah. And now I get my reward.

Leaning back against the side of the shower, he lifted her into his arms. She cried out as he filled her, holding her against himself as he turned on the water again with his mind so that it pounded down on them once more. His movement was restricted by his braced hips. But as he held her, she moved her body, the friction taking them to a high peak where the air was almost too thin to breathe.

She loved the intensity on his face—in his mind—as she quickened the pace.

His exclamation made her raise her head as she stared at the water pouring down on them. She had stopped thinking about the water, but now it was pulsing in time to the movements of her body.

She drove them to a sharp, all-encompassing climax that radiated to every part of her body while the shower seemed to explode in a cascade of water.

She felt Craig follow her into ecstasy, and as they came back to themselves, the shower settled down to a normal flow.

She heard Craig's silent laugh. *That last part was...*

Unexpected, she finished as she collapsed against him and he lowered her to her feet.

Proof we can do more with our minds than we thought.

I don't believe we can count on sexual arousal every time we need to generate psychic power, she answered.

He reached for a towel and trapped it around her shoulders, then began to dry her off.

As he did, she caught the thought in his mind.

You're full of ideas, she answered.

You don't think we should try it?

Is it ethical?

We're not going to harm anyone. We're just going to have a practice session.

THEY GOT DRESSED, left the room and stopped at the office to ask for lunch recommendations.

Mrs. Marcos suggested several restaurants, and they decided on a place with a deck along the bayou and an extensive seafood menu.

On the way over, they discussed Craig's plan.

The restaurant was pleasantly decorated with rough-hewn wood on the walls and old-time photographs from the twenties and thirties. The dining room was about half-full, with plenty of tables available both inside and out.

They walked in and stood together waiting for the hostess to return to the podium. She was a young woman with curly blond hair and a bright smile.

"We'd like a table," Craig said without volunteering any other information. But silently he was asking to sit out on the deck—along the railing.

"I have a lovely spot on the deck along the railing," the hostess said.

Craig gave Stephanie a satisfied look. "That would be great," he said to the hostess.

They followed her outside, to the only prime spot left at the edge of the deck.

"Your server is Julian, and he will be right with you," the woman said before she left.

"That went well," Craig said when they were alone.

"It doesn't prove anything. She could have just decided to give us this spot."

He shrugged. "Okay, we'll see what we can get the server to do."

A dark-haired young man wearing a black T-shirt and black pants approached the table carrying a pitcher of water.

"Hi, I'm Julian, and I'll be your server this evening."

They'd silently agreed that Craig would get him not to pour the water and ask if they wanted tea instead.

As he lifted the pitcher, she fed Craig energy.

Julian's hand shook for a moment, and he lowered the pitcher, a strange expression on his face.

"Uh, I was wondering, would you prefer iced tea?" he asked.

"Why, yes, we would," Craig answered.

"Sweetened?" he asked.

"Correct again."

"I'll be right back with your tea."

When the young man had departed, Craig wiggled his eyebrows suggestively at Stephanie.

She laughed. "Okay, that was pretty good. Maybe we can work up a stage act."

"Yeah, it *was* good, and you can't argue that he was pushing tea instead of water."

She nodded and opened the menu, scanning the entries. "Now what?"

"Get him to suggest that we try the popcorn shrimp?"

"Too easy. He's probably already thinking about them."

CRAIG RAN HIS FINGER down the menu. "Get him to sell us the fried okra."

"Have you ever tasted it?"

"No."

"It's an acquired taste. Let's try something else."

He turned back to the menu. "Okay, buffalo wings."

When the server returned and set down their glasses of tea, he asked, "Can I get you started with an appetizer?"

"What's good?"

Again Stephanie let Craig make the silent suggestion to the man while she added her power to his mental push.

"I think you'll love the buffalo wings," Julian said.

"Excellent," Craig answered. "Bring us an order."

He slid his foot along the deck boards and rested his shoe against Stephanie's. "Score another one for us."

Making food selections isn't that hard. Do you think we could have made those thugs who kidnapped us put down their guns?

Not then. Maybe now, Craig answered.

You'd bet your life on that?

No. That's why we're practicing.

We're just playing games, she shot back.

That's all we can do—unless you want to get some-one in town to rob a bank. It's got to be stuff that's within bounds of the law.

I don't think you're going to get that guy to jump into the bayou. And I don't want to suggest something that would get him fired—like tossing the buffalo wings over the rail-ing. What if we see if we can get him to deliver them to the wrong table?

Okay.

They relaxed at their table, sipping their iced tea. When Stephanie saw the waiter come back with the wings, she sent Craig a silent message. *He's here.*

Craig let her direct the next part, but she felt him lend-ing energy. She told the guy to deliver the appetizer to the table in back of them, and she saw his face take on a con-fused look. He stopped for a second, then walked past them to the next table.

Behind her she heard the couple telling Julian that they hadn't ordered the wings. In fact, they were waiting for their dessert.

He did a quick about-face and came back to Craig and Stephanie, his cheeks flushed.

"Sorry about that. I don't know how I got mixed up."

"Don't worry about it," Craig said.

We have to stop playing with him, Stephanie said when he'd left the food and departed.

Yeah, poor guy.

They ate the wings and ordered shrimp étouffée and grilled snapper, which they shared before returning to their cottage for some more intimate practice sessions.

Worn-out, they fell asleep, but the events of the past few days had taken their toll.

JOHN REYNARD PICKED UP the phone. The police detective on the other end of the line said, "I have some information for you." The caller was the guy he'd sent over to the dress shop earlier who took substantial amounts of money under the table to keep Reynard informed on police-department business.

"Go ahead."

"I have a fingerprint report on the man who called himself Craig Brady."

"That's not his name?"

"He's Craig Branson. He's a private detective out of the Washington, D.C., area."

"What the hell is he doing here?"

"I'm working on that. He made an inquiry about a body that turned up in the bayou. A guy named Arthur Polaski."

John felt a frisson go through him. How did Branson know about *that?*

"You think Branson is in New Orleans investigating Polaski's death?"

"Or what he did before he was killed."

"Yeah, thanks for the heads-up."

The cop hesitated. "I think one of the other guys in the department gave Branson the heads-up about Polaski."

"Why?"

"Apparently Branson made it his business to keep in touch."

Oh, great, John thought. But then he supposed if you had a police department full of informants, you couldn't control who was giving out information to whom.

"You need anything else?" his contact asked.

"Can you find out if Branson has used his credit card recently? Maybe I can get a line on where he went."

"Okay. Do you want him arrested?"

"For what?"

"He's down here using an assumed name. We could have him brought in for questioning."

"Yeah. That might be good. If you can find him."

"There could be an accident while he's in custody."

"Even better."

STEPHANIE KNEW she was dreaming, but there was nothing she could do about it and no way she could stop the course of events her mind had conjured up.

The dream started at her father's house. She and Craig climbed out the window and down to the ground. Then she rounded the corner and ran into the two thugs with the guns. Only this time was different. This time she was alone.

They hustled her to the van, and she kept crying out in her mind, crying out for Craig, but he simply wasn't there. She was totally alone. The way she had been all her life. Only now she knew what it was like to be bonded with her soul mate. But he wasn't there. He had vanished. And she couldn't go on alone. Not after what she'd found with him.

The two thugs were there, but they weren't her only captors. John Reynard stood over them, telling them to tape her hands and feet. He was telling them to take her away, to a place where Craig could never find her.

His eyes met hers, and she felt ice forming in her chest and throat.

"You betrayed me with that man."

"No," she lied.

"You belong to me," he said. "I'll take you back, but only if you promise never to see that other guy again."

Her mouth worked, but no words came out. How could she make that promise? How could she say she would never see Craig again? That would be as good as death.

Chapter Twelve

In the dream, the two thugs were holding her down in the back of the van, and she struggled against them, knowing that if they drove away with her, she was dead. Desperate to escape, she kicked out with her foot, making one of them gasp.

Good.

Someone was calling her name, and it didn't sound like either of the men who had taken her captive, or like John.

"Stephanie. For Lord's sake, Stephanie."

She heard the words in her ears—and in her mind. And they finally penetrated through the dream.

It was Craig. He was here, calling her, holding her.

Her eyes blinked open, and she stared up at him, catching his relief.

Stephanie.

Craig, she answered. *I was so scared. I was dreaming those men had me, and John was there.*

I know. I caught the edge of the dream as you started to wake up.

I thought I'd lost you.

You'll never lose me.

She sighed deeply as she held on to him, overwhelmed with gratitude that he was here—with her. Yet she knew he couldn't make the promise to be with her always. He could be yanked away from her, the way his brother had been yanked away from him.

No. I promise.

Despite his reassurance, her thoughts were racing. *Something awful is going to happen. We have to get away before it does. Can't we leave Louisiana? Go somewhere nobody knows us?*

She caught his reluctance to consider the desperate suggestion. *I understand why you want to run, but we won't really be safe until we find out who's after us.*

How do we do it?

The answer must be in Houma.

She shuddered. *I don't want to go there.*

I know. He gathered her closer, running his hands up and down her back, combing his fingers through her hair, stroking his lips against her cheek.

She relaxed into his embrace, so grateful to have him.

The feeling's mutual, he murmured in her mind.

He rocked her in his arms, and when he began to make love to her, she brought her face up for a long, heated kiss.

JOHN REYNARD RANG the elder Swift's doorbell and waited, impatiently tapping his foot on the floorboards of the wide front porch.

It was early in the morning, earlier than he liked to be making a business call, but he had spent a restless night worrying about Stephanie. She'd disappeared, and he had to find her.

He'd gotten a call back on the Craig Branson credit card. It hadn't been used, which meant that the guy was being careful about revealing where he was.

The last John knew, Stephanie was with him, and he meant to find her. And get her away from the guy.

Was she a prisoner? Or had she willingly gone with the

bastard? And what had Branson told her to get her to go along with whatever the bastard had in mind? Had he told her about the body of Arthur Polaski?

But why would he? Unless he was trying to turn her against her fiancé.

One thing John knew was that she'd left her car at home. Of course, there was no absolute proof that she was with Branson, but it was John's best guess.

In the middle of the night, he'd sent a message to a P.I. who worked in the D.C. area and started the guy checking into Branson's background, looking for something that would explain why the man had shown up to investigate a twenty-two-year-old murder. And why he was dragging Stephanie around.

When no one answered the door, he rang again.

"I'm coming," a voice called from inside.

The crackly old voice sounded like Henri Swift.

Half a minute later, a shadow appeared behind the lace curtain that covered the glass panel in the middle of the door. Finally the barrier was pulled open, and John and one of his men stepped inside.

Swift blinked at him. He was wearing an old burgundy satin dressing gown. His hair was mussed, and his cheeks were covered with gray stubble. Obviously his visitor had gotten him out of bed. "What are you doing here at this time in the morning?"

"Looking for my fiancée."

"She isn't here."

"Maybe not now. But was she?"

When Swift hesitated, John wanted to smack him upside the head. "Answer yes or no."

"I think she was here."

The answer elicited a curse. "Are you saying you don't

know for sure? Are you saying she came in and didn't speak to you?"

"I was out."

"Doing what?"

Swift's face tightened. "Getting supplies."

"Liquor?"

"I was running low."

John made a disparaging sound.

"I came home, and I thought she was in the house. But when I looked for her, she'd snuck out. If she was here at all."

"What makes you think she was here?"

Swift shifted his weight from one foot to the other. "I don't appreciate your barging in on me like this."

"Oh, you don't? Well, you don't have much choice."

"We have an agreement."

"That's right, and I don't know where the hell to find your daughter. If she was here, I want to know why and where she went."

"All right. I heard someone upstairs, but nobody was there. When I investigated, I saw that the bedspread in her mother's room was mussed."

John felt a wave of anger sweep over him. She hadn't made love with him, but had she come here to do the deed with Branson? "You mean she was on the bed with someone?"

"I don't think so. I think she took a bunch of boxes out of the closet and put them on the bed."

"You're quite the detective."

"It's my best guess."

"Show me the bedroom." He turned to the bodyguard he'd brought along. "Wait here."

"Yes sir."

John was already barreling up the stairs, then had to wait for the old man to come huffing after him.

He led the way down the hall to a bedroom that looked as if it hadn't been touched in years.

"What boxes? Why?"

Swift opened the closet and pointed to the top shelf. "That's stuff my wife kept around. Stuff I couldn't throw out."

"And why do you think Stephanie was into it?"

"The boxes aren't piled up exactly the way they were."

"I mean, what was she looking for?"

"I don't know."

John marched to the closet and pulled the boxes down. He could see folders and piles of old papers. Photographs and schoolwork from when Stephanie had been little. He wasn't interested in the sentimental crap, but he looked at the pictures anyway, trying to find something that would give him a clue.

There were photos of the family when Stephanie was little. He hoped he wasn't going to find that guy Branson's smiling face.

That thought gave him pause. She didn't know him from her past, did she?

He looked up, seeing Swift watching him.

"Get me some coffee. No cream. No sugar."

He could see the man wanted to say he wasn't John Reynard's servant, but he kept his mouth shut and shuffled out of the room. John could hear him rattling around downstairs, then a few minutes later Swift brought a mug of coffee. At least it was a strong New Orleans brew laced with chicory. John sipped while he looked through folders, wondering if anything would strike him. And wondering why he was bothering. Maybe because if he couldn't have Stephanie with him, he could at least paw through her past.

The notion made him snort. John Reynard didn't settle for less than he was due. But in this case, he'd have to settle until he could change the equation.

He came across some forms and instructions from a place called the Solomon Clinic in Houma. Apparently it was a fertility clinic. And it looked as if Stephanie's mother had gone there for treatments before she was born. That was interesting. Did it mean that Stephanie would have trouble conceiving children? He hadn't considered that when he'd decided he had to marry her because it certainly hadn't been his main reason for wanting to keep her close. Kids would be good, though, because it was a way to keep hold of her. If she was worried about losing custody of her children, she wouldn't be quick to leave her husband. But that was all in the future. It didn't give him a clue to where she was now. He put the folder back into the box and kept looking for information he could use.

"Do you have a second home?" he asked Swift.

"Yes."

"Where?"

He gave the location.

That might be a possibility.

When his cell phone rang, he looked at the number with annoyance, displeased to be interrupted in the middle of his search.

Then he recognized the area code and knew it was the guy in D.C. he'd hired to dig up stuff on Craig Branson. Maybe he'd found something that would be more useful than these piles of old papers and pictures.

He got up, walked into the hall and answered the phone.

"Mr. Reynard?" the detective said.

"Yeah."

"I've been digging into Branson's past."

"Have you found any dirt?"

"Not anything illegal that he's done, but he was involved in an incident a number of years ago."

John felt his heart leap. Was this something he could use?

"What?" he demanded.

"He and his family were eating dinner in a restaurant when a mob boss named Jackie Montana was gunned down."

John felt the hairs on his arms prickle.

The man continued, "The guy and two of his bodyguards went down. It turns out Branson's twin brother, Sam, was collateral damage."

An exclamation of disbelief sprang to John's lips. "You mean at a place called Venario's?" he managed to ask.

"You know about it?"

"It made the news," John answered. He'd ordered that mob hit because Jackie Montana had been trying to muscle in on John's New Orleans operation. John had known that there were some civilians hit, but he'd never paid attention to the names of the victims. That hadn't been his concern.

"You're sure about that?" he asked now.

"Yes."

John's head was buzzing, but something the man was saying penetrated the swirling thoughts in his brain.

"What did you say?" he asked.

"Which part?"

"About the clinic."

"Okay. Yeah. After Sam died, the mother tried to get in touch with a place called the Solomon Clinic. Down your way, in Houma."

"Okay. Thanks. You have the address."

"I have the old address, but the place burned down."

They talked for a few more minutes before John hung up.

"Thanks for your help," he said to Swift.

"I didn't do much."

"You noticed."

When he started out of the room, the older man called out, "Hey, what about all that stuff on the bed?"

"I'm sure you can put it away."

He knew Swift was angry, which pleased him.

Outside he turned to his man. "You and Marv are going down to Houma."

"For what?"

"Stephanie and that bozo she's with might show up there."

"Like where, exactly?"

"There was a clinic down there they might want to check out. I'll get you the address."

"WE CAN LEAVE our things here and drive over to Houma," Craig said.

"And do what, exactly?"

"We could start with the archives at the local papers, or we could try something else."

When she asked for details, he said, "I'll tell you about it on the way over."

They walked to the main house, where Mrs. Marcos was in the dining room.

"I hope you slept well," she said brightly.

"Yes, of course," Stephanie answered. "The cottage is charming."

"You can sit anywhere you like. Breakfast is served buffet-style."

They took a table by the window, then helped themselves to the buffet on the sideboard, indulging in the coffee cake and muffins that Mrs. Marcos had set out—along with her spinach quiche and strong Louisiana coffee.

"I didn't see you at breakfast yesterday. Are you enjoying your stay?" the B and B owner asked as they were finishing their breakfast.

"It's perfect," Stephanie answered.

"And we enjoyed your accommodations so much that we're hoping to keep our room for another night," Craig added.

"That would be fine. Where are you off to today?"

"We thought we'd drive over to Houma."

"It's a lovely little town."

"Didn't I read about some kind of explosion there?" Craig asked.

Mrs. Marcos's expression clouded. "Yes. At an underground research lab," she said, then pressed her lips together, indicating that she didn't want to continue the subject.

What do you mean by "underground"? Craig asked.

"Nobody in town knew Dr. Solomon was still doing research." The woman stopped, looking confused. "Well, I guess some people did know. Like his nurse, Mrs. Goodell. She worked for him at the old clinic...." Her voice trailed off. "I don't know why I'm prattling on like this. I have things to do in the kitchen."

"You're just being friendly," Stephanie said in a pleasant voice when her heart was pounding. She added her psychic power as she let Craig direct the message he sent the B and B owner.

If you know anything more about the Solomon Clinic or Dr. Solomon, tell it to us now. He repeated the suggestion, waiting tensely for what she would decide.

The outcome wasn't a sure thing. Stephanie could see the woman going through a debate in her mind, and she felt Craig pushing the idea.

"So who was this Dr. Solomon?" Stephanie asked.

"Thirty years ago, he had a fertility clinic," she said

as though she didn't really want to speak the words. "My friend Darla Dubour went to him, and she was so appreciative when she got pregnant. She had a little boy. David."

"It's always nice when medical treatment works out," Stephanie said brightly. She caught a stray thought from Craig and asked, "Where is her son now?"

The woman's eyes clouded. "He died."

Stephanie sucked in a startled breath. "What happened to him?"

"I should stop talking about this."

"I'm sorry. I don't know how we got on the subject. I guess we were just looking for information about Houma so we could plan our day."

"You can get that from the chamber of commerce or the town hall."

"Yes, thanks," Stephanie said, but the other woman was already bustling toward the dining-room entrance, where another couple was waiting to be seated.

I guess we hit some kind of nerve, Stephanie said to Craig when they were alone again.

Yeah. There must have been some blowback from the Solomon Clinic.

Or it's because that woman's son died.

I think we should go see her.

You think she'll talk to us? Stephanie asked.

Maybe we can use the same method, Craig answered.

I hate doing that to a grieving mother.

I don't love it, either, but if it saves our lives, I'm willing to try it.

She winced.

They went back to their room, where they used the computer to look up Darla Dubour in Houma, Louisiana, and found that she lived in a small community outside of town.

"Should we call her?" Stephanie asked.

"I think it's better if we just go over unannounced."

They were in the car and on their way a few minutes after they'd looked up the location.

Stephanie felt a chill go through her.

Craig reached to cover her hand with his. "You're thinking we're going to find out something bad about ourselves when we talk to that woman?"

"Yes."

WAYNE CHANNING and his partner, Buck Arnot, Harold Goddard's men, had arrived in Houma the evening before.

Because they'd been ordered to stake out the location where the Solomon Clinic had been located, they had spent an uncomfortable night in their car in a grocery-store parking lot where they could see the target location.

"Got to pee," Wayne said as he moved restlessly in his seat.

"There's a gas station a couple blocks down."

"But we're supposed to keep the building in sight."

Channing sighed. "This is a real long shot."

"But we got our orders."

"Okay, I'll drive down to the gas station and do my thing. You stay here and watch the building."

"And get arrested for loitering."

"Walk up the sidewalk and back again, like you're out for your morning constitutional."

"Yeah, right. Come back with coffee and doughnuts."

"What flavor?"

"Surprise me." Buck climbed out and watched his partner drive off. When he was out of sight, he ducked around by the Dumpsters. He didn't need a smelly gas station to relieve himself. Then he started down the block, looking in shop windows.

When he got to the cross street, he turned and walked back, then did it again.

He was going to call Wayne on his cell and ask if he'd fallen into the gas-station toilet when he saw something interesting.

A car turned in at the grocery-store parking lot where he and his partner had spent the night. As he watched, two tough-looking men got out and stretched, as if they'd just finished a long drive.

Their gazes were fixed on the building that he and Wayne had been watching.

When he saw his partner coming back, he flagged him down and climbed back into the car.

"I can go into that parking lot and we can switch. You can drive to the gas station, and I'll wait here."

"I already done it out by the Dumpsters."

Wayne made a disgusted sound. "Didn't your mama teach you better?"

Ignoring the comment, Buck said, "Keep on drivin' past that parking lot."

The urgency in his voice made Wayne glance toward the lot, then speed up.

"Two tough-looking guys," he said.

"Yeah. I'm thinkin' they might have the same assignment we do."

"Why?"

He shrugged. "Must be a lot of interest in Swift and Branson."

"So what are we gonna do?"

"Call the guy who hired us and ask for instructions."

"He's probably still sleeping.'

Buck's voice took on a nasty tone as he turned toward his partner. "Well, we got reason to wake him up."

Chapter Thirteen

"I thought we'd take a look around town before we talk to Mrs. Dubour's," Craig said as he pulled out of the driveway of the B and B.

Stephanie closed her hand around his arm.

"Don't go there."

His gaze shot to her, then back to the road as he tuned in to her thoughts.

"You think it's dangerous to go into Houma," he said aloud, considering the implication of her words.

"Yes."

He silently debated her assessment. "You think the men who kidnapped us might be looking for us there."

"Yes."

"Which would mean they know something about the Solomon Clinic."

She nodded.

"Okay, we can go straight to Darla Dubour's."

"How are we going to approach her?"

"I think honesty is best. We tell her that we found out we were born as a result of treatments our mothers received at the Solomon Clinic and came to Houma to see if we could find out more about the clinic. We were talking to Mrs. Marcos, and she told us about David, and we'd like some more information, if she can give it to us."

"And if she doesn't want to talk to us?"

"We try our new technique."

RACHEL HARPER SHUFFLED a deck of tarot cards and laid one of them on the table.

Her husband, Jake, took in the worried expression on her face.

"It's the Hierophant, isn't it?" he said.

"Yes. He's the archetype of the spiritual world. The card can refer to a person who holds forbidden or secret knowledge."

"Which means what, in this case?"

She sighed. "You know how relieved we were when Solomon and Wellington were killed."

Jake nodded.

"Suppose there's someone else who knows about the children from the Solomon Clinic?"

"And he's trying something similar to what Wellington was doing?"

She clenched and unclenched her fists. "Yes."

"Which means we should stay away from him."

"Or it means we need to reach out to that other couple. Unless they turn out to be our enemies."

"Try another card," Jake suggested.

Rachel fanned out the deck and pulled out the Ace of Cups. When she smiled, Jake stroked his hand over her shoulder. "The start of a great love," he murmured.

"You're learning the cards."

"I like knowing what you know."

"A great love—ours or theirs."

"Let's see one more card," Jake said.

Rachel pulled out the Five of Swords and caught her breath.

"What?"

"Well, it usually means you are defeated, cheated out of victory by a cunning and underhanded opponent."

"You think it refers to that other couple?"

"Or to the person who is going against them and us. But sometimes with the Five of Swords, you are that victor. You're the one who wins over your opponents by using your mind."

"That sounds like us."

"And them."

"And you still don't have enough information to trust them?"

She shook her head. "It's not just us who would be at risk. It's also Gabriella and Luke," she said, referring to Gabriella Bordeaux and Luke Buckley, another couple who'd been born as a result of treatments at the Solomon Clinic. Rachel and Jake had come to their rescue, and they had formed a little community, using the plantation property Gabriella had inherited from her mother. Rachel and Jake lived there part of each week and commuted to New Orleans so that they could each maintain their business interests in the city, Rachel with her shop and Jake with his antiques and restaurant businesses.

"Can you at least try to figure out where they are?"

Rachel closed her eyes and leaned back in her chair, sending her mind outward.

"If Mrs. Dubour won't talk to us, we're no worse off than we were before," Craig said.

They drove away from town, turning off onto a secondary road that led to a small community at the edge of the bayou, checking the house numbers on the mailboxes as they drove.

When they came to number 529, they turned into a rutted gravel drive that was about fifty yards long. At the end was a white clapboard house with blue shutters surrounded by a trimmed lawn and neatly tended flower gardens edged with white painted rocks.

A car was parked in front, and they pulled up behind it and walked to the front porch that spanned the front of the house.

It took several moments for them to hear movement inside after they knocked. Finally an old woman opened the door. She looked to be in her late seventies, with wispy gray hair and a lined face. She was wearing slippers and a faded housedress.

"I'm not buying anything," she said as she stared through the screen door. "And I'm not interested in any religious lectures."

Stephanie shook her head. "We're not selling or preaching. Are you Mrs. Dubour?"

"Yes."

"We'd like to talk to you about your son, David."

She stiffened. "What about him?"

"We're staying at Mrs. Marcos's bed-and-breakfast, and we were talking to her this morning. She told us that you were treated at the Solomon Clinic before David was born."

"What about it?"

"Our mothers were both treated at the same clinic, and we wanted to find out what you knew."

Her expression had become less hostile as she'd listened to Stephanie speak. "I guess you'd better come in," she said.

Craig let out the breath he'd been holding as the older woman stepped aside. They followed her into a small, neat sitting room furnished in old maple pieces and a bulky sofa and overstuffed chairs.

"Sit down," she said, gesturing toward the sofa.

They sat, and she took one of the chairs opposite, where she watched them with speculative interest.

"You say your mothers went to the same clinic that I did?"

"Yes."

"How do you know?"

"It goes back to my twin brother being killed by mobsters in a restaurant when I was eight."

The old woman sucked in a sharp breath. "I'm so sorry."

"After Sam died, I remember hearing my mother trying to contact someone at the Solomon Clinic, but it was already closed by then."

"She wanted to have another child?"

"That's my guess."

"Weren't there other clinics she could have gone to?"

"Maybe she only had faith in Dr. Solomon."

"Yes, he had a way of projecting strength and reassurance."

Stephanie got back to the original question. "We looked through some of my mother's papers and found literature and application forms from the clinic."

"And how did the two of you get together?" Mrs. Dubour asked.

"I got some information on who might have caused my brother's death. I came down to New Orleans to investigate and found Stephanie," Craig explained, giving an abbreviated version of how they'd happened to hook up.

The old woman looked from one of them to the other. "Did you think it was odd that the two of you ended up meeting each other?"

"I wasn't thinking about it," Craig said.

Mrs. Dubour shook her head. "Maybe you should have," she said in a hard voice.

Craig kept his gaze fixed on her. She looked like a typical aging housewife, but she obviously had spent a lot of time thinking about what happened to her son. And she'd come to some interesting conclusions.

"Something similar happened with my David."

They both stared at her. "What do you mean?"

"David was living at home and working at the hardware store in Houma when he got an email from a woman who said she'd gotten his name from a lawyer who was investigating inequalities in fees charged at the Solomon Clinic. She said her mother had paid thousands to be treated there, and his mother had gotten her treatment for free. The woman was all hot under the collar, and she came charging down here to see David. She was a weird, kind of flighty girl. I took a dislike to her right away, but as soon as she and David locked eyes on each other, something changed with him. With both of them, I guess. I mean, you could see sparks flying between him and that girl."

"What was her name?" Craig asked.

"Penny Whitman."

"What happened?"

"I saw them outside under the willow tree, holding hands and looking like they'd been hit by a meteor or something, like they were having some kind of secret communication nobody else could tune in on."

Craig nodded, understanding perfectly.

"David was so happy. I'd never seen him like that before. They took off, and I never saw David alive again. He and the girl were found in a motel room in bed together—both of them dead."

Stephanie sucked in a sharp breath. "What happened to them?"

"The coroner said it was like both of them had had a cerebral hemorrhage."

"My God," Stephanie whispered.

"I'm sorry for your loss," Craig said.

Mrs. Dubour nodded. "Losing him would have been more of a shock if I hadn't felt that I'd lost him years ago. Or that he never really belonged to us."

"What do you mean?" Stephanie asked.

"I was so excited to have a child," she said, her voice low and wistful. "But he never was, you know, normal. He always kept to himself. He wasn't affectionate with me or my husband. He never did date much when he was a teenager." She gave both of them a sharp look. "Am I telling you things you understand about yourselves?"

"Yes," Stephanie whispered.

Craig also nodded in agreement.

She kept looking at them. "But you met each other, and something changed for you?"

"Yes."

"You went off together, like my David and that girl, only it turned out different for you."

"Yes," Craig said.

"You're alive, and he's dead."

"I'm sorry he died."

"Because he hooked up with that woman. Why did it kill them?"

Craig wasn't going to tell her that it had to do with forming a telepathic bond that might overwhelm the two people involved.

"I don't know," he said.

Mrs. Dubour kept her gaze on them. "I guess you two should be careful."

"Yes," Stephanie whispered, although Craig knew from her mind that she was sure they had made it past the dangerous phase of bonding.

"Did you ever find out anything about the lawyer who sent the woman down here?"

"I didn't pursue it."

"Do you happen to know his name," he pressed.

She hesitated, probably coping with all the sad memories he and Stephanie had dredged up. It would be kindest to let her be, but because they had come here for information, Craig gave her a push. *If you know who the lawyer was, you should tell us. We'd really appreciate the information.*

She was silent for several more moments, then said, "She came down here with the email."

"You mean from the lawyer?"

"Yes." Mrs. Dubour got to her feet and left the room. While she was gone, they both waited tensely, wondering if she'd really be able to put her hands on the evidence. Finally she returned holding a piece of paper. "Here it is."

When she handed over the paper, Craig scanned it. It was from a Lewis Martinson in Washington, D.C.

"Thank you so much," Stephanie said. "We really appreciate this."

They talked to Mrs. Dubour for a few more minutes. When the woman stood up, her shoulders slumped.

"I'm sorry to have brought all this up for you," Stephanie murmured.

"I hope it does some good."

When they were back in the car, Stephanie turned to him, and he felt the relief in her mind.

"We could have ended up like David and that woman."

"Yeah."

"We both had a headache when we first made love. I guess that was a symptom of…"

"Getting ready to have a stroke," he finished for her.

"What was the difference for them?"

"We can't know for sure. Maybe the pain was too much for them to focus on the pleasure. Maybe they lost their nerve at the last minute, and when they didn't bond, they'd already set the process in motion."

When he saw a shiver go through her, he reached for her hand, holding tight.

"We got through it," she said. "Thank God we didn't understand the danger."

"I guess it's a crap shoot—how it turns out," he said.

"I prefer to think that we had something they didn't."

He laughed. "We were hornier."

She grinned, then sobered. "It looks like somebody wanted to get David and that woman together. Maybe to find out what would happen."

"I don't like being manipulated."

"Likewise. How did you happen to come down to New Orleans?"

"I never gave up the idea of finding out who was responsible for Sam's death, which was one of the reasons I maintained connections with police departments all over the U.S."

"Interesting that the body turned up after all these years."

"You think…"

He let his voice trail off, but he knew where her mind was going. Somebody had deliberately arranged for him to receive the information because they wanted him to come down to New Orleans and investigate the man responsible for Sam's death—which would mean that he would meet Stephanie Swift.

"Which meant they knew investigating John Reynard would lead you to me," she murmured. Then she added, "It's someone who knows there's something…strange about the children from the clinic." She looked at him. "How, exactly, did you find out about Arthur Polaski?"

"I got a call from a contact at the New Orleans P.D., Ike Broussard."

"You think he's working with Lewis Martinson?"

"I'll be surprised if it's that simple."

"Then what are we going to do?"

"We could talk to Broussard and look up Martinson. Unless you want to go poking around in Houma."

She thought about that. "I think that would be dangerous, because Martinson already knows we're likely to come to Houma."

"Agreed."

"And I wouldn't have any more contact with Broussard."

"You could be right about that."

They stopped to pick up lunch at a fast-food restaurant, then returned to the bed-and-breakfast, where Craig booted up his computer and looked up Lewis Martinson. There were several people with that name, but none of them was a lawyer in Washington, D.C.

"Now what?" Stephanie asked.

"I'm thinking."

Chapter Fourteen

Ike Broussard swiped his shirtsleeve across his forehead and sat for a moment in his unmarked car, postponing the moment of reckoning. A lawyer in Washington, D.C., had paid him to make sure a guy named Craig Branson got some information about a cold case. Now he was realizing that he could have put his balls in a wringer.

He'd thought John Reynard would never know who had given Branson the information. But somehow it had gotten back to him, and now Ike was in deep kimchi.

Finally he opened the car door and hoisted his two-hundred-fifty-pound bulk to the cracked sidewalk.

He didn't count it as a good sign that Reynard had asked to meet him at one of his warehouses.

He buttoned his sports jacket over his bulging middle, then decided it looked better unbuttoned.

Glancing up at the redbrick building, he saw that a couple of video cameras were tracking his approach to the warehouse door. So if he didn't come out of here alive, would Reynard destroy the tapes?

Trying to look confident, he walked through the door, which led directly onto a dimly lit space half the size of a football field stacked with boxes. But there were no men working the forklifts that sat along the left wall. He looked upward, locating the metal balcony on the other side of the room. Up there was an office where he'd been told to meet Reynard.

His footsteps echoed on the cement floor as he crossed the room, then clanged on the metal stairs. At the top, he looked toward the lit office.

Two bodyguards were in the waiting area. They gave him a knowing look as he knocked on the door to the inner office.

"Come in," Reynard called out.

His heart was pounding as he went in.

"Close the door."

He did as the import-export man asked.

"Thank you for coming," Reynard said.

Ike nodded.

"I assume you thought I wouldn't find out who told Branson about Polaski."

When Ike started to speak, he waved him to silence. "You made a mistake. Every man is entitled to one mistake."

The observation didn't stop the pounding of his heart.

"But you have a chance to redeem yourself," Reynard said.

Ike waited to find out what he had to do.

"I want the location of Branson's cell phone."

Ike didn't bother saying that giving out information was against the law. He only said, "Yes, sir."

"I want it by the end of the day," Reynard clarified. "And when you've got it, you're going to do something else for me."

AT THE COTTAGE, Craig pushed back his chair and stood up.

"What now?" Stephanie asked.

When he sent her a very explicit picture, she flushed. "Is that all you think about?"

"I'm a guy. When I'm locked in a room with a beautiful woman, I can't help thinking about making love to her."

"You're not locked in."

"Not technically, but I think we need to stay out of sight. Which means staying in here. Do you have a better suggestion for how to use the time?"

"Do you think Dr. Solomon was trying to create telepaths?" she asked.

"I don't know."

"It's kind of a stretch."

He nodded.

'So what if he was trying to do something else, and this is what happened?'"

"Work before pleasure. Let's do more research on the Solomon Clinic and see if we can figure it out."

"THIS IS THE ADDRESS," Tommy Ladreau said.

"Like the boss said, it's a bed-and-breakfast." He looked behind him at another car that had pulled up. It was a detective from the New Orleans P.D., a guy named Ike Broussard, and Tommy didn't like having him on the scene. But it had been the boss's orders.

"We don't know if they're in the main house or one of the cottages," his partner, Marv Strickland, said.

"Go see if you can spot his car."

Marv climbed out and made his way through the bushes to the main house, checking the cars in the parking spots. When Branson's car wasn't one of them, he started down the lane that wound through the property.

When he located Branson's rental, he stopped, then moved into the shrubbery again.

His orders were to bring Stephanie Swift back, and if he had to kill Craig Branson to do it, so be it. But Marv was hoping to avoid an outright murder in broad daylight.

He went back to the car and climbed into the passenger seat.

"You saw him?"

"I saw his car."

"Tell Broussard to do his thing."

Marv climbed out again and walked back to the car behind theirs.

"Go for it," he said.

CRAIG AND STEPHANIE came up with several more articles about the clinic, but nothing that would tell them what Dr. Solomon had been doing.

"I'm wondering if he was operating with government funding," Craig said.

"What about it?"

"That might be a way to get a line on whoever's after us."

"We also have the names of several women who worked there," Stephanie said. "Nurses."

"Yeah." Craig thought about that. "What if I talk to some of them? There's one who's living in a nursing home in Houma, for example."

"What do you mean—you? If you're going, so am I."

"You're the one who pointed out that it was dangerous to go into Houma."

"Yes, but…"

"You stay here, and I'll be back in a couple of hours."

"Don't go unless you know she's really there."

"Okay." He looked up the number and dialed the nursing home, asking if he could speak to Mrs. Bolton.

"She's not feeling well this evening," the woman who answered the phone said.

He felt Stephanie's sigh of relief.

"So you don't have to go see her."

Almost as soon as Craig clicked off, his cell phone rang and they both went rigid.

"Who could that be?"

He looked at the unfamiliar number.

"Don't answer."

"I'd better do it."

When he clicked the phone, the man on the other end of the line turned out to be Ike Broussard, the police detective who was responsible for his trip to New Orleans.

"Branson?" he said.

"Yes."

"I've got some information for you."

"What?"

"Not over the phone. I want you to meet me."

"Where?"

"At the Bayou Restaurant in Houma."

"You know about the Houma connection?"

"Uh-huh."

"What do you have for me?"

"I'll tell you when I see you."

"Something to do with the Solomon Clinic?"

The detective hesitated for a moment, then said, "Yeah."

"Okay."

He clicked off and looked at Stephanie.

I'll be back as soon as I can.

I was hoping you wouldn't leave.

I know.

He reached for her, and she came into his arms, clinging tightly. "I just found you. I don't know what I'd do if I lost you."

"You won't lose me."

They held each other for long moments, and he had to force himself to ease away.

"I'll be back as soon as I can."

He stepped outside the door of the cottage and stood for a moment, feeling the barrier between them. He couldn't see Stephanie now, but he could still feel her mind, and that was comforting. Even when he walked to the car and climbed in, he was still in contact with her.

Craig, he heard her whisper his name.

I don't like leaving you.

Then don't.

He didn't answer because there was nothing he could say. Still, he had to fight the need to turn around and go back as the contact with her faded and then vanished altogether.

He flashed back to the horrible moment when Sam had died and the contact between them had snapped.

This was the same, only Stephanie wasn't dead; she was just out of range. He would finish his mission and come back to the cottage, and she would be there waiting for him.

He turned on the engine and drove away, heading for the restaurant where Broussard had said he was waiting.

STEPHANIE WALKED BACK to the bedroom, where she and Craig had made love. While they'd been out, Mrs. Marcos had remade the bed.

Stephanie sat down, smoothing her hand across the spread, thinking that if she folded back the spread and climbed under the covers she'd feel closer to Craig. Maybe she could just sleep until he came back.

A knock at the door interrupted her thoughts.

"I'll be right there," she called out as she walked into the living room. Thinking it was someone from the B and B staff, she opened the door.

The two men she'd seen in the car across the street from her house barreled in, a mixture of triumph and relief on their faces.

As CRAIG DROVE into Houma, he kept alert for the men who had kidnapped him and Stephanie. He'd struggled to keep his thoughts to himself as he'd discussed this trip with Stephanie, but now that he was alone, he was aware that he was at risk. And as he thought about it, he couldn't be sure if Lieutenant Broussard was on the up-and-up. He drove slowly past the Bayou Restaurant, looking in the window, trying to spot Broussard. Although he'd never met the man, he was pretty sure he could identify a police detective.

But as he glanced in his rearview mirror, he saw a van in back of him, a van a lot like the one the two thugs had used when they'd kidnapped him and Stephanie.

He cursed aloud, speeding up, wishing he knew the city better. He'd insisted that Stephanie stay at the B and B, and now he realized he'd given up the one advantage he'd had. Together he and Stephanie had psychic powers they could draw on. Alone, he was the way he'd been for all the years since Sam had died.

He drove across a bridge that spanned a bayou, then across another, surprised at how much water flowed through the city. The van stayed behind him as he turned down a side street, then came to a screeching halt when the blacktop ended at the bank of a river.

There was nowhere to back up, no escape in his vehicle. Throwing open the door, he sprang out and started running along the edge of the bayou.

He heard running feet behind him and then the sound of a bullet whizzing past his head.

He ran down a short pier, then dived in, swimming deep underwater as more shots were fired. His only option was to keep going, trying to put as much distance between himself and the men with the guns while he veered downstream to make it harder for them to figure out where he would surface.

Finally, when his lungs were bursting, he swam to the surface and dragged in air.

He heard a shout, then bullets hit the water around him, but he was already diving.

He let the current carry him farther downstream. When he came up again, low-hanging branches shielded him from view.

Looking back, he saw the two men running along the bank, but it appeared that neither one of them was going to plunge into the bayou.

When he heard a splash, he looked to his right and saw an alligator slipping into the water.

Teeth gritted, he used a cypress root to pull himself out of the water, putting a tree trunk between himself and the men with the guns.

His clothing was dripping. His shoes were covered with mud, and he was out in the open. If he turned around, he would likely run into the men.

His only option was to keep walking, his shoes sucking in the mud as he put space between himself and the two men. He had left civilization behind. There was only dense vegetation on both sides of the water, cypress and tupelo and saw palmetto, until he came to a shack near the water. In front of it was a pier, and tied to the pier was a pirogue, one of the small boats that the local residents used.

He looked behind him and across the water. The men had lost him in the swamp, and he thought it would be safe to cross the water again. The shack in front of him looked deserted.

Turning toward the pier, he walked onto the weathered boards, heading for the boat.

Before he had gotten more than a few feet, a voice rang out behind him.

"You—hold up, or you're a dead man."

STEPHANIE FACED the two men, determined not to give them anything Reynard could use against her. "Thank God you're here."

"Oh, yeah? Looks like you were pretty cozy here with Branson."

"I thought his name was Craig Brady."

"Craig Branson," one of the men corrected.

"He was using a false name?" she answered, as if she was shocked.

"What were you doing here with him?" the shorter man asked.

"He was holding me captive."

"What did he want with you?"

"I'll talk to Mr. Reynard about that," she said, hoping she could come up with a story he would believe.

The guy snorted, and Stephanie fought to project the impression that she was telling the truth.

"Come on, we're getting out of here."

"Going where?"

"Mr. Reynard is waiting for you."

"Let me get my stuff."

He hesitated for a moment, and she struggled to project the idea that he had to give her a few more minutes here—time to leave a clue for Craig.

CRAIG TURNED to see a grizzled old man with a week's growth of beard, wearing a camouflage shirt, torn blue jeans and combat boots. He was holding a shotgun pointed at Craig's chest.

"Don't shoot. I need help," Craig said, raising his hands above his head.

The guy's face turned a shade less hostile as he took in Craig's appearance. "What happened to you?"

"Two guys with guns were chasing me."

"Yeah, why?"

Craig took a chance and asked, "Have you heard of the Solomon Clinic?"

"You one of the bastards who was runnin' that place?"

Craig shook his head. "I'm one of the children who was born as a result of Dr. Solomon's treatments. Somebody knows about us and is going after us."

The guy lowered the rifle. "Yeah. My nephew was one of them kids. He's dead."

Craig sucked in a sharp breath.

"He was one of the ones who got together with another kid from the clinic—and croaked in bed with her."

"I think my…girlfriend and I lucked out on that part. But somebody's been chasing us since we met."

"Where is she?"

"I left her at a B and B outside of town and came here to talk to a police detective who said he had some information for me."

"Don't never trust the cops."

Craig was already having bad feelings about Broussard. "You may be right."

His benefactor said, "You need dry clothes and a ride."

"I'd surely appreciate it," Craig allowed.

"I think I got something from my son that you can wear." He turned and walked toward the shack.

Craig followed, sloshing as he went, then hesitated at the doorway.

"I'll get your place wet."

"The water will go through the cracks in the floor. Come on in."

Craig followed the man inside. The interior looked a lot more comfortable than the ramshackle facade suggested. A lantern sat on a wooden table, illuminating a narrow bed, several chairs and a small kitchen area, all neatly arranged.

The old man opened a chest of drawers and pulled out a shirt like the one he was wearing and another pair of jeans.

Craig shucked off his wet clothing and put on the dry replacements. The pant legs were an inch too short, but they were better than what he'd been wearing. His shoes were still a muddy mess, but there was nothing he could do about that at the moment. His cell phone was ruined, and his wallet was soggy, but the money and credit cards inside would dry out.

"You got a way to get back to your place?" his benefactor asked.

"I left my car on the other side of the river," Craig answered.

"I can take you across."

They walked down the dock where Craig climbed into the boat and the old man cast off, using a paddle to propel them.

Craig looked back, seeing the dense swampy area where the shack was almost hidden from view.

"Thank you," he said when they got to the other side. As he reached for his wallet, the old Cajun shook his head.

"No need."

Craig climbed out and started along the shore, watching for the men who had chased him. It seemed they had given up the chase for the moment, but what about Stephanie? He made it to his vehicle and climbed in, torn between caution and speeding as he headed back to the B and B.

He wanted to rush to the cottage, but instinct had him stopping down the block and proceeding on foot, casting his thoughts before him, trying to contact Stephanie. He knew she had to be worried—and probably angry that he'd left her alone.

There was no mental sign from her as he approached the cottage, and he felt his chest tighten.

Then he saw something that stopped him in his tracks. It was Ike Broussard climbing out of a car and heading for the cottage.

As far as Craig knew, the bastard hadn't kept the appointment at the restaurant. What was he doing here now?

Craig sped up, calling out a mental warning to Stephanie as he watched the man push open the front door.

He'd barely disappeared inside when a massive explosion shook the little building, throwing Craig to the ground.

Chapter Fifteen

Craig covered his head with his arms as debris rained down around him. As soon as he could, he scrambled to his feet and ran toward the building.

"Stephanie. Oh, Lord, Stephanie," he called out as he surveyed the damage. The building simply wasn't there, and the man who had stepped inside had vanished.

Craig's whole body was shaking. He'd left Stephanie here when she'd begged him to take her with him. He'd thought he was doing the right thing, and now she was gone—the way Sam was gone. That had been the worst thing that had ever happened to him. This was a thousand times worse.

He heard a siren in the distance. The fire department and probably the cops. Instinct told him to get the hell out of there before the authorities arrived.

Quickly he backed away and ran down the block to the spot where he'd left his car.

"She's in the car. We're on our way," the man in the back-seat said into his cell phone. He listened for a minute, then said, "We expect to be there in forty-five minutes."

Stephanie knew that John Reynard had a number of residences. One was a plantation house about forty miles from New Orleans. Which was where they were going, Stephanie surmised.

After one of the men had hustled her out of the cottage, the other had gotten something out of the trunk and gone back to the cottage, but she'd had no idea what he was doing.

He'd given his partner the thumbs-up when he'd climbed back into the car. Then the three of them had sped away. Toward her doom? Or could she somehow save herself— and get back to Craig?

She modified that thought. She had to get back to Craig. She belonged with him, not with the man she'd promised to marry because of misplaced loyalty to her father.

She'd felt guilty about her relationship with him, and she'd told herself that was her fault. Now she knew it wasn't true. It had as much to do with him as with her, and it was too bad she hadn't seen that a long time ago.

But her father wasn't her immediate problem. *That* was John Reynard. Every time the car slowed to take a curb or stop at a traffic light, she thought about jumping out and making a run for it. But that would only confirm her guilt. And what was the chance that she could actually evade these men?

She would have to face John, but what could she say to him that he would want to hear—and that he'd believe?

It was hard to make her mind work coherently, and she was still trying to figure out what she was going to say when the car stopped at the gate across the access road. Once the house had sat in the middle of cotton fields. Now it was a fortified compound, guarded by men and a fence that circled the area around the house.

The barrier slid open, letting the car through, then slid closed behind her—like a prison gate clanging shut. The long drive was lined with live oak trees, making a majestic approach to the restored plantation house that had been newly painted white. It had a portico across the front that reminded Stephanie of Tara in *Gone with the Wind,* except that the entrance was on the second floor as in most Louisiana plantation houses.

When the car pulled up beside the wide front steps, Stephanie dragged in a breath and let it out, preparing for what was coming next.

Unable to move, she simply sat in the passenger seat.

"Get out," the man in back said, climbing out and opening her door.

There was no point in trying to stay in the car. It wouldn't do her any kind of good. She climbed out and stood on shaky legs, looking up at the steps.

When a figure appeared, she blinked. It was Claire Dupree, the woman who had been helping her in the dress shop for the past few months. Once the shop had been her life, but she hadn't thought about her business or her assistant in days. Now she tipped her head as she stared at Claire.

"What are you doing here?" she asked.

"John thought you'd appreciate having some female companionship."

"John asked you here?"

"Yes."

As Stephanie tried to work her way through the implications, a lightbulb suddenly went off in her head. Claire had come to the shop looking for a job not long after Stephanie had met John Reynard. She'd offered to work for almost no salary.

Now it was pretty clear why. Stephanie had been paying her a small salary, but she'd really been working for John Reynard. He'd sent her to Stephanie so that he could keep tabs on his fiancée.

"We've been waiting for you. Why don't you come in?"

Claire said, as if she was the owner of the house inviting in a guest.

With no other choice, Stephanie followed the other woman up the stairs and into the house, which had been furnished with many antebellum antiques as well as some comfortable modern pieces. The wide front hall boasted a sideboard imported from England with a gilt mirror hanging on the wall above. Like her father's house, but in much better condition. On the polished floorboards was a rich Oriental rug.

"Where's John?" she asked.

"He's in the lounge. There's some very interesting news on television."

The edge in Claire's voice made her wary, but she followed the other woman down the hall to the sitting room that John had set up like a room in a turn-of-the-century men's club, furnished with comfortable leather chairs and couches.

The walls were wood-paneled, and the only piece of furniture that looked out of character in the room was the flat-screen TV on the wall across from the sofa.

John, who had been sitting in one of the leather chairs, stood up.

He looked from her to the television, where an announcer was breathlessly reporting some catastrophe and it took Stephanie a few moments to orient herself. First she realized it was in Houma. Then she saw it was at a bed-and-breakfast. The reporter was pointing to what must have been a house or a cottage; nothing was left but a blackened hole in the ground.

"Police say there are no survivors from the explosion that destroyed one of the cottages at the Morning Glory B and B about an hour ago. At the time a Mr. and Mrs. Craig Branson were registered at the cottage."

Stephanie tried to take that in. In the background she could see the main building, and it looked as if the blackened ruin was the cottage where she and Craig had been staying.

"Sorry to report that your friend Craig Branson was blown up in an explosion while you were en route here," John said, the tone of his voice making it clear that he wasn't sorry at all.

Unable to catch her breath, Stephanie swayed on her feet. Claire caught her arm and eased her onto the couch, where she sat gasping for air.

John tipped his head to the side as he stared at her. "It isn't confirmed that your friend was in the cottage, but I presume that he rushed back home to you, opened the door and triggered an unfortunate incident."

"No," Stephanie whispered.

John glanced at Claire. "Go get Stephanie a glass of brandy. I believe she could use a drink."

Stephanie watched the other woman leave the room. Then she swung back to John when he said, "You're in a delicate position now."

She answered with a small nod, wondering exactly where this conversation was going. She was still struggling to come to grips with her new reality—back in the clutches of John Reynard. If it was her new reality. The explosion was real, but what if by some miracle Craig was all right?

She had to cling to that. It was her only option, because if she admitted that he was dead, what was the use of her going on? Or to put it another way, what did it matter what John Reynard did to her?

He was speaking, and she struggled to focus on his words. "So whatever you've been doing with him, it's over. And now we can take up where we left off."

"Yes," she managed to say.

"You refused to sleep with me until we were married," he said suddenly, his words and his tone lancing through the wall she had tried to build around her emotions. "A very old-fashioned attitude, I must say. Did you sleep with him?"

She should have been expecting the question. Well, perhaps not so bluntly. Now she froze, knowing that she was skating on very thin ice.

Raising her head, she looked John square in the eye, calling on all the salesmanship she'd learned at the dress shop. "No," she said aloud, and as she spoke, she did something else, as well—gathered her mental power and put it into her silent order to him. *You believe me. You believe I didn't sleep with Craig Branson. You believe it because you want to believe it. That's the answer you want to hear, and you believe me.*

Would it work? She certainly hadn't been able to do anything like that before she'd met Craig. The power had developed as a result of her connection to him.

A stray thought danced in her mind, a thought that gave her hope. Or was it false hope?

She brushed aside that last part. If she'd developed this power with Craig, could she still use it if he was dead?

She clung to that as she kept shooting her silent message to John, and maybe her faith that Craig was still alive made the suggestion stronger.

HAROLD GODDARD HELD UP the duct tape he'd asked his man to leave for him at the shopping center. It was the tape that had been used to restrain Swift and Branson. It was stretched slightly out of shape, as if it had somehow been melted. How had that happened? Had Branson or Swift done something to it? And if so, what and how? The speculation was cut off when his cell phone rang. He put down the tape and clicked the on button.

"You have them?"

"No," Wayne answered.

"You followed him, but you weren't able to get your hands on him?" Harold clarified.

"We had him cornered, but he dived into the bayou."

"And then what?"

The man on the other end of the line hesitated, and Harold could picture the scene.

"Did you shoot him?" he asked.

"We tried to wound him, but he got away."

"And he didn't go back to the bed-and-breakfast?"

Again the man seemed reluctant to answer. Finally he said, "When we didn't find him, we went back to the place where they were staying."

"And?"

"There was an explosion," Wayne said.

Harold shouted a curse into the phone. He walked across the room and snapped on a news channel. A breathless reporter was giving the details of a mysterious explosion in Houma.

"I'll get back to you later." Harold advised.

"You want us to stay in Houma?"

"Yes." He clicked off and focused on the report. It seemed that the man and woman who had rented the cottage were Craig Branson and his wife. Unless they'd gotten married in the past couple of days, that was a polite fiction.

But were they really dead?

He'd keep checking to see if they surfaced somewhere. Meanwhile, he'd look around for another couple he could send into each other's arms.

FOR THE SECOND TIME in his life, Craig Branson was completely devastated. Sam's death had almost killed him. He'd survived. But now he was facing unimaginable heartbreak.

He had no idea where he was going as he put distance between himself and the terrible explosion. He simply drove aimlessly, wanting to get away from the place where Stephanie had died.

Moisture clouded his vision, and he finally pulled over to the side of the road, thinking that he was a menace to other drivers if he couldn't see straight.

He sat for long moments, gripping the wheel and trying to get his emotions under control. But grief rolled over him, drowned him, making him wonder if there was any use going on without Stephanie. What if he just drove his car into a bayou? There would be no one to miss him. No one to mourn him.

He'd lived his life a certain way because he'd thought he'd never find a woman he could love. Never marry. He'd found Stephanie, and it had been wonderful, except for the serious complications. Not just because she was supposed to marry the man responsible for his brother's death, but because someone had tried to kidnap them. He'd tried to find out who it was and hadn't succeeded. It flickered through his mind that figuring out who they were would give him a goal.

If he could pull himself together again. For the moment, he was too paralyzed with grief.

He started to swing back onto the highway, then stopped short as a car horn blared, and he realized he'd almost plowed into another vehicle.

Sorry, he mouthed when the other driver gave him the finger. After that he drove slowly to the next town and found a downscale motel where he could hole up.

He debated using his credit card, then decided that if he was supposed to be dead, maybe staying dead was the best way to go, for now. He paid in cash, then pulled back the covers on the lumpy bed and threw himself down, wondering how long he was going to be there and what he was going to do next.

He let the notion of getting a gun and shooting himself swirl around in his head. That was what you did with an animal in pain, wasn't it? It had a lot of appeal, but at the same time he hated the idea of giving up everything he had ever worked for.

Yeah, but what was it worth now? Without Stephanie.

JAKE HARPER CRADLED his wife in his arms. An hour earlier, Rachel had been struck by a thunderbolt. Not literally, but the effect was the same. She'd been standing in the kitchen loading the dishwasher when something had made her whole body jerk. Thank God he'd been there to catch her and take the plate out of her hand when she'd fallen.

He'd picked her up in his arms and asked her what was wrong, but she hadn't been able to answer him, either aloud or in her mind. So he'd struggled to suppress his own fear as he cradled her in his lap and rocked her, waiting until the storm passed and she was able to function again.

Finally she raised her head and looked around as though she didn't recognize her surroundings—although they were in one of the apartments Jake owned in New Orleans. Long ago he'd gotten into the habit of moving around the city. He had several comfortably furnished places, and he and Rachel split their time among them and the plantation in Lafayette where Gabriella Bordeaux and Luke Buckley lived. With funding from Jake, Gabriella had turned her family's plantation house into a showcase restaurant called Chez Gabriella. She and Luke lived upstairs in the plantation house, and Rachel and Jake had one of the cottages on the property, where they stayed part of the week. All four of them were children from the Solomon Clinic. And all four of them often joined forces to practice their psychic powers together.

Jack stroked Rachel's hair. "What happened?" he asked.

"There was an explosion near Houma. Turn on the television set."

Jake picked up the remote from the end table and clicked on a news channel. Instantly, they were in the middle of a breathless report from the affiliate in Houma.

"It is believed that Mr. and Mrs. Craig Branson were killed in the explosion that destroyed a cottage at the Morning Glory B and B," the reporter was saying. "Authorities are still not sure what caused the explosion."

"A bomb," Rachel whispered.

Jake shuddered. "And the couple are dead?"

Rachel closed her eyes and pressed her fingers against her forehead. "No."

He stared at her. "What happened?"

She dragged in a breath and let it out. "They escaped. Craig was out trying to get some information about the Solomon Clinic. Stephanie…"

"Their names are Craig and Stephanie?"

"Craig Branson and Stephanie Swift."

Jake's eyes narrowed. "Doesn't she have a dress shop on Royal Street?"

"Yes."

"And…isn't she supposed to marry a nasty piece of work named John Reynard?"

Rachel nodded. "Yes. Only that was her father's idea. Then she met Craig, and she knew she couldn't marry Reynard." Rachel gripped her husband's hand. "Reynard found out where she and Craig were staying. He found a way to get Craig out of the house. He kidnapped Stephanie and had his men set the cottage to explode when Craig came home. Only someone else set off the bomb."

"And you know all this—how?" Jake asked in a rough voice.

"It...came to me." She looked at her husband. "Stephanie and Craig each think the other is dead. Both of them are devastated. Think about how you'd feel if you thought I was...gone."

"Don't say that."

"I'm trying to make you understand why this is so urgent."

Jake's chest tightened as he imagined his own grief if he somehow lost Rachel.

He knew she followed his thoughts and emotions, knew from the way she wrapped her arms around him and from her own churning mind that she was imagining the same terrible situation—in reverse.

We can't leave them like that, she silently whispered.

We agreed that contacting them could be dangerous, Jake argued.

Are you saying you can leave them in so much pain?

Jake let the question sink in. *No. What do you want to do?*

They're far apart now. I think I can boost the signal between them. Let them talk to each other.

She turned to her husband. *But I can't do it alone. Will you help me?*

He hesitated, caught by the urgency of her request and the need to keep both of them safe. Not just themselves, but Gabriella and Luke, too.

They'd made a commitment to the other couple; now Rachel was saying they should act on their own.

Can't we wait?

They might go mad or kill themselves if we just wait.

Chapter Sixteen

Stephanie rarely drank anything stronger than wine. Now she sipped the brandy John had given her, welcoming the fiery sensations as it slid down her throat. Wanting to be alone with her private agony, she kept her gaze focused on the television, hoping against hope for some scrap of news that would tell her Craig had survived the blast.

"We should move up the wedding," John was saying. "I want the chance to be close to you, to make up for what you've just been through."

Her gaze swung to him, and she knew he was watching for her reaction to that bit of news.

"Yes," she said.

"We can have the ceremony here at the plantation. We'll just invite a few friends—and your father, of course. I'm thinking a morning ceremony, then lunch around the pool."

She nodded numbly. Was there any escape from this lovely plantation that was really a fortress? And where would she go if she could get away? It would have to be somewhere John could never find her. Out of the country for sure, but why bother if Craig was dead?

"Claire has been very helpful. She's been making a guest list, which she'll share with you. And she tells me that your wedding dress arrived at your shop."

"Yes."

"I'll arrange to have it delivered here."

"And we can contact a catering company," Claire added brightly. "And a florist. That's all you need."

"And a license and man of God," John added. "But all that's easy to arrange." He made a dismissive wave of his hand.

She tried to take all that in. Everything was moving too fast, and she wanted to scream at John to slow down, but she had to act as if she loved the idea of marrying him right away—because anything less was dangerous.

And then what? She imagined kissing him. Imagined his hands on her body, and she had to keep herself from screaming.

As she fought to look normal, something happened that made her head spin, and she gasped.

John tensed. "Stephanie, what?"

She tried to speak, but she couldn't get the words out. John's face swam before her, and she saw the panic in his eyes.

"I'm sick. Migraine headache. Need to lie down," she whispered.

"I didn't know you had migraines."

Neither did I, she thought, but she only said, "Yes."

Because she needed to be alone. Now.

JOHN HELPED STEPHANIE to the bedroom, taking in her pale face as she kicked off her shoes. She looked sick. No doubt about it, but he was having trouble believing anything she said now.

She hadn't slept with Brandon? He wanted it to be true, but he couldn't be sure.

She was such a beautiful, desirable woman—from an old family that had seen better days. Probably her social standing had been one of the reasons he'd been willing to wait until marriage to make love to her. That and the convenience of having Claire as a willing bed partner. It had amused him to sleep with the woman who was spying on his fiancée. He'd even entertained some fantasies of taking the two of them to bed. He knew Claire would be totally okay with that. Maybe it would take some persuading to get Stephanie to agree.

She was a lady, and he'd thought she was adhering to what she considered proper.

His mind circled back to the moment when he'd decided to marry Stephanie Swift. It had been at one of the damn charity events that he was expected to attend. This time at the St. Charles Country Club. One of the other men there, Larry Dalton, had called him aside to ask about their business transaction. Larry had gone in with John on an import deal, two million dollars worth of heroin packed in toys coming in from Taiwan. Only someone must have tipped off the Feds because they'd sent in an inspector to check the shipment. And it had been the guy's bad luck.

John's men had caught him on the boat while it was at sea, and the federal agent had ended up overboard in the Pacific Ocean.

John had gotten a report about it before he'd left for the reception, and when Larry had approached him at the event, he'd been in a bad mood. He'd told him about it, watching the man's face as he realized he was a party to murder.

John had enjoyed spoiling the man's evening. And then he'd turned around and seen Stephanie Swift in back of him. Had she heard? He wasn't sure, and she certainly hadn't said anything, but he wasn't going to take a chance on her telling anyone about it. Which was why he'd started keeping her close.

He'd decided that if she married him, she couldn't testify against him, and he'd been glad when she'd agreed to the marriage, because he'd rather screw her than kill her. But maybe he was going to end up doing both.

Of course, now he had other things to think about. Like why had Branson been dragging her around? Had he talked about the long-ago death of his brother—and of Arthur Polaski? If she knew about any of that, she was more dangerous to him. But he'd find out after the wedding. After he took what she owed him.

CRAIG HAD DOZED OFF. He jerked awake when he heard a voice in his head. A woman's voice.

Craig Branson.

Hope flared inside him.

Stephanie? Oh, Lord, is that you, Stephanie?

No. I'm a friend.

He tried to cope with the instant wave of despair and with the confusion swirling in his mind. Had grief driven him mad, and he had invented an invisible friend to compensate for the loss of the woman he loved?

The voice pulled him back to her. *You aren't crazy. This is important.*

I doubt it.

Stephanie isn't dead.

His whole body went rigid as the words blasted into him, yet he couldn't allow himself to believe. Sitting up, he looked around the motel room, confirming he was alone.

Who are you? he repeated.

Rachel.

She was speaking to him—the way Sam had spoken to him. And Stephanie.

Do I know you? he asked in an inner voice that he couldn't quite hold steady.

No.

Is this a cruel joke?

No. I understand what you are suffering.

He scoffed at that statement. *How could you? How could anyone?*

Because I am one of the children from the Solomon Clinic, and I bonded with another one of us.

He made a low sound. Of course, he should have realized why she could reach his mind.

You must rescue Stephanie.

He scrambled off the bed, ready to charge out the door, if he only knew where he was going—and what had happened.

How did she escape?

Two of John Reynard's men captured her after you left. Then they set the explosive charge to kill you. Only someone else was caught in the blast.

Ike Broussard. I saw him. I didn't understand why he was there. He said he was going to meet me at a restaurant.

I think Reynard ordered him to meet you.

How do you know?

My husband knows which cops are corrupt in New Orleans. Ike Broussard was one of them.

Then why did he come to the cottage?

I can only guess at that. What if he hated being under Reynard's thumb and thought that the two of you could work together to take him down?

Craig considered that. It might fit the facts, and he was sorry the man was dead, but his main focus was Stephanie.

The woman named Rachel must have read his thoughts. *I can boost the signal between you.*

And then, all at once he caught Stephanie's silent voice. *Craig?*

Yes.

Oh, my God, you're alive! Reynard said you were dead.

I'm fine.

Thank God, but how are we talking?

Someone's helping us. Another one of the children from the clinic.

Yes, I...heard her in my mind. I didn't know what was happening.

Where are you? Craig asked.

At the plantation Reynard owns, near Morgan City.

I'm on my way now.

Be careful. It's heavily guarded. With armed men.

We'll figure something out, he said, wondering what it was going to be.

I can't hold the connection...the woman who had made the long-distance contact between them said, and suddenly there was silence inside Craig's head—leaving him dazed and confused.

JAKE HARPER SWORE aloud as he picked up his wife from the couch. Lowering himself to a sitting position, he gathered her limp body in his arms.

"You hurt yourself," he whispered as he stroked his hands over her back and shoulders.

"I'm...okay," Rachel managed to say.

"You..."

She closed her eyes and clung to him. "They had information to give each other—and I was the only way they could do it."

"And now you're going to stay away from them," he said in a hard voice.

"They may need us."

"I'm not going to lose you because you feel some sort of obligation to two strangers."

She raised her head and looked at him. "Jake, they're two of Dr. Solomon's children."

"So were Tanya and Mickey," he bit out, referring to the telepaths who had tried to kill them.

"Craig and Stephanie are different. They're good people. They just want to be free to live their lives."

"So we can stay clear of them."

"Maybe that's not going to work."

"Maybe it has to," Jake said, punching out the words. He tipped Rachel's body so that she was looking up at him. "I was along for the ride on that mental conference call. Something you're not saying is that someone was after Craig. Not Reynard's men. There's something else going on."

He saw her swallow. "Yes."

"Maybe someone who knows about the clinic."

She gave a small nod.

"Wellington and Solomon are dead. So who is it?"

CRAIG BRACED HIS HAND against the wall, fighting to stay on his feet. His head was swimming as though he'd just suffered a blow to the jaw. But he didn't care.

He knew Stephanie was alive. And she knew he was okay, too. That was important, because Reynard had her, and if she thought Craig was dead, there was no telling what she'd do.

And he knew where she was. At least the general location. He started to charge out of the motel room, then checked himself. Men had chased him around Houma. If they didn't think he'd been blown up in that explosion, they would be searching for him again.

First he looked out the window to make sure nobody was lurking in the parking lot. Then he cautiously stepped outside.

He climbed into his car and used the GPS to set a course for Morgan City, driving below the speed limit so as not to call attention to himself. All he needed was to get stopped by a cop and have them find out he was still alive. If they did, they'd probably hold him for questioning in the death of Ike Broussard—when they found out he was the guy who'd gotten caught in the explosion.

Hopefully, that wasn't going to happen anytime soon because the big advantage Craig had now was that Reynard thought he was dead. If he could keep it that way, he'd have a better chance to get Stephanie out of there.

And then what? He'd worry about that after he sprang her.

When he reached the approximate vicinity, he stopped at one of the gas stations. After filling his tank, he went inside the station. As soon as he saw the racks of junk food, he realized he hadn't eaten anything since breakfast. He put a soft drink and some peanut-butter cheese crackers on the counter and paid for them, along with the gas, glad that he'd brought a fair amount of cash with him—and that he also had the use of the thugs' money. But eventually he was going to need more cash. Maybe he could rob the gas station, he thought with a snort before turning toward the cashier.

He ran his hand through his hair and looked around as if he thought the interior of the station would answer a vital question.

"I'm supposed to be delivering an important package to the Reynard estate," he said as he put his wallet back into his pocket, "but I'm not sure of the address. Can you tell me where it is?"

"It's about five miles south of town on the Old River Road," the man answered. "But you won't get in unless they're expecting you, because there's a guard at the gate."

"Thanks for the information," he said.

Before leaving town, he stopped at a dry-goods store and bought a tractor cap and a work shirt, which he put on in the men's room. He would have to stop to buy some more clothing, because he'd lost everything in the explosion. But he had brought his computer along in the car, which kept him from having to make a major purchase.

After doing what he could on short notice to disguise his appearance, he used the GPS to find Old River Road, then drove south. As the gas-station attendant had said, the Reynard estate was surrounded by a high chain-link fence, topped with razor wire, and a gate, with several men in attendance, controlling access to the property. As he drove past without stopping, he glimpsed a stately plantation house through the live oaks lining the drive.

How much surveillance equipment did Reynard have? he wondered as he put a mile between himself and the gate. Pulling off the road, into a small clearing, he tried to send his mind to Stephanie, but he was too far away and couldn't reach her.

He'd have to come back at night and hope that he could get close enough without alerting the guards.

A KNOCK AT THE DOOR made Stephanie go rigid. When the door opened, she expected to see John, but it was only Claire.

"How are you feeling?" her assistant asked.

"Better."

"Dinner is in an hour. I'm sure you want to look your best. Why don't you take a nice hot shower? And there are clothes in the closet."

"Thank you," she said as she climbed out of bed and headed for the bathroom, which turned out to be large and luxurious—a place she would have enjoyed if her stomach hadn't been tied in knots.

A shower and nice clothing. Was John thinking about

taking her to bed after dinner? If he was, she prayed she could derail that plan.

Once she'd showered, she dried her hair and tamed it into a style she knew John admired. Then she went to the closet to see what clothing was available.

There were a number of tasteful gowns and dresses, probably chosen by Claire, who was using the knowledge of style she'd learned at the shop.

Stephanie ground her teeth when she thought about her sweet little assistant. It went to show that you couldn't always tell a person's real motivations. She should have thought about that when she'd let John Reynard into her life. Well, it was too late to worry about what she should have done. She had to think carefully about what she was going to do now.

After looking through the dresses, she selected a pale green dinner gown, then did a careful job with her makeup, trying to present herself as the happy bride who had finally moved into the very well-appointed home of her fiancé.

But she hesitated at the door to her room, wishing she could stay locked away where John couldn't touch her.

"Stop it," she muttered to herself. "You have to face him, and you have to make him absolutely sure that you're relieved to be here."

After taking a deep breath and letting it out, she stepped into the hall and headed for the stairs.

John and Claire were waiting for her in the drawing room, sitting with their heads together, speaking in low voices. She stood for a moment in the doorway, observing the intimacy between them and confirming her earlier thought that they were probably sleeping together. That would have made her angry if she'd cared about her relationship with John Reynard. Under the circumstances, she couldn't help thinking that the other woman was doing her a big favor, letting John blow off sexual steam with her instead of his fiancée.

They stopped talking abruptly when they noticed her in the doorway, and she suspected they had been talking about her.

John looked her up and down, taking in the makeup and the dress she'd chosen.

"I must say, you look lovely, my dear," he said, getting up and coming over to plant a kiss on her cheek.

"Thank you."

"Can I offer you some wine? I remember you like Merlot."

"Yes," she answered. She wasn't going to drink much because she needed to keep her wits about her. But she'd gotten an idea when John had offered her a drink.

She looked toward the glass he'd left on the end table and saw amber liquid and ice cubes. Probably bourbon, which was his whiskey of choice.

Have some more bourbon, she silently told him. *Drink more bourbon. You want to drink a lot of it tonight—to celebrate your impending marriage.*

She waited with her heart pounding while he poured her a glass of the red wine, then hesitated for a moment at the bar.

Again she sent her message and felt a thrill of relief and satisfaction when he reached for the bottle of Jack Daniel's and poured himself a drink.

He brought her the wine, then did a double take when he realized he already had a glass of whiskey sitting on the side table. Quickly he took it away and put it in the sink.

"We should eat," he said. "Matilda has prepared a delicious dinner for your homecoming. All the Creole treats you love. We're starting with Oysters Bienville. Then we have jambalaya, and we're finishing with bananas Foster."

"That sounds wonderful," she said, when she wondered how she could swallow any of it.

Bring your drink, she told John, and he obliged her by picking up his glass and carrying it into the dining room.

They took their seats at the table, where the staff gave everybody speculative looks, and she wondered what had been going on between John and Claire. Had they flaunted their relationship, or had the servants simply picked up on the intimacy between them?

The maid brought the baked oysters, the shells resting on a bed of hot salt, then served each of them two.

As Stephanie started to scoop the contents out of the shell, using the small oyster fork, a jolt of mental energy made her hand shake and the shell clatter against the dish.

John gave her a sharp look. "What?"

"I...just touched the hot oyster shell by accident," she lied.

"Let me see."

"Really, it was just enough to startle me," she said as she held out her hand, fighting madly to stay calm.

Craig had just contacted her.

Sorry, he apologized.

Where are you? she asked as she bent to fork up the oyster in its creamy sauce, hoping her face wasn't flushed. Craig was close by. Close enough to contact her.

I'm at the edge of the plantation. Around back.

Be careful, she warned, marveling that he could speak to her from so far away. Maybe something that woman Rachel had done had boosted the signal between her and Craig.

I am being careful. I just wanted you to know I'm here.

She forced herself to eat the oyster, then smile at John. "This is so good."

"I'm glad you like it."

"I'd like some more wine," she said. *And you want more bourbon. Lots more bourbon.*

They finished the meal, and when they got up from the table, John approached her, putting his arm around her shoulder so that his fingers brushed the top of her breast.

She caught her breath, knowing that she was playing a dangerous game. The whiskey had made him amorous, but had he drunk enough to keep him from performing?

"Let's have a nightcap in the lounge," she murmured, reinforcing the invitation with a mental suggestion, which she expanded to include Claire. The longer she could keep the other woman with them, the longer she could keep John from pawing her, she hoped.

The three of them sat together in the lounge. To avoid conversation, she suggested, *Let's watch a movie.*

"I wanted…" John said, then trailed off as though he had forgotten that he was hot to take his fiancée to bed.

Stephanie silently pushed the movie idea as she brought everyone a drink.

John picked an action-adventure, which was better than something sexy. But he crowded against her on the sofa, his lips brushing her cheek and his hand touching her leg or the side of her breast.

She fought not to cringe as she kept making suggestions that he drink, and by the time the movie was over, he was unsteady on his feet. Yet he clamped his arm around her as they walked to the stairs.

Her heart was in her throat as she let him walk her up the steps. Inside she was screaming, *You're so sleepy. All you want to do is fall on your bed and sleep. You'll enjoy making love to Stephanie so much more when your head doesn't feel so fuzzy.*

She held her breath as they passed her room, then continued on to his.

He stood wavering in the doorway, and she helped him inside, easing him onto the bed. He closed his eyes as she pulled off his shoes. Then his eyes blinked open and focused on her.

"Did you hear me talking about that murder?" he asked.

"What?" she gasped. "What are you talking about?"

"At that reception at the…what was it…the St. Charles Club. You know, where we first met. I was talking to Larry Dalton about…you know."

Her heart was in her throat.

"I know what?"

"That drug-enforcement agent who went into the ocean when he was messing with my shipment from Taiwan."

"No," she breathed.

"Got to keep you close," he muttered, "in case you heard."

Her heart was already pounding so hard she could barely breathe. Then, as his hand reached for her, she felt her heart leap into her throat.

Chapter Seventeen

As John made a grab for Stephanie, she stepped out of the way.

Sleep. Just sleep. You need to sleep, and you'll feel so much better in the morning.

To her profound relief, he accepted the suggestion and sank into sleep, and she exited his room, then hurried to her own, her pulse pounding.

She'd thought he'd wanted to marry her because he wanted entrée into an old New Orleans family. Apparently it was more than that. It seemed he thought she'd overheard a conversation about a murder he'd ordered.

She hadn't heard him. But now she knew. In the morning, would he remember that he'd told her?

"Oh, God," she whispered, thinking that she was in more trouble than she'd even known.

As soon as she closed the door, Craig was in her head.

Thank God.

You were watching that.

Yeah.

You heard about…a murder.

Yeah.

What am I going to do?

Hope to hell he doesn't focus on it when he wakes up.

As she caught the raw edge in his silent voice, she shuddered. Then she picked up that he was thinking about her in bed with Reynard, not about the man's murderous past. He already knew about that.

But now the dark and dangerous images swirling in his mind made her gasp. *You can't break in here. Don't try. They'll catch you.*

I'm coming in for you.

Wait

I will. I'll figure something out.

She pulled off her gown and shoes and found a long T-shirt she could wear—something very unsexy, if John appeared in her room.

She knew Craig caught that thought and tried to ignore his instant flare of anger. But then she walked to the desk, picked up a letter opener she'd seen there and set it on the bedside table.

She heard Craig catch his breath.

You think you could get out of there alive if you stabbed him?

You have a better idea?

Wait for me to get there.

Praying that was possible, she washed her face, brushed her teeth and used the toilet before climbing into bed.

Closing her eyes, she imagined Craig lying beside her.

Soon, he whispered in her mind, and she hoped it was going to work out the way they wanted.

She made a strangled sound when she felt his lips against hers.

Her eyes flew open, but the room was empty.

How did you do that?

In the darkness she heard him chuckle.

It's like moving books in the bookcase. Only more fun. As she heard his voice in her mind, she felt his invisible fingers stroking her hair, her arms. When he cupped his palms around her breasts, she caught her breath.

What are you doing?

What we both want to do.

You shouldn't. When she tried to sit up, he pressed his hand against her shoulder. *Don't run away from me.*

But you're making me hot. And what can I do about it?

He laughed again. *I can do something about it. You've had a terrible day. Let me make it up to you.*

It's not your fault.

You begged me to take you with me. I wouldn't listen.

She swallowed hard. *But that might have gotten you killed. I think that blast at the cabin was meant for you.*

Yeah. And the poor cop was just at the wrong place at the wrong time. But let's not focus on that now.

As he spoke, he brushed his invisible lips against hers as he lifted and shaped her breasts. She closed her eyes, unable to pull away from the sensations. And as she enjoyed his kisses and his touch, it was difficult to remember that he wasn't there in the bed with her. When his thumbs and fingers closed around her nipples, she had to take her lower lip between her teeth to keep from crying out. That was all she needed—to bring someone charging down the hall. She didn't allow herself to actually name who that might be.

She squirmed against the mattress.

Stop.

You don't like it?

You know I do.

Than let me give you pleasure.

But...

He stopped her protest with a long, passionate kiss as he tugged at one nipple while his other hand drifted down her body toward the juncture of her legs.

She didn't have to open them for him. Using his phantom

hands, he had complete access to the most intimate parts of her, and she caught his satisfaction in knowing what he was doing to her.

Her hips rose and fell as he stroked a finger through her folds, dipping into her and turning his finger in a maddening circle, then traveling upward to the point of her greatest sensation. He kept up the arousing attentions, making it impossible for her to focus on anything else as he drove her up and up toward a climax that burst over and through her, making her gasp as she struggled not to cry out in pleasure.

And when he was finished, he whispered in her mind, *Sleep now. You need your rest.*

What about you? she managed to ask.

That was good for me, too. And it gives me something to look forward to. When I get you back, we'll finish what we started.

She prayed that he was right. Prayed that he would be able to get her away from the man who refused to allow her to escape from him.

STEPHANIE WOKE with the memory of making love with Craig and a smile on her face. She'd dreamed of having a relationship like that, but she'd been sure it would never happen for her, until she met Craig.

She whispered his name and turned her head, expecting to see him lying beside her. Then reality slammed back like a prison door clanging behind her.

She wasn't with Craig. Not at all. She was in a bedroom in John Reynard's house. Thank the Lord, not Reynard's bedroom.

She clenched her hands into fists, wanting to pound them against the walls for all the good that would do her.

When she glanced at the bedside table, she saw the letter opener she'd put there—which looked as if she'd been expecting to be attacked in the night.

Hoping that no one had checked in on her, she put the weapon back on the desk and went to the bathroom, where she got ready and pulled on jeans and a T-shirt.

People were moving around the house when she came down, and John and Claire were sitting at the dining-room table, talking as intimately as they had been in the lounge the night before.

As she watched them together, she wanted to ask why John just didn't marry Claire, since they were so obviously suited to each other, but she kept the question to herself.

"There she is," Claire said.

"Yes, we let you get your beauty sleep," John added as he gave her a considering look. "I'm sorry I drank so much last night. It won't happen again."

While she was scrambling for a reply, he said, "The wedding will be this afternoon."

"What?" she gasped, feeling as if the breath had been knocked out of her. "I thought you wanted a morning wedding."

"I changed my mind," he answered.

"Yes. We have almost everything arranged," Claire said brightly.

Unable to stand, Stephanie dropped into a chair at the table. She'd known that John wanted to move quickly, but she'd had no idea the wedding would be today.

Claire bustled over and set a notebook in front of her. "Since you were asleep, I took the liberty of making some selections. I thought Prestige would be an ideal caterer. They're bringing the food from their kitchen in New Orleans. But I know there's a branch of Just for You Flowers about twenty minutes away, so we can use them. I've sent out email invitations to a number of John's business associates, and I've already received some replies, but I think we can expect a small group—perhaps twenty guests. And we'll have your father picked up and brought here. We decided that a justice of the peace was the easiest choice for an official. Mr. Vincent Lacey will be here at five."

Stephanie fought a wave of dizziness. "Five? The ceremony is at five?"

"Yes. Your dress has also arrived. And I can do your hair and makeup. That's what I used to do—for one of the local TV stations before I came to work for you."

"Oh" was all Stephanie could say, ordering herself not to start shaking. She had to hold it together but knew she was on the edge of a meltdown. And the worst part was that when she tried to contact Craig, she couldn't locate him. He seemed to have fallen off the edge of the earth again.

HAROLD GODDARD ENDED the phone call with a broad grin on his face. He had some good news for a change. He'd known from his men that someone else was looking for Stephanie Swift and Craig Branson in Houma.

There was a chance it could be someone who knew about the clinic's purpose, but he doubted it. Maybe this had to do with her fiancé, John Reynard. Harold had used the old Reynard murder connection to get Craig and Stephanie together. But it looked as if Reynard wasn't prepared to give her up.

And now there was a massive mobilization at Reynard's country estate. Mobilization for a quickie wedding. Caterer, florist, a justice of the peace. The works.

Which made it pretty clear that Stephanie wasn't dead. Reynard must have taken her back to the plantation. Maybe his men had even blown up that cottage and killed Branson.

Now Reynard was going to make sure his bride didn't escape again. Harold tapped his finger against his lips, thinking. He'd sent two guys to Houma, but it looked as if Reynard had a lot more than that at the plantation. Harold had better get some extra help and send them down there.

The plantation was fenced in—with a gate. But the guards would be expecting wedding guests, which meant it wouldn't be that hard to crash the gate and snatch the bride.

Of course, Branson was out of the picture now, but it would be very instructive to see what had happened to Stephanie with her lover gone. He'd examine her mental state, then put her out of her misery.

CRAIG HAD BEEN BUSY. Last night he'd spent some time in the bathroom of the cheap motel where he was staying, using a clipper on his thick dark hair and then shaving his head. He'd cut himself a couple of times, but the effect of the hair removal was startling. He didn't recognize the ugly-looking man who stared back at him in the mirror. Hopefully, Reynard wouldn't, either.

Next he took a chance and wired five thousand dollars from an account he kept under another name to a Western Union office in a nearby town.

He'd used some of the cash to buy spy equipment to monitor phone communications at the plantation, and that had already paid off. Reynard was planning his wedding for that afternoon.

Craig swore. The bastard was moving fast. But as he listened to the preparations, he got an idea.

After learning Reynard's plans, he stopped at a discount department store and bought some extra shirts, which he put on in layers, bulking up his body to change his physique a little. As he passed the cosmetics department, he had another couple of ideas. He bought a dark eyebrow pencil and fake tanning cream. He spent some time in the men's room putting on the tanning stuff and doing his eyebrows, trying to make them look thicker but natural. Next he stopped in the hardware store and bought some little rubber rings, which he stuck into his nostrils to make his nose look bigger. After altering his appearance, he ran a couple more errands. With the state's lenient gun laws, he was also able to pick up a SIG semiautomatic with a couple of spare clips—plus some other equipment he was going to need.

When he was as prepared as he could be, he drove to Just for You Flowers, where the staff was frantically working to get the Reynard order ready in time.

He'd asked for a wedding bouquet of white roses and baby's breath plus several vases of flowers in stands to decorate the pool area where the wedding was being held.

"Hi, I'm Cal Barnes from the New Orleans store," he told the woman behind the counter. "When they heard you were doing a job for John Reynard, they sent me down here to help."

She gave him an annoyed look, and he was pretty sure that with his bald head and heavy eyebrows, he looked like a thug.

"No need. We have it under control," she said.

But I'm going to drive the van that brings in the flowers, Craig said, putting in every ounce of mental energy he could muster. He'd done this before with Sam. He'd done it with Stephanie. He'd never done it on his own, but he knew Stephanie had been pushing John in the direction she wanted, and if she could do it, so could he. He reinforced the silent observation with a second repetition.

The woman's expression was still doubtful. "I'm just going to call Phil at the New Orleans shop and check on that."

"It was Phil who sent me."

She reached for the phone, and he sent her a fast and

furious message. *Don't call Phil. Don't call Phil. You need Barnes to drive the truck.*

He kept repeating the message, waiting with his heart pounding. If she didn't take him up on the offer, he'd have to go to plan B, and he had no freaking idea what that was. But he *had* to get inside that plantation compound, if he had a chance of rescuing Stephanie before she ended up in Reynard's bed tonight.

"We could use a driver. Some of the stands we'll need are heavy, and we only have women in the shop today."

"I'm glad to help with that," Craig said.

"And while you're here, there are some deliveries that need to be put in the refrigerator."

SEVERAL MILES AWAY, Rachel and Jake Harper were tuned in to the preparations at the estate.

"He's going to marry her this afternoon," Rachel said, a note of disgust in her voice. "And Craig Branson is ready to go in there and rescue her."

"He could get himself killed," her husband answered.

"I know that. And I want this to come out okay for them. What can we do about it?"

"I should say—nothing," Jake answered firmly.

She gave him an incredulous look. "You'd leave two of the children from the Solomon Clinic in terrible danger?"

"I didn't say I'd do that, but we have to think carefully about what we're risking."

"I know. But maybe we'd better start making some contingency plans."

He answered with a tight nod, and she knew he would go along with her plans—if he didn't think they were too dangerous.

She also knew he had grown up on the streets, committed to no one but himself. Caring about no one but himself.

He'd bonded with her because of the telepathic link they'd forged, but it was still difficult for him to see the importance of extending that bond to the others. Especially after the first children from the clinic that they'd met had started off by attacking them.

Chapter Eighteen

Trying to act as if his brain wasn't going to explode from tension, Craig went to work helping unload roses and gladioli. Then he tried to look busy while he watched the woman who was putting together bouquets, hoping he could do a credible job of flower arranging. It looked like the trick to making them stay in place was anchoring the stems in some kind of rigid foam stuff.

And all the time he kept projecting the message that nobody had to check up on him at the New Orleans office. He was supposed to be at the local shop. He couldn't be sure if it would work, and he kept thinking that if it didn't, he might have to pull a gun and herd the two women into the refrigerator, while he stole the van and went to the wedding.

Every minute that ticked by made him feel a little closer to pulling off the delivery scheme. But that didn't stop his mind from churning, because there was no way to know if his plan would work until after he got into the estate. More than that, he knew Stephanie had to be sick with worry about the upcoming wedding, but there was too much activity around the plantation for him to risk going until closer to the big event. The best he could do was to keep sending messages, telling her he was coming. Telling her it was all going to turn out okay, even when he was pretty sure she couldn't hear him.

Unfortunately, he wasn't picking up anything from her, and that had him worried, even though he kept telling himself they were simply too far apart.

STEPHANIE'S CHEST was so tight that she could barely breathe. While she ate breakfast, she covertly watched John. But he gave no sign that he remembered anything from the evening before.

Of course, that could all be an act. One of his main goals was to never have anyone think less of him. Even her and Claire, so he put up a good front.

After she'd done her best to pretend that she was hungry, he pushed back his chair and stood up.

"I should leave you ladies to the preparations," he said, his voice casual, though she knew he was hiding his own tension.

"We'll be ready for you at five," Claire said in a chipper voice.

Right, Stephanie thought. *Why don't you just stand in for me, since you're apparently enjoying sleeping with him?*

"I'll be in my office if you need anything," he added.

Stephanie nodded.

As soon as he was out of the room, she felt marginally better.

"You have nothing to worry about," Claire said.

"Mmm-hmm," she answered, wanting to scream at the woman who had been betraying her all along.

"Do you know how lucky you are?" Claire asked.

"Yes," she said. She was thinking she was so lucky to have met Craig, and he was going to get her out of this.

Or die trying? That stray thought had her insides going cold. She knew he was going to try to get in here, but she didn't know how.

"You should start with a nice relaxing bath," Claire said.

"I'm thinking about what order we should do stuff in. First the bath. Then we can do your finger- and toenails. Then your hair and makeup. What color do you want for your nails?"

From the sideboard she brought over a box of nail-polish bottles. "I think a pale pink would look good with your coloring."

Stephanie agreed because she had no interest in the color. Or maybe bloodred would be best. Then it wouldn't show on her hands if she ended up in bed with John and scratched her nails down his face.

She canceled that thought as soon as it surfaced, knowing it was dangerous to give Claire even a hint of her real feelings.

Instead she said, "Yes, let's go with pink." At least getting herself all prettied up would give her something to do until the hateful ceremony.

And then what? She kept thinking of something she'd heard about the 1950s. Back then, the Soviet Union had been the major threat to America, and people had debated "Better dead than red or better red than dead?"

In other words, if you succumbed to the enemy, could you bide your time and hope to free yourself?

She knew that was true for the countries that had been Soviet satellites. They'd stuck it out and come through the dark period. And many of them now had democratically elected governments.

All of that was well and good in theory. But could she stand to go to bed with John Reynard? Stand to have him kiss her, touch her? Be inside her? And what else would he want her to do to him?

When she couldn't stop herself from shuddering, Claire touched her arm. "I know you've been through a terrible experience," she murmured. "Maybe it would help to tell me about it."

So you can report to John, Stephanie thought, but she only shook her head. "I don't want to dwell on it."

"I understand."

Yeah, I'll bet you do, she thought with a note of sarcasm. Aloud she said, "I'd like to take that bath now."

If they had to have a wedding night, maybe she could get him drunk again. Or would that work twice in a row? And she couldn't do it every night of her life. Eventually…

She cut off that thought, because she couldn't let it come to that.

HAROLD GODDARD WAITED impatiently to hear from the men he was sending into the Reynard compound.

When Wayne finally called, he snatched up the phone. "What?"

"There's a lot of activity at the estate. Delivery trucks going into the compound. Two catering trucks."

"And anyone going in and out is getting stopped at the main gate?"

"Yeah."

Harold thought for a moment. Were they really expecting an attack, or was Reynard just taking precautions because that was his M.O.? Finally he said, "I think he's not really expecting trouble. I mean, who would go up against him? I've hacked his email. The wedding ceremony's at five. Wait till then, then crash the gate. You'll know where the woman is, and you can take her and run."

"What about collateral damage?"

"Do what you have to."

Chapter Nineteen

The flower delivery was scheduled for three-thirty in the afternoon. Craig's tension mounted as the departure time approached. And he breathed out a sigh when he finally drove away from the loading dock in back of the flower shop. He made one more stop, at a spot where he'd left the extra equipment he was going to need, packing it into the back of the panel truck behind the flowers.

He said a silent prayer that he wasn't going to get Stephanie killed, then headed for the main gate of Reynard's estate and waited with his heart pounding while he sized up the operation. At the gate there were three guards. One of them asked for his credentials and checked them over carefully, as if the president of a foreign country was staying here and needed special protection.

"I'd like a look in that truck," the man said.

"Sure," Craig agreed as though he didn't have a thing in the world to hide. Like, for example, that he was here to kidnap the bride. Climbing out, he walked around to the back and opened the door.

There's nothing in here but flowers. All you see is flowers, Craig said over and over as the guy climbed inside and poked around.

Flowers. Just flowers. And I'm just the delivery guy, doing his job.

The guard jumped out. "You're good to go," he said.

"Thanks." He waited a beat.

"Yes?"

"Where should I park?"

"Around the side of the house. The ceremony is out by the pool."

"Okay. Thanks."

He would have liked to ask more questions about the lay-out of the estate, but he assumed he was supposed to know. He still wasn't sure what "around the side of the house" meant, but when he spotted a catering truck pulled up near the triple garage, he breathed out a little sigh. Before parking, he turned around so that he was facing outward, poised for a quick getaway. But he figured that would look normal because he was unloading the flowers from the back.

After climbing out, he followed one of the catering guys to the back of the house. Chairs had been set up on either side of an aisle, facing a bank of bushes. Over to the side were six round tables, with snowy-white cloths where china and cutlery had already been set out.

He tried to remember what he knew about wedding ceremonies, which wasn't much. Probably they wanted a big bouquet of flowers on either side of the open space in front of the bushes, because presumably that was where the ceremony was being held.

Someone came hurrying out of the house. He turned, hoping against hope to see Stephanie.

Instead it was a dark-haired woman that he recognized immediately. She was Stephanie's assistant, the one he'd met at the dress shop a lifetime ago.

He forced himself to stand in a relaxed posture with his hands at his sides as she gave him a long look. As he faced her, he furiously sent her the message. *You do not know me. You never saw me before in your life.*

She tipped her head to the side. "Do I know you?"

He kept projecting the silent message as he lowered his voice an octave. "No. Are you the bride?"

She laughed. "No, I'm Mr. Reynard's assistant."

Mr. Reynard's assistant. Last time he'd seen her, she'd been Stephanie's assistant. It seemed she'd come up in the world, or maybe she'd been working for Reynard all along.

"Let me give you the bride's bouquet," he said, leading her back to where he'd left the van. "And then you can show me where you want the flowers placed."

"You do have the centerpieces, right?"

"Of course," he answered quickly. Yeah, there would be flowers on the tables.

He led her to where he'd parked the van, then opened the back door and got out the box with the flowers the bride was to carry, feeling a pang as he handed them to her. A wedding bouquet for the woman he loved, only it wasn't *their* wedding.

She gave the flowers a brief inspection. "Very nice."

"Thank you," he answered, thinking, from her expression and the tone of her voice, that she wished they were hers. Too bad Reynard couldn't have picked a bride who wanted to marry him, but probably he was too obsessed with the prestige of marrying into an old New Orleans family, and with thinking Stephanie had heard him discussing murder.

As soon as she took the flowers away, he dragged in a breath and let it out. This might be the best time to contact Stephanie. She'd be alone. At least, he didn't think Reynard would be with her.

He sent his mind out to her. *Stephanie.*

He felt her jolt of recognition when she heard him.

Craig?

Yes.

Thank God. Oh, thank God.

I just saw Claire. She came down to get the flowers.

Yes, she was apparently working for John all along.

I think she's on her way back to you—with your bouquet.

But I have to tell you some stuff while we have a chance. I'm the guy delivering the flowers.

Apparently his previous words had registered.

Did you say she saw you?

Yes, but she didn't recognize me. I have on a few shirts to bulk me up. And I'm the bald guy with the splotchy tan and the dark eyebrows.

She caught her breath.

Yeah, I look like hell, but so far the disguise is working. What are we going to do?

You've been manipulating his mind, right?

Yes. Like when I got him drunk last night so he couldn't... Her silent voice trailed off.

We're going to do it again. And I've got something else planned.

When he told her what he'd brought with him, she sucked in a sharp breath. *Claire's back.*

I'll see you in a little while.

Light classical music had begun to play as he carried the large vases of flowers to the spot where the bride and groom would stand and fluffed up the arrangements, then began taking the smaller arrangements to the tables, setting one in the center of each. The effect was quite nice. Too bad it was going to be screwed up when the guests stampeded.

And here they were. As he worked, he saw well-dressed men and women arriving and gathering in an area at the side of the pool where a bar had been set up. One of them was Stephanie's father, who was holding a glass of clear liquid.

Water? He remembered that the old guy drank too much. Maybe he was trying to be on his best behavior today.

Craig saw Reynard at the edge of the crowd and sent him a message. *Go get yourself a nice big drink.*

He was elated when the man approached the bar and got a glass of whiskey. But instead of drinking, he looked at it for a long moment and left it on the bar.

Craig felt his stomach muscles tighten. Apparently Reynard didn't want to repeat last night's nonperformance.

He was focused on Reynard and his guests when he felt a tingling at the back of his neck.

Turning, he saw one of Reynard's guards stoop to pick up the knapsack he'd left at the edge of the patio. When the man started to open it, Craig strode over.

"That's mine," he said aloud. Silently he added, *There's nothing you have to worry about in there.*

"What's in it?"

"I'm from the florist. That's extra stuff I might need."

Nothing to worry about.

"I'll just take a look."

Too bad the mental push wasn't working on this guy.

"We should step around the corner so we don't disturb the guests," Craig said.

The man looked toward the crowd at the bar where Reynard was chatting to a group of men and women. "Yeah."

They rounded the corner of the house.

When the guy bent to look inside the knapsack, Craig chopped him on the back of the neck, and he went down. But now what?

He pulled the guy into the bushes and opened the knapsack, where he'd stowed some duct tape. He used it to tape the guy's mouth and secure his hands and feet. Then he hit him on the back of the head with the butt of the SIG, hoping that would keep him quiet.

His heart was thumping inside his chest as he rushed back to the pool area.

Men in uniform moved through the crowd, apparently telling the guests to take their seats because they began to find chairs.

When everyone was seated, a rotund gray-haired man clad in black walked to the front area and stood between the tall vases Craig had placed there.

Then the music switched to the traditional wedding march.

As all eyes turned to the patio door, Craig's breath caught. Stephanie was standing just inside the entrance in a long white dress, gripping her father's arm. She looked achingly beautiful, and also pale and breathless. Her father looked like a cat that had finished a saucer of cream.

From the corner of his eye, Craig saw Reynard take his place at the front of the assembly and look back toward his bride, his expression a mixture of relief and satisfaction.

Stephanie and her father were about halfway down the aisle when one of Reynard's guards came running toward his boss. He shouted, "Intruder alert. Intruder alert."

Reynard looked up as the man scanned the crowd, then pointed to Craig. Oh, Lord, maybe they'd caught the incident with the other guy and the knapsack on a security camera.

It wasn't time for the diversion he'd planned, but he had no choice now.

Reaching into his knapsack, he pulled out some of the fireworks he'd bought in town, touched a lighter to the fuse of one and tossed it beside the pool. He did the same with several more.

They began shooting off sparks and smoke, sending panicked screams through the crowd as they mowed down chairs in their haste to get to safety.

Craig could hear chairs crashing to the ground. One of

the fleeing guests bumped into a table and tipped it over. And at least one splashed into the pool.

As he'd planned, people were creating chaos as they tried to get away before they got burned.

Over here. I'm over here, Craig shouted in his mind. There was as much smoke as sparks now, and it was hard to see, but he also knew that he could bring Stephanie toward him by using their mind-to-mind contact.

He drew his gun, hoping he didn't have to start shooting, because innocent bystanders would get hurt.

To his relief, Stephanie came stumbling out of the smoke, and she was also holding a pistol.

Where did you get that?

I asked one of the guards, and he gave it to me—to protect myself.

Stupid of him, given the circumstances. But then, Reynard still thinks I'm dead.

As he spoke, he was leading her around the pool toward the side of the house where he'd left the van.

He ached to pull her into his arms, but there was no time for that.

This way.

He directed her toward the waiting delivery van, praying that they could get out before Reynard realized where they'd gone.

Stephanie jumped into the passenger seat, and he saw her clawing at the white dress. She tore a rip down the front and wiggled out, throwing the dress into the back of the van. Underneath she was wearing a pair of shorts and a halter top.

He had started the engine and was headed for the gate when a group of men came running out of the woods, shooting at the van.

Lord, who were they? Not Reynard's security men.

Stephanie gasped.

I see one of the men who kidnapped us, Stephanie shouted in his mind. *They're here, and there are more guys with them.*

He tried to cope with that, tried to reason how they had gotten here. They must still be after Stephanie, and they must have seen him lead her toward the van.

The invasion force ran toward the van shooting, and behind the vehicle, Reynard's men were also charging forward and also shooting, and Reynard was with them, firing along with the rest.

"Duck down," Craig shouted as he plowed forward, turning left and driving in a zigzag pattern, hoping he could keep himself and Stephanie alive long enough to escape.

Intruder alert. Intruder alert, Stephanie shouted beside him. *Shoot at the invaders. Shoot at the invaders, not the van.*

He took up the chant, adding his voice to hers. Some of Reynard's men got the message and began firing at the men who had poured onto the property. The newcomers returned fire. But others kept aiming at the van.

And then another voice, louder and stronger, added force to the order.

Shoot at each other, not the van.

Who's that? Stephanie asked.

No idea. Could it be the woman who put us in communication?

Maybe.

For a heart-stopping moment, nothing seemed to change. Then Reynard's men began blasting in earnest at the others, and the invaders blasted back.

Craig looked behind them and saw Reynard still coming, determined not to let his bride escape.

He knew Stephanie caught the thought because she gasped as she followed his line of sight.

Craig kept aiming for the gate. And for long moments he thought they would get away. Then, to his horror, the van began to sputter, and he knew the engine had been hit. Finally it coughed and stopped.

Chapter Twenty

"We have to make a run for it, but wait until I throw more
fireworks," Craig shouted, opening the driver's door and
ducking behind it as he set off two more cones and lobbed
them behind him.

Reynard leaped out of the smoke, murder in his eyes as
he raised his gun at Craig.

Before he could fire, Craig heard the crack of a pistol.

Reynard's eyes took on a look of shock as he went down.
When Craig turned his head, he saw Stephanie had shot
the man.

She gasped as she stared at her former fiancé.

"I had to do it."

"Thanks for saving my life."

They both crouched low, running forward as the gun battle raged behind them, but there was still a guard at the gate.

"Halt or I'll shoot."

"I'm trying to get Miss Stephanie out of the line of fire,"
Craig shouted back.

"The hell you are." He gestured toward the uproar in
back of them. "I think you caused whatever's going on
back there."

"No," Craig denied, but the man advanced on them,
gun drawn.

"Drop your weapons."

With no choice, Craig and Stephanie dropped their guns. They had gotten this far, but they were still inside the compound.

The man held the pistol on them, using his walkie-talkie to call the other stations.

"What's going on back there?" he asked.

Static crackled on the line.

"Intruder came in to kidnap the bride. Fox is down. Repeat, Fox is down."

Fox must be the code name for Reynard, Craig thought.

Be ready to drop, he said to Stephanie. He knew she had picked up on what he was doing and was getting ready to send him power, but she stayed on her feet.

Craig had dropped his gun, but he still had the lighter in his hand. While the guard was distracted by the walkie-talkie message, Craig flicked the lighter on, using his mind to shoot out a tongue of flame toward the guard. When the man screamed and jumped back, Craig ducked low and rushed him, plowing his head into the guy's middle and bringing him down.

As they grappled for the weapon, Stephanie rushed in and kicked the guy in the head, stunning him.

Craig grabbed the gun and slammed it into the guard's face. As he and Stephanie started for the gate, he saw two figures had emerged from the wood, a man and a woman, advancing slowly.

Hurry, the woman shouted inside his head.

He and Stephanie picked up speed, but he heard running feet behind them. Guards who had escaped the gun battle were closing in.

As they pelted toward freedom, a bullet whizzed past his head, apparently shot from too far away for accuracy.

The woman raised her hand, lightning crackling at her fingertips. She sent it flying toward the cameras at the guard post. They sizzled and exploded, hopefully wiping out a visual of what had happened at the gate.

Power, give me power, the woman shouted inside his head.

Craig wasn't sure what he was doing, but both he and Stephanie tried their best to send her additional energy, just as they had done with each other.

When he heard roaring, crackling noises, he turned his head and saw a wall of flame erupt, creating a barrier between them and the advancing guards.

Shouts of fear and curses of anger reached him, but none of the bullets were getting through.

You can't keep that up forever. Let's get the hell out of here. This time it was the man speaking.

As the fire burned behind them, the man grabbed the woman's arm and pulled her away. Craig and Stephanie followed.

The four of them raced into the woods, then into a clearing where a four-wheel-drive SUV sat. The man and woman climbed in front, with the man behind the wheel. Craig and Stephanie climbed in the back.

Before they'd clicked their seat belts, he took off, jouncing along a dirt road. The ride smoothed out as they came out onto a two-lane highway.

In the backseat, Craig pulled Stephanie close and slung his arm around her shoulder, still trying to process everything that had happened.

"You're like us," he breathed, speaking to the people in the front seat.

"Yeah," the man answered.

"Thanks for showing up."

"We couldn't leave you in danger," the woman said as she turned around. "We haven't officially met. I'm Rachel Harper, and this is my husband, Jake."

"Again, thanks," Stephanie said.

"Who was after you?" Rachel asked. "I mean besides John Reynard's men."

"I don't know, exactly," Craig said. "But I think it had something to do with the Solomon Clinic, since they apparently knew to show up in Houma."

Jake Harper cursed and glanced at his wife. "I thought we were done with that."

"Why?" Stephanie asked.

"Dr. Solomon is dead. And so is Bill Wellington, who funded the project through a Washington think tank. That should have laid the past to rest. But it appears that someone is still hunting us."

"It looks like it," she murmured.

"Why are they doing it? What do they want?" Stephanie asked.

"The Howell Institute fronted the money for a lot of pie-in-the-sky projects for the Defense Department and other agencies. Solomon convinced them he could create superintelligent children by manipulating fertilized eggs."

"So his clinic was a source of the eggs."

"Exactly. And when the kids turned out to have normal intelligence, Wellington shut the project down."

"Why isn't that the end of it?"

"Because of what we are," Jake answered. "We've got powers they don't understand. Which makes us a threat, or maybe an asset that someone can exploit."

Stephanie shuddered.

"One good thing about the situation—whoever was stalking you sent an invasion force to the wedding."

"Why is that good?" Craig asked.

"Because they took out a lot of the guards, and the guests saw the battle. They know the invaders are responsible for anything bad that happened."

"Like Reynard's death," Stephanie murmured.

"Exactly," Craig said.

"But that's the only upside. Until we figure out who is after us this time, I think it's best if you stay at the Lafayette plantation."

"You have a plantation?" Stephanie asked.

"It actually belongs to Gabriella Bordeaux. She and Luke Buckley are also products of the clinic. They were on the run, too. And hooked up with us."

As they drove west, Stephanie slumped against Craig.

We don't know what happened back at Reynard's estate. I don't even know if my father is all right.

He is. I saw him duck under a table.

Well, he got what he wanted. Reynard paid his debts, and I didn't have to marry the man.

She let her head drop to Craig's shoulder, and he held her close, marveling that she was in his arms and the two of them were finally safe.

Rachel broke into their silent conversation.

"The plantation's a good place for you to hide out—until we get the mess straightened out."

"You think we can?"

"Yes," she answered with conviction. "And I hope you want to join us in our group defense efforts."

"Of course," Craig said. "What you did back there was pretty impressive. How did you do that trick with the lightning bolt?"

"It's not difficult. We can teach you." She huffed out a breath. "I'm sorry we didn't come to help you sooner, but we had to be sure about you."

"About our being children from the clinic?"

In the driver's seat, Jake made a wry sound. "No. That part was pretty obvious. She means sure that you were friendly. The first people we met from the clinic tried to kill us."

Stephanie gasped. "Why?"

"They thought they were the only ones with our kind of mental powers, and they couldn't stand the idea of anyone else having them."

"Nice," Craig answered.

"You were a twin?" Rachel asked Craig.

"Yes. My brother, Sam, and I must have developed powers together right from the beginning. When he was killed, I thought I'd never find that again." He pulled Stephanie closer as he spoke. "Then I found Stephanie and discovered there was more than what Sam and I had shared."

As they drove to Lafayette, Jake and Rachel told them about the plantation. And they spoke about the clinic.

"Right now, the two of you probably want to decompress," Jake said.

"There are guest cottages on the grounds," Rachel said. "You can have one."

Craig was still feeling dazed as they pulled onto the Lafayette plantation property. He blinked when he saw the sign for Chez Gabriella.

"She was a pastry chef in New Orleans," Jake explained. "She's funding the plantation with this restaurant in the main house—where she grew up. But it's only open on the weekends. That gives us the run of the place the rest of the time. We're going to move the housing farther from the restaurant, but we haven't gotten around to it."

When he pulled up in front of a semicircle of cottages, another man and woman came walking down from the main house.

"Gabriella and Luke," Jake said.

They climbed out, and the newcomers hurried forward.

Jake made the introductions.

"It's so great to meet you. We wanted to come along, but Jake said we needed to stay here," Gabriella said.

They all shook hands, and Craig cleared his throat. "Try to imagine me with hair. I shaved my head for a disguise."

"We'll wait for the real you to emerge," Stephanie said. "Trust me, he's a handsome guy. And twenty pounds lighter than he looks."

"There's so much to tell you," Gabriella said, "but I know the two of you want some alone time."

"The restaurant's closed today, but I'm cooking for us. Come over around seven and we'll all have dinner."

"Thank you so much," Craig answered.

Gabriella showed them to one of the cottages. They stepped inside, and Craig had only a vague impression of antique furnishings because he was too focused on Stephanie to notice anything else. He reached for her and folded her into his arms. They hugged each other fiercely, both of them hardly able to believe that they'd escaped from Reynard's compound.

"Thank God you got there," Stephanie murmured.

"Thank God you kept your head and helped me."

He cut off the conversation by lowering his mouth to hers for a kiss that spoke of all the powerful emotions surging through him.

You were alone for so long. You never have to be again. I have you.

And you showed me what it is to have a partner who is everything two people can be to each other—and more.

It's just sinking in how much danger you put yourself in—for me.

For us.

I had to. You know I had to. And it worked out.

When they finally came up for air, she ran her hands up and down his arms, over his back, and he knew she was re-assuring herself by the contact with his strong body.

"This place must have a bedroom."

"I hope so."

Linking his hand with hers, he led her into the next room and stepped far enough away to look at her outfit.

"How could you put on a halter top and shorts under your wedding gown?"

She laughed. "I did it while Claire was out of the room. I knew I couldn't run very far in that gown."

"You looked so beautiful, and then you ripped the dress apart."

"We'll get another one—for us."

He laughed. "Is that a proposal?"

When she flushed, he kissed her. *I'm just teasing. You know I want the same thing you do.*

He untied the halter. *Convenient. No bra.*

His eyes were warm as he looked at her.

She reached for the buttons of his shirt, then found another layer underneath—and another. "Not so convenient."

He helped her unbutton the shirts and shrugged out of them.

She ran her hand across his broad chest, winnowing her fingers through the crinkly hair she found there.

He sighed and pulled her close, swaying her breasts against his chest.

His mouth came back to her, his tongue playing with the seam of her lips. She opened for him, closing her eyes as he deepened the kiss while he cupped her breasts in his hands and slid his thumbs over the taut peaks, wringing a glad cry from her.

JOY SURGED THROUGH STEPHANIE. She was free to be with Craig now, and that thought sent hot, needy sensations curling through her body.

He unbuttoned her shorts and lowered the zipper, pushing the garment down her legs, along with her panties, so he could touch her intimately, sending heat pounding through her.

He had brought her to climax the night before. Now she needed more. And she needed to return the pleasure he had given her.

She pulled back the covers, bringing him down to the surface of the bed with her, clasping him to her before rising up and trailing kisses along his body, moving ever downward, knowing he was tensing with anticipation. And when she found his erection with her mouth and closed around him, she felt his pleasure zinging through her.

He didn't have to tell her when to stop. She knew. And she knew when to straddle his body and bring him inside her.

She was dizzy with desire. And she knew he was, too.

She had kept things slow. Now an explosion of need had her moving in a frantic rhythm that sent them both flying off into space.

When she came down to earth, he was there to catch her.

Emotions flooded through her as they looked at each other.

"This is so much more than I ever expected from my life. Oh, Craig, I love you so much."

"I love you. And I'm going to make sure nobody can snatch you away from me."

"You think we're still in danger?" she breathed.

"I think we have to stay hidden until we find out who was after us." He dragged in a breath and let it out. "I came to New Orleans to punish my brother's killer, because I thought that satisfaction was all I could expect. Then I met you, and I knew that there was so much more."

"Never alone again," she whispered as she snuggled against him, marveling at what she had found with this man. Now and for the rest of her life.

* * * * *

"Something tells me that down deep, you don't agree with what you have to believe."

Her touch spilled heat into Zac's gut. He was no saint, but he could honestly say he hadn't felt that kind of fire in a long time. Whether it was wishful thinking or plain wanting action, he didn't know, but he liked it. Given his current status as the prosecutor on her brother's case, thinking like that would lead him nowhere good.

Emma snatched her finger back. He smiled and her cheeks immediately flushed. Too damned cute. Even if he should be running like hell.

"I need to go," she said.

For safety, Zac stepped far enough out of reach so he didn't do something stupid and touch her. "Yes, you do."

Acknowledgments

Thank you to my husband, who continually offers support and incredibly corny jokes that make me smile. You are the love of my life and I'd be lost without you. To Gigi Giordano Pallitto, you rock, girlfriend! Thank you for your never-ending patience while I tackled legal research. I've always said it's good to have a lawyer in the family. Hopefully, I haven't mangled the massive amount of information you provided!

To John Kocoras, I so appreciate your early input while I plotted this story. Who knew I'd find Brady and Giglio material so fascinating?

And now for my usual suspects, whom I couldn't complete a book without. Thank you, Theresa Stevens, for once again pushing me on the tiny details in my writing. I wish I could bottle all you've taught me and share it with other writers. You're the best! To Tracey Devlyn and Kelsey Browning, thank you for your constant support and for traveling this road with me. It's been an amazing ride. Lucie J. Charles and Misty Evans, you always allow me to disturb your day with critiques and brainstorming ideas, and I'm continually thankful for your help.

John Leach, there aren't enough words to thank you for sharing your law enforcement knowledge. With each book, you give me new possibilities for my stories.

Thanks to my editor, Denise Zaza, for joining my lunch table the day we met. I'm thrilled to have the opportunity to work with you. It's been a wonderful experience. To Dana Hamilton, thank you for your guidance throughout production on this book.

Finally, to my son, who reminds me every day why love is so important. I love you.

THE PROSECUTOR

BY
ADRIENNE GIORDANO

© 2012 Adrienne Giordano

MILLS & BOON

Published in Great Britain 2014
by Mills & Boon, an imprint of Harlequin (UK) Limited,
Eton House, 18-24 Paradise Road, Richmond, Surrey, TW9 1SR

© 2014 Adrienne Giordano

ISBN: 978 0 263 91353 8

46-0314

Harlequin (UK) Limited's policy is to use papers that are natural, renewable and recyclable products and made from wood grown in sustainable forests. The logging and manufacturing processes conform to the legal environmental regulations of the country of origin.

Printed and bound in Spain
by Blackprint CPI, Barcelona

For Elisa and Chris, who make the complexities
of sibling relationships easy to navigate. I love you.

Chapter One

Assistant State's Attorney Zac Hennings leaned back in his chair the second before a newspaper smacked against his desk.

"If there's any blowback on this," Ray Gardner said, "it's yours."

Zac glanced at the newspaper. On page one, below the fold, was a photo of a young woman—*brunette*—gazing out a window framed by a set of gold drapes. Someone's living room. The headline read Fighting for Justice. He skimmed the first few paragraphs. The Chelsea Moore murder.

A burst of adrenaline exploded in Zac's brain. *Big case.*

Turning from the newspaper, he looked back to his boss. Ray's generic gray suit fit better than most he wore but still hung loose on his lean frame. Once in a while, to keep his staff sharp, Ray would show up in a blue or black suit. Regardless, the guy needed a good tailor, but Zac wasn't going to be the one to suggest it. Not when Ray led the Criminal Prosecutions Bureau, the largest of the six divisions of the Cook County State's Attorney's Office.

Ray gestured to the newspaper. "The Sinclairs got traction with this. Steve Bennett—"

"The detective? The one who died last week?"

"That's him. Brain cancer. He apparently refused to

face his maker without clearing his conscience. He sent Emma Sinclair a video—starring himself— telling her the witness who ID'ed her brother wasn't sure he got the right guy. According to Steve, detectives pressured the witness into saying he was positive."

Zac took his time with that one, let it sink in. "We locked up Brian Sinclair for murder and now we've got deathbed revelations?"

"Something like that. The State's Attorney called me at six this morning after seeing her newspaper. She wants the office bulldog on this. That's you, by the way. You'll have all the case files this afternoon."

More files. Every open space in Zac's office had been jammed with stacks of folders containing all the lurid details of crimes ranging from robberies to murders. Where he'd put more files he had no idea, but as one of nine hundred assistant prosecutors in Chicago, a city plagued with over five hundred murders last year, he had bigger problems than storage space.

Not for the first time, his responsibilities settled at the base of his neck. He breathed in, gave that bit of tension its due diligence and put it out of his mind. Unlike some of the attorneys around him, he lived for moments like this. Moments when that hot rush of scoring an important case made him "the man," marching into court, going to battle and kicking some tail.

The cases were often brutal, not to mention emotionally paralyzing, but his goal would always be telling the victim's loved ones they got a guilty verdict. No exceptions. In this case, they'd already convicted someone. Zac had to make it stick.

Adding to the drama was Chelsea's father, Dave, who was a veteran Chicago homicide detective. A good, honest cop who'd lost his child to a senseless act of violence.

In short, Zac wanted to win.

Every time.

"We're already behind the curve with this article," Ray said.

"I'll get us caught up."

When Chelsea Moore's murder occurred, Zac had been grinding his way through misdemeanors. After getting promoted to felonies, he'd worked like a dog to win his cases and it paid off. Big-time. Ray had just assigned him a politically and emotionally volatile case that he'd bleed for in order to keep Chelsea's killer behind bars.

No matter how hard Emma Sinclair came at them, Dave's daughter deserved justice. And Zac would see that she got it. He'd study the trial transcripts and learn the facts of the case.

"The P.D. will go to the wall for Dave Moore," Ray said.

"Yep. The guy breaks cases no one else can. He won't tolerate his daughter's murderer going free. His buddies won't, either."

Ray pointed. "Bingo."

If Emma Sinclair managed to get her brother's conviction overturned, the Chicago P.D. would not only be angry, they'd also make sure Helen Jergins, the new State's Attorney who'd promoted Zac, got run out of town. Hard.

Ray shifted toward the door then turned back. "Whatever you need, you let me know. We have to win this one."

"I got this," Zac said. "Count on it."

EMMA STOOD IN FRONT of the huge whiteboard she'd rolled to her mother's basement wall and contemplated her revised list of target defense attorneys. Given the newspaper article, today would be the day to once again get cracking on Project Sinclair.

Eighteen months ago her twenty-two-year-old brother,

a guy who had nothing but love for those around him, had been convicted of strangling a young woman outside a nightclub. Unable to withstand the injustice of the circumstantial case—no fingerprints or DNA—Emma started banging on the doors of defense attorneys all over the city, trying to win a reversal. No matter how many times she was told no, she would not be silenced. Not when her innocent brother was rotting in prison.

She flicked her finger against the whiteboard. The new video evidence would lure one of these lawyers in. It had to. The case suddenly had all the political melodrama—corruption, false witness testimony, withholding information—defense attorneys thrived on.

She spun back to the oblong folding table, shoved aside an open banker's box, grabbed the binder with her latest set of research and made a note to study up on *Brady* and *Giglio* material. Being a first-year law student, a field she'd never imagined for herself, she hadn't yet mastered the concepts, but they involved impeaching a witness and items prosecutors were required to share with the defense. Maybe in the next few days she'd have a defense attorney—preferably pro bono, considering that she was broke—to help her slice through the technical aspects of the case.

Above her head, the exposed water pipe clunked. Her mother flushing the toilet. Emma sighed. She should move all this stuff upstairs to Brian's old room, but her mother didn't need to see a daily reminder that her son was a convicted murderer. Bad enough the poor woman had to think about it, never mind see it every time she walked upstairs.

So Emma and her effort to free her brother would stay in the cold, dreary basement, surrounded by cobwebs that, no matter how many times she brushed them away, kept returning. When the time came for her to move out on her own again, she'd have a finished basement. No doubt about it. For now, she'd left her cute little apartment in Wrigleyville so her widowed mother wouldn't have to face her demons alone.

A rapid click-click-click of heels hitting the battered hardwood came from the first floor. Emma had spent countless hours listening to her mother's footsteps above. Whether early morning or the darkness of night when sleep eluded them, Emma recognized the sound of her mother's shoes. The ones she'd just heard didn't belong to her mom. *Someone's here.*

"Emma?" her mother called from the doorway.

"Yes?"

"There's a Penny Hennings here to see you."

Emma froze. *Penny Hennings.* She perused her whiteboard, where she'd alphabetized the lawyers' names. Hennings. There it was. Not Penny, though. Gerald, from Hennings and Solomon.

Maybe Penny was a relative sent to check her out for Gerald Hennings, who might want to take the case. And if said relation fought downtown traffic on a weekday morning and hauled herself to the North Side, to Parkland, it had to be serious. Emma linked her fingers together and squeezed. *Please, let it be.*

"Be right up, Mom."

She glanced down at her sweats, torn T-shirt and pink fuzzy slippers. Great. She'd have to face some snazzy lady from a big-time law firm in this getup. She plucked a rubber band from the little bowl with the paper clips. Least she could do was tie back her tangled hair.

Rotten luck.

Forget it. She had to put her appearance out of her mind. For all she knew, Penny Hennings could be a cosmetics saleswoman.

But what were the chances of that? Particularly at 9:00 a.m. on the morning an article about Brian ran?

"Emma?" her mother called.

"Coming."

She straightened. If Penny Hennings *was* from Hennings and Solomon, Emma had to go into full sales mode and convince this woman that her firm should take Brian's case. After eighteen months of studying overturned convictions and hounding lawyers, it was time for their odds to change. And Hennings and Solomon could make that happen.

Emma ditched her slippers at the base of the stairs and marched up. She looked like hell, but she'd dazzle this would-be-lawyer-slash-cosmetics-saleswoman with her powers of persuasion.

The basement door stood open and Mom's voice carried from the living room. Emma closed her eyes. *This could be it.* After a long, streaming breath, she stepped out of the short hallway.

A minuscule woman—maybe late twenties—with shoulder-length blond hair sat on the sofa. The plaid, overstuffed chair tried to swallow her, but her red power suit refused to be smothered. No, that puppy screamed strength and defiance and promise. Could be a good sign.

Plus, to the woman's credit, she kept her gaze on Emma's face and not her attire. One cool cookie, this blonde.

Emma extended her hand to the now standing woman. "Hello. I'm Emma Sinclair."

"Good morning. I'm Penny Hennings. I'm an attorney from Hennings and Solomon. I'm sorry to barge in, but I saw the story on your brother this morning."

Emma glanced at her mother, took in her cloudy, drooping brown eyes and flat mouth. A heavy heart had stolen her mother's joy. Ten years ago, at the age of forty, the woman had been widowed and learned that hope could be a fickle thing. Emma, though, couldn't give in to that defeatist thinking. There was a reason she'd been left fatherless at sixteen and now, with her brother in prison, had assumed the role her father would want her to take. To watch over Mom and free Brian.

Some would say she didn't deserve all this loss. Why not? It turned out their family had crummy luck. Her father's sudden death from a brain aneurysm had left a void so deep she'd never really acknowledged it for fear that she'd be consumed by it and would cease experiencing the joy the world offered. Ignoring that vast hole inside her seemed easier.

Then Brian went to prison—more crummy luck—and the hole inside grew. The thing she held on to day after day, the thing that kept her focused and sane and standing, was the fight to free her brother.

Whatever it took, she'd find a way to put their family back together.

"Ms. Sinclair?"

Make this happen. "Forgive me. I'm…well, I'm trying not to get ahead of myself, but you're the first attorney to contact me in eighteen months and I'm really, *really* happy to see you."

Penny offered a wide smile and instantly Emma's pulse settled. "Please, have a seat. Would you like coffee?"

"No, thank you. I can't stay long. I spoke to my father—Gerald Hennings—on the way over. He indicated that you'd contacted him about this case some months back."

Emma sat on the love seat and rested her hand over her mother's. Maybe they'd finally get the break they deserved. "Yes. He was kind enough to review the case, but said there was nothing he could do."

"At the time, that was true, but I'm intrigued by this video you've obtained. If the video is accurate, we might be able to prove that your brother's constitutional rights were violated. Any information regarding witness testimony should have been turned over to the defense before trial."

"It's *Giglio* material, right?" Emma asked.

Penny cocked her head. "You've brushed up."

"Yes. I'm also a first-year law student at Northwestern. I left a job at a public relations firm so I'd be available during the day to work on my brother's case. With the hands-on experience, I figured I might as well go to law school. I waitress at night and work my classes in around everything else."

"Wow. You're good."

Emma shrugged. "Not really. My brother is innocent and he's slated to spend the next twenty-five years in prison. I can't let that happen."

Penny's expression remained neutral, her lips free of any tightening or forced smiles. No pity. Good. They didn't need pity. They needed a shrewd legal rainmaker.

"That's why I'm here. I'd like to review the information you've collected and possibly take your case. Pro bono. I'm not going to lie: this will be tough. The victim's father is a Chicago P.D. detective. The State's Attorney will go to war with us to keep your brother in prison, but I won't back down. If Brian's rights were violated, I'll prove it. Besides that, I'm hungry for a big case and I think yours might just be the one."

Suddenly, Penny Hennings seemed young. Idealistic maybe. Not the battle-hardened defense attorney her father was. Did it matter? Her wanting to step out from under her father's shadow and make a name for herself was a great motivator.

She's a rainmaker, smart and determined.

Emma gestured down the hall to the basement door. "Would you like to see what I have on the case?"

Penny smiled. "You bet I would."

ZAC PUSHED HIS ROLLING cart stuffed with case files from the courtroom to his fifth-floor office. Along the way he passed other prosecutors dragging their own heavy loads and their stone faces or smirking, sly grins told the tales of their wins and losses.

Zac's day had consisted of jury selection for a murder trial he was scheduled to prosecute. The pool of candidates wasn't ideal, but his evidence was strong and he'd parlay that into a win.

He nudged the cart through his doorway and turned back to the bull pen for Four O'clock Fun. On most days, prosecutors coming from court gathered to compare notes, discuss the personalities of judges and opposing lawyers, anything that might be good information for one of the other ASAs. Some days, Four O'clock Fun turned into a stream of stories that would scandalize the average person, but that prosecutors found humorous. For Zac, gallows humor was a form of self-protection. A way to keep his sanity in the face of the day-to-day evil he grappled with.

"Zac," Stew Henry yelled, "Pierson got his butt kicked by Judge Alred today."

"Seriously?"

Alred had to be the easiest-going guy on the bench. It took a lot to aggravate him. Two steps toward the bull pen, Zac's cell phone rang. He checked the screen. Alex Belson, the public defender on the Sinclair case, returning his call.

"Have to take this," Zac yelled to the bull pen before heading back to his office. "Alex, hey, thanks for getting back to me."

"No prob. Got to say, screwy timing since your sister called me today, too."

"My sister?"

What's that about?

"Yeah. She's taking the Sinclair case. Wants copies of all my notes."

Zac dropped into his chair to absorb this info.

"You didn't know?" Alex asked.

Penny had left a voice mail earlier in the day, but he'd been in court and hadn't had a chance to get back to her. "I haven't talked to her today."

Another call beeped in and Zac checked the screen. Penny. "Alex, let me call you back." He flashed over to his sister. "Pen?"

The sound of a horn blasted. Outdoors.

"Hi," she said. "Are you in your office?"

"Yeah."

"I'm walking into the lobby. Be there in two minutes."

She was here. "What's this about your taking the Sinclair case?"

"Word travels fast. How'd you know?"

"The PD told me. Pen, I caught this case."

Silence. *Yeah, little sister, soak that up.* If this case went forward, Zac would be battling his baby sister in court. At twenty-nine, only two years his junior, she was equally competitive when it came to winning her cases. Plus, she had their legendary father as co-counsel.

In short, it would be a bloodbath.

Unfortunately for his sister, Zac planned on winning and giving Dave Moore justice for his daughter.

"So," Pen said, "I guess my calling you to find out who Ray assigned proved fruitful."

"You don't want this case. It's a dog."

"Not a chance, big brother. See you in a minute."

Zac hung up and stared through the open doorway where raucous laughter from Four O'clock Fun raged on. That Alred story must have been a good one. He should have stayed and listened. He could use the laugh.

Two minutes later, Penny swung into his office. Behind her strode a woman wearing tan pants and a black sweater. Emma Sinclair. He'd never met her, but had seen photos of her, including the one from the morning paper still sitting on his desk. That photo hadn't done Emma any favors. In person, her dark hair extended below her shoulders and, when Zac took in the soft curve of her cheek and her big brown eyes, something in his chest pinged. Just a wicked stinging that reminded him he was in desperate need of a woman's affections.

Except she was his opponent.

Why the hell was Penny bringing her here?

"Hello, *Zachary,*" Penny said in that sarcastic, singsong way she'd been addressing him for years. She stepped forward to give him the usual kiss on the cheek, but caught herself.

Yeah, welcome to Awkwardville. For the first time, they were squaring off against each other in the professional arena. Considering that his father and his two siblings were all attorneys, Zac had known he'd eventually face one of them in court. The only thing that had saved him thus far was the Chicago crime rate providing enough cases to go around.

Until now.

Pen gestured to Emma. "Zachary Hennings, meet Emma Sinclair. Brian Sinclair's sister."

Zac stepped around the desk and shook hands with Emma. What he expected, he wasn't sure, but for some reason her warm, firm grip surprised him. Their gazes met for a split second and the intense, deep coffee brown of her eyes nearly knocked him on his butt. But he couldn't think about Emma Sinclair and her alluring eyes and how they affected him. He had to think of Chelsea Moore.

Dead Chelsea Moore.

He released Emma's hand and stooped to clear the files off the second chair in his office. The place was a mess. "Have a seat."

On his way back to his desk, he shot Penny a *what-the-heck?* look. She grinned. She wanted to play, he'd play.

While doing so, he'd also remind his baby sister that he wasn't a guy who liked to lose.

EMMA WATCHED ZACHARY HENNINGS—did he really want people calling him *Zachary?*—head back to his desk while she took the seat he'd cleared for her.

He relaxed back in his desk chair, Mr. Casual. As if she'd believe he could be comfortable with Penny as the attorney on a high-profile case and the sister of the convicted sitting in front of him. He certainly looked the part, though. Then again, he had that yacht-club look about him. His short, precisely combed blond hair and perfect bone structure just added to the patrician image. The only thing slightly ruffled about him was the unfastened top button on his shirt and his loose tie. The look fit him, however. Country-club rugged.

If she'd met him elsewhere, she'd have steered clear of him. In her experience, men who looked like that were either arrogant and patronizing or ignored her altogether. Being Miss Completely Average, she didn't have the high-maintenance looks men like him went for and that was just fine with her. What she needed was a dependable, rock-solid man who could roll with the insanity of her life.

Something told her Zachary Hennings had no interest in a woman with complications. Maybe that was an unfair judgment, but it wasn't for her to worry about.

"So," Penny said. "Let's talk about this video."

Zachary held up a hand and gave a subtle nudge of his chin in Emma's direction. "Is this appropriate?"

"She's my intern."

Her intern. Funny.

"Say what?"

"She's a law student who knows this case better than anyone. Trust me, in her first year at Northwestern she knows more about the law than the two of us combined did as first years. Suck it up. She's staying."

Obviously amused by his sister's antics, he cracked a wide grin. Emma cut her gaze to Penny, then back to Zachary before biting her lip. Down deep, the warrior in her wanted to join the fray, but watching these two hammer away at each other would be just as much fun.

"You were saying about the video? I need a copy, of course."

"Of course." She pulled her phone, hit the screen a couple of times and stuck it back in her purse. "On its way. I'm planning on filing a PCR." Penny turned to Emma. "Post-conviction relief." Emma nodded and Penny went back to her brother. "A video like this, you know we'll get our hearing based on newly discovered evidence."

He shrugged. "No judge in Cook County will vacate a sentence in the murder of a cop's daughter without something better than that video. And hello? Did the detective not have brain cancer? How do we know disease hadn't brought on hallucinations?"

"Please, *Zachary*. You'll need to try harder than that." Penny stood and adjusted the hem of her jacket. "Anyway, I only stopped to see which lucky prosecutor would face me in court. Now that I know, I'm off to make notes on this new evidence. Better start thinking about the State's reply, big brother. See you at dinner on Saturday." She gave him a finger wave. "Toodles. Love you."

Emma sat speechless as Penny strode from the office. Her attorney was one crazy chick, which might not be a good thing, considering that Brian's freedom rested in her hands. But Penny had something. Maybe it was her brash attitude or her willingness to take a chance on Brian, but whatever it was, Emma liked it. A lot.

From his desk chair, Zachary snorted. "She's nuts. Get used to it."

Emma stood. "Maybe so, but I like her spunk."

"She has plenty of that."

Before she turned for the door, Emma stared down at him. "My brother is innocent."

"He was convicted by a jury of his peers."

"And juries never make mistakes?"

No answer. It didn't matter. "I've studied the evidence," she continued. "The public defender blew this one. I can promise you my brother didn't strangle anyone. I'd know."

According to the prosecution's theory, Brian had left Magic—the nightclub—to meet the victim in the alley beside it. After he murdered her, apparently using the belt from her jacket, he supposedly went back into the club and partied for another hour.

"Were you with him that night?"

"No. But I know my brother. He stole four dollars from my wallet when he was twelve. An hour later the guilt drove him mad and he confessed."

Zachary shrugged. "He was twelve. He's a man now. People change."

"Not my brother. He was living at home with my mother at the time of the murder. Want to know why?"

"Is it relevant to my case?"

"My brother is in prison. Everything is relevant."

Zachary tapped his fingers on the desk. "I'll bite. Why was he living at home?"

"Because our father died ten years ago and I'd moved out. He didn't want our mother to be alone. He had a good job and could have easily afforded to be on his own, but he couldn't stand the idea of his mother being by herself. That's not a man who commits murder."

Emma stopped talking. The past year had taught her the value of silence. Silence offered that perfect span of time when each person decided who would flinch. She stared down at Zachary Hennings.

A fine-looking man she desperately hoped would flinch.

Finally, he stood. He was a good six inches taller than she was, but she held her ground and kept her head high. "No offense, Ms. Sinclair, but you're far from impartial and the daughter of a good cop is dead. Any one of us, given the right circumstances, has the capability to commit murder."

"Not my brother, Mr. Hennings. You'll see." She turned to leave.

"It's Zac. My father is Mr. Hennings. And I can tell you I'll study the case file. I love to win, but I have no interest in keeping an innocent man in prison. That being said, twelve reasonable people heard evidence and decided his fate. I'm not going to go screaming to the judge that it was a mistake. Prove it to me and we'll take it from there."

Chapter Two

In the beat-up hallway outside Zac's office, Emma spotted Penny waiting for her. The moment she got close, Penny headed for the elevator, the two of them moving at a steady clip.

"I'll get started on the petition," Penny said. "What's your schedule the next couple days?"

"I have a class in the morning and then I work tomorrow night. On Saturday, I work at four, but I have all morning and early afternoon open. Sunday I have to study. What do you need?"

"We need to analyze the video and compare what he says to what we know happened around the time of the murder. There has to be something else that will support our case. I think we'll get our hearing anyway because that video is pretty darn compelling, but it wouldn't hurt to have more."

Emma pushed through the lobby door and a burst of cold, early-April wind blew her hair back. Penny remained unruffled, her hair perfectly intact as she whipped through the doorway. Emma would have loved to be that put together, but she didn't have a sense of fashion so she stuck with the basics of slacks and sweaters. Basics were easy and kept her from looking like a fashion disaster.

Penny stopped on the cement steps of the towering

building. Behind them, the early rush of employees leaving for the day funneled by.

"I already have a time line built," Emma said. "I'll go through the video and do a second time line with what the detective says. And, oh, I'll get myself on the list to visit Brian tomorrow. I can squeeze that in before work and show him the two time lines. Maybe he can help."

"Good. Anything that seems off, note it and I'll have one of our investigators check it out."

Investigators. All this time, Emma had been trudging around town, fighting every step of the way, begging every defense lawyer, reporter, blogger, anyone who could help, and finally, finally, someone believed in her. Her breath caught and she smacked a hand against her chest.

Penny drew her eyebrows together, marring her perfect porcelain skin. "You okay?"

Maybe. "You have investigators."

"The firm does, yes."

Months of exhaustive, energy-sapping worry erupted into a stream of hysterical laughter. "*Investigators.*"

Penny's eyes widened. Poor woman must have thought her client was insane. Emma laughed harder and grabbed her lawyer's arms. "I've been alone with this for so long. No one has helped. No one. Even my mother has been too depressed to lend a hand, and now you tell me you have investigators. And it won't cost me anything. You have no idea what that means to me."

Finally, the tears came. A flood of them gushing to the surface and tumbling down her face. God, she was tired. Insanity might not be far behind after all.

Penny stepped an inch closer. "Listen, we've got a long road. I'm good, but we're dealing with the murder of a cop's daughter. We're about to climb Everest with no oxygen. Can you make it?"

Emma nodded. This one she knew for sure. "I've already climbed to ten thousand feet without oxygen. I'm not stopping now."

"Good. Then let's do this. Call me with any updates. I've got to go."

Penny charged down the cement steps and Emma pulled her phone from her jacket pocket. Two missed calls. One from Mom. She dialed. "Hi."

"Hi. You had a call. That Melody. The one Brian was dating."

Brian's old girlfriend—well, she couldn't really be called a girlfriend. Melody, according to Brian, was more like a friend with benefits. The fact that this *friend* had called their house on the day an article ran about Brian could not be a coincidence. Particularly since Melody, again according to Brian, had spent a few minutes with him around the time of the murder. He'd left the club and walked Melody to her car around 12:30 a.m. that night. The defense never called Melody as a witness and, with Brian not testifying at trial, Emma assumed this information had been deemed irrelevant. Not that she understood it, but she didn't understand a lot of the nuances about Brian's trial.

"What did she want?" Emma asked her mother.

"I don't know. She started talking, then stopped and said she needed to speak with you."

"Did she leave a number?"

"Yes."

Her mother read off the number and Emma repeated it to herself. "Got it."

She disconnected and entered the number into her phone before she forgot it. Pedestrians continued to stream from the building and she moved to the side. Another gust of wind caught her coat and she yanked the zipper up to shield herself from the cold air. Stepping away from the pedestrian traffic, she pressed the TALK button, heard the phone ring and waited for Melody to pick up.

Brian's public defender had been no help when it came to Melody. He'd never even pursued her claims because she couldn't prove that Brian had been with her that night. According to the lawyer, she could be covering for him.

As if a casual friend would risk a perjury charge. *Whatever.*

Emma didn't want to revisit her frustrations with Bri's public defender. Unless she could prove his incompetence, it was best left alone. Instead, she'd remind herself that she now had Hennings and Solomon on her side.

"Melody? It's Emma Sinclair."

"Hi, Emma. Thanks for calling me back."

"Sure. What can I help you with?"

"How's Brian?"

He's in prison. "He's holding up."

"I saw the article in the paper."

"They did a nice job." She wasn't about to give an outsider too much information.

"Is there anything I can do to help? I told the prosecution and the defense lawyer that I'd testify. They never contacted me, even after I gave the detectives the receipt from the parking garage."

Suddenly, all movement around Emma ceased—a huge, jarring halt that caused her body to stiffen. "There was a receipt?"

Breathe. Get loose. Too many hopes had been bludgeoned by the cruelty of injustice and she'd learned to temper her optimism. Whatever this receipt was, it couldn't have been anything stunning or the public defender—she'd hope—would have uncovered it.

"Yes," Melody said. "I used a credit card to pay for the garage. It was one of those machines. You stick the ticket in, put your credit card in the slot and you get another ticket that lets you out of the garage. Brian was with me."

Emma paused a second, let the cold air wash over her

while she mentally played find-the-missing-receipt. She'd amassed boxes and boxes of notes on the case and had never heard about a parking receipt. Didn't mean the thing wasn't sitting around somewhere, but she would have remembered seeing it. *If* she'd seen it.

Oh, and she could just hear the prosecutors moaning about how it wouldn't prove that Brian had been with Melody and unless they had solid proof, Melody could be protecting her lover.

"Unfortunately, none of this proves where Brian was at the time. I've hired a new lawyer, though. Can I have her contact you?"

"Yes. I mean, he shouldn't be in jail. He didn't do it."

"I know. I'm not giving up." She gripped the phone tighter. "Thank you for calling, Melody. I appreciate it. I know Brian will, too."

Emma hung up and stared at the phone. Now she had a receipt to chase down, another lead to work with. People continued to file out of the building, their voices and footsteps clicking against the cement.

4:40.

By the look of the mountain of files in his office, Zac Hennings would probably still be at his desk. He struck her as the diligent type—a man who'd sit and study his notes, losing all track of time. Maybe she'd march up and demand—no—*ask* about the receipt. Playing nice with the new prosecutor might get her a little cooperation.

If not, too bad. She wanted answers.

ALREADY, ZAC HAD DETERMINED one thing. The video had to be deep-sixed. On a decent day, a detective's deathbed confession was a nightmare scenario. Couple that with Zac's rabid sister and the persistent Emma Sinclair and he had one hell of a problem. Emma didn't have his sister's flashy clothes and sarcastic manner, but she obviously had a quick mind and adjusted to conflict easily. With these two, he'd have his hands full.

First thing was to obtain copies of all the case files and interview the detectives.

Still at his desk, he tapped the screen again and the dying detective's face appeared. Damn, he looked bad. It could be a major problem in court. Who wouldn't be sympathetic to someone dying of cancer?

He set the phone down and jotted notes as the now-deceased detective spoke. *Witness unsure. Alley dark. Couldn't positively ID. Showed a six-pack*—the old photo lineup where the witness was given photographs of possible suspects and asked if he could identify any of them. In this case, according to the dying detective, the witness *thought* that *maybe* Brian Sinclair *could be* the guy.

All of it should be documented in the case files.

Zac shook his head as the detective confessed to coaxing the witness with leading questions. *He had dark hair, right? And a white shirt, correct?*

Zac studied the detective's sallow face, seeking anything that might indicate that brain cancer had caused mental impairment. Outside of the papery, sagging skin that came with chemo treatments, his speech was clear and he seemed rational. Zac checked the date on the bottom of the screen. Six weeks ago. He'd have to research the effects of brain cancer in the weeks prior to death. To refute this evidence, he'd simply need to prove that the man had lost cognitive brain function. In which case, everything on the video would be thrown out.

Problem solved.

Next. Identification of the white shirt worn by the accused might be something for Penny to run with. The murder happened in March. It could have been cold. Did the assailant wear a jacket? That had to have come up in court.

Again, all this information should be in the case files,

which Zac didn't have. He scooped up his desk phone and dialed his office assistant. "Hey, Beth. Have you seen the files from the Sinclair case yet?"

"I put them in your office. They're in a box by the corner window."

On the floor sat one square file box, maybe eleven by thirteen inches. A corner of the lid was torn, as if someone had tried to lift it and it ripped. "That's it?"

"That's all that was delivered."

One box. On a six-month investigation. There should have been stacks and stacks of reports particularly General Progress Reports—GPRs—where detectives recorded notes. Those GPRs were what he needed. Typically handwritten by the detectives, the reports told the story of who said what. Anything on the investigation's progress should have been documented for use in trial.

So why did Zac only have one small box?

He'd have to track down the old prosecutor—the one who'd been fired by the new State's Attorney—to see what happened to the rest of the documentation. *Yeah, he'll be more than willing to talk.*

Zac stood, grabbed the box and set it on his desk. At least it had some weight to it. Inside he found a few supplementary reports, along with a lineup report. He perused one of the pages for any mention of a white shirt. Nothing. He checked the next page. Nothing.

Not off to a good start. He continued flipping through the files. Nothing about a white shirt. He dropped the stack of papers back in the box and propped his hands on his hips. He'd have to read through every document and study it.

Someone told the detectives that Brian Sinclair was wearing a white shirt that night and it wasn't their star witness. That guy had only confirmed the shirt's color. Zac considered the guy's statement, rolled it around in his mind. *Massaged* it. What he came up with was that the detectives, in a typically aggressive move, had convinced the witness they had Brian Sinclair dead to rights and all they needed was corroboration on the white shirt.

Which they got. *Hello, video.* If he couldn't discredit this sucker, Penny would argue that Sinclair's constitutional rights under *Giglio v. the United States* had been violated. In *Giglio* the Supreme Court ruled that the prosecution had to disclose all information related to the credibility of a prosecution witness, including law enforcement officials.

Bottom line, if the cops had pressured the witness into falsely identifying Brian Sinclair, his testimony could be thrown out.

And then they'd be screwed.

EMMA FOUGHT THE STAMPEDE of people exiting the building and rode the elevator to the eighth floor. As suspected, Zac was still at his desk, his big shoulders hunched over a legal pad as he took notes. A fierce longing—that black emptiness—tore at her. She'd always been drawn to men with big shoulders and the way her smaller body folded into the warmth and security of being held. *Pfft.* Right now she couldn't remember the last time she'd gone out with a man, never mind been held.

Dwelling on it wouldn't help her. She'd have to do what she always did and keep her focus on Brian. Then she'd pick up the pieces of her life.

She knocked on the open door.

"Enter," Zac said, his gaze glued to his notes.

"Hello again."

His head snapped up and a bit of his short blond hair flopped to his forehead. A sudden urge to fix the disturbed strands twitched in her fingers. Wow. Clearly she'd been without male companionship for too long. Even so, this was the man who wanted to keep her brother in prison. She had no business thinking about her hands on him.

"Ms. Sinclair?"

She stepped into the office, keeping back a couple of feet from the desk. "Hi, Zac. And it's Emma."

He dropped his pen and reclined in his squeaky chair. "Can I help you with something?"

You sure can. She waggled her phone. "I just took a call from a friend of Brian's."

The idea that she should have checked with Penny before talking to the prosecutor flashed through her mind. Maybe she'd been too hasty, but that had never stopped her before. Her brain functioned better this way, always moving and jumping from assignment to assignment. Fighting her brother's legal battle, until now, had been a solitary endeavor, and she had simply not considered that she had an ally. Next time, she'd consult with Penny. Next time.

She stepped closer to the desk and met Zac's questioning gaze. "Melody was with my brother around the time of the murder."

Zac opened his mouth and Emma held up her hand. "Let me finish. I know what Melody says doesn't prove anything, heard it a hundred times. However, she told me she turned over a receipt from the parking garage near the club."

"And?"

So smug. "I have boxes and boxes of information regarding my brother's case. Eighteen to be exact. They're stacked in my mother's basement. Three high, six across. I guess you could say I've amassed one box for every month since his conviction."

"Really," Zac said, his voice rising in a mix of wonder and maybe, just maybe, respect.

Not so smug anymore, huh? "I've never seen a receipt from a parking garage."

"With eighteen boxes, you don't think you could have missed it? And I'm sure you realize that a receipt won't prove his whereabouts."

There went the respect. Lawyers. Always vying for the mental edge.

"I do realize that. My concern is why I didn't know about this receipt and what other information I might not know about. I'd like a copy of the receipt."

He remained silent, his gaze on hers, measuring, waiting for her to cower.

"Zac, I'm happy to call Penny and make her aware of it. I'm sure *you* realize that all evidence must be shared with the defense." For kicks, she grinned at him.

He sat forward, his elbows propped on the desk, all Mr. I-won't-be-taken-down-by-a-law-student. "You and my sister will get along great."

"Excellent. I'd like the receipt, please."

"Sure." He pointed at the open box on his desk. "It's probably in here."

Slowly, she turned toward a brown banker's box sitting on the desk. The lid was off, but nowhere in sight.

One box.

A small box at that.

"Those are my brother's files?" She surveyed the office. "Where are the rest of them?"

Zac stood, his tall frame looming over the desk, his focus on the files. "We'll start with this one."

A niggling panic curled in Emma's stomach. "Tell me there's more than this. *Tell me* my brother wasn't convicted of murder based on half a box of files."

The prosecutor wouldn't look at her. Not even a glance. He busied himself sifting through the box. Her brother's freedom rested on the contents of one minuscule box. How dare they. Eighteen months of keeping Brian from descending into emotional hell, eighteen months of her digging in, eighteen months of begging anyone who'd listen for help—it all bubbled inside. Emma locked her jaw and gutted her way through an explosion of anger that singed her. Just burned her alive from inside. These people were so callous.

She grasped the upper part of the box and yanked it toward her. Finally, he looked at her and if his eyes were a bit hard and unyielding, well, too bad. "Tell me there's more." But darn it, her voice cracked. Emma Sinclair wasn't so tough.

He continued to stare, but something flicked in his blue eyes and softened them. "Right now, this is all I have. There's more. On a six-month investigation, there has to be more."

"Where is it?"

He propped his hands on his hips and shook his head. Emma folded her arms and waited. She wanted to know where those files were.

"Emma, I'm not about to go into court without every scrap of evidence from the first trial. A young woman is dead and I want her killer locked up, but if your brother is innocent, I'll be the first one to say so."

Brief silence filled the room. He hadn't answered her question about the whereabouts of the rest of the files. She could argue, kick up a fuss about the injustice of it all, but what was the point? All she'd do was alienate the man responsible for keeping her brother in prison. That didn't seem like a class-A plan.

Plus, for some reason, she believed him. Maybe it was his eyes and the way they snapped from hard to sparkly or the way his confidence displayed strength and a willingness to fight, but above all, Zac Hennings screamed of honor and truth.

Emma imagined that not much rattled him and she suddenly had a keen desire to see him in action, in front of a judge and jury, arguing his cases. Maybe she'd make a research trip to the courthouse and size up the enemy. She'd always believed there were multiple ways to win any brawl. Pinpointing her opponent's strengths—and weaknesses—was one of them.

Yes, a trip to the courthouse was definitely in her near future.

She shoved the box back at him. "I still want a copy of that receipt. If you don't have it, I'll have Melody call her credit card company. Either way, I'm getting that receipt."

After a long stare, one where the side of his mouth tugged into a brief smile, he dug through the box and pulled out a thick manila envelope. "I *should* advise you that I'll have everything copied and sent to Penny's office. That's what I *should* do."

"But you're not going to?"

"No. And it's highly improper. The receipt you want is probably in this envelope. I'll go through it with you. Document everything. That's the best I can do."

THERE WAS NO DAMN RECEIPT. Zac sat back and watched cute, pain-in-the-butt Emma Sinclair sift through the last stack of papers from the banker's box. They'd gone through the whole box—not that there was much of it—and nothing.

What was it with this case? He'd barely started and already everything felt…off.

Emma restacked the pages she'd just gone through and shoved them back into the envelope. "No receipt."

"I'll look into it. Right now, in fact." He picked up his phone and dialed Area 2 headquarters to speak with John Cutler, one of the detectives who had investigated the case. This guy was legendary in Cook County. The cops often joked that he could squeeze a confession out of a brick. Problem was, some of those confessions got recanted. In this particular case, Brian Sinclair had never confessed.

Detectives had kept him in an interview room—some would call it an interrogation room, but cops didn't like to use that term—and questioned him for more than a day, never letting him rest, never letting him eat and never hearing a confession.

Then the first of his four public defenders showed up. From what Zac remembered, one PD died—died for God's sake—one got fired, the third quit and finally, Brian Sinclair wound up with Alex Belson, an attorney Zac had faced in court many times and had no problems with. Some of the PDs were tough, never willing to stipulate to anything. Belson, though, was reasonable. Zac could call him up, talk about a case and they'd hammer out a deal to take to the judge. He never minded calls with Alex.

Zac was not a fan of Detective Cutler, however. His tactics were too rogue. Any confession pried free by Cutler always received extra scrutiny. Zac wasn't about to head into court and have the confession thrown out because the suspect's rights had been violated. No. Chance.

He waited on hold for Cutler. Emma sat across from him, her back straight and her dark eyes focused. Maybe her shoulder-length brown hair was rumpled from her fingers rifling through it, but otherwise, she was all business, and he pretty much assumed she wouldn't leave until he gave her something. And a dinner invitation probably wouldn't do it.

As a man who liked a challenge, he appreciated her ferocity. Her determination to find justice in a case that had more turns than a scenic drive. It didn't hurt that he found her easy on the eyes. Not in a flashy, made-up way, like a lot of the women he'd dated. Why he went for those women was no mystery and it was definitely nothing deep. Guys were guys and Zac supposed most enjoyed the company, among other things, of a beautiful woman.

Emma was different. She had a no-frills, natural beauty

that left his chest a little tight and if she'd been anyone else, just an average woman he'd met, he'd have asked her out. Plain and simple.

Judging by the intensity of her beautiful brown eyes, she wanted to skin him.

The receptionist came back on the line and informed him that the detective was out. *Of course he was.*

"Thanks," Zac said. "Have him call me ASAP." He rattled off his work cell phone number and disconnected the call. "He's on a case," Zac told Emma.

She nodded then stood. "Obviously, Penny will need a copy of everything in this box."

She turned to leave, her body stiff and distant, and something pulled Zac out of his chair. Damned if he'd let her leave like this. Why he cared, he didn't know, but he did—massively. He hustled around the desk. "Emma, look, I don't know what's going on with the case files, but I'll figure it out. One way or another, I'll figure it out."

"Yeah, because your job is to keep my brother in prison. You want to *win.*"

"If he's guilty, you bet I do. But if he's innocent, if his rights were violated and you can prove that, he'll get a new trial. That's the way our system works. Nothing I can do to change that. Nor do I want to."

She eyed him. "What do you think?"

"About?"

She waved at the files on his desk. "Looking at that box, do you think my brother's rights were violated?"

Not a chance I'm answering that one, sweetheart. "I think we're missing the rest of the files. *I* think we'll find them and then I'll get a clearer picture of this case. Until then, I believe his rights were not violated and he was convicted based on solid evidence."

She smiled. "Right. That's what you have to believe. Something tells me that, down deep—" she placed her index finger in the center of his chest and pushed "—right here, you don't necessarily agree with what you have to believe."

At her touch, heat radiated through his gut. He was no saint and willing women weren't all that hard to come by when he put some effort into it, but he could honestly say he hadn't felt that kind of fire in a long time. Whether it was wishful thinking or simply wanting action, he didn't know, but he liked it. Given his current status as the prosecutor on her brother's case, thinking like that would lead him nowhere good.

Emma snatched her finger back. He smiled and her cheeks immediately flushed. *Too damn cute.* Even if he should be running like hell.

"I need to go," she said.

For safety, Zac stepped far enough out of reach so he didn't do something stupid and touch her. "Yes, you do."

He watched her leave the office while his pulse triple-timed. A career-making case and he was having carnal thoughts about the convicted man's sister. Talk about a brilliant way to screw up.

Time to refocus and get organized. Zac dialed Alex Belson to find out where all the evidence for this case was. In a matter of one business day, Zac had fallen way behind on a case that should have been a slam dunk. A damn murder conviction and he had no files.

"Alex, hey, it's Zac Hennings."

"Hang on." Alex said something to someone on the other end then came back to him. "Sorry. Madhouse. What's up?"

"The Sinclair case. What the heck happened here? I've got one box—half full. I should have a truckload."

Alex groaned. "I feel for ya, man. I inherited exactly what you got."

"And?"

"And what? I was the fourth PD to handle this guy. I backtracked, though. The first guy died—as in keeled over out of the blue. And the other two guys aren't with the PD's Office anymore. I'm guessing when the first guy crapped out, some of his files were never recovered. Then the other two guys left and all I could salvage was what was in that box."

A murder case with no evidence. Zac dug his fingertips into his forehead. He'd have to track down the two remaining PDs, wherever they might be. If he had a knife, he'd gut himself. "You're telling me that one box is all there is?"

"As far as I know. I don't have investigators just sitting around here. Plus, we're dealing with a cop's daughter as the victim. Dude, I knew going in I was going to lose. The blue wall wasn't coming down on this one."

Cops in Chicago were legendary for their ability to keep quiet about crimes involving other cops. Chicago's blue wall wasn't cement—that sucker was solid steel—and the detectives didn't bend over to help the defense. For the most part, Chicago detectives were honest investigators who worked until they reached logical conclusions. In some cases, hunches, whether right or wrong, guided them, made them feel someone's guilt deep in their bones. Magicians that they were, they found a way to organize the evidence so it helped get a conviction.

In the case of Chelsea Moore, detectives chipped away until the evidence fit. They would have made it fit for Dave. In a way, Zac understood.

And that scared the hell out of him.

"I'll tell you one thing, though," Alex said. "Emma Sinclair made for a great investigator. She hammered me about the victim's boyfriend. Ex-boyfriend. Ben Leeks Jr."

Zac wrote down the name. "What about him?"

"His father—Ben Leeks—is an Area 1 detective."

Zac's stomach pitched. He shot a glance at the box of

evidence. There had to be something in there about the boyfriend. "Was he questioned?"

"According to the detectives, he was cleared early on. The PD before me talked to the kid. Nothing there."

"I'm guessing Emma wasn't happy."

"She thought it was too convenient. Can't say I blamed her. I went with what I had."

After three other PDs had already gone with it. Total snake pit. Zac made another note to look into the boyfriend. "What happened with the boyfriend?"

"Chelsea's friend said the kid was abusive. Smacked her around some."

"And he was *cleared*?"

"The blue wall, my friend, the blue wall."

Zac wrote *blue wall* on his notepad and then slashed a giant X through it. If it took a blow torch, he'd burn through that steel wall.

Chapter Three

After blowing off class on Friday morning and visiting Brian, Emma flew down the expressway toward home. Lately it seemed she was always in a hurry to get somewhere while never really reaching the place she wanted to be. Today however, her optimism had hit a two-year high. During their visit, Brian had made adjustments to her time line. How those adjustments would differ from the video and trial transcripts, she wasn't sure, but she'd find out soon enough by comparing them.

Emma sang along with the radio. She felt as if things were looking up. Even if the gray sky, in complete contrast to her mood, hung dull and lifeless, it wouldn't dampen her sunny mood. Brian had stayed subdued about their new lawyer. *Defense mechanism.* Her younger brother lived in a six-by-six cell. Hope ran thin for him.

Emma's cell phone rang and she punched the Bluetooth.

"Helloooo?" she sang.

"Penny Hennings here. Where are you?"

Hello to you, too, Penny. Then again, Emma didn't need her pro bono lawyer to be her friend. She needed her to give Brian his life back.

"I'm coming from seeing Brian. Thirty minutes from downtown. Why?"

"I'm heading to court. I need my intern's help. Can you get to the parking garage next to Magic?"

Emma stuck out her bottom lip. "The nightclub?"

"The one and only. I had one of our investigators call the garage owner about the missing receipt. He has an office across the street from the garage above the sub shop. He also has five years of security backups and can pull the date we need. I love technology."

Now this could be good. "He's willing to let me look through them?"

"Yes. And if you find anything, he'll give us a copy. I'll call Zac. I want someone from the State's Attorney's Office to be with you so they can't accuse us of tampering. The chain of custody on this will be rock solid. Ha! My brother will have a cow. I cannot wait. Seriously, I love my job sometimes."

Maybe Zac was right about his sister being nuts. Sanity issues aside, this might be another lead. "I'll take care of it."

Emma arrived at the garage, parked and made her way across the street. A lunch rush descended on the sub shop and, with her metabolism reminding her that she'd only had a banana for breakfast, she contemplated grabbing a sandwich on the way out. Next to the sub shop was a door marked ENGLAND MANAGEMENT. She swung through the door and walked up the stairwell.

At the top of the stairs she found a second glass door. The receptionist glanced up and waved Emma in.

"Hi. I'm Emma Sinclair."

The receptionist smiled. "He's expecting you. Come in."

Emma was ushered down the short, carpeted hallway to an office where a man sat at a metal-framed desk. The receptionist waved her in and the man stood up. He wore khaki pants and a long-sleeved golf shirt that stretched across his protruding belly. She guessed his age at about fifty, but she never was any good at figuring out a person's age. His lips curved into a welcoming grin and the wrinkles around his eyes bunched. Nice smile. Emma returned the gesture. She'd come to appreciate someone smiling at the sister of a man convicted of murder. Even if that man were innocent, most people didn't take the time to think of her feelings in that regard.

"I'm Emma Sinclair. I believe Penny Hennings told you to expect me."

"Sure thing. I'm Glen. Glen Beckett. Have a seat." He waved her over to one of the two chairs in front of the desk. "You know the date you're looking for?"

I sure do. "Yes. March 21st—two years ago. Not last March."

Glen swung to the computer and grabbed the mouse. Emma leaned forward. "On second thought, Glen, would you please wait one second? Someone is meeting me here and I don't want to start without him. Let me make a quick call."

She dialed Penny, who picked up on the second ring. "He's coming."

"Who?"

"Zac."

"Really? Not an investigator?"

"Zac's court appearance was continued and my brother is no fool. If I'm requesting someone be with you, he knows I'm not playing games. My extremely smart brother wants to see for himself what evidence I'm going to hit him with."

The door behind Emma flew open and Zac Hennings, all wide shoulders and six-foot-plus of him, marched into the office. For reasons she didn't understand herself, Emma stepped back. Zac certainly knew how to enter a room and command it.

"He's here." Emma disconnected and shoved the phone in her jacket pocket. "Hi."

Zac nodded. "Emma." He turned to Glen, held his hand out. "Zac Hennings. I'm an Assistant Cook County State's Attorney."

"Holy…" Glen shot a look at Emma then went back to Zac.

"I'm only here to authenticate the video *if* we find something."

"Oh," Emma said. "We'll find something. My brother said he walked Melody to her car and she drove him back to Magic."

Glen faced his computer again. "Then we should have it. The camera by the exit records all vehicles as they leave. Do you know what time?"

"Somewhere around 12:30 a.m."

A few clicks later a video popped onto the screen. Emma jumped out of her seat and crashed into Zac, her shoulder nailing him right in the solar plexus as they both attempted to round the desk. He let out a whoosh of air and clasped both her arms to keep her from stumbling. Emma stared down at his hands—good strong hands that had to be capable of all sorts of things—and sucked in a breath.

"Sorry!" she said. "So sorry. Are you okay?"

"I'm fine." He waved her through. "Go ahead. You'll recognize him before I will."

She wedged herself between Zac and the desk and stood next to Glen, who scrolled through a video while checking the time stamp.

"I can stop it around 12:25, if you want. Then you can watch it in slow motion."

"Thank you," Emma said.

Behind her, Zac inched up, his body not touching hers, but close enough that an awareness made it hard to focus. He had that way about him. Commanding, but reserved. Somehow she didn't think Zac Hennings had to beat on his chest and holler in order to control a room. He had a sense of authority about him that completely unnerved her.

She kind of liked that. Or maybe she was just lonely. Either way, she couldn't think too much about it. Her loneliness depressed her and she had no interest in analyzing that fact. Or the fact that he was the prosecutor on her brother's case. What a mess that would be. Allowing herself to want him darn near guaranteed another heartbreak.

"Do we know what kind of car we're looking for?" Glen asked.

Emma stepped forward, adding space between her and hunky Zac Hennings. "It's a Dodge Neon."

Zac nodded and three pairs of eyes focused on the screen. Three minutes later, Emma checked the time stamp again. 12:35. No Dodge Neon. No Melody. No Brian.

Come on. Inside her shoe, she wiggled her toes. Her head pounded as the seconds ticked away. *Please be there.*

"There it is!" Glen yelled.

Emma brought her gaze to the car on the screen. The pounding in her head tripled and she squeezed her fingers into fists. *This could be it.*

Zac leaned closer, his chest nudging Emma's shoulder. "Can you slow this down?"

Had they been anywhere else, she would have poked him with her elbow and given him the back-off-buddy look, but she refused to take her eyes off that screen.

Glen tapped at the mouse and the car slowed to barely moving as it proceeded through the open gate.

"Here we go. This should be it," Emma said as two figures—one male and one female—came into view. As the car rolled forward, the camera finally captured their faces and—bang—there was her brother's smiling face. Energy roared into her, made her a little lightheaded, and moisture filled her mouth. She swallowed once, twice. *He's there.*

"Freeze it," she yelled before the car drove off screen. She turned to Zac. "That's him. That's Brian. And Melody."

"12:37," he said. "Okay."

"Okay? Okay what?"

Zac shrugged. "We have him on tape. This gets admitted into evidence." He turned to Glen. "I'll need a copy of this video."

Clearly, the prosecutor didn't want to say another thing in front of Glen. Fine. She'd wait. At least until they got outside. Then they'd chat.

"Make it two," Emma said.

ZAC STEPPED ONTO THE sidewalk and contemplated jumping in front of the bus pulling up to the curb. His sister would go crazy over this video. Not only would she smell the blood, she'd swim faster to get to it.

Emma had stayed on his heels on the way down to the building exit and parked herself in front of him. Forget the impending self-inflicted death.

"12:37," she said. "That proves where he was."

"Yes. At 12:37. Doesn't necessarily help, though. We have the time of the murder narrowed to an hour. He could have done it *after* Melody dropped him back at the club."

She flapped her arms. "Oh, please. This is a guy who worried enough about his friend to walk her back to her car and then ride out of the garage with her. You think he goes from there to killing someone? It makes no sense."

The bus pulled away with a whoosh and left a batch of engine fumes to poison Zac's lungs. Once again he contemplated the bus. *Should have jumped.* He looked back at Emma. "Nothing ever makes sense in my job. I go with the evidence. Tell me about the victim's ex-boyfriend and the abuse."

Emma jerked her head back and stared up at him with those big brown eyes that made him think of liquid chocolate and all the things he liked to do with it. Now he'd have to figure out a way to get *that* thought out of his mind.

"Yeah," he said. "I know about that. I talked to your brother's public defender. He said you hammered him about the ex-boyfriend. So tell me because there's nothing in that box of files about it and that doesn't sit right with me."

Emma hesitated, twisting her lips for a second and—yeah—he'd have to get those lips, along with the liquid chocolate, out of his head, too.

"I was upset that the police weren't talking about the boyfriend. Brian knew Chelsea Moore casually. They were the same age and were regulars at Magic. Brian told me she'd texted him a few times after she'd broken up with her boyfriend. I don't think Brian was interested in her in a—well—sexual way so he didn't pursue her. When he was questioned, he asked the police about her ex-boyfriend. They did nothing with it."

"How do you know?"

"I asked the public defender. The guy before Alex Belson. He didn't have anything on it."

"Then how do you know the ex was abusive?"

"Well, Zac," Emma said, layering on the sarcasm. "I did something that was pure investigative genius. I did something the Chicago P.D. never thought of doing."

Here we go. "Ditch the drama, Emma. I get it."

She held up a finger. "I talked to the victim's friends. Miraculous, isn't it?"

Zac rolled his eyes, but he couldn't blame her for the attitude. If it had been one of his siblings on trial, he'd feel that same burning, festering anger. This whole thing stunk of cops trying to protect the ex-boyfriend, who also happened to be the son of a cop.

The blue wall.

He grabbed Emma's elbow and ushered her to the corner. "Are you parked in the garage?"

"Yes. I need a sandwich first. I haven't eaten all day."

"Fine. I'll wait for you and then walk you to your car. Then I have a couple of detectives to talk to."

DETECTIVE JOHN CUTLER marched into Zac's office wearing a wrinkled blue sport coat and a scowl. The man didn't like being summoned to an ASA's office in the middle of the day. Zac didn't care.

Not when one of Cutler's investigations was about to be sliced and diced in court and Zac would be the one taking the hit.

He tossed a pen on his stacked desk and leaned back in his chair. "Have a seat, detective."

Cutler stared down at the two chairs, curled his lip at the one with the stack of file folders and dropped his bloated body into the vacant one. He spent a few seconds shifting into what would have to pass as a comfortable position, then stretched his neck where loose skin spilled over his collar.

Zac waited. Why not? No sense giving the detective the ever-important mental edge. Nope. Zac would control the festivities.

Finally, Cutler held up his hands. "What do you need?"

Zac leaned over, scooped a box off the floor and set it on the desk. "The Sinclair case. These are the files. On a *six-month* investigation. Am I missing something?"

Cutler's gaze tracked left then came back to Zac. "How do I know what your office did with the files?"

Not an answer. "Is this box everything? If you tell me *yes,* then I work with what I have. If you tell me no, we have missing evidence."

Cutler folded his hands across his belly and tapped

his index fingers. "I'd have to look through the box. See what's there."

"Sure." Cutler got up to leave. "I'm not finished, detective."

The man made a show of checking his watch, and Zac nearly laughed. He'd grown up in a household that produced three lawyers. He thrived on conflict.

Cutler reclaimed his seat.

"Couple of things," Zac said. "What do you remember about a parking garage receipt given to you by Melody—" he checked his legal pad "—Clayton? She's a friend of Brian Sinclair who claims he was with her around the time of the murder."

Slowly, Cutler shook his head.

Patience, Zac. Patience. "You don't remember a receipt?"

"No. She could have given it to Steve and I wasn't aware."

"Steve Bennett? The other detective?"

"Yes."

Sure, another dead guy to blame. This case was rife with dead guys. "I'll look into that. I'm assuming you viewed the video I sent over. What do you remember about the witness?"

Cutler shrugged. "It's not like we coerced him. We showed him a six-pack, helped him narrow it down."

Helped him narrow it down… "And what about the white shirt? Who told him Brian Sinclair was wearing a white shirt?"

"I don't know anything about that. That must have been Steve."

Of course.

Zac jotted more notes and the detective tugged on his too-tight collar again. *Yes, detective, you should be nervous.* The truth was, Zac scribbled gibberish. The Area

2 detectives weren't the only ones who knew how to play mind games.

"The victim's friend told Emma Sinclair that Ben Leeks—I'm sure you're aware he's the son of a Chicago P.D. detective—was abusive."

Cutler shot Zac a hard look. Well, maybe *Cutler* thought it was a hard look. Zac thought it was more of a desperate, defensive man's way of trying to intimidate an opponent. "The kid was cleared early on."

"Cleared how?"

"He was inside the club. We had witnesses who saw him getting busy with some brunette. He didn't leave the club until closing. When he did leave, he left with a group and they all went to the diner down the street."

Zac nodded. "I need names. They're not in the case file."

Cutler grabbed one of the armrests and shifted his big body. "I told you I don't have anything. I turned over all the reports."

"Even the GPRs?" Zac smacked his knuckle against the box. "I didn't see any GPRs."

"I turned over *everything*."

"Did you write up any GPRs?"

Again the detective tried a hard look and Zac angled forward. "I'm aware that you're not happy being questioned. I don't care. I'm about to get hauled into court to defend your work. My guess is you want me to feel confident about that work. I'm far from confident. Cut the nonsense and answer my questions."

Cutler sighed. "I wrote up GPRs. I don't know what happened to them."

"Did you make copies?"

"No."

"Of course you didn't. Does it shock you that reports

pertaining to the allegedly abusive son of a detective were not submitted into evidence for a murder trial?"

Cutler stayed silent. The blue wall.

Zac eased his chair up to the desk and put the box back on the floor. "I think we're done. For now."

The detective sat across from him, his breaths coming in short, heavy bursts and his cheeks flamed. He was obviously steaming mad.

Good.

Zac was about to get his butt handed to him—by his baby sister, no less—and he wasn't going down alone. Ignoring the about-to-be-raging bull across from him, he flipped open one of the many file folders on his desk and began reading. Cutler finally pushed himself out of his chair.

"That Sinclair kid is guilty," he said. "No two ways about it."

Zac didn't bother to look up. "A video of him leaving the parking garage at 12:37 might say otherwise. Buckle up, detective. We're about to go for a rough ride."

EMMA PULLED INTO THE driveway at 12:15 that night after enduring Friday-night chaos at the restaurant. As usual, Mom had left the porch and overhead garage lights on. Even now, with a son in prison, Mom worried about her children being out late.

It never ends for her.

Emma gathered her apron and shoved the car door open. Her feet hit the pavement and she nearly groaned. Hauling trays all night had left her arms and back aching and, combined with her beat-up feet, she longed for her bed.

Nothing about waitressing was easy, but the money was good. Better than good since she'd gotten lucky and landed a job in an upscale steak place. Still, she craved the day when she'd go back to an office job, sit behind a desk and leave the body aches behind.

Soon, Emma. If her plan worked and Brian came home, she'd have her life and a chance at a normal schedule back. She could attend law school at night, allowing her to take a nine-to-five job. Heck, maybe Penny would hire her as an assistant.

Emma hip-checked her car door shut and hit the LOCK button. A loud beep-beep sounded. Out of habit, she glanced behind her. Nothing there. Their neighborhood had always been safe, but she'd learned to be cautious wherever she went. Criminals didn't necessarily care what neighborhood they were in if the target appeared easy.

Humming to herself for a distraction until she reached the front door, she tossed her apron over her shoulder. She'd throw it and her uniform in the washer before bed so she'd have it for tomorrow.

"Ms. Sinclair?"

Emma froze, her body literally halting in place, unable to move. Deep—*male*—voice behind her. *He knows my name.* An onslaught of blood shot to her temples. Car key pointed out, she spun around. A man wearing an unzipped brown leather jacket, dark shirt—no buttons—and jeans stood in the tiny driveway directly under the garage light. He wasn't tall, but he appeared fit. Muscular. Tough.

Get a description.

Short, darkish hair that was almost black. No gray. She guessed he was in his late forties. His nose was wide and crooked, broken a few times maybe.

He stepped toward her. *Don't let him get too close.* She backed away, key still in hand, ready to poke an eye, if necessary. He grinned. A disgusting I've-got-you grin that pinched Emma's throat. She swallowed once, gripped the key harder.

"Ms. Sinclair, relax. I'm Detective Ben Leeks, Chicago P.D."

Emma let out a long breath, but paralyzing tension racked her shoulders. No straight-up detective would be visiting her house at this hour, particularly the father of a guy whose girlfriend had been murdered. With her free hand, she reached into her jacket pocket for her phone. Worst case, she'd hold the panic button on her key ring to trigger the car's horn and then dial 9-1-1.

"Detective, it's late. This is inappropriate."

Slowly, she backed toward the porch. A car drove by. *Scream.* That's what she should do. Except she might wind up looking like a lunatic and lunatics never got their brother's convictions overturned.

The detective didn't move. Simply stood there, arms loose at his sides, posture erect, but casual, completely nonthreatening. "No judge in Cook County will overturn *that* conviction. Get comfortable with your brother in prison and stop making trouble. Troublemakers in this city get dealt with. Sometimes the hard way."

Emma stood in a sort of detached shock. Tremors erupted over her body, that nasty prickling, digging into her limbs and making her itch. He strolled out of the driveway, just a man enjoying an early spring night. *Get in the house.* She ran toward the door, shoved the key at the lock with trembling hands and missed. She glanced over her shoulder again, saw no one and breathed in. *Get inside.* On the second try, the key connected and she stormed into the house, throwing the dead bolt then falling against the door.

He'd just threatened her.

Maybe it wasn't an overt threat. Without a doubt he'd deny it if she flung an accusation his way, but they both knew he'd just delivered a message.

All that was left now was to decide what she'd do about that message.

Chapter Four

One thing Zac didn't expect to hear at seven o'clock on a Saturday morning was his crazy sister pounding on his door. The sound drove through his skull like a pickax. What the heck was she doing? Couldn't a guy get a break and sleep in on his day off? He should never have given her a key to the first-floor entry. And for that matter, why didn't she use her *other* key to open the inside door?

He rolled out of bed, blinked a few times against the shaft of sunlight seeping through the blinds and grabbed a pair of track pants from the chair. Too damn early for this. The way she was carrying on she'd wake up the other two tenants in the house. Worse, he was on the second floor, so the two remaining apartments would have equal opportunity to hear the racket. After jamming his legs into his pants, he grabbed last night's T-shirt from the floor and decided it would do. Temporarily.

"Zachary! Open this door."

"Keep your skirt on, Pen. I'm coming. Why didn't you use your key?"

Prepared to broil her, he ripped open the door and there she stood in a blinding bright pink coat. He closed his eyes, drove his fingers into them. "You look like a popsicle. Seriously, you need to tone that down."

When he opened his eyes again, his gaze shot to movement behind the popsicle. Instantly his face got hot. A sizzling burn straight to his cheeks because his crazy sister had brought Emma Sinclair—in a knit cap and white trench coat that made him think about stripping them off her—to visit.

Pen pushed by him, stomped into his apartment and jerked her thumb behind her. "She's why I didn't use my key. How did I know if you'd be naked in here? Or if you had company."

Emma remained standing in the hallway and he waved her in. "You might as well come in. Excuse the mess. And that I'm not appropriately dressed for a business meeting." He turned to his sister. "In my *apartment*. On my day *off*."

"Blah, blah, blah," Penny said. "You won't believe this one, Zachary."

"I'm sure you'll enlighten me."

"Bet your butt, I will. Detective Ben Leeks visited Emma last night at her house. He was waiting for her, *stalking* her, when she came home from work at one o'clock in the morning."

Zac shifted his gaze to Emma who stood quietly in the middle of his living room, staring at him and his bed head. He might be a little slow on the uptake this morning but last he'd checked, his hearing was pretty good and he thought his nutty sister had just told him Emma had received a visit from a potential suspect's cop father.

"He did *what?*"

The thing he did not need in this already puzzling case was some amped-up detective with a direct link to the proceedings screwing around.

Penny, ever the drama queen, threw her hands up. "Marched right up her driveway and scared the daylights out of her."

Zac went back to Emma, studied her face for any sign of trauma. Nothing there. Only soft lips and those lustful wide eyes. "Are you okay?"

Pen's phone rang. The theme from *The Godfather*. "Ooh," she said. "This is Dad. Hang on." She retrieved the phone from the suitcase-slash-purse she carried. "Hi, Dad."

He faced Emma. "She gave my father *The Godfather* theme as a ringtone. I told you she was whacked."

Penny's eyebrows hitched up. "Sure. Got it. I'm on it, Dad." She disconnected. "I have to go."

"What?" Zac said for what felt like the tenth time. "You drop this on me and you're leaving?"

He gestured to his clothing, then to Emma.

"I have to go. The son of one of our clients got arrested. Mom and Dad left for Wisconsin early and they're already at the lake house. He needs me to get the guy out of lockup and I'm not telling our father no." She turned to Emma. "I'm sorry to do this to you. Can you fill Zac in and then grab a cab home?"

Emma slid her gaze to Zac, hesitated, then went back to Penny. "Um, sure."

In a blur of pink, Penny strode to the door and Zac pulled it open for her. Leave it to her to install Emma and her gorgeous brown eyes in his apartment and then bolt. Bad enough that his thoughts had been dropping to the gutter ever since Emma had put her hand on his chest a day-and-a-half ago, now he had to be alone with her in his apartment. Did he mention alone? *Damn Penny.* "I'll take her home. Why should she take a cab?"

His sister patted his cheek. "Good boy, Zachary. Don't forget, we have to be at the lake by five today. Don't be late. Mom will kill you. And me because you're my driver."

"I won't be late."

He shut the door and faced Emma, the woman he was terrified to be alone with in his apartment. Only slightly awkward, this situation. "Sorry about waking you up," she said. "I made the mistake of telling your sister I had the morning and early afternoon open. Apparently she thinks that means it's okay to call me at 6:00 a.m."

Zac laughed. "I swear she's a vampire. She's always been this way. She can function on five hours' sleep and I need a ton. How is that fair when we come from the same gene pool?"

"I don't know. Don't get me wrong, I'm not complaining. I appreciate her dedication."

"She's dedicated all right. I love that about her. Just not on a Saturday. When I'm sleeping."

Emma glanced around the apartment. Her stare landed on the kitchen doorway at the end of the hall. Excellent idea. Safest room. He could throw a pot of coffee together. The caffeine would jump-start him and give him something to do with his hands. Considering his hands wouldn't mind stripping that coat off Emma Sinclair. "How about coffee?"

She nodded and followed him into the kitchen where his table sat buried under case files, reminding him that he should get a damn life and invite people over once in a while.

"I guess you don't eat in the kitchen much?"

"There's one spot cleared. I usually sit there and read while I'm eating." He cleared a second spot. At least now they could both sit.

"So, the files in your office and all of these—" she pointed "—are all your cases?"

"Yeah. No time to be bored."

He scooped coffee into the basket, filled the reservoir and hit the button. "Tell me about the detective."

"Creep. He was waiting for me when I got home last night. I didn't see him when I pulled in, but by the time I got near the front door, he was in the driveway."

Zac leaned against the counter and folded his arms. "What time was this?"

"About twelve-fifteen."

Of all the idiot things. Sure he was some hotshot detective everyone in the P.D. either feared or worshipped, but if the guy thought Zac would let him interfere with his case, Ben Leeks had another think coming.

Zac nodded. "Putting aside the fact that it's not all that safe for you to be driving around by yourself so late—"

A flush of red fired Emma's cheeks and she snapped her head up. "*Excuse* me? Some rogue detective pays me a visit in the middle of the night and it's *my* fault?"

"I didn't say that. And you didn't let me finish."

But—wow—the woman was steamed in a big way. He'd better fix this quick. He held his hands up. "I'm sorry. None of my business. What he did was out of line without question. I'll deal with him."

"That's more like it, Mr. Prosecutor."

Now he was Mr. Prosecutor. Perfect. Maybe he deserved that blast of frigidness. Pointing out the obvious—that a woman should not be out alone late at night—was apparently unacceptable. With the cases he'd seen—maimed women, dead women, women who'd been violated in unspeakable ways—suddenly he shouldn't warn someone the world could be an ugly place?

Or maybe his already jaded view of the world got knocked further into submission by such atrocities. Someone like Emma Sinclair, with her can-do, won't-be-beaten attitude, didn't see the world the way he did. She saw a problem and tried to fix it. Zac saw a problem and wanted to know who he could lock up.

The coffeemaker gurgled. Finally. He spun to the cabinet, pulled out two giant mugs and poured. The potent aroma of the strong brew drifted toward him and something in his brain popped. "Milk or sugar?"

"Black with sugar."

From the same cabinet he grabbed a few packs of sweetener and handed the steaming mug over. "Tell me what Detective Leeks said."

She dug into her coat pocket and pulled out a folded piece of lined paper. "I wrote it down."

She wrote it down. Emma Sinclair would be an A-list lawyer. Before reading, he took a hit of coffee, one good gulp that burned his throat. He set the mug down, unfolded the paper and read.

Get comfortable with your brother spending his life in prison and stop making trouble. Troublemakers in this city get dealt with. Sometimes the hard way.

His neck went tight. Bam. Solid ache. He cracked it and let some of the tension snap free. In an effort not to miss anything, he went over the note a second time.

After a third read, he glanced up at Emma who had her luscious eyes focused on him. "This is exactly what he said?"

"Yes. I wrote it down the minute I got into the house. He also said no judge in Cook County would overturn Brian's conviction. I didn't write that down, though. It was too much to remember and I wanted to document the part about troublemakers before I forgot."

Zac took another two swallows of coffee and dumped the rest in the sink. He needed to nix this quick. "Wait here. I'm grabbing a quick shower then I'll pay a visit to the good detective. You good with that?"

"Am I going with you?"

"If you want to. Otherwise, I'll take you home. This is the kind of garbage—this pressuring witnesses—that got us into this mess in the first place. He needs to be called out."

A smile crept across Emma's face. Obviously she had developed an affinity for conflict, for the clashing of wills. For *war.* Zac understood the intoxicating pull. No matter how gruesome the case, he experienced a natural high every time he stepped into a courtroom.

"I'll wait for you," Emma said.

ZAC HENNINGS MIGHT BE as crazy as his sister.

Emma loved it. Every inch of it. The look on his face when he read the note, all rock-hard and vicious, showed Emma a side of him she hadn't seen before. He may have been the enemy, but he wanted to win fair and square. She appreciated that in him. Or maybe she was looking for something to like beyond how good his butt looked in track pants.

She seriously had to get her head in the game. This guy could keep Brian in prison and pulverize what was left of her family. Thinking about him in a physical way, no matter how deprived of male attention she might be, would only destroy her.

Focus was what she needed now. She'd been fighting for justice and now she had a chance. An attraction to Zac Hennings couldn't derail that.

Not today.

Not tomorrow.

Not any day.

She took another swig of coffee. Sludge, really. Who could drink coffee so unbelievably strong?

Splayed in front of her were stacks of folders and for no other reason than idle curiosity, not to mention boredom, she itched to take a peek.

Not happening, though. He'd left her here, trusting her not to invade his privacy. She wouldn't betray that trust. She glanced around the room. Just feet away stood the refrigerator, a plain white one with French doors and an ancient stove that anchored the laminate countertop. A no-fuss kitchen for a bachelor. Somehow she'd expected fancier from a guy whose father was a big-shot attorney. That'd teach her for prejudging.

Needing a distraction, she went to the sink, poured the sludge down the drain and heard the shower go off. Talk about idle curiosity. She wouldn't mind taking a gander at the country-club-rugged prosecutor wrapped in a towel. No shirt, skin still slick. She grunted. The way he filled out his shirts, she was darn sure it would be a pleasant experience. Yep. That would be a sight.

"Wow, Emma," she muttered. "You are a mess."

Mess or no mess, she stole a glance down the hall to see if he'd come out of the bathroom in a towel. Nothing. Not even a glimpse.

Rotten luck. As usual.

So I'm desperate. Big deal. Between the files and Zac naked, she had to move. The living room might be a better spot. On her way down the hall, she slowed when she reached a room with a half-open door. Bedroom. For kicks, she snuck a glance. Hey, if she couldn't see him in a towel, she'd check out his bedroom. The room was surprisingly uncluttered, considering what his office and kitchen looked like. Maybe he'd thrown a pair of jeans into a corner, but the heavy cherry dresser was neat and polished.

Behind her, the bathroom door flew open and even if her mind and body brawled over whether or not to sneak a peek, she scooted away. "I'm moving to the living room," she called over her shoulder.

"Everything okay?"

Risking the sight of him in a towel, she spun around and found him fully clothed in jeans and a crisp button-down shirt. "Yep. Your files were distracting me."

He angled back to the kitchen, the potential error of his ways hitting home and she held up her hand. "I swear I didn't look. I removed my overly curious self from the area."

For many reasons.

"Thank you for not looking. None of them are your brother's files, but…"

"I know," Emma said. "As much as my brain likes activity, you trusted me. I wanted to respect that."

Zac moved closer and the smell of his soap, something clean and pure—*salt air*—reached her. His blond hair was still damp and somehow, even more than if she'd seen him in that towel, Zac Hennings drew every ounce of her attention.

"You are something else, Emma. Straightforward. No drama. I like that."

The compliment burrowed inside and a rush of happiness lit into her. *He's not the guy for you.* Even if she had thousands of arguments, none of them could be justified. Not if Brian's freedom became the casualty. She shrugged. "I am what I am. Life hasn't exactly gone as planned, but I refuse to give in to it. There's a happy ending for my family somewhere. I'm not sure when or how, but I know it's out there."

He watched her for a few seconds, his eyes intense and unwavering and all that determined male attention made her legs a little wobbly. She needed a man. Preferably one like Zac Hennings.

Soon.

Finally, he broke away. "I hope you find that happy ending. Your mother and brother are lucky to have you."

Down deep, she knew that. Sure, there were times she admitted to herself, she'd like to run away, just disappear somewhere, hit the RESET button and start over, but she didn't have it in her to walk away. She loved her family too much.

But suddenly, the small space of silence between her and Zac filled with crackling energy and Emma's pulse jackhammered. She couldn't take it anymore. All this thinking about naked, hot prosecutors and running away and freedom, it was almost too much. A prize dangling just out of reach.

"I...um." She shook her head. *Don't know.*

Zac looked away. *Thank you.* He turned to the small side table and scooped up a set of keys. "Let's hunt down our rogue detective."

Chapter Five

After calling and confirming Detective Leeks was working, Zac left Emma in the car and climbed the few stairs leading to Area 2 headquarters. The short walk gave him a minute to clear his traitorous mind because, seriously, how many times would he have to shut down thoughts of Emma under him and moaning. He had no business wanting that. Not when a botched murder investigation was involved.

Once inside the building, he identified himself and told—no asking—the desk sergeant he wanted to see Detective Leeks.

Five minutes later, he was directed down a long hallway and told to take the last doorway on the left. That last doorway, not surprisingly, was an *interview* room. These dopes thought they'd play him by letting him stew in an interrogation room. This stunt only added fuel to his already raging fire.

He yanked out a chair, settled into it, threw his shoulders back and took a breath. *He* would control this conversation. Not Leeks.

Ten minutes they made him wait. With each ticking second, Zac got more steamed, all that negative energy spewing in his mind. Contain it. That's what he'd do. Contain it and channel it. He'd been raised by a master strategist. He'd carve Leeks to pieces before he let this chump play mind games with him.

Finally, Leeks stepped into the room. The guy was a good four inches shorter than Zac, so Zac made sure to stand and greet him. Let the shorter man get a feel for looking up at him.

Leeks stared at him with dark, vacant eyes. Nothing there. No life. No anger. Nothing. After a brief stare-down, he must have come to the realization that intimidation tactics were useless. *No dice, pal.*

Leeks pursed his lips and made a smacking sound before dragging out the chair opposite Zac's.

Zac waited for him to sit, hesitated a few extra seconds, then reclaimed his chair. The detective smirked. Yeah, he knew the alpha war game of standing over someone as long as possible. At least they understood each other.

Leeks pushed up the sleeves on his sweater. Most detectives wore sport coats and dress slacks. Maybe during the week Leeks did, too. Today he wore jeans and an expensive-looking sweater.

Zac sat forward. "I'll make this quick, detective. I'm the prosecutor handling the Sinclair case. My guess is you know that already."

"Affirmative."

"Good. Let me also inform you that you are to stay away from anyone involved in this case. *Anyone.* Do you understand?"

Leeks shrugged.

"I'll take that as a yes because the next time you threaten Emma Sinclair, I'll dig up enough dirt on you that your superiors will have no choice but to relieve you of your badge."

Leeks finally sat forward, all tough-guy shrugs and grimaces. "Listen, Ivy League, I didn't threaten Emma Sinclair."

Excellent. Precisely what Zac wanted to hear. He slapped Emma's note on the table. "You didn't say this?"

Leeks eyeballed him then picked up the paper. After reading it, he tossed it back and it floated in midair for a moment, crackling in the silence.

Leaning in, Zac mirrored the detective's body language. "You expect me to believe Emma Sinclair lied when she said you walked up to her home in the middle of the night and told her troublemakers in this city get dealt with. You didn't say that?"

"Hey, Ivy League—"

"Hey, *detective,* I'm not interested in having a conversation. I'm *telling* you what you need to do. Am I clear?"

Leeks slouched back—almost retreating, but then defiantly folding his arms across his chest. The guy's body language was all over the place.

"Yeah. You're clear. Crystal. But you better find a way to keep this guy in lockup. He murdered a young woman and his cute, defenseless sister is getting this city all churned up. Do your job, counselor."

As if he'd let this scumbag lecture him. "After the garbage you've pulled, you think I'll let you sit there and tell me how to do my job? Screw off, detective. Last I checked, my conviction rate was rock-solid. As long as I don't have overanxious cops mucking it up, we'll have a murderer behind bars." Zac stood and headed for the door. "By the way, I went to Loyola. And make sure your son is available to me."

Leeks shot out of his chair, sending the legs scraping across the cheap linoleum. *"What?"*

That extra four inches Zac had on Leeks played nicely here. It was tough to get large with someone taller and carrying an extra thirty pounds.

"You heard me. Have your son call me. I have questions about his relationship with Chelsea Moore. The sooner those questions are answered, the sooner this case goes away. I'm extending you a courtesy here. If you and your

son choose not to take advantage of that courtesy, I'll subpoena him. Your choice, detective, but either way, your
son will talk to me."

EMMA SAT IN ZAC'S sleek BMW, one just like Penny's—
and how cute was that?—thinking he should be coming
back any second. As curious as she was about his meeting, boredom had set in more than ten minutes ago. How
long did it take to go in there, tell this loser detective to
back off and come back?

Her cell phone rang. *Thank you.* Penny. "Hi."

"Hi. How'd it go with Zac?"

"Not sure yet. He's in talking with the detective now."

"OMG," Penny squealed. "I love my brother. He's so
darn predictable. He's probably tearing that guy apart as
we speak. Listen, Emma. Good trial lawyers know their
opponent's weaknesses and use them. It doesn't hurt that
our opponent happens to be my brother and he has a streak
of honor in him a mile long."

"You manipulated him?"

"So harsh! I utilized my knowledge of his personality.
Guaranteed he'll come out of that meeting and say he's
subpoenaing Leeks's kid."

"Well, we should know shortly. I'm waiting in the car.
I think it's cute that you two have the same car."

"His is two years older than mine. Our parents gave
each of us one when we graduated from law school. Our
older brother totaled his a year in. Those cars are the only
ones they bought us. We had to pay for our first cars on
our own. It was a good lesson in managing money."

Emma glanced up and spotted Zac jogging down the
few steps in front of police headquarters, his long legs
moving fast. "Here comes Zac. Want to hang on until he
gets here?"

"You bet."

He swung into the car and Emma put the call on speaker. "I have Penny on the phone."

"Hey," he said. "Did you spring your guy?"

"I did. He got picked up on a drunk and disorderly. How did you do with Leeks?"

"I've alerted him that he should steer clear of my case. He's also bringing his son to me for questioning."

Emma's heart lurched. "You're kidding?"

Zac started the car, checked oncoming traffic and entered the fray known as the Saturday-morning rush. "I want to talk to that kid."

"And he's just bringing him to you?" This from Penny who obviously didn't believe it.

"I'm good, Pen, but I'm not that good. I gave him the choice to either bring the kid to me or I subpoena him. Let's see what they decide."

"You're a good man, Zachary."

"Yeah, yeah, yeah. You don't think I know you played me? Pen, you've been doing this to me since you were twelve. I know you as well as you know me. In this instance, it works in both our favors, but I still can't figure out why I let you get away with this nonsense."

"It's because of my powers of persuasion, big brother." Zac waved his hand, but his grin stretched a mile. "Pick me up at four for dinner with the 'rents. And whatever you do, don't try to sleep with my client."

Emma made a gagging sound and Zac rolled his eyes. "Nice, Pen. Nice."

"Going on record that I've advised you both. I'm not blind and I'm certainly not stupid."

Zac made yapping gestures with his free hand. "Goodbye, Pen."

Emma clicked off and dropped the phone in her lap. "Well, that was…awkward."

"Nah. She's just being Penny. You may have noticed that she likes to stir things up."

"I noticed."

"She's unbelievable. Sometimes I think she'll give me a stroke, but she's funny as hell. That's the problem with the men in our family. We've spent her lifetime letting her get away with things we shouldn't let her get away with because she entertains us."

"You've created a monster."

"We have indeed," Zac said.

He stopped at a red light and turned to her, his blue eyes twinkling too much for Emma's comfort. Maybe Penny was onto something with that warning.

Plus, all that sibling banter had opened up the emotional sinkhole inside of Emma. Once upon a time, she and Brian had ribbed each other in much the same way. Now? Kind of hard to do with a glass wall between them and thinking about it pressed in on her. *No sadness.* Not now when they were making progress.

Soon things would change. She felt it. Finally, someone would question the victim's boyfriend. "Thank you."

"For what?"

"For pursuing the boyfriend. No one has done that for us."

He stopped at the traffic light on the corner, let out a breath and turned to her. "No problem. Thank you as well. If it weren't for you, the guy would be off the grid. Now, at least, we get to hear what he has to say."

"Yes, we do."

Their gazes locked again and the same crackling silence from earlier returned, making Emma long for something, anything that would offer a distraction.

A car horn blared—distraction granted—and Zac checked the stoplight. Green. "I'm hungry," he said. "You hungry? We can grab a bite."

She shouldn't do it. He *was* the prosecutor on her brother's case. And, well, the towel fantasy still looped in her mind.

When she didn't answer, he gave her an earth-to-Emma look that earned him a swat on the arm.

"We can always discuss your brother's case."

She gasped. "Oh, so dirty. You know I can't resist that one."

"Part of being a good lawyer is knowing your opponent's weakness."

Unbelievable. "Your sister just said that to me! Right before you got into the car. I'm not kidding."

He shrugged. "We learned from the master. Now, where shall we eat?"

Chapter Six

Emma set the steaming hot plate of pasta in front of her last customer and did the can-I-get-you-anything-else spiel. As usual, her feet and body ached from the Saturday-night rush, but she'd go home with a fat wad of cash to plop down on her next tuition payment, so there wasn't a lot to complain about.

From the corner of her eye, she spotted someone sliding into a booth. Really? Closing in thirty minutes and people were still being seated in her section? She headed to the new customer and analyzed the back of his blond head. Couldn't be.

Then he turned sideways and—yep—Zac Hennings. Her heart seized, along with every other part of her. Why would he be here when he'd told her he and Penny would be spending the night at their parents' lake house? *Something's wrong.*

The creepy detective. His son probably fell off the face of the earth. Or they cleared him.

Wouldn't that be her luck?

In the back of her mind, a nagging, paralyzing, incessant fear that sometimes dulled, but never truly vanished, roared with full force. Images flashed through her mind of Brian's bloody body, laid out on a prison floor where he'd bled to death after a prison brawl.

Don't think about it.

Zac shifted sideways and peered over his shoulder, his expression neutral. If he'd at least smile, her fear would go back into hibernation. *Come on, Zac.* But his lips remained…well…flat. He waved, but she stood still, half-terrified to step closer and hear whatever news he had to deliver.

Then, as if sensing her panic, he finally waved her over. She breathed in, ignored her pounding heart and forced her feet to move. Perhaps whatever he had to say wasn't so bad after all.

She stopped in front of his table. He wore navy slacks and a white dress shirt, no tie. Must have come straight from dinner with his folks. Translation: bad news. Horrible news, if he'd driven from Wisconsin to deliver it.

He squeezed her wrist and the connection, all that warm male heat, sparked.

"Everything is fine," he said.

Emma dropped her chin to her chest and breathed. With each exhalation, her pulse slowed a notch and she focused on releasing the tension that had wound her body so tightly. How had she gotten so accustomed to bad news that her mind always went straight there? After a few seconds, her composure restored, she lifted her head. "I got nervous when I saw you."

"I can tell."

She stole a glance at her customers. Everyone was busy eating. She went back to Zac. "I'm sorry. Prosecutors usually bring bad news. I've been conditioned."

"I understand." His lips quirked in a subtle, mischievous way and tingles shot up her arms. "Maybe I can break the trend."

We can't have that. She had no room left for personal sinkholes and Zac Hennings was one giant sinkhole waiting to swallow her up. If her brother's freedom weren't involved, there would be no question that she'd be on this man like nobody's business. But right now, Zac's job was to keep her brother incarcerated.

She could flirt with the charming prosecutor, though. No harm in that. "If anyone can, it's you. Why are you here? I thought you went to Wisconsin."

"I did. We had dinner and I decided to come home. Penny stayed with my folks. They'll all come back tomorrow."

"So you're not here for dinner."

He grinned. "Wicked smart you are."

Oh, that smile—charming and slick and devilish. The man knew his way around a woman's heart. And most likely other body parts as well.

Bad, Emma. Bad.

"I'm here because I don't want you going home by yourself. I'll follow you and make sure you don't have any unexpected visitors."

If ever there was something to make her shamelessly sigh, it was that statement right there. After what had happened to her the night before, knowing how alone she was, Zac Hennings, the guy who could destroy her family, wanted to protect her.

I'm in trouble. Deep trouble.

Nothing about this situation would roll into a happy ending. Her luck didn't hold that long. Not even close. She'd fall for him and he'd wind up keeping Brian in prison. Recovery from that emotional devastation would be unlikely. This, she understood.

Intellectually.

Physically, she craved a connection. Several connections. On an ongoing basis.

Bad, Emma. Bad. She had to get her head together. "Hang on. I have to check this table."

Her customers might have been a lame excuse, but she needed to consider the fine-looking prosecutor with gorgeous eyes and a build she wouldn't mind seeing sans clothing offering to escort her home.

Had Penny told him to do this?

Could be. Or he was just a nice guy, which wouldn't be hard to believe because she'd seen that side of him already. That morning over breakfast—his treat—he'd regaled her with stories of childhood antics involving Penny and her hijinks. Emma had laughed and laughed and laughed and, for the first time in two years, she'd allowed herself an hour of fun. To shut her mind off and not think about Mom and Brian and working on finding a solution for the mess that had become her existence.

Now, tonight, fun time had ended. She had to forget how late it was and the fact that she hadn't been held by a man in an excruciatingly long time.

She checked in with her customers. They were fine. Just fine. Figured. A trip to the kitchen wouldn't have been a bad stalling tactic. Again her luck had gone bad. Back to the charming prosecutor she went. "Sorry about that. Duty called."

"No problem. Do I need to order something while I wait for you?"

"Nah. I'll just tell them you're my ride. The cheesecake is pretty awesome, though, if you want dessert."

"No cheesecake. Anything chocolate?"

Emma propped a hip against the side of the booth and nudged his arm with her elbow. "We have a ferocious brownie à la mode."

Again came the devilish smile. "I love ferocious."

I'll bet you do. Bad, Emma. Bad.

"Okay then. One ferocious brownie for the ferocious prosecutor. Be right back."

One of the other waitresses, Kelly, sidled next to Emma on her way to the kitchen. Work and school and Brian's case had sucked away every last bit of Emma's time, but

Kelly had been a constant and the closest thing Emma had to a friend.

Kelly pushed the kitchen door open and held it. "Who's the guy?"

"Prosecutor on my brother's case."

"Shut. The front. *Door.*"

"Truth. I think I have a mad crush on him. He's so flipping hot and I'm a girl who hasn't had a man's hands on me in…a while." She pulled Kelly aside. "I'm crazy, right? Should I feel this way about a guy who wants to keep Brian in a cell?"

"Considering I've never experienced this scenario, I can't really say if you're crazy or not, but yeesh, that guy could melt asphalt. I'm thinking you're crazy if you *don't* sleep with him."

Emma aimed for a laugh, but it came out more like a panicked, hysterical squeak. "This is nuts."

"Don't get nervous. See where it goes. You might wind up hating him."

Yes. She barely knew Zac and getting ahead of herself about the nature of their friendship—or whatever it was—wouldn't help matters. His coming here could be a matter of doing Penny a favor by making sure Emma got home safely.

That's all this was. A guy offering a kind gesture because his sister asked. "You're right. By the time we're done with Brian's case, I'll probably despise him."

Emma nodded to emphasize the point. One solid jerk of her head. Total control. She had it.

Too bad she didn't believe any of what she'd just said.

ZAC TURNED ONTO EMMA'S street, trying to convince himself that he knew exactly what he was doing. Sure did. He also knew it was an epic—beyond epic—mistake. Bulldozing himself into believing he was a nice guy for getting his sister's client home safely wasn't a problem. That was easy enough. The problem was that under all that chivalry he'd buried a guy who wanted to get Emma Sinclair into bed.

And not just once.

Certain things he couldn't deceive himself about.

All through dinner he'd wondered if Ben Leeks would pay a repeat visit to Emma's. He could see that scumbag doing it just to mess with him. Throw in the chivalrous, but horny guy—the one buried under the professional veneer—and Zac found himself logging the miles back to Chicago.

He parked in the minuscule driveway—a luxury in Cook County—behind her ancient compact and studied the house. He'd always liked the cultural diversity of Parkland. Certain streets had a small-town feel while still being part of the city.

The Sinclairs' small colonial with the sagging covered porch could use more outdoor lighting, but he supposed two women living alone didn't necessarily have the ambition or funds to take on major maintenance projects.

Emma kicked open her car door, held it with one foot. *I know what I'm doing.* Zac got out, sucked cold air. *Focus here.* She reached over to the passenger seat for her purse and the bag of food from the restaurant and bungled it all. He snatched it from her before it hit the pavement.

"Got it."

"Thanks. My mom wouldn't want her dinner for tomorrow splattered on the driveway."

She locked the car and leaned back on it. The garage spotlight illuminated those luscious brown eyes. Fantastic eyes.

"Do you always bring her food from work?"

"Yep." She shrugged. "She doesn't go out much anymore."

"That's too bad."

"It sure is."

The cold, quiet air whipped around him and he breathed in, let it soak his body and, perhaps, if he got lucky, freeze his lascivious thoughts. He gestured to Emma's unbuttoned jacket. "It's cold. You should button up."

Plus, it would be another layer between them. The now frozen *and* buried horny guy wasn't too thrilled with the chivalrous guy's suggestion.

"It's just a short walk to the house."

Unless I keep you out here. "Let's get you inside. I'll carry this to the porch for you."

She stared up at him with those eyes that slayed him every time and then a small smile split her full lips. Perfect lips. The top one a hair bigger than the bottom and enough to bring a man down. Horny, frozen guy had big trouble because every inch of him ached to show her how he could put a bigger smile on those lips.

Instead, he gave her a light push toward the door and surveyed the area for a particular detective who had better not be in the vicinity.

Emma climbed the three steps to the wooden porch. Zac spied a loose board on the middle step and stooped to check it. The board flipped up when he pushed on the end. "Hey, you need to get this nailed down. Someone'll break a foot."

"I know. It came loose last week and I haven't had time to deal with it. I'll take care of it."

He stepped over the board and gave Emma the bag. "One of my buddies is a contractor. I'll get him to swing by."

"Thanks, but don't go to the trouble."

"No trouble. He won't mind." He grinned at her. "He owes me."

Emma stared down at the fractured step and sighed. "It

sounds dumb, but even getting a stupid board fixed feels like a monumental task."

A gust of wind blew a sliver of hair out of her pony-tail and, on instinct, he reached for it. She flinched and he paused with his hand in midair. Her gaze ricocheted to it then back to him and he waited for her to either back away or green-light him. His baser needs hoped for the green light.

I know what I'm doing.

Except they were standing on the porch where any rat-faced detective might be watching. Tree branches smacked against the house and twigs cracked. Zac breathed in and—how about that—she didn't back away.

Green light. What that green light entailed he wasn't entirely sure, but he'd never been a guy afraid to take a chance. Particularly when it came to women he wanted naked and under him doing wicked things. Slowly, he tucked the loose strand behind her ear. "Houses need maintenance."

"Yeah, but so do people."

Oh, honey.

She slapped her free hand against her forehead, her big eyes horrified. "Wow. That came out so wrong."

Dang, she was cute. Laughing at her, he set his hand on her shoulder and pulled her in for a friendly hug. Maybe it was more than friendly in his mind, but he made sure to keep it PC in case his radar was way off and Emma Sinclair hadn't given him the *go* sign.

His radar was pretty good, though. He kissed the top of her head and visions of her sprawled across his bed, tangled in his sheets, tangled in *him,* filled his mind. Totally cooked. That's what he was. He wanted her—no two ways about it—and horny, frozen guy didn't much care who might be watching.

She rested her forehead on his chest and rolled it back

and forth while he held her there. A few seconds passed.
Then a few more. He'd stand there all night. Emma in his
arms got his engines firing in a way he hadn't experienced
in a long time. He relaxed his shoulders, tried to stay loose
and control his raging body. Something was happening
here. Something good and hot and satisfying and he always wanted more of anything good and hot and satisfying.

"This is bad," she said.

"Probably."

She snuggled closer and he slid his arm farther around
her shoulder, stroking the back of her neck.

"No probably about it, Zac."

"I won't argue, but I generally don't walk away from
something this good."

Finally, she retreated. "It's more than good. I'm not
sure we should do anything about it, though. You're the
prosecutor on my brother's case. You have the ability to
destroy my family. I can't risk that."

He leaned down, got right next to her ear and she stiffened when his lips brushed her skin. "You're convinced
he's innocent. Convince me and I'm the guy who puts your
family back together."

Again, the tree branch smacked the house and twigs
crackled. Suddenly the air was harsh and charged and his
skin started to flame. She grabbed a handful of his jacket
and pulled him closer. He shifted his head, his lips hovering just over hers. And right then he decided that if they
were being watched, he didn't give a damn.

Her breath hitched and she blinked a couple of times.
"I guess I'll have to convince you then."

He dipped his head lower, waiting for her to meet him
halfway. She lifted her chin and their lips touched. A light
brush that made him groan and then he made his move,
hauling her in and sweeping his tongue over her bottom lip.
She gripped his jacket tighter and pulled him even closer.

Clunk. Her purse hitting the porch. Still holding the food bag, he wrapped his arms around her and held her close to him, her smaller body molding to the curve of his, while he feasted on her lips, nipping and tasting and wanting more and more and still more.

Something about Emma had buried itself inside him and every minute he spent with her didn't seem long enough.

Slowly, she backed away, but he stole one last nip of that lush upper lip before releasing her. She laughed. "You're a devil, Zac Hennings."

"I'm greedy for sure." He rubbed his hand over her arm. "It's cold. You should go in."

She glanced at the door. "Yeah, I should. I don't necessarily want to, though."

"I know. We have time, Emma."

With the places his mind was going, there'd never be enough time, but he'd figure it out. He wanted her. Job or no job, wrong or right, he'd figure it out.

"Zac, this—whatever it is—will be complicated."

"Yep. I don't know how to get around that. Not going to try. We'll take it a step at a time. See where it goes. Deal?"

She nodded. "Deal."

Chapter Seven

Sunday mornings were always Emma's favorite. Her schedule didn't allow much downtime, and with all the studying she had to do, Sundays were no exception. At least hitting the books could be done in her pajamas with a steaming cup of peach tea.

She sat at the dining room table, tea in hand, flannel PJs keeping her warm and her books sprawled in front of her. If civil liberties and constitutional law weren't the most stimulating reading, she had no one to blame but herself. Typically, she'd be engrossed. Today, though, her mind repeatedly wandered to that soul-scorching kiss Zac Hennings had plastered on her.

Total charmer, that one. But nice. The nice part was the problem. If he'd been a jerk, she could justify hating the prosecutor handling Brian's case. If he'd been a jerk, she could let her anger fester, eat away at her and push her to work harder to free her brother. If he'd been a jerk, she'd have been disgusted by that kiss.

Because he was a good guy, Zac ruined everything.

Above her, a floorboard squeaked. Mom in her bedroom, probably changing the sheets. Another thing that happened every Sunday. Routine kept her mother from thinking too much about Brian.

Emma sighed and went back to her constitutional law

book. It was easier than contemplating her mother's state of mind.

The house phone rang and Emma pushed out of her chair to grab the cordless. "Got it!"

She checked the display and saw the too familiar prison phone number. Brian calling. Each inmate paid for calls using his commissary account, which for Emma and her mother, saved a ton on the phone bill.

"Hello?"

"Mrs. Sinclair?"

Not Brian. Throbbing panic shot up Emma's neck into her head. "No, this is her daughter, Emma."

The sound of shuffling paper drifted through the line. "Yes, Emma, this is Trent Daniel."

Brian's prison caseworker. They'd spoken before. Emma's head continued to pound and she pressed her fingers against her temple. *Please, let him be okay.*

"We've had an incident with your brother."

He's not okay. "Is he sick?"

"He was attacked this morning in the prison laundry. The nurse believes he has several broken ribs. We've sent him to the local hospital."

Emma leaned against the counter, thinking prison caseworkers should be required to take classes on bedside manners.

He's alive. She focused on that. Everything else she could deal with.

"Why was he attacked?"

"We're still looking into it. It appears he didn't initiate the fight."

"What hospital has he been sent to?"

"Good Samaritan. They may keep him overnight."

An overnight stay would give him time to rest. She squeezed the phone tighter and, for the first time in years, wondered why their family had to endure so much. But that kind of self-pity never yielded any solutions. Typically, Emma found it a useless endeavor and a complete waste of energy. She relaxed her grip on the phone. "Can we visit him?"

"Yes."

"Thank you." She hung up and stared at the ceiling. Her mother hadn't come down yet. Should she even tell her? Would withholding that information make her a horrible daughter? Or a humane one? Since Penny had taken their case, Mom's mood had lifted some. This news might send her spiraling back into depression.

And Emma wasn't sure she could handle that. Selfish? Yes. Right now, though, with this latest development, she needed to deal with the immediate problem. She needed to protect herself until she could tell her mother that Brian would be fine.

She scrolled back to the prison number, ran her thumb over the SELECT button and considered her options again. None appealed.

DELETE.

Hoping Mom hadn't looked at the upstairs phone—she'd clear that one in a minute—she charged down the basement steps while speed dialing Penny. It went straight to voice mail. Plus, it was only ten o'clock, so Penny was most likely still at the lake house with her parents. Emma left her a voice mail regarding Brian's condition and that she'd be heading north to visit him.

After hanging up, Emma stood among her boxes of research, wondering what she'd tell her mother about rushing out.

Studying…with a friend. A lie she hoped would be forgiven, but at that moment, standing in that basement, the place where she'd spent countless hours strategizing how to get her brother out of prison, Emma couldn't come up with a compelling reason why she should tell her mother that Brian had been attacked.

She marched up the stairs and found Mom in the kitchen making a fresh pot of coffee. "Hi. Do you want coffee?"

"No. Thanks. I need to shower and run out."

"Why?"

Emma held the phone up. "That was a friend from school. We're studying together. Will you be okay for a while?"

Mom shrugged. "Sure. Take your time. You should go out for something to eat. Have a little fun."

"I could say the same about you."

"Maybe we'll do that this week. The two of us."

Wait. *What?* Had her mother, the shut-in, just agreed to go out for dinner? "Really?"

"Really." Mom glanced around the kitchen she'd called her own for thirty years. "The house is closing in on me."

Emma rushed to her, wrapped her in a fierce hug and a spurt of tears welled in her eyes—what a morning so far. "Thank you. I hate that you stay in all the time." She backed away from the hug. "Let's do it. One night this week. We'll go someplace nice for dinner. How's that?"

"I'd like that."

Headway. Finally. All Emma could hope was that her mother's optimism, like every other time, wouldn't get snatched away.

Thirty minutes later Emma made the left off their street. Her cell phone rang and, not bothering to check the ID, she pressed the button on her earpiece. "Hello?"

"It's Zac."

Had he heard about Brian? "Hi."

"Where are you?"

"On my way to Wisconsin because my brother was injured in a fight and he's in the hospital."

"I know. Penny called me. Stop by my place. I'm going with you. She'll meet us there."

Too much information flew at her and Emma shook her head. Suddenly, she had all these people worried about her brother. A good thing she supposed, but unusual. "Wait. What?"

"Penny called me. My folks are thirty minutes from that hospital. She'll borrow a car and meet us there."

"You don't have to come."

He hesitated. "I want to. Besides, I need to confirm that this incident doesn't have something to do with his case."

"You think someone beat him up because of that?"

"I don't know. I'll find out, though. He's been an exemplary inmate—yes, I checked. Suddenly he's attacked. It's not sitting right."

Emma pulled to the side of the road and parked. *Deep breath here.* Her work on Brian's case might have gotten him injured. God help her.

"Emma?"

"What if it's my fault?"

"It's not. Get to my place and I'll drive. It'll give you a break."

Emma sat quietly, her brain processing the events of the last hour. The hole inside opening wide, ready to claim her. Not only had she lied to her mother, but Brian might have gotten hurt because of her.

"Emma?"

Don't think about it. She shifted the car into gear and pulled from the curb. "I'll see you in twenty minutes."

ZAC FOLLOWED A CHARGING Emma down the hospital hallway where she'd almost taken out a nurse and apologized profusely, but it didn't slow her down. People should know better than to get in her way when she was on a mission. Yeah, he loved that about her.

An armed guard stood outside Brian's room and Emma halted in front of him. After showing her ID, as well as Zac's credentials, they were allowed into the room.

Penny sat in the chair next to a battered Brian Sinclair. Having only seen pictures of the guy from the trial, Zac wouldn't have recognized him. His face looked like a harvesting tractor had torn through it. His bottom lip was swollen and stitched together, the black thread menacing and violent. His right eye didn't look much better. Ugly, black bruises marred the upper lid, the side and underneath.

Emma stopped short and gasped at the sight of him. "Oh, Brian. I'm so sorry."

To his credit, Brian held up a hand. "Don't freak."

Penny nodded her agreement. "The doctor was just in. He has a couple of broken ribs, but that's the worst of it."

Zac stepped around Emma and extended his hand to Brian. "I'm Zac Hennings."

"Yeah," Brian said. "Your sister told me you were coming."

"Zachary," Penny said. "Don't think you're going to interview him."

Cripes. Penny wouldn't give him a break. "Relax, Pen. I only want to know what happened. Then I'll leave the room so you all can talk."

"Fine, but don't pull any funny stuff. I know how you are."

"Pen! I get it. Go back to your lair and let him tell me what happened."

Brian turned to Emma. "They're funny, huh?"

"This is nothing. I can't wait to see them in court." She bit her bottom lip, slammed her eyes closed for a second and squeezed his hand. "I'm so happy to see you. Are you sure you're okay?"

"I'm good. Don't worry. Does Mom know?"

"I couldn't do it to her. Maybe later I'll tell her, but I wanted to see you first." She glanced at Zac, then went back to her brother. "Zac's a good guy. You can tell him what happened."

"I'll keep him in line," Penny cracked.

His sister never gave up, which was probably a good thing. If she had, he'd have to send her to a shrink because something would be seriously wrong. He shook his head at the thought of his sister harassing a psychiatrist. Poor guy would run from the room screaming. *Crazy, Penny.*

"Whatever you're thinking, Zachary, stop it."

He waved her off and leaned against the wall, his body loose and unthreatening, while Emma took the second chair on the opposite side of the bed.

Penny tapped her hand on the bed rail. "Go ahead, Brian."

After boosting himself in the bed, he winced. "I was in the laundry room. That's my work detail. One of the inmates, I don't know who he was, but he was big and sure not happy with me, came up behind me." Brian pointed to the back of his head. "He smacked me on the head with something. Next thing I knew, I was on the floor and he was pounding away at me."

"Any idea why?"

Brian glanced at Emma then looked away. This kid would be a terrible poker player.

Immediately, Emma's eyebrows shot up. "What?"

"Nothing."

"Brian," Penny said. "Tell them what he said."

From where Zac stood, he watched Emma's posture go completely erect. Stiff. *She knows.*

"You can say it," Emma said.

"Don't get nuts on me."

She offered a poor excuse for a smile. "Good luck with that."

Brian nodded. "He knew my name, told me to tell my sister to shut up. That's it."

The words came out fast, like a ticking bomb he wanted to toss. Not wanting to give Emma time to overthink the situation, Zac boosted himself off the wall. "That's all I needed. I'll dig around. See if I can figure out who this guy has a connection to."

Emma spun around to him, threw one hand out. "No. He has to go back to that place. You'll make it worse."

"Hey," Brian said, "I'll live with it."

"Brian!"

"Forget it, Em. Whatever you're doing is shaking things up. If I have to take a beating to get me out of that hellhole, I'll do it. No problem there."

She gaped at her brother—*yeah, she's not happy.* Zac gave Penny the do-something look, but his conflict-loving sister ignored him.

"They'll kill you." Emma's voice rose, the sound breathy and panicked. "Is that what you want?"

"If it means proving I'm innocent, I'll take it. What kind of life do I have? Being locked up for something I didn't do? I liked Chelsea. She was a nice girl and I hate that people think I did that to her…and I miss her."

Apparently, Penny had heard enough. She stood and waggled her fingers at Zac. "I want him segregated from the other prisoners. At least until this is over. Will you back me up on it? It'll carry more weight if the prosecutor agrees."

Zac shrugged. "Of course. We can't have this happening to him. I'll make some calls."

Emma spun around to him, her face, for the first time, not so pinched and he wanted to think maybe he'd helped with that. "Thank you."

Yeah, he'd helped.

He jerked a thumb toward the door. "I'll be outside. Take your time."

"Zac?" Brian said. "Or Mr. Hennings? What do I call you?"

"As I told your sister, Mr. Hennings is my father. I'm Zac."

"Okay, *Zac*. This has got to be weird with your sister being my lawyer, but thanks."

Weird was probably the best description out there. Zac grinned. "It's definitely weird. But rest assured, she'd like nothing more than to pin me to the courtroom floor."

"Ha!" Penny said. "And you don't want that?"

"Hell, yes. But if you win fair and square, I got no beef." He turned back to Brian. "She's a pain in the butt, but she'll take care of you."

Penny batted her eyes. "Oh, Zachary, how you flatter."

Brian pointed at his sister. "Emma says she's a rain-maker."

That sounded like Emma. "She's tough and she'll make sure your rights are protected. That's about all you can ask for."

Zac touched Emma's shoulder. "Take your time. You're good here until visiting hours are over."

EARLY EVENING HAD ALMOST succumbed to darkness when Emma strapped her seat belt on. While waiting for Zac to turn on the engine, she stared at the neon hospital sign sitting atop the six-story cement building. Ironically, for the first time since Brian's incarceration, she'd sleep tonight knowing her brother would be safe.

She rested her head back, closed her eyes and willed the twinge in her neck away. Every muscle ached. And she still had to face her mother, whom she'd lied to and kept in the dark about her son's condition. Maybe Emma could slip into the house, head straight for her bed and not tell Mom about Brian tonight. The worst of it was over and, at this point, maybe she shouldn't tell her at all.

Did a mother *need* to see the brutal remnants of a beating that had left her son's face swollen and held together by harsh, black stitches? Would she want to see it?

A slow prickle moved up Emma's spine. *What have I done?* Keeping Brian's condition from their mother may not have been fair. *God, I don't know.* A mother would act on basic parenting instincts by going to her child when that child needed care. Emma had stolen that opportunity, ripped it from her mother's hands.

Her stomach twisted and she held her breath. *What have I done?* Panic, slow and vicious and cutting, flooded her system and her heart slammed, just hammered, hammered, hammered at her. Then she felt it. Tears. *Don't cry.* Not here. She bit her bottom lip, squeezed her eyes closed.

Zac backed out of the parking spot and glanced at her. "You okay?"

No. "Yep," she croaked, turning away from him. *Don't let him see.* "Just tired. Long day."

"That it was. Can I get you anything? I'm hungry."

Food. She hadn't had any since that morning. "I guess we should eat." She threw her hands in the air. "Oh, and I'm such an idiot. We should have brought Brian some decent food. What am I doing? I've screwed this whole thing up."

"Hang on." Zac guided the car from the middle of the lot and parked behind a group of empty cars. "Screwed what up?"

Emma hit the window button and sucked in cold air, let it fill her lungs and quiet her battered conscience. She couldn't look at Zac. Not now. He wouldn't understand. How could he? He was Mr. Perfect Family. Mr. I've-got-it-all-together.

Stop. Of all people, he didn't deserve that. If anything,

he'd been nothing but helpful. Not many prosecutors would help a convicted man.

"Hey." He rubbed the backs of his fingers over her cheek, a soft, brushing motion that eased the pounding in her body. "Talk to me."

Even in the dark, she saw it, the compassion in his eyes, the driving need to help. She tilted her head, pressed her cheek against the warmth of his fingers. Being touched was underrated. Or maybe she just hadn't been touched this way in ages. "I rushed into a plan, and robbed my mother of seeing her son outside of prison. Now, I can't decide if I should tell her or just let it be. Either way, I'll probably break her heart. I wouldn't blame her if she was furious with me."

He didn't look away, didn't roll his eyes and didn't judge her. *I could love him.* And, yeah, that was big trouble. Thinking like that would lead her smack-dab into the middle of heartbreak when Zac convinced a judge that her brother should stay in prison. That sinkhole inside her would have a huge payday.

"First off," Zac said, "there's not a right or wrong answer. You had no idea what his condition was. You wanted to protect her."

There he goes, Mr. Perfect. "When I saw that he was okay, I should have called her. I *should* have gone home and gotten her so she could see him."

He dropped his hand from her cheek. "Come on, Emma. How much are you supposed to do?"

Mr. Perfect wasn't so perfect. *Thank you.*

"It's a ninety-minute drive," he said. "By the time you'd have gotten home and back, visiting hours would have been over."

"Then I should have gotten someone to drive her up here."

He let out a harsh breath. If he thought *he* was frustrated, he should climb inside her brain. He had nothing on her.

She unfastened the seat belt and shifted to face him. "You think I'm being ridiculous?"

He turned his head toward her, his blue gaze shooting daggers. "I didn't say that." The edge in his voice, so quiet and controlled, took on a gritty, strangled tone. "If I thought that, I'd have said it. I think you're exhausted and you're overanalyzing."

"And rightly so."

"Wrong!" he yelled.

"Hey!"

He held up his hand, pressed his lips together for a second. "My point is you should give yourself credit for managing an unmanageable situation. There's no instruction manual for this. How would anyone know what the right move is? What it comes down to is you took care of your brother and you saved your mother from worry. Beating up on yourself doesn't help you, your brother or your mother. *That's* what I think."

Emma stayed silent, but folded her arms. Because down deep, tearing away at her, nibbling like a slow-moving cancer, was the urge to crawl across the console and smack him. Just let him have it. She didn't want him making sense of her life right now, trying to fix every damn thing. What she wanted was sleep, and food and a way to forget about her life for a while.

Zac blew air through his lips and rested his head back. "I'm sorry I yelled. I want you to understand that there's no playbook, Emma. No playbook. Don't beat yourself up. You're extraordinary and you don't have to do this alone."

Mr. Perfect returns. "You can't help me, Zac. Your job is to keep him locked up."

"My job is to go into court and prove he did it."

Now they were getting to the meat of the issue. "Do you think he did it?"

He stared out the windshield, drummed his fingers against his thigh. After a minute, he turned to her. "I don't know. Honestly, I don't. I need to talk to witnesses, find the rest of the damn reports that should have been in that box and figure out what's going on with this case."

His being unsure could work for her. Maybe he wasn't committed to finding the real killer, but it was more than she'd gotten from any prosecutor or law enforcement official thus far. "I can help with that."

Light from the dashboard illuminated his narrowed eyes. "How?"

"You told me to prove it to you. I'll give you copies of all my notes. If Penny wants to use them at trial, we'll have to turn them over anyway, but I'll give it all to you. Even the stuff we don't use."

For her brother, she'd do that. She'd even help Zac sort through it all and explain it to him.

He eyeballed her. "You said it was eighteen boxes. You'll give me all eighteen boxes?"

"I'll give you copies. Not that I don't trust you—you and your sister are the only ones I do trust. Everyone else terrifies me. I need to protect my originals, but I have no problem going over it all with you. I'll show you the inconsistencies in your *rock-solid* case."

Zac grinned at her. "You'll give me everything? Leave nothing out?"

"I have nothing to hide."

He turned and shifted the car into gear. "You, Ms. Sinclair, have a deal."

"Excellent. My brother is innocent. You'll see."

Chapter Eight

Zac stepped into his office carrying his jumbo coffee in one hand and his briefcase in the other. He flipped the light on with his elbow, did his usual scan of the mountains of files stacked in every available spot and wondered if he would ever come in and have an empty desktop.

In a city this size?

Probably not.

He set his cup on the desk and opened his briefcase to sort through the files he'd need for court.

A familiar knock sounded and he glanced up to see Ray Gardner striding toward him. The boss first thing on a Monday morning couldn't be good.

"Hey," Zac said, still pulling folders from his briefcase. "What's up?"

"What's the story with Ben Leeks?"

Zac snorted. Of course the detective went to his superiors about Zac's visit. He probably left out the part about his inappropriate visit to Emma. Zac snapped the briefcase closed, set it on the floor and motioned his boss to a chair.

The two of them sat, just a couple of buddies and no bull. "Ray, this is a mess. How these guys got a conviction baffles me."

His boss shifted in his seat. "How so?"

"There's no evidence. I got one half-filled box of files. No GPRs, no witness statements, nothing. I've got Leeks showing up at Emma Sinclair's at one in the morning and telling her to back off."

"He did that?"

"Yeah, I paid him a visit on Saturday and told him to knock it off and to have his son call me. This kid is the ex-boyfriend of Chelsea Moore and was supposedly abusive. They cleared him within hours. What is that? You can add to that Brian Sinclair spending the night in a hospital last night because someone wanted to send his sister a message. You think that's a coincidence? With the gang contacts Ben Leeks has?"

Ray drummed his fingers on the armrest and twisted his lips. A few long seconds passed—nothing unusual for his boss—while Ray mulled over this new information.

"Look," he finally said. "The SA is all over me on this. She got a call from Grossman over the weekend and he's about to blow his top. I need you to make this go away."

Leeks had taken it all the way to the superintendent of police. Zac should have expected nothing less.

"And what? We don't care that the *investigation* was a joke? I'm not saying Sinclair is innocent, but I have questions. I've also got a copy of a security video showing Sinclair leaving a parking garage down the street from the club at 12:37 that night."

Ray's eyebrows shot up. "What video?"

"My sister tracked it down from a witness statement. A witness who was never called at trial, but who was with Sinclair in the parking garage and drove him back to the club. According to the time line, he would have left his friend's car and walked into that alley to murder Chelsea Moore. Is it a solid alibi? Not necessarily. But why wasn't the friend's testimony admitted into evidence? Something is wrong here."

Ray's secretary appeared in the doorway and Zac held his hand to her. Ray angled back, spotted her and stood.

"I've got a meeting. Figure out how to make this go away. Quietly. Please."

Someone was on something if they thought this case would go away quietly, especially with his sister in charge. Kicking up a frenzy was her specialty. She'd mastered the art of manipulating that frenzy in her desired direction at the age of ten. She was, in fact, brilliant at it.

His desk phone buzzed and he hit the speaker button. "Zac Hennings."

"Hi, Zac," the office assistant said. "I have Dave Moore to see you."

Dave Moore. The day couldn't have started off any worse. What would he even say to the man? *I'm sorry, Dave, but your daughter's murder investigation was completely botched.*

No way to win this one. Zac checked his watch. An hour before his first court appearance and he still had notes to review. He'd give Dave some dedicated time—he owed the man that much—and then excuse himself.

"Send him back."

Two minutes later, Dave stepped into Zac's office looking like he'd aged ten years in the couple weeks since Zac had last seen him. His thick head of gray hair was neat and gelled in place, but the loose flesh under Dave's eyes told the story. The man was seriously lacking sleep. Zac rose from his chair and extended his hand.

"Zac, thanks for seeing me unannounced."

He waved the comment away and pointed at the guest chair. "Have a seat."

Dave's large frame dwarfed the chair, but he shifted until he found a suitable position. "These chairs never get any better, do they?"

"Not in my experience."

Dave nodded then looked around at the stacks of folders. Oddly, his gaze landed on the unmarked box on the floor. His daughter's box. No way for him to know what was in it, but his focus sent goose bumps up Zac's arms.

"Dave, talk to me. What do you need?"

The detective tore his attention from the box. "I need you to tell me Chelsea's murderer won't walk out of prison. After that Steve Bennett video, the article in the paper and now I'm hearing noise about your going at it with Ben Leeks, I have concerns."

That dog. Ben Leeks had tapped into every available resource. Even the grieving father.

Zac sat back, his squeaking chair adding to the aggravation of the morning. "I did have a conversation with Leeks. He made an inappropriate visit to Emma Sinclair. This is a politically charged case and he's not doing us any favors." *Neither am I with that whole kissing-the-defendant's-sister thing.* Total mess all around. "I'm working this case, Dave. I'm looking at witness testimony, reviewing evidence, talking to the PD, but I want to be honest with you. There are problems."

Dave's eyes went sharp. "What kind of problems?"

"A serious lack of an investigation for one. I should have a mountain of evidence. I've got half a box. But I promise you, I'll figure this out. Your daughter deserves that and I'll give it to her."

"You think we locked up the wrong guy? That because she was my daughter, the case was fast-tracked?"

Zac wasn't about to tell a detective that his buddies behind the blue wall had manipulated evidence to gain a conviction. "I don't know yet. He was convicted. Something swayed the jury. I've got the trial transcripts on the way. I'll study everything and if Brian Sinclair deserves to be where he is, he'll stay there. I can promise you that."

"But you're wondering."

"I have questions. I won't lie to you. If Sinclair is innocent, the person who did this to Chelsea is walking around.

Neither of us wants that. Right now, I need to talk to the Leeks kid and see what was up with his relationship with Chelsea."

Dave nodded. "I'll make sure that happens."

"Don't. I've already spoken to his father about it. He knows I'll subpoena the kid if I have to. For now, I need you to not be a detective working your contacts. I need you to be Chelsea's father. If Brian Sinclair gets a hearing on this new evidence, I want to walk into court with everything aboveboard. No cops cashing in favors. My sister, who's representing Sinclair on the PCR petition, will tear us apart if there's a whiff of impropriety."

"Sinclair did it, Zac. I can feel it. We've gotta get him for good. My wife is a wreck and I don't know what to tell her. We need it to be over."

This poor guy. His daughter murdered, his coworkers screwing up the investigation and now his family would have to go through it again. How the hell was the man supposed to cope? "I'm sorry this is coming back. I give you my word that the investigation will be solid. By the time I'm done, there won't be any questions."

The detective stared at him for a long minute, then, with great effort, pushed himself out of the chair. "I know you're the best they've got. I appreciate what you're doing. If you need my help, let me know."

Zac waited for Dave to leave, then picked up his desk phone and dialed Emma. Her files were looking like the Promised Land right now. Pressure had never been an issue for him. Part of him lived for it, the rush of energy, the high that came with battle. For him, it meant euphoria. It meant walking into court and decimating the opposition.

Except he had a thing for Emma Sinclair—also known as the opposition. Worse, she might be right about her brother's innocence—damned if he knew—and it would rock a city already rife with political scandals.

Emma picked up on the third ring.

"Hey, Emma."

"Hello, *Zachary*."

And wow, that spot-on imitation of Penny was bizarre. Zac laughed for the first time today. *Hell*. Another reason to like her. She made him laugh when everything else gave him an ulcer. "You sound just like her. That's nuts."

"I've been practicing. I can't help myself. She's such a character. How are you?"

"I'm good. You okay?"

"You mean after my trip to psycho-land last night?"

He laughed. "I wouldn't call it that, but yeah."

"I am. I had decent sleep. I'm taking your advice and not beating myself up. What's done is done."

Good for her. "What did you decide about your mom?"

"I didn't tell her. Brian's caseworker just called and he's on his way back to the prison. I didn't see much point in telling my mother now."

"Probably the right move."

"I hope you're right, *Zachary*." She laughed. "I'm sorry. I'm punchy. I've been studying constitutional law since five."

On top of all this, she was a law student keeping up with her studies. "Oh, that's good stuff right there."

"You think?"

"I know. We're talking about the foundation of our country. Constitutional law is all about our society's fundamental relationships."

"Well," Emma said, "since you're an expert, you can help me study for my test on Friday."

"Anytime. I love that subject. I know it every which way. That's not what I'm calling about, though."

"Somehow, I figured that."

Well, shoot. He should have called her this morning to check on her. That would have been the right thing to do after the day she'd had yesterday. The lines of separation on this case were starting to shift. To *blur*. Regardless of his feelings for Emma, he had to focus on winning. On giving Dave Moore and his family the answers they deserved. "When can I get a look at your files?"

"*Zachary,* you're so forward."

Again, he laughed. *Those shifting lines are nonexistent now.* "You don't want to go there with me, Emma. I take dirty talk to a whole new level."

Silence. Yeah, he thought so. So did his erection. *Dammit.* "The files?"

She cleared her throat. "Right. The files. After the copy machine gets here."

"What copy machine?"

"The one your sister insisted on because she refuses to let you take one slip of paper from this basement. She told me she'd have a copy machine sent over so you can make dupes of whatever you need."

Leave it to Penny. At least it was coming out of her budget and not the state's.

"That'll be convenient," Zac said. "When is it getting there?"

"She said sometime today. I'm off tonight if you want to come by."

He checked the calendar on his phone. Pickup basketball game at seven. He'd have to skip that. "Tonight works. I'll swing by after work. I'll even bring dinner."

"Perfect. Bring enough for three. My mom will be here."

EMMA SWUNG THE FRONT DOOR open and found Zac standing on the other side juggling his briefcase and enough pizza to feed a small army. She grabbed the two pizza boxes from him. "Zac, we're only three people."

"I figured there'd be enough for leftovers."

Leftovers. How incredibly sweet. "Well, don't just stand there. Come inside."

He stepped into the living room and looked around. Just days ago his sister had been in the exact spot. Of course, her reasons for being there were about defending Brian whereas Zac's were about prosecuting him. No one had ever accused Emma of leading a boring life.

She led Zac to the kitchen where she set the food on the despised and scarred Formica countertop. One day, they'd rip it out and give their homey kitchen the update it deserved. Some of Emma's most cherished moments— family breakfasts, her father's corny jokes, fresh-baked cookies with Mom—occurred while sitting in this kitchen. No wonder her mother refused to give up the circa-1985 table. The table held memories of a life that no longer existed. A life stolen by death and injustice.

Emma pointed to the floor where Zac was about to step. "Don't trip. The linoleum is coming up."

Being the fixer he was, he squatted and pressed it back into place.

"Thanks, but it'll only come up again. It's one of the projects on Brian's to-do list when he comes home. He's handy that way."

Zac nodded, seemingly unmoved by her declaration that Brian would be coming home. "Where's your mom?"

"She went out for a bit."

"Doesn't want me here, huh?"

Might as well tell him the truth. Smart man that he was, he'd figure it out anyway. "It's not that. I told her you were a nice guy."

He cracked a grin. "Did she call you a liar?"

"No. She loves Penny, so it wasn't hard for her to believe. I think it's more about not wanting to like you."

"Come again?"

Needing a minute to align her thoughts, Emma set one

of the pizza boxes on the table and flipped it open. "I think she's afraid she'll like you and then you'll keep her son in prison."

Kind of like me.

"There's an angle I never considered."

"I'm not sure how she'd reconcile those two things. She's used to life kicking her to the curb, but that might be too much."

Emma grabbed a couple of plates from the cabinet, found the necessary silverware and arranged everything on the table. Yes, she was stalling and they both knew it. "What do you want to drink? Pop, iced tea? I could probably scrounge a beer from the back of the fridge, but I can't vouch for how long it's been there."

His lips quirked and Emma got that little rush—the zipping heat—that had distracted her too many times over the last few days. "Pop is good. Thanks."

She busied herself with two cans of pop while Zac pondered the pizza. "We can eat and then head downstairs. No food down there. I once bumped a bowl of chili and it splattered all over my notes. It's now a no-food zone. And if you drink down there, it needs to stay away from the work space." She grinned. "Evidentiary rules."

"You're cute, Emma Sinclair."

"Compliment me all you want. You're still not bringing food or beverages into my work space."

"I'm fine with your rules. They're good ones."

Pizza devoured, Emma loaded the dishwasher and led Zac to the basement. A sudden whoosh filled her head. For the first time, she'd be allowing the enemy to see her notes. That alone was a monumental step and she took comfort in knowing she trusted this man enough to give him access to her life.

At the bottom of the stairs she flipped the wall switch and her corner work area lit up.

His eyes feasted on the boxes. "Yowzer."

"It's the Operation Sinclair command center."

The copy machine Penny had sent over stood in the farthest corner beside the boxes, a bright white beacon against the gray cement wall. "I hope you know how to use that copy machine because it's got way too many buttons for me to figure out."

"It's probably the same one they have in their office. I'll show you how to use it." He stepped over to the boxes—*three high, six across*—and scanned the labels. "Emma, this is unbelievable."

"I told you I had eighteen boxes."

"Seeing them is different. I've seen teams of detectives that can't gather this much information."

Teams of detectives didn't have a brother in prison and a mother stranded in the grip of depression. "When it's personal, you work harder. Where do you want to start? I have three boxes of statements from people who were at the bar that night." She pulled one of the boxes off the stack and set it on the long folding table she used as a desk. "This is the first set. There are two others."

Zac lifted the top and spotted the individually marked folders. He lifted a few out and opened them. "You have statements like this from each person?"

"Yep."

"Emma, you'll be an amazing attorney."

All the hours she'd spent in this basement, poring over notes, studying cases, organizing files, not one person had ever said that to her and her chest locked up, seizing in a way that stole her breath.

"Thank you. Coming from you, that's tremendous praise." She waved her hand toward the files. "I found all of Brian's friends who were at the club. Then I found Chelsea's. Some of them weren't thrilled to talk to me. I understood, but I kept at it and eventually I found more and more people who were there. Oh, and I ran an ad in the paper looking for witnesses. I'll never do *that* again. You should have seen some of the crackpots."

"Tell me you didn't put your phone number in the ad."

"No. I set up a dedicated email account. Still, I came across some nutcases."

"I'm sure."

"It was worth it, though. I have over two hundred statements."

Again, he shook his head. "I'm in awe. Too bad Penny snatched you as *her* intern. I could use you."

"Except you're the enemy."

He glanced at her, his gaze suddenly serious. "Right now, I'm just a guy trying to figure out what the hell is going on with this case." He picked up a file. "Where do I start?"

Someone on the other side wanted to help. After all these months of contacting the press, stalking attorneys, *begging* for assistance, she still had trouble believing it. "Well, *Zachary,* that depends on what you're looking for."

"The white shirt is bugging me."

She knew exactly which shirt he was referring to. "The one Brian wore that night?"

"Yes. The witness said the man in the alley wore a white shirt. It was March. I checked the temperature that night. Forty-three degrees. Did Brian wear a jacket?"

Her answer wouldn't help them. She knew it, but it was the reality and something she'd learned not to fear. At this point, there were too many other things worth fearing. "He said he left it in the car. It was a nice leather one and he didn't want to take it into the club."

"Blows that theory." Zac unbuttoned his shirtsleeves and rolled them up. "I guess I'll dig in."

"Thank you."

"For what?"

Their gazes met and held for a long minute and Emma felt that same heat, that yearning to do something she shouldn't do. *Bad, Emma. Bad.* "For everything. For taking the time to figure this out."

He shrugged. "It's my job."

"Not all of what you've done is your job. Bringing me home the other night, driving me to the hospital yesterday." *Kissing me.* "You didn't need to do those things."

A slow smile eased across his face. "Maybe I have a thing for the defendant's sister."

Feeling a little playful—and when was the last time that happened?—Emma fanned herself. "I might have a thing for the prosecutor, too."

"Could be fun."

"Could be an awful mess."

They both knew it—no sense ignoring it. Awkward silence was shattered by the furnace kicking on. Not necessarily a bad thing, considering that they needed a distraction from exploring their mutual attraction.

Zac tapped a finger on one of the folders. "I'll find out what happened with Chelsea, but you may not like the outcome. You need to be ready for that. My sister is a great lawyer and she's got my father to help, but…"

Emma held her hand up, then dropped it again. "I know what you're saying. You don't want us to get our hopes up."

"I don't want you to get hurt."

Silly man. She was an ace at hurt. Hurt had no teeth left except when it came to him. That she wasn't so sure about. "Zac, all we have left is hope. If it doesn't go our way, we'll deal with it. The Sinclair family, unfortunately, is used to disappointment."

The electric charge of moments ago roared back and his gaze swept over her. From head to toe, he quietly took her in and the stillness, all that power and control he was so good at unnerved her. She wiggled her fingers and he glanced down at her hands.

I don't know what to do.

Finally, he stepped toward her, pulled her against him and kissed the top of her head. "This is complicated."

Complicated. Good word. Under her cheek, his heart-beat thumped and Emma settled there, enjoying the much-missed comfort of a man's arms around her. She fiddled with the button on his shirt, flicking her finger back and forth. They could just stand here like this for a while. A few more minutes was all she wanted.

He backed away. Of course he did. When had she ever been lucky enough to get what she needed or craved out of life? She looked up at him and those baby-blue eyes gazed down at her. Gripping his shirt, she pulled him down and kissed him. Softly at first, but when he tightened his hold, something inside her shifted. For once, she—the caged twenty-six-year-old woman who hadn't experienced af-fection in…well, she wouldn't dwell on how long—didn't feel like rushing to the next item on her to-do list. Particu-larly with Zac's hands finding their way under her sweater to bare skin and—*yes*—her body detonated. A veritable explosion of fire and loneliness and yearning all bursting free, frying her from the inside.

She pulled him closer, clutching his shirt, hanging on while he nipped at her lips, making her want more and more because—oh, it had been so long since she'd felt this scorching need to be close to someone. Had she *ever* felt this?

I'm boiling. Not good. The loneliness, the neediness. It was all too much. *Overload.* Her skin got tight. *He'll destroy me.*

She gripped his shirt harder, willed her mind to silence. *It'll hurt when he leaves.* No good.

With one last peck, Zac backed away. "You okay?"

She darted her gaze over his face. Such a fine face. Strong and angular and oh so touchable. "No." *Really, Emma?* What was wrong with her?

But Zac smiled that million-dollar smile of his and ran a hand over her hair. Just a gentle touch that let her know he understood her brand of kooky. And didn't that do her in completely? Somehow, she'd found safety in this man. Or maybe all the nights alone had simply made her think she'd found safety.

"I'm sorry. My mind is raging. But I love every second of kissing you. I'm alive again and that's a gift." She tugged on his shirt. "A gift I want a whole lot more of."

He pulled her in again and she rested her head against his chest while he stroked her back. Up and down. Up and down. Up and down. A gentle, repetitive motion that did wonders for her frazzled senses. His chest rose and fell under her head as he let out a giant breath. "I think that can be arranged. Show me your files first."

"Kinky, *Zachary.*"

Stepping back, he shook his head. "Seriously, you have to stop talking like my sister. It's freaking me out."

"You're no fun." She waved toward the boxes—*three high, six across*—she was about to let the prosecution have access to.

And to *her.* In the last ten minutes she'd sliced her life open and exposed every vulnerable artery to the enemy. Now she had to prepare for the consequences. But she'd do that later. She smacked her hands together. "Let's get to work."

Chapter Nine

After hours of reviewing case files and breaking down time lines, Zac knew there was more than thirty minutes when Brian's whereabouts were unaccounted for. From the sudden silence in the basement, he'd guessed that Emma knew it, too.

Brian had left Melody's car around 12:45. His friends all made statements that he was with them, but no one could pinpoint the exact time, at least not until 1:20, when one guy received a text and remembered showing it to Brian.

Thirty-five minutes. Plenty of time for someone to slip out of a nightclub, walk to the alley next door, strangle a woman and return. Zac kept his eyes glued to the witness statement in front of him, not really reading, but not ready to look at Emma yet.

As good as Penny and their father were, those thirty-five minutes would work to Zac's favor. Even with the holes in this case, he could create enough of an argument to satisfy a judge, make his boss happy, give Dave Moore his so-called justice and keep Brian Sinclair in prison.

Assignment complete.

But was it the right thing? For the first time in his career, a career filled with emotional cases that he'd both won and lost, he found himself questioning his own judgment because he wanted to get laid. *Moron.*

Seated next to him at the long folding table, Emma sighed and the soft sound hit him square in the chest. He wanted her, no doubt about it. His problem was that he didn't just want her. He cared for her. This was a woman who'd put her life on hold to salvage the remaining rubble of her family. Emma saw problems as opportunities. Whatever the issue, she found a way to strap it to her back and carry it. What man would be crazy enough *not* to want her?

Which was why his reasonable self—knowing he was messing with something he shouldn't mess with—turned tail and ran. *Hell with it.* He grabbed the bottom of her chair and rolled it closer so he could snuggle her neck. "It's 10:30. I should go."

Rather than shoo him away, she tilted her head, exposing her neck. "Yes, you should. My mother will be home any second now. I feel like a sneaky teenager. You're a bad boy, *Zachary*."

"Ah, yes, my sister's voice."

Emma cracked up. "Sorry."

But Zac kissed her, one of those long, slow ones that would torture him long into the night. "So, yeah, I'm going to leave before I try to convince you to hop into bed with me."

She waggled her eyebrows. "Right now, sailor, that wouldn't take much convincing."

"How you wound me."

"You'll survive, I'm sure." She gestured to the stack of folders he'd set aside. "Do you want me to copy everything in those folders for you? I have a class in the morning and then I'm working the lunch shift. I'll have time after that."

He stood up, grabbed his jacket from the back of the chair and slid it on. "Emma, between work and school, you don't have time to be copying notes. I'll send someone over to do it."

"If it'll help my brother, I'll make the time." She went up on tiptoes and kissed him quick. "Besides, I don't want anyone touching my notes. Not that I don't trust you. I do, but accidents happen and something could disappear."

"You don't have to explain to me. I'm a prosecutor with half a box of evidence. Thank you. How about we go through more of this stuff tomorrow? At my place so your mom doesn't have to leave."

Emma bit her lip, looked down at her feet. "I don't know."

Losing her.

"My sister will insist on armed security for the folders, but I'll talk to her, convince her that I won't abscond with evidence."

Laughing at him, she looked up and rolled her eyes. "She let you in here, didn't she?"

"Maybe she trusts me after all. How about you? Do you trust me?"

"I let you in here, didn't I?"

He shrugged.

Again, she bit her lip. Indecision was a wicked thing. Finally, she shook her head. "I don't want to do anything stupid. Penny is our hope in all this. Then you come in here and kiss me and I think *Penny who?* That bothers me."

He tugged the front of her shirt. "If it makes you feel better, it bugs me, too." He grinned. "I like kissing you, though."

"Such a man."

"Can't help it. What do you say? Tomorrow night?"

"You'll behave?"

"Realistically? Probably not."

She laughed and the sound lit something in him that would keep him awake the whole damn night.

"Then I guess I'll see you tomorrow," she said.

He leaned over and, already blowing his quest to be-have, kissed her again, nibbled those lush lips. Her lips could drive a man insane, thinking about all the uses for them. "I guess you will."

AFTER ZAC LEFT, Emma checked on her mom who had parked herself at a friend's house and was now on her way home. If nothing else, it was good for Mom to get out some. Emma stacked the folders to be copied on the tray table she'd set up next to the copy machine. Starting on them now would save time in the morning.

Plus, she was too keyed up to sleep. Intimacy, she de-cided, was a beautiful thing. She'd gone too long without this tingly, happy feeling that came with having the right man touch her.

Zac Hennings, for many reasons, might not be Mr. Right, but he was definitely Mr. Right Now. Setting aside the fact that he was the opposition, he was a good man. A good man willing to look beyond the surface of her broth-er's case when others had turned away.

She stood in front of the copy machine and picked up the first folder. The one containing her notes about the white shirt testimony. Zac seemed a little obsessed with the white shirt. She wished she could have told him Brian hadn't been wearing white that night. That it was all some dumb mistake and that he'd worn blue. The case would have fallen apart if he'd simply worn blue. Such a simple thing could have changed it all. *Why didn't you wear blue?*

No use dwelling on it. Emma opened the folder and read her notes. Witness at end of alley. Saw man coming toward him. Moved on. Her gaze shot left again.

End of alley.

On a moonless night. She remembered that from her in-vestigation. She'd checked on it. It had, in fact, been heav-ily overcast that night. Dark. Really dark.

End of alley.

Emma dropped the folder and papers scattered in a blanket of white at her feet. "Oh, my." She scooped up her phone, charged upstairs to her bedroom and grabbed one of her white work shirts, a jacket, her purse and keys and flew out the door.

As she ran to her car, she scrolled her contacts for Zac's number. Hopefully he'd meet her there because only stupid women walked in dark city alleys late at night. Emma wasn't stupid. At the same time, this mission could only be done in the dark. The call went straight to voice mail and she hung up. She'd call back from the road.

Once en route, she tried Zac again, but the phone beeped. On the line. She'd leave a message. "It's Emma. On my way to the crime scene to check something. Can you meet me there?"

She drove past Magic where even on a Monday people headed in for a night of partying. A sign with bright red letters indicated dollar draft night so the college kids probably showed up en masse. On the busy main street, cars stacked up at the traffic signals. Half a block down, one of the many city bridges spanned the Chicago River, its lights twinkling against a black sky. She stopped in a no-parking zone at the alley entrance and slapped her hazards on. A cabbie flew by, sitting on his horn and the sharp blare grated up her neck.

"Take it easy, mister," she muttered.

Her phone whistled and she checked it. Voice mail from Zac. She punched the button and his deep voice filled the car. "It's me," he said. "Three minutes out. Wait for me."

Another car whooshed by and she chomped her bottom lip. Sooner or later a cop would move her along. The dashboard clock blinked. Another two minutes and Zac would be here.

Someone knocked on the passenger window. The banging sent blood slamming through her and she swung her head sideways. One of the bouncers from the club jerked his thumb. "Lady, you gotta move."

Emma grabbed her purse, jumped out and shut the door before a passing car ripped it off. She worked her way to the curb and stared up at the massive security guy. "Hi. I'm an investigator." *Investigator?* "Working on a murder case. I need to check something in the alley. Real quick. Promise." Digging into her purse, she fished out a twenty. "Will you keep an eye on the car a minute?"

"Lady—"

"Two minutes. That's all I need."

The bouncer glanced around, snatched the twenty out of her hand and nodded. "Go. Fast."

"Thank you." From the passenger seat she grabbed the white shirt and headed into the alley.

So much for smart girls not going into dark alleys alone. Desperate measures, right? Besides, Zac would show up any second.

Still, she headed in, moving slowly at first, letting her eyes adjust to the blackness. The only lights were halfway down the alley over two adjacent doors on each building. From the street behind, a car horn honked, then screeching tires. Prickles coursed up her arms and even in the cold, the air felt hot against her. The sides of the buildings pressed in and her eyes darted left and right. Anyone could be hiding here and she wouldn't see him. *Take a breath.* She turned back. No bouncer.

Was this what Chelsea heard right before she died?

For that matter, Chelsea must have had a reason for coming into this scary place alone. Emma would have to study her files for any pertinent info on that. Yes. Focus on the case.

A light wind blew and the stench of ripe garbage forced

her to scrunch her nose and gasp. A garbage container was somewhere close.

She stopped in the approximate area where Chelsea Moore spent her last moments. Between the rancid smell and visions of the young woman trapped against the wall, her throat being crushed, Emma's stomach churned.

Closer to the lights now, she spotted the offending container overflowing with garbage. Probably the weekend pile-up. On her right was a thin electrical pipe running up the side of the building. Not a great test subject, but it would suffice. Emma shoved the white shirt into the gap. There. All she had to do was run back to the alley entrance and verify that the shirt could be seen from there.

Behind her came the squish of rubber on damp pavement. *Zac.* She started to turn and a hard shove sent her sailing into the brick building. Her cheek smacked the cold, rough surface. A ripping sensation tore into her and her lungs froze. No air.

Stupid girl.

"You don't learn, do you?" a guttural voice whispered and the sound, so low and ugly and hard, sent a violent burst of panic up her throat.

She opened her mouth to scream. Nothing. Paralyzed. The man's hot breath snaked over her skin and she gasped. *Don't let him win.* Her eyes watered. She blinked, fought the tears seeping free. *Breathe, Emma.*

Chaos and fear whirled through her mind. *Turn around.* Look at him. Her minimal self-defense lessons flashed into her head. If she could get to his throat or his eyes, she'd have a chance. She shifted, tried to spin, but he shoved her against the wall, his bigger body leaning into her, crushing her.

"Help!" she croaked.

Her attacker laughed and pushed his body further into hers. "You wanna die right here like Chelsea Moore?"

Vomit heaved into her throat and she gagged, swallowed it back. *Someone, help me. Should have waited for Zac… Fight. Don't let him win.* Messages and warnings came in a rush, battering her oversensitized system, shredding what was left of her nerves.

Elbow.

She jerked her elbow back and connected—his arm maybe—but it skidded off.

And then she got mad. Mad enough to show this jerk that she wouldn't be an easy victim. Not ever.

"No!" she hollered, her voice suddenly coming to her aid. *Thank you.*

"Emma!" Zac from the alley entrance.

"Here."

The pressure from the man's disgusting body eased up and she sucked in a breath, all that rancid air flooding her lungs. She turned and swung. Nothing there. A shadow sprinted to the back exit of the alley. The clomp of shoes— Zac's dress shoes—sounded from behind her.

Catch him. Knowing Zac would follow, she gave chase. "Did you see him?" she hollered over her shoulder.

"No."

She had to find him, see who he was and what he knew about Chelsea Moore.

Zac caught up to her, his longer legs making the task easy. "Emma, hang on."

He grabbed her arm and halted her, but she struggled against his hold as her attacker fled. *No. No. No.* "He's getting away."

She yanked free and ran to the far end of the alley, looking both ways. *I've got to find him.* Crushing disappointment, like rising water, overtook her, stole her breath. *I blew it.* Whoever it was, he'd disappeared. "No!" Her echoing rage bounced off the surrounding buildings and she squeezed her fingers into tight, knuckle-popping fists. So much pressure.

Then Zac was next to her, sliding his arms around her and pulling her in for a hug so fierce it sparked that same heat that she'd felt earlier. *Concentrate, Emma.*

"What happened?" he asked.

Not wanting to be babied—who needed that?—she elbowed away and stared into the blackness where her attacker vanished. *Damn it.* She shook out her hands, let her aching fingers recover. "He pushed me."

Zac set her back and squeezed her arms. "Mugger?"

"No. He said…"

What *did* he say? *Think, Emma.* She spun around, pointed. She'd been standing there, right there, shoving the shirt into the pipe and then—bam—he'd shoved her. As she stared at the spot and envisioned the attack in her mind, his voice came back to her, low and mean and vile, and she focused. *Think.* The words tumbled in her brain and she separated them, gave them order. "He said, 'Do you want to die like Chelsea Moore?'"

"Oh, honey. I'm so sorry. Did he say anything else?"

Zac hugged her again, holding her against him and the warmth of his bigger body drew her closer. After all the battles she'd fought alone, someone wanted to take care of her.

"Yes." Emma backed up, waggled her hands as the words came back to her. "He said, 'You don't learn, do you?'"

In the darkness, Zac's arm moved. "I'm calling 9-1-1."

Emma stilled his hand, kept him from dialing. "Wait. We must be getting close to something someone doesn't want us to find. He followed me here."

"Lady!" The club's security guard. "You gotta move this car!"

"Be right there!" She turned back to Zac. "The bouncer

was rushing me. I paid him twenty bucks. That's why I didn't wait for you."

"What *are* we doing here?"

"Lady!"

"We're coming," Zac yelled back, his voice carrying an unmistakable don't-screw-with-me message.

Grabbing his hand, Emma dragged him back to where she'd shoved her shirt. The stingy light illuminated them and she pointed at it. "I wanted to see if we could see the white from where the witness was standing. Maybe that's what's bugging you about the shirt."

For a full ten seconds, he stared at the shirt then turned to the alley entrance. He grabbed her hand. "Come with me."

The two of them strode back to her car, Emma double-timing to keep up. At the entrance, Zac whirled around. She did the same thing. Behind them traffic whooshed by as they gazed into the darkness where the meager light showed two doorways. Only two doorways.

No white shirt.

ZAC KNEW THAT SOMEONE had to stand in the alley with that shirt on. Except it was Emma's shirt and he wasn't about to send her back in there.

"Dude," the bouncer said. "You gotta move these cars. It's a fire lane."

But Zac was distracted by a white shirt he couldn't see. He studied the bouncer. Big, but not huge. A size or two bigger than Zac.

I'm wearing a white shirt.

Following Emma's lead, he peeled a fifty from his money clip. "My name is Zac Hennings. I'm a Cook County Assistant State's Attorney. We're investigating the homicide that occurred here two years ago."

"The cop's daughter?"

"That's her." Zac held the fifty between two fingers. "This is yours if you'll put my shirt on and stand in the middle of this alley. That's it. Fifty bucks. It'll take two minutes."

Come on. Take the money. He needed to see for himself if that shirt was visible from his vantage point. If not, he'd haul the detectives back here and prove to them that it couldn't be seen from this distance. Something they should have done and something the SA's office should have confirmed.

Dammit.

Zac didn't know what to feel right now. Frustrated with shoddy investigating? Sure. Terrified that his case was coming apart? Definitely. Worried about Emma? Absolutely.

And yet, if the evidence fell apart, it would help her. But this was his job and his boss wanted to save face for the SA.

The bouncer glanced at the club's doorway. *Losing him.* Zac flicked the fifty at him. A second later, the bill was gone. Zac hurried out of his jacket and Emma took it from him, watching as he stripped down to his undershirt. Did she have to do that? Talk about a distraction. Cold air blasted his bare skin, bringing his mind back to his task rather than taking his clothes off in front of a woman he'd like to see do the same.

Emma held his jacket up and he slipped his arms into it. "Thanks." He went back to the bouncer. "Go halfway down the alley and stop."

While the security guard made his way down the alley, Zac glanced at Emma and the red scrape he'd failed to notice when they'd first come out of the alley. His face got hot and his typically reined-in temper flared. *Should've gotten here faster.* He'd never considered himself a chest-pounding alpha male, but another man putting his hands on Emma made him want to gut someone.

And he was the prosecutor.

What a mess.

He propped his finger under her chin and tilted her head up. "You've got a scrape. Did he hit you?"

"No. He shoved me into the building, and my cheek crashed into the brick."

"I'm sorry." He leaned down, dropped a kiss on the spot. "I'm sorry you're hurt and that I didn't get here sooner. We have to be more careful."

She squeezed his wrist. "I should have waited. Next time I'll wait."

"This good enough?" the bouncer yelled from the middle of the alley.

"Yeah. You're good. Hang there a sec." Zac took a few steps left, separating himself from Emma. He had to focus on his job, on not letting his growing feelings for this woman sway his judgment. He stared into the blackness. Nothing. He took two steps closer to the alley entrance.

"You remember where the witness was standing?" he called to Emma.

"He said he was walking past the club on his way to the garage so he'd have been on the sidewalk and crossing. You're probably closer than he was."

Then she was next to him, her energy an electric current zapping him hard. The two of them looked into the black mouth of the alley, not seeing a thing.

Now Zac had a problem.

Chapter Ten

After her eight o'clock class, Emma drove to the North Side to meet Penny at Stanley Vernon's home. Mr. Vernon, the star witness for the prosecution, had identified Brian as the man wearing the white shirt in the alley and Penny wanted to shake him up.

Considering Emma informed Penny of the white shirt test the night before, Penny, being Penny, sensed blood gushing from Zac's case. If they could get Mr. Vernon to recant, Penny felt sure their request for a post-conviction relief hearing would be granted and Brian would have a chance at a reversal.

This meeting was crucial to their effort. Emma breathed deep and squeezed the steering wheel. Moisture from her hands made the surface slick and she scrunched her nose. *Relax. Let Penny do the talking.*

On her first pass around the city block, she spotted the spunky lawyer in her pink coat—not hard to miss—waiting for her two doors down from their intended target. Remembering Zac's cross-eyed irritation from the morning he'd spotted that coat gave Emma a moment of respite from the giant knot between her shoulders. *Popsicle Penny.*

As siblings went, Zac and Penny were a funny pair. Clearly, their affection ran deep, but she imagined that when they fought, they fought hard.

Being attorneys, Emma assumed they were used to the

conflict, but she wasn't sure she could face her brother in court. Her protective instincts would kick in and she'd worry about beating him.

Zac and Penny didn't have those issues. Not with their kill-or-be-killed instincts. They craved the slaughter. The *win*.

Emma found a parking space half a block from Mr. Vernon's home. The short walk and fresh air would help clear her mind for the conversation about to take place. Part of her wanted to run screaming from this encounter. In a few moments, she'd have to face the man who'd helped tear her family apart. Maybe, at the time, he'd felt he was simply doing his civic duty, but she now knew that he'd lied on the stand.

And she had proof in Zac's white shirt.

Emma stepped onto the sidewalk, straightened her trench coat and ran a hand down the front. She'd opted for a knee-length navy-blue skirt and light blue sweater for this meeting. Not too lawyerish or bold. She took one step and—*whoops*—her thin heel sank into the crack in the sidewalk, the soft dirt holding her hostage. Terrific.

Outside of special occasions, she never wore heels and now knew why. She slid out of the shoe and squatted to free it.

"What?" Penny called from four houses down.

"Keep your panties on. My shoe is stuck."

Obviously enjoying the show, Penny shook her head. "I do love you, Emma."

"Yeah, whatever."

She plucked the shoe free and used a tissue from her purse to wipe the heel. Upsetting the Vernons by leaving a trail of mud in their home certainly wouldn't help their cause. Her shoe clean once again, she half walked, half jogged to where Penny was standing. "I'm sorry. I hate heels. I'm never good in them." She pressed her hand to her head where a sudden throb nearly split her skull. *I'm a wreck*.

Penny squeezed her arm. Not hard. Just a light, reassuring gesture. "Relax. I've got this. You sit and look sincere. The guilt alone will kill this guy."

"I'm afraid I'll screw up. What if he refuses to talk in front of me?"

"Then I'll send you outside, but I have a hunch that won't happen. When I tell him we tested the white-shirt theory, he'll take one look at you and cave. Trust me. We'll be fine."

Emma smacked her eyes closed. Penny, the only lawyer in town with enough faith, or maybe it was nerve, to take their case, needed her and she was having a meltdown. Not smart. The knot in her shoulders tightened and Emma rolled her head side to side. She could do this. Hadn't she interviewed over two hundred witnesses? Some of whom had literally run from her, but she'd kept at it, hour after hour. She'd hounded them. And persuaded them to talk to her.

I can do this.

She opened her eyes and jerked her head. "Thank you. And, no pressure here, but my brother's life is in your hands."

"Oh, please. As if *that* would work on me." She linked her arm with Emma's. "Let's eat this guy alive."

Lawyers.

They climbed the four brick steps leading to a two-story, aluminum-sided, single-family home. The porch columns looked recently painted and Emma felt a pang of guilt over the neglected maintenance on her mother's home. There was always so much to do. Penny knocked on the front door and the repetitive thunk refocused Emma.

I can do this.

A plump woman with bleached-blond hair—maybe

fiftyish—opened the door. She spotted Penny in the popsicle coat and smiled. Then she turned to Emma. The smile evaporated. *I can do this.*

Penny shoved her hand out. "Mrs. Vernon? I'm Penny Hennings. We spoke on the phone."

The woman's gaze slid back to Penny and her smile returned. "Yes. Hello. Come in. My husband will be right down."

"Thank you."

Penny followed the woman in, but swiveled to Emma and crossed her eyes. Emma cracked a smile, thankful her lawyer's energy was strong enough to handle any grim task.

Mrs. Vernon ushered them into a sitting area at the back of the house. Three large windows of the converted porch overlooked a patch of yard with wisps of early-spring greenery. In the summer, it would be a quiet, comforting spot for reading. Not that Emma did much pleasure reading anymore. Who had time?

The woman motioned them to the upholstered love seat, offered them coffee and went about all the niceties required when guests arrived. A valiant effort, but Emma imagined that their presence wasn't all that welcome.

While Mrs. Vernon tended to the beverages, Penny sat erect and unmoving, her hands in her lap. Even in a motionless state, her crackling energy suffused the room. Pink coat and fair-haired beauty aside, this was a panther ready to pounce.

A man entered the room. Mr. Vernon. Emma recognized him from court, but he was thinner now, somehow smaller than he'd been when she'd seen him during Brian's trial. As if life had beaten a few inches off him. She could relate.

For a moment, she remained buried in the shock of seeing him. His testimony had decimated her brother's future

and torn away another chunk of her family. *Don't go there.*
Penny popped off the love seat, slapped the glamour girl
smile on her face and stuck her hand out.

"Hello, Mr. Vernon. Thank you for seeing us. So kind
of you." Emma unglued herself from the chair and stood.
"Allow me to introduce Emma."

Funny how she left off the last name. Mr. Vernon held
out his hand. His gray-blue eyes narrowed a bit, not mean,
more questioning. Within seconds his eyebrows lifted.
Recognition complete. The poor man made an effort to
smile, but it came off stiff and unyielding.

Apparently, Emma wasn't the only one feeling the pressure.

"Nice to meet you, Emma."

Liar.

"You, too, sir."

Liar.

Penny smacked her hands together. "Shall we sit?"

"Yes, please. My wife offered you a drink?"

"Yes, thank you." Penny settled back into her seat and
waited for Emma and their witness to park themselves.
"Mr. Vernon, as I mentioned on the phone, we'd like to
ask you a few questions about your testimony."

His gaze shifted to Emma, then back. "I'm not sure how
much more I can tell you."

How about that you lied? Emma clasped her hands in
her lap, determined to keep her trap shut.

Penny reached into her briefcase for a legal pad. "Do
you mind if I take notes?"

"That's fine."

The Popsicle Penny smile, all sweet and gooey, broke
loose. "Thank you. I'd like to ask you about the white shirt
you said you saw on the man in the alley."

Vernon's throat bulged from a swallow. Interesting.

"Sir, we did a re-creation in the alley."

"I don't understand."

Penny flipped her palm up. "A man wearing a white shirt stood in the alley where Chelsea Moore's body was found. We did this at night, of course."

Mrs. Vernon entered the room with two coffee mugs and handed one each to Penny and Emma. "Thank you, ma'am," Emma said.

Penny set the mug on the table next to her. "Mr. Vernon, I don't mean to be argumentative and I'm not questioning what you saw—" She smiled that sweet-girl smile that had probably destroyed an army of men. "Well, maybe I am. You understand. I need to clarify the details."

"What details?"

"About the shirt. When we did our test, the man wearing white could not be seen from where you said you stood."

"How can that be?"

"I'm not sure, sir. Are you certain of your location? Or perhaps the man in the alley was closer than you thought."

Mr. Vernon glanced at Emma, then shook his head. "No."

Liar.

Trap shut. Emma sipped her coffee, but oh, how she wanted to rage and scream at him to tell the truth. Her brother's future had been ripped to shreds, *stolen,* and this man dared to sit in front of her and lie?

Her hands trembled and, fearing a spill, she set the mug down, then flexed her quivering fingers. A total wreck. But she'd keep quiet and let Penny handle it. For once, someone else could do the dirty work. Right?

Right.

Except someone else hadn't lived with her mother night after night and listened to the never-ending weeping. Sometimes, on the really rough nights, the weeping turned into sobs and Emma shoved earplugs in because she couldn't stand the torture her mother was enduring.

Even now, eighteen months after her younger child had been found guilty and shoved in a cage, Mom still cried herself to sleep.

Emma bit her lip. *Let Penny handle it.* But, but, but how hard would it be to tell the truth?

She couldn't do it. Couldn't sit here simply accepting the lies. *Nope, can't do it.* "Mr. Vernon, are you a parent?"

Ever so slowly, Penny inched around and gave Emma the wide-eyed, don't-make-me-kill-you glare.

"I have three children," Mr. Vernon said.

Emma nodded. "Sir, I know you wanted to help find a murderer by testifying and I appreciate your willingness to do that."

"But?"

"But my mother has a son in prison. If someone were to accuse one of your children of a crime, a crime that would send them to prison for the better part of their adult life, wouldn't you want that person to be sure of what he saw?"

"I am sure."

Emma gripped the sofa cushion and squeezed. "I don't think you are, sir. I stood outside the alley myself last night and couldn't see the white shirt. There were two of us. Neither of us saw him."

Penny scooted forward. "Mr. Vernon—"

He held his finger up. "Are you accusing me of lying?"

Uh-oh. Penny would skin her. "No, sir. I'm trying to figure out what it is you saw."

Penny set her hand on Emma's arm. Okay. Point taken. Emma was shutting up now.

"Mr. Vernon, I'm sure you're aware that a video has surfaced that shows one of the detectives confessing to pressuring witnesses." Penny dug in her briefcase for her phone. "I have a copy of the video if you'd like to see it."

"Don't need to."

"No?"

"No."

She dropped her phone back in the purse. "That's fine. Let's talk about the night the police questioned you. You were shown a series of photographs, correct? Six, if I'm not mistaken."

"Yes."

"After that you were taken to view a lineup, correct?"

Vernon shifted away from Emma and her pulse kicked. The man couldn't even look at her. His body language all but screamed it. This was getting good.

"Yes."

"And you identified Brian Sinclair?"

"Yes."

"Mr. Vernon, how many of the men in the photo lineup were wearing a white shirt?"

Vernon opened his mouth then stopped, tilted his head as if stumped.

"Sir?"

Go, Penny.

"Just one."

Penny made a note and Mr. Vernon's eyes bounced every which way. God, she was good.

"I see. The only one in a white shirt was Brian Sinclair?"

"Yes."

"And at what point did the white shirt enter into the conversation?"

Again, Mr. Vernon shifted, his shoulders slumping a bit. His entire body seemed to fold and Emma's heart banged. *Please, let this be it.*

"Before the photo lineup," Mr. Vernon said. "The detectives asked me if I remembered the person in the alley wearing a white shirt."

"So the detectives suggested that to you?"

"Well, they asked me."

"And you remembered that."

Vernon licked his lips. "I identified the kid. That's who I saw in the alley." He turned to Emma. "I'm sorry for your family. I wouldn't wish it on anyone. I can't help you, though." He stood. "Thank you for coming. I'll show you out."

Emma gawked, her mouth literally hanging open while Mr. Vernon hurried from the room. Just that fast, everything had derailed. How?

She glanced at Penny who shoved her notepad back in her briefcase then held her finger to her lips. "It's okay," she mouthed.

Emma nodded. What else could she do? At this moment, she had to be a professional. She couldn't be a grieving, heartbroken sister. She followed Penny through the house and nodded at Mr. Vernon as she strode out the front door.

"Well, that was a bust," Emma said when they reached the sidewalk.

She glanced back at the house where she'd blown her chance to help her brother. Penny charged in the direction of Emma's car. She must have been parked in the same general area.

"Since when are you so negative? Buck up, sister. I told you we were about to climb Everest. We're barely at the first camp and you've got a long face."

Oh, and now she was gonna start? "Excuse me? You forget who's been doing this climb for two years now."

"Yeah, without a Sherpa. I'm the Sherpa. I'll get your butt to the top. You can't give up." She stopped, hefted her briefcase higher on her shoulder and folded her arms. "That was our first go at him. I didn't expect to walk out with a confession. We presented our case. We rattled him. Now we let him stew on it. He'll cave. Did you see the way he looked at you when you gave him that parent speech? Girlfriend, you're gonna be an amazing lawyer."

Wasn't that what Zac had said? Coming from these two, with their lineage, she might even start to believe it.

"I thought I blew it."

"I'll admit that you scared me for a second, so let's stick to the script next time, but it worked. Obviously, he's a man with a conscience. My guess is that at this very second he's dialing his detective buddies wanting to know if they manipulated him."

She spun around front and started walking again. "I love this job, Emma. It's such a rush."

Emma did her half walk, half run thing to catch up. Penny had to be one of the tiniest women Emma had ever laid eyes on, yet she moved like a ninja. "I think you're insane."

"You're not the first to accuse me of that. Here's my car. Just so you know, I'm sending an investigator to talk to Chelsea's ex-boyfriend."

"Really?"

"Yep. I figure after his father paid you that visit the other night and with Zac pressuring him from the SA's side, it couldn't hurt to get under the kid's skin. Who knows if anything will come of it? I'm guessing not because Daddy will tell him to keep his lips buttoned, but, hey, you never know. It would be interesting to know if he was the one in that alley with you last night."

Emma closed her eyes, let her mind drift back. "I'd remember his voice. Mean. Nasty."

"Good. That's important. You need to be careful, okay? My dad thinks you need protection. I tend to agree."

"I can't afford that. I'll be careful. No more stunts. I promise."

"We could probably help with the expenses for protection. I'll ask my father."

Absolutely not. There was only so much charity she

could handle. "I'm not taking money from you. You're doing enough."

Penny fished her keys from her briefcase and hit the UNLOCK button. "Think about it. Great work today. Don't worry. This is all good. Just hang in there with me, okay?"

Emma nodded. "I will. Thank you."

"No. Thank *you*."

"For what?"

"For making me look like a superstar, of course. And whatever you do, don't have sex with my brother."

Emma's feet fused to the ground and it had nothing to do with a stuck heel. *What?*

Penny opened her car door and tossed her briefcase in. "I know my brother and he wants to jump you. A sexual relationship between the two of you would be emotional warfare. He wants to win as much as we do. If he wins, you lose. If you win, he loses. Either way, one of you gets hurt."

ZAC KNOCKED ON HIS boss's half-open office door and stuck his head in. "Got a sec?"

Ray looked up from the document he'd been reading, dropped his glasses on the desk and sat back. "Whatcha got?"

Aggravating his boss required privacy so Zac shut the door.

"Oh, hell. You're gonna ruin my day, aren't you?"

A little bit, yeah. Zac sat on the miserable love seat against the wall. Not that the place had room for a love seat, but he supposed being the boss meant Ray wanted something no one else had. Something like a love seat in an office already crammed with an overstuffed bookcase.

"I went to the alley. Where Chelsea Moore was murdered."

Ray groaned.

"Yeah. We got a witness saying he saw Brian Sinclair

in that alley wearing a white shirt. Last night I had the bouncer from the bar stand in the alley in a white shirt."

Ray groaned louder. He understood exactly where they were headed.

"I think we need an investigator on this. My sister is all over the shirt."

The SA's office had its own investigative bureau, which handled specialized offenses, including official misconduct. They were the impartial eyes of Cook County and if ever a case warranted an impartial eye, it was this one.

"Hang on. You told your sister?"

"No. Emma Sinclair was with me. She told my sister."

Ray jerked his head. "What?"

Go easy here. The boss popping his cork wouldn't help. "She called me last night with this theory about the white shirt. She wanted me to authenticate her experiment." *Close enough to the truth.* "I met her there. The shirt couldn't be seen. If I know my sister, she's already leaning on the witness trying to get him to recant."

Ray grabbed a notepad and pen and started writing. "We've got the video and the shirt. And let's not forget Ben Leeks's stunt with Emma Sinclair," Zac's boss said.

"No GPRs in the case file. What there is of a case file."

More notes. "Right."

"Ray, these detectives phoned it in. There are too many holes. They latched onto Brian Sinclair and made it fit. Right now, I'm not sure the kid did it."

Ray snapped his head up. "Whoa."

"I'm not saying he didn't. I'm saying we don't have enough to know. If I was working Felony Review and the cops came to me with this case, I'd say they don't have the horsepower."

Ray slapped his pen down and ran both hands through his short black hair. Tension Zac hadn't felt all that often filled the cramped office. He waited. Talking now would be suicide.

The baseboard heater clunked. Zac ignored it. He refused to move. Finally, Ray gave up on his hair and set his hands on the desk, his fingers tapping the memo he'd abandoned. "All you had to do was make this go away. Now you're telling me you can't."

A sharp stab hit the back of Zac's neck. *What the hell?* Busting his tail on this and his boss is miffed because the case is a stinker. Forget about the guy they locked up, the one who might be innocent. "Am I supposed to concoct evidence? Talk to the detectives and see what the hell they were thinking by not writing up any reports?"

"There's gotta be something."

Sure. Right. No sweat. Zac grunted. "This case is a disaster. And, no, I can't make it go away."

"It's been less than a week. How can you know that?"

Unbelievable. "Come on. I know a dog when I see one. This is a *crippled* dog."

"Then work it harder. Make something happen."

For the first time, a picture of his boss formed. A picture Zac didn't like. One that pitted a political system against a twenty-two-year-old kid convicted of murder. Sickness rolled in his belly. What was wrong with these people that they let politics dictate the outcome of trials? He was far from an idealist, but this sizzled him.

Zac shot out of his chair and threw the door open. It hit the wall hard and Ray stared at it, his cheeks turning a flaming red.

"Don't you walk out of here."

To hell with that. "I think we're done."

"Hennings!"

But Zac kept moving. No sense stopping. He'd just alerted his superior that they had catastrophic problems with a murder conviction and the only advice he'd received was to make it go away. As if it would be that simple. As if he'd be able to live with himself knowing they put this kid away on bogus evidence. Well, he couldn't. Call him the last good guy standing, but if his boss wanted to reprimand him, demote him, so be it. He wasn't about to risk his law license by rigging a case.

Chapter Eleven

Emma climbed the stairs to Zac's second-floor apartment and a sudden case of the jitters sent her pulse twitching. She paused in the center of the staircase.

Run.

Being here with him—alone—was probably a mistake. *Probably?* No question about it. This was a colossal risk. After the scorching kiss-fest a few days ago she might have lost a few brain cells. Either that or her body and its lack of male attention had taken over and decided not to heed Penny's warning about Zac.

But hey, they were adults capable of controlling themselves. She glanced at the folders tucked in her right arm.

It's fine.

She hefted the shopping bag in her other hand to her wrist, grabbed the knob at the top of the polished oak railing and pulled herself up. She loved these old houses with all the dark wood trim. The door to his apartment opened and there stood Zac, wearing black track pants and a T-shirt that hugged his shoulders in all the right ways. He never wore tight clothes, but somehow they always molded to the long, lean muscles that spanned his upper body. His blond hair was wet and combed back, revealing those perfectly angular cheeks and—yep—Emma needed a man.

Pronto.

So much for not thinking about it.

Total mistake.

Zac grabbed the stack of file folders from her. "Something wrong?"

Everything. What was she doing letting herself get involved with the prosecutor on her brother's case? Brian's only chance in eighteen months and Emma was hormonal about the hot prosecutor. She should march right down the stairs and out the door. No harm done. Except she couldn't discount the kisses they'd shared. Those were definitely something.

She hadn't slept with him, though. Even if the way Zac Hennings moved turned her liquid and made her fantasize about things they could do together.

"Emma?"

Walk away.

She handed him the bag of takeout. *Too late now.* "Sorry. Thinking too much."

"I know the feeling. Come in." He shut the door behind her and set the folders on the side table. When he turned back to her she spotted it, the hardness in his eyes, the taut cheeks and locked jaw. Standing this close, his raw energy, primal and predatory reached her, sending a burst of heat to her core.

Is it hot in here? "Bad day?" she asked.

"My day stunk."

"Sorry to hear that."

He stepped closer, staring down at her for a second while his gaze moved over her face, stalled at her lips and then went to her trench coat. Zac had something on his mind and—being the smart girl she was—she could make a good guess as to what it was.

Walk away.

"You feel that?"

Sure do. She swallowed. "Um—"

"It's crazy. The minute I get close to you, it's an explosion."

He slipped his hands into the neckline of her coat, pushed it off her shoulders and down her arms, and caught it before it hit the floor. He tossed it over the living room chair.

But his eyes were on her lips again. Her stomach dropped and heat surged and—*wow*—she got a little woozy. *Two rational adults.*

He dipped his head closer, teasing, testing to see if she'd meet him halfway.

No. She stepped back, hunched her shoulders. "We're not behaving. Either one of us."

It shouldn't have been wrong. Not when it felt so right and good and natural. Since Brian's nightmare began, she'd been denying herself the basic human need to be touched. To be loved. And now she had her chance. For Emma. Not for anyone else but her. For once, only she should matter. *I need a man.*

This man.

Zac straightened, shook his head. "You're right. I'm sorry. My fault." He banged his hands on his head. "I'm all screwed up. I know it's wrong, but I want what I want."

He wasn't the only one. Maybe just once what would be so bad about that? No strings. Even if she'd never been the no-strings kind of girl, she'd make this one exception. *I want what I want.* That want pushed her to her tiptoes, stretching toward him, angling her head until her lips hovered close enough to feel his breath on her face. She waited, hoping he might stop her.

I need a man. Screw it. She clamped her hand on the back of his neck and hauled him closer. His lips slid across hers and she mangled his shirt in her fist while Penny's warning blared in her head.

Penny who?

She focused on the feel of his perfect lips on hers and pressed closer, needing the contact, the feel of his body against her. So long she'd been without affection, without the caress of hands. Then her skin caught fire, every inch sizzling, and she wrapped both arms around his waist and pulled. How close could she get? She wasn't sure, but she knew it wasn't enough. Enough of this didn't exist. She'd always want more.

He broke away and kissed across her jaw. Emma lifted her chin, exposing her neck.

"Atta, girl," he said.

"Penny says we shouldn't have sex."

"Penny is a pain in the ass."

More kisses and his hands moved under her blouse, his thumb stroking her belly. *Penny who?* "You could be right about that."

Apparently that was all he needed because he lifted his head and gave her his million-dollar country-club smile.

She glanced down as he worked the buttons on her blouse, one button, two buttons, three buttons. And then her shirt was open and his hands were on her breasts, detouring as they moved to push the blouse off her shoulders, those fantastic fingers moving down her arms until the shirt was off and Emma's chest hitched.

He wanted her. Somehow she believed it was more than sex. Maybe it was the gentleness of his touch or the brief hesitation that gave her a chance to follow Penny's orders, but it was there, urging her forward. *Penny who?*

He gave her a playful push toward his bedroom. *One of us will get hurt. Most likely me.* Right now, though, with all this crazy lust roaring inside her, she'd risk it. All this time she'd taken a backseat to everyone else. If she could have one night that was all hers, one night to forget all the problems and heartache, one night of ecstasy, she'd live with potential heartbreak. When it came to a broken heart, she was a pro.

In the bedroom, Zac yanked his shirt off and tossed it. Light from the hallway threw shadows and she watched the shirt sail through the air and land on a high-backed chair in the corner of the room. She reached for him, giving herself a minute to explore the planes of his chest and shoulders. Yes, it had been too long. Closing her eyes, she let the moment drift and stretch and settle in her mind so she'd always remember.

"You okay?" he asked.

"I'm great. It's…" Her voice trembled and she stopped. *Don't lose it now, Emma.*

He backed away, cupped her face in his hands. "What?"

"Fun. It's fun. And I've been without fun for a long time."

"Fun is good." He nudged her backward and her calves smacked the edge of the bed.

She sucked in a breath, her arms flailing as she flew backward and landed with a whoosh. The prosecutor wanted to play. From the bed, she placed her foot on his belly and pushed. "You're going to get it for that, *Zachary.*"

"Bring it on, Emma. Bring it on."

Slowly, he lifted her foot and ran his hands along her leg, his long fingers skittering over her jeans as they made their way up. So good. Inside, little by little, she came apart, abandoned all control.

He settled one knee on the bed and went to work on the button at her waist.

"I've got it." She flicked the button and worked the zipper down.

Again, Mr. Prosecutor went to work, removing her jeans, those dangerous hands slowly moving over her bare legs. He glanced up and the slant of light from the hallway illuminated his face and the slow, easy smile quirking his lips. Her chest hitched again. She was gone. So gone.

He'll destroy me.

But she didn't care. She shot to a sitting position, clamped her hands on the waistband of his pants and shoved. "Get these off."

Then something happened, like an eruption of energy, the air around her crackled and her skin tingled and snapped and she breathed in just as Zac kissed her, his tongue doing magic things to her. Needing the contact, Emma dug her fingers into his back.

Zac broke away, flipped her over and unhooked her bra. She flipped over again, still in her underwear, but letting him see her. Even in the dark, she saw that gleam in his eye. "Get naked, Zac. I'm a chick in need."

He cracked up, but did as he was told. How she loved a man who followed directions. He reached across her to his bedside table and his erection poked her leg. *Wow.* It had definitely been a while since she'd felt *that*. The crackle of foil drove away the silence and Emma tried not to think too hard about him keeping condoms in his bedside table. Or the women who'd been here.

Not going there.

Within seconds, he was back to her, trailing kisses over her chest, those luscious hands moving over her breasts and stomach and she slapped at the bed, squeezing the blanket. Surely she would die from all this attention.

She opened her legs and watched him slide between them. God, he was gorgeous. She wanted this, wanted him. Grabbing his cheeks, she pulled him to her and kissed him. Long and soft and then he pressed into her and she gasped. Too good.

They moved together, her locking her legs around him and gliding her hands over his back, then his face and chest, and when he settled himself on his elbows and kissed her again it was all too much. She'd been alone for way too long.

She held on and moved with him, their bodies in perfect unison, and then her stomach clenched and she sighed. Zac licked behind her ear, teasing her. He got as good as he gave because the muscles in his back tensed under her hands and he picked up his pace, racing, racing, racing until her mind whirled and her body turned frantic while she held on, wanting to prolong this moment before it all went away.

Too late.

Her world exploded into enormous flashes of light and ecstasy. She focused on breathing, enjoying the long-denied release of a good, healthy orgasm. Her world wasn't the only one exploding. Zac collapsed on top of her, his breaths coming in heaving bursts while she ran her hands over his back, along the quaking muscles.

"Heck of a way to end a rotten day," he said.

"I'll second that."

After a few moments, he rolled off her, taking all the warmth with him, and a blast of cold sent goose bumps up her legs. Zac lifted his arm, an obvious invitation for her to snuggle into his side. She wouldn't complain. She curled into him and ran her hand through the wispy blond hair in the center of his chest.

"Emma Sinclair, somehow I didn't figure you for a snuggler."

"Usually I'm not." Loneliness did that to a girl. "So you figured right."

He nibbled her neck. "I'm a snuggler."

Oh, this man is a total destroyer. But she wrapped her arms around him and squeezed because it all felt so right. So effortless.

Perfection.

Don't go there, Emma. Perfection didn't exist. At least

not for her. She eased her hand over his hip, drew tiny circles and loved the feel of being so close. "We have food out there. We should eat."

"There's food, too?"

Smarty-pants. "Yes, there's food. And then we have work to do, so no funny stuff."

Finally, with great effort, Zac rolled away. Part of her hated it, wanted him to stay close, let her feel loved a bit more. When had she turned into such a needy person?

Maybe since she'd been without affection for so long.

Who knew? She watched Zac gather his clothes and slide into his pants, already wondering if they'd do this again.

"Emma, quit looking at me like that or you won't get food. I'll keep you in this bed all night."

Promises, promises.

ZAC TUGGED HIS SHIRT ON and from outside the bedroom, a cell phone chirped. Good distraction before carnal thoughts coaxed him back to bed.

"That's my phone," Emma said.

"I'll grab it for you. In your coat?"

"Yep. Pocket."

He left the room in search of the phone and to give his brain a minute to catch up to what just happened. If there were any more ways to annihilate his career, he wasn't sure he could find them.

But, yeah, Emma Sinclair was worth it. She had to be because he'd never crossed the line when it came to his job. Right now, he didn't care, didn't anticipate caring in the near future, either.

More of Emma was what he wanted.

He retrieved her phone, grabbed the bag of food and headed back down the hall. He'd heat up dinner while she got dressed. Give them both a little privacy. By the time he stepped into the bedroom she'd already slipped on her blouse. "Don't get dressed on my account."

She swatted at him and bent to pick up her jeans. "Yeah. Whatever, mister."

"Can I turn on the light?"

"Sure."

Zac flipped the switch, flooded the room with light and found Emma with her eyes closed. She slowly opened them and he imagined lazy mornings watching her roll out of bed. *Easy now.*

He handed her the phone and she checked the screen. "Oh, this is funny."

"What's that?"

"It's a text from Penny. What timing." Using her thumb, she hit a button. "Oh. Oh, wow."

This should be good. He waited, wondering if she'd share whatever news Penny had sent. Was that fair? To wonder? To expect it?

Hell if I know.

After a second, the silence morphed into awkward and he held up the bag. "I'll nuke the food."

Emma finally lifted her head. "Zac?"

"Yes?"

"She got a call from Ray Gardner."

Son of a gun. If he were being taken off the case, he'd have been told. Maybe not. Ray had been pretty steamed at him earlier. Zac waited, the silence tearing his brain to shreds. "Ray is my boss."

"He's assigning an investigator from the SA's office to Brian's case."

Air flew up Zac's throat and came out in a whoosh. If it was relief or satisfaction, he didn't know. Either way, his boss had redeemed himself. Zac leaned against the doorframe and stared at Emma's face, where a tentative smile appeared. Her eyes filled with tears and she blinked them away.

"It's okay to be happy," he said. "You've worked hard for this."

She lifted the phone then let her hand drop again. "I know. I just can't believe it. Someone is listening."

"And you made it happen." He held up the bag. "I'm on the food. Take your time."

He turned from the doorway, hoping she wouldn't press him on what he knew about the investigator. In short—and overdue—order he had to separate his job and this case from his feelings about Emma. It was all too intertwined and…muddy.

"Zac?"

He popped his head back in the bedroom and she held the phone up. "Did you have anything to do with the investigator being assigned to this case?"

"I may have suggested it as a precaution."

"You think my brother is innocent."

Trouble. Part of him wanted to tell her he agreed with her, but the truth was, he didn't know. The prosecutor in him wanted to believe the jury got it right and hadn't convicted an innocent man. But he'd also been an ASA long enough to know that, sometimes, justice got sidetracked. Things went wrong. Innocent people went to prison.

He tapped his hand against the doorframe and stared into her big, hopeful eyes. "I think there are inconsistencies with Brian's case that need to be looked at."

If she was disappointed, she didn't show it. Nothing moved. No slumping shoulders, no dramatic sigh, no pinched eyebrows. Nothing. Emma Sinclair, rock star.

Finally, she ran her hands over her legs and drummed her fingers. He should say something. Even if he wasn't ready to admit that Brian might be innocent, he should say *something*. But that was the tricky part.

"Emma—"

She held up her hands and attempted a brief smile that screamed of indecision. "It's okay. You're a prosecutor. I know what your job is. And thank you for suggesting the investigator. It's more than anyone from your office has done since this nightmare began. That means a lot to me. By the end of this, you'll see that Brian is innocent."

For her sake, he certainly hoped so.

Chapter Twelve

After her morning class on Wednesday, Emma headed to her mother's favorite Italian restaurant, a little hole-in-the-wall near the United Center. With her crazy schedule, she and her mom hadn't managed to arrange a dinner out together, so they'd found a sliver of time to squeeze in lunch.

As she drove, Emma turned up the volume on the radio and sang along. At the traffic light, still wailing, she glanced at the car next to her and found the driver, a young guy wearing a baseball cap, howling at her. *Hey, whatever.* She threw her arms up and wiggled them. Still laughing, he shook his head and waved her off. Fun stuff, that. It had been too long since she'd allowed herself to lighten up, to keep from being so serious about every darn thing.

Blame it on the orgasms—as in multiples. Thanks to one Zachary Hennings, whom she couldn't seem to stop thinking about today. A total stud.

Bad, Emma. Bad.

Emma made a left on a tree-lined street where the homes, in typical city fashion, had roughly six inches of space between them. She found a parking space a block away from the restaurant and called it a done deal.

Not a bad day for a short walk. She tightened the belt on her coat and faced the unseasonable cold. Even if the temperature hadn't made it out of the forties yet today, the sun's warmth poured over her. She'd take it after the vicious winter they'd had. Above her, a few birds chirped and the clear blue sky stretched as far as she could see. She stopped, tipped her head up and the damp smell of early spring tickled her nose.

Two years of her life had slipped away, two years of not taking a few seconds to enjoy a pretty day or belt out a song. Two years of being smothered under the blanket of a wrongfully accused brother.

As was typical of her life, the piercing shriek of a police siren interrupted her moment of grateful appreciation. Out of curiosity, she spun toward it and spotted a Chicago squad car near the corner, where he'd made a traffic stop. A car that looked suspiciously like her mother's. *Oh, come on.* Mom finally leaves the house and she gets pulled over? And for what? The woman barely drove the speed limit. If anything, she'd be cited for driving too slowly.

To be sure, Emma moved closer and—yep—that was her mother in the driver's seat. The officer hadn't gotten out of his car yet and as Emma got closer, she found her mother digging through the glove compartment, probably looking for her registration and insurance card. Emma pulled off her glove and tapped the passenger side door. Her mother flinched, glanced up and slammed her hand against her chest.

"Open the window," Emma said.

From the driver's side, her mother lowered the window and Emma stuck her head in. "What happened?"

"I don't know. He just signaled me over."

"Did you run the light or something?"

Mom scoffed. Perhaps the timing stunk, but Emma laughed. She had to. "Sorry. Stupid question."

The cop finally heaved himself from his car, slipped his cap on and headed their way. Emma backed out of the window and stood tall. "Hello, officer."

"Step away from the car, please."

He wore a light jacket, obviously padded with a vest underneath. In this town, any cop would be nuts not to wear one. This was her home, but it was still a city and cities had gangs and drugs and guns that could steal a life.

"This is my mother." Emma jerked her thumb down the street. "We're meeting for lunch."

"Yeah, fine. Step away from the car." The cop's nasty gaze focused on her and he pointed to an area in front of the car. "Move. Now."

What the heck? A second officer—this one younger and not as tall, but bigger-chested—got out of the car and walked toward her. "Ma'am, step to the side."

Mom leaned over to the passenger side and spoke through the window. "Emma, it's fine."

The second cop puckered his lips, glanced at the other cop and gave a subtle nudge of his chin.

Emma eyeballed them both. "Why are you pulling her over?"

"Broken taillight. License and registration, please."

Emma angled around the second cop to check the taillights. If Mom had a broken taillight, it had just happened because they were fine this morning. Both taillights were intact. She pointed to the taillights. "They're fine."

The first cop wandered to the back of the car and stared at the driver's-side taillight. "This one is burned out. I saw it when she made the turn."

"Mom, hit the brakes."

Both taillights lit up. Emma gave the first cop a hard stare, daring him to argue with her. "It seems you're mistaken."

The cop shrugged. "She must have a short in the wiring. Better get it checked before she has an accident, *Emma*."

And the way he said her name, sarcastic and taunting and drawing out the m's. She jerked her head back and then came the "aha" moment. Her mother didn't have a broken taillight. Her mother had a daughter making the CPD look bad. Clearly, they didn't like that because not only had they pulled her over on a trumped-up violation, they'd suggested that her mother might have an accident.

That, Emma would not stand for. She threw her shoulders back, held her head higher. "Are you threatening us?"

The cop placed his hand over his chest in mock horror and Emma thought her blood would seep clear through her pores. She'd like to climb over the car and pummel him. Just beat him senseless for being an idiot.

"Ma'am," the second cop said to her mother from the passenger side, "we'll let you go with a warning today, but you need to get that light checked."

A warning. They'd given the warning all right.

The second cop stepped around Emma and headed back to their car. She watched him for a second and zeroed in on his name tag. *Collins.* Gotcha. She brought her attention back to jerk number one. She hadn't gotten close enough to catch his name, but she had his partner's. She'd find them.

Jerk number one tipped his hat. "Enjoy your lunch, *Emma.*"

With all the crime happening in a city the size of Chicago, these creeps had nothing better to do than harass a widow whose son was in prison, wrongfully convicted.

Despite the brisk air, hot stabs punctured Emma's skin. They weren't harassing her mother, they were harassing her. First it was the detective coming to the house and now this. From the curb, Emma watched the lights on top of the police car move down the street. That crazy detective and his friends were trying to scare her by targeting her loved ones, by letting her know they could find them wherever they happened to be. Well, guess what? She was out of loved ones.

Emma stooped down and looked at her mother through the still-open window. "Are you okay?"

"I'm fine. I don't understand what happened with that taillight. I'll have to have it checked."

Part of Emma wanted to tell her mother that it wasn't about the taillight, but what was the point? Why give her another thing to worry about when she was finally finding her way out of depression? Giving her mother any questionable news might send her back to that joyless, mind-numbing state she'd been in for too long.

Emma opened the car door and slid in. "I'll take care of it. Let's find a parking space and have a nice lunch. Maybe we'll even have a glass of wine. What do you think?"

Her mother grinned. "Drinking at lunch?"

"It's one glass."

"Why not? It wouldn't kill me."

Yes, and right after lunch, from the privacy of her car, Emma would put a call into their pit-bull lawyer and let her know that certain members of the Chicago Police Department were harrassing her.

THE JUDGE TOOK PITY and called an early recess for the day. Zac had no issues with that and lugged his stuffed file cart out of the now-empty courtroom. Two o'clock and he hadn't eaten lunch yet. Reminding him of his crashing blood-sugar levels, a nagging ache thumped at the center of his forehead. He needed food. Fast. He'd run his cart back to the office and hit the corner deli for a bite. Then he'd study his cases for the next day.

From his right jacket pocket, his phone—the personal one—buzzed. Office phone was left pocket.

He checked it. Penny. "Hey."

"*Zachary,* I just thought you'd like to know I'm about to file a complaint against the City of Chicago."

Zac rolled his eyes. *Let the drama begin.* "Okay, Pen, I'll bite. What is your complaint?"

"It starts with the Chicago Police Department harassing Emma Sinclair. From there, I'm sure I'll come up with plenty of other misconduct violations."

Zac's headache pounded away and he closed his eyes. What the hell was Penny talking about? "What happened?"

At the elevator bank, he swung into the corner alcove and leaned against the windowsill. Afternoon sun shot rays of light against the marble floors and he centered himself in its path to soak up the heat.

"Emma and her mom had a lunch date and her mother got stopped for a broken taillight. Guess what, Zachary?"

The headache suddenly went nuclear, his skull nearly coming apart. "No broken taillight?"

"Excellent guess."

"Emma was with her?"

"They were meeting at the restaurant. Emma had just parked and saw the whole thing."

"What'd the cops say?"

Obviously reading from notes, Penny recited everything Emma had told her. He stayed quiet, listening, absorbing it all, ignoring the spine-busting grip of tension and remaining focused while the warm sun made him think of needing a vacation. "Hang on."

"What?"

"The part about the accident. They said she'd have an *accident?*"

"They implied it, yes." Paper shuffling came from Penny's end of the line. "They said she'd better get it checked before she had an accident."

That made him boil. It was one thing to pull her over, but to imply that someone would get hurt? Epic fail. Zac stood tall, stretched his shoulders to crack his back. "You're sure that's what they said? No paraphrasing?"

"Yes. That's what Emma said. Her mother heard it."

"I'll take care of it."

"Have him hold," Penny said to someone on the other

end. "Well, how about that, *The Herald* is on the other line. They're returning my call."

Damn, Penny. "You went to the press?"

"You bet your butt I did. I'm done playing. Gotta go."

The line went dead and Zac squeezed the phone hard enough to snap a knuckle. This damn case. He couldn't get a break. Witnesses, *Emma* being threatened. He didn't know how the hell to deal with that particular issue. Well, he did know, but he'd definitely lose his job if he dug his fingers into someone's throat and tore it out. Add to that his boss being mad at him for not controlling the spin and he was cooked.

And worse, he'd gotten emotionally involved with Emma. Whom he'd made love to last night, a couple of times, which he wanted to do again in the very near future.

He ran his free hand over his face. "What am I doing?"

At the window, he tilted his head to the bright sun hoping it would calm his rioting brain. *Think.* But the headache reminded him that he needed fuel. He opened his eyes and stared down at the street where a steady flow of pedestrians came and went from the building. The lunch truck was still parked at the curb.

First things first. He'd grab a sandwich from the truck, go back to his office, call Emma and get the story from her.

Then he'd kick some tail.

At least he had a short-term plan. An excellent plan. With the way this case was going, that plan would probably be blown in the next five minutes but for now it would do.

After jamming the sandwich down his throat and settling in at his desk, Zac popped three ibuprofens. Excessive, but he had King Kong tap-dancing in his head. He hit Emma's number on his personal cell. Voice mail. She might already be at work. She'd mentioned it the night before.

Next he dialed Detective Leeks, that scumbag. If Leeks

wanted mind games, Zac would bring it on. This guy would not threaten Emma. Not without some backlash, and Zac had enough firepower to grab the detective's attention.

Another voice mail. No one wanted to answer today. He waited for the beep. "Detective Leeks, this is ASA Zac Hennings. Have your son in my office at 9:00 a.m. tomorrow. If he doesn't show, I'll get a subpoena. Your choice, detective."

Pleased with the message, he hung up. That'd rattle some cages.

"What the hell are you doing?"

Ray stood in the hallway, hands on his hips, his fingers drumming. *This is a problem.* Keeping his focus on his boss, he sat back, forced his shoulders down and did his best to appear casual.

"Hey, finished up early in court."

Ray stepped into the office, his face pinched and red enough that his already high blood pressure had probably spiked a couple hundred points. When he closed the door behind him, Zac tapped a foot. Ray didn't often close doors. When he did, people got a few extra holes ripped into them.

Here we go.

Ray jabbed a finger. "You're not the investigator. I talked to the SA and we assigned an investigator. You're not him. *He* will question witnesses. You want answers from the Leeks kid, you can watch from another room." Ray stopped, took a breath and dropped his hands. "I don't know what's going on with you, but you're too close to this. It's killing your judgment."

Zac stood and got eye to eye with his boss. He wouldn't yell, wouldn't wisecrack, wouldn't take an attitude. He'd just lay it out, as he always did. "What's killing my judgment is detectives and cops threatening witnesses. Emma

Sinclair's mother—her mother, for God's sake—got pulled over today on a bogus stop."

"What bogus stop?"

"A busted taillight that's not busted. Emma was there and the cop told her they'd better get it fixed before her mother gets hurt."

Ray sighed.

Yeah, right there with ya, pal. "So, if I'm whacked out it's because I've had it with a small group of Chicago's finest. We need to get this Leeks kid in here and ask him if he wore a white shirt the night of Chelsea Moore's murder. Fairly simple."

Ray put his hands up. "Okay. Okay. Relax. Let's get the Leeks kid in here tomorrow. We'll have the investigator talk to him. A conversation only, nothing too hard, and see what happens. Give me a list of questions you want answered and we'll have the investigator ask."

"Ray—"

"That's the best I can do. I'm not letting you question that kid. Hell, I'm not letting you in the room. Whatever is going on with you and this detective, it's not going ballistic on my watch. Do us both a favor and back off. Got it?"

Zac didn't answer.

"I'll take that as a yes."

Ray left the office and Zac stared at the now-open doorway, pains shooting down his neck from clenched teeth. Back. Off. Handed an explosive case and the minute he uncovered something questionable, he was supposed to ease up. What they should be doing is touting a political win for the new State's Attorney, a woman who campaigned for honesty in a city plagued by corruption.

Whether Brian Sinclair was guilty or not, this case deserved a second look. Justice demanded it. Justice for Chelsea Moore, for Brian Sinclair and for Emma, who'd been fighting this battle for so long.

Maybe his emotions *were* getting in the way, but someone had to ferret out the truth. If for no other reason than to figure out what had happened to a young woman in a dark alley, Zac wanted answers.

Either way, he wanted answers.

THIRTY MINUTES BEFORE closing time, Emma stood at the bar waiting for her customer's drink order when Zac strolled through the door. Immediately, relief flashed and spread through her. His presence did that to her, brought a sense of comfort and security to a life that had very little of either.

He spotted her, tilted his head and their gazes locked. This time, she didn't have that panicky feeling at the sight of him coming into the restaurant. After what had happened this afternoon, she'd half expected him. Penny was right about her brother. He was indeed predictable in all the ways that mattered.

But something was off about him tonight. At this late hour, he still wore his suit, minus the tie. His shirt collar was unbuttoned and his jacket could have used a good pressing. So not Zachary. His body language wasn't right, either. Sure he'd slapped a smile on his face, but his shoulders slumped and that was one thing she'd never seen. Zac always, always, entered a room with his head high and shoulders back, his aura screaming power and control. But tonight that aura was utterly absent.

The bartender loaded drinks on her tray and she detoured in Zac's direction on her way to the table.

"Hi," she said. "I'll bet you're looking for another ferocious brownie."

"Thought I'd escort you home after your run-in with the P.D. today."

She nodded, thankful for his thoughtfulness. "I'd like that. You look sad, *Zachary*."

That got a smile out of him. *When all else fails, do the Penny voice.*

"I'm fine. Tired."

"Everything okay?"

He glanced around the nearly empty restaurant. "Yep."

She jerked her head to the bar. "Have a seat. I'll send you a brownie."

Barely a smile out of him. Yeesh, this boy was in a world of hurt. She delivered her drinks and swung back toward the kitchen to get Zac his dessert. On the way, she noted the hostess, a perky sex kitten of a blonde, sniffing around the bar. *Hands off my man, honey.* Really, though, Emma couldn't blame the girl. Zac was definitely sniff-worthy.

Her friend Kelly marched into the kitchen behind Emma and backhanded her on the butt. "I see the hot prosecutor is back. I think Miss Emma has a boyfriend."

Emma rolled her eyes. "Emma has something. She's not sure what it is, but it definitely makes her toes curl. And that's all I'm giving you, so don't bother asking."

"Come on. Give me a little more." She squeezed her thumb and index finger together. "Just a little."

Emma put Zac's brownie into the microwave and grinned. "He looks great naked."

"I knew it!"

The microwave dinged. She retrieved the brownie, gave it an extra scoop of ice cream and finished it with chocolate sauce, whipped cream and a cherry. He'd love this.

"Bye, Kelly."

"Oh, come on!"

"Nope." She pushed through the kitchen door, swung around the bar and slid the brownie in front of Zac. "Here you go, handsome. I made it myself." She leaned in and ran one hand over his shoulders. Locked up tight, they were.

The man needed to de-stress. "It looks like you had another rough day so I gave you an extra scoop of ice cream."

"You're too good to me, Emma."

She glanced at her table then back at him. "I don't like seeing you with a long face. It's not you."

"I'm okay."

Not for a minute did she believe it. But she had two tables to close out and she'd have to quiz him about his day when they were out of here. "I have customers. Enjoy your brownie."

Ninety minutes later, Emma parked in her minuscule driveway with Zac pulling in behind her and temporarily blocking the sidewalk. Home. Safe and sound. What a day. She'd checked on her mother a few times throughout the evening and all was quiet. No lurking cops to be found.

Zac yanked open her door, held his hand out and she grabbed it. "Thank you, sir."

"My pleasure. You gave me a brownie. Least I could do."

Once out of the car, she eased her hand away, but Zac held on, entwining his fingers with hers. Nice. They walked to the door hand in hand and Emma slowed to a crawl, wanting to prolong this feeling of being attached, of being a couple. When was the last time she'd had a casual stroll while holding hands? And was it pathetic that such a simple gesture should make her feel so desperate for the moment not to end?

Loneliness had apparently turned her into a sap because there was most likely a hateful detective watching them, taking note of the prosecutor getting friendly.

At the door, she stopped and faced Zac. "Thanks for coming home with me."

For a minute, he simply stared at her, his gaze traveling over her face until he lifted his hand and ran the back of it over her cheek. "You should have called me this afternoon. I would have helped."

She shrugged. "I wanted to."

"And what?"

"I couldn't decide if I was calling you because you're the prosecutor on my brother's case or because you're the guy I went to bed with last night. It's confusing."

He eased his hand away from her face. "Sure is."

"What happened today, Zac? Why are you sad?"

"I'm not sad. I'm frustrated. My boss thinks I've let myself get emotionally involved in this case and I can't dispute that." He puffed his cheeks up and blew out a breath. "That's tough for a trial lawyer to admit."

"I can imagine."

He leaned in, dropped a light kiss on her lips. "I worry about you. I won't apologize for that. I'm standing on this porch knowing someone could be watching and I'm not sure I care because I haven't done anything I wouldn't have done before getting involved with you. I've done my job."

Was she dreaming? Had to be. Things like this didn't happen to her. People like this, folks who fought for her, took care of her and made her believe life wasn't always a matter of handling one crisis after another. "But I don't want you risking your job for me. That's why I didn't call you today. It's not fair to you. Penny has a handle on it."

"I know she does. And, you'll find this out, but Leeks's son is coming in tomorrow. That's what got me in the penalty box."

"Oh, Zac."

He shrugged. "I was aggravated. I know Leeks is behind those cops pulling your mom over. I figured I'd up the pressure on him. Ray heard me on the phone and reamed me out."

"I'm sorry."

"It needs to be done, Emma. It's the right thing. Someone has to question this kid without his father influencing the interview."

A girl had to love a man willing to rail against the establishment. "Obviously, I agree, but maybe you shouldn't be the one to do it."

"I'm not. Ray told me to forget it, which, at the time, aggravated me even more. Now? I agree with him. I have to be careful here. A neutral party should question that kid and I'm not neutral anymore. Not with the way I feel about you and definitely not with the way I feel about that scumbag Leeks."

Emma threw her hands up. "Okay, Mr. Prosecutor. Let's take it easy now. Don't destroy your career for me. The guilt would kill me and then I'd spend the next two years figuring out how to save *you*, too." She cracked a smile, hoping he'd grasp the sarcasm. "I'm a little tired of saving everyone. It's exhausting work."

He grabbed her around the neck and kissed her—bam— all heat and tongues and crazy, lovable passion and everything inside her burst open. *I'm crazy about him.*

Since he'd come into her life, she didn't feel so alone, so at war with the world. Being with Zac brought her peace and a sense of calm. How he did it, she wasn't sure, but he was one of those men who gave people hope.

The front door opened. "Oh!"

Emma jumped back and turned to her wide-eyed and horrified mother about to slam the door closed. Emma shoved her hand against it.

"I'm so sorry," Mom said.

"It's okay. I want you to meet someone. This is Zac. Hennings. Penny's brother."

Mom's gaze slid to Zac, then back to Emma. "He's the…"

The prosecutor. "Yes."

Zac stuck his hand out. "Mrs. Sinclair, nice to meet you. You have an amazing daughter."

"I'll agree with you there." Mom took his hand and shook it. "Nice to meet you as well. Thank you for all you've done. It has to be awkward."

Emma coughed. Then, as if sensing her misstep, Mom's eyes got big. "I mean with Penny being our lawyer. Not with…" Mom ran her palm up her forehead then held it there for a second. "I think I'll shut this door. I'm sorry, Emma. I heard you pull in and wondered where you were. I didn't know you had company."

"Zac met me at work. He didn't want me to come home alone."

Mom stared at her, a slight smile threatening before she looked at Zac. "Thank you for taking care of her."

"No problem, ma'am." He squeezed Emma's arm. "I should go. Busy day tomorrow."

The Leeks kid. Right. "I know. Thanks for bringing me home."

She wouldn't ask him to keep her posted. He was still the prosecutor and she was still the defense. *Confusing.* Besides, Penny would have her spies out and would fill her in.

Zac nodded. "Make sure you lock up. I'll call you tomorrow."

Chapter Thirteen

Ben Leeks Jr. was a bigger weasel than his father. What a conniving piece of trash this guy was. Zac watched on an oversized monitor in an office adjacent to the conference room where investigators *conversed* with Junior.

Watching this particular interview, Zac silently seethed. He wanted nothing more than to tell the kid and his lawyer to cut the nonsense and answer the flipping questions.

They'd been responding, but those responses had been in an abstract, vague way that failed to completely answer the questions. Junior's whole demeanor, the relaxed, mocking posture, the eye-rolling, all of it, stank. At least he came dressed to impress in slacks and a pressed shirt, probably his lawyer's doing. But this guy knew—*knew*—he'd be walking away a free man even if he was guilty.

His father would make sure of it.

Ray stood beside Zac, studying the screen, his arms folded. "He's not giving us anything."

"Yeah, because the lawyer isn't letting him. They've admitted he was at the club and that he left with a group. Knew that before he walked in here. We need to push harder, see if he and Chelsea argued that night."

Ray ignored the comment. No shock there. He'd made it clear he had no interest in pushing.

Zac focused on the monitor and Leeks Jr. Massive kid. Muscular and strong. Zac hit the gym four or five times a week, pumping serious iron, and yet the guy being interviewed was at least double his size. Freakishly big. *Unnatural.* "Ask him if he uses steroids."

"*What?*"

"Chelsea's friends said he was abusive. Look at his body. He's huge. If he's taking steroids, Chelsea may have been a victim of 'roid rage."

Ray sighed.

"It happens."

"I'll have the investigator ask. Right after we get him to admit that he was wearing a white shirt that night."

Now Zac rolled his eyes. Conveniently, Junior couldn't recall what color shirt he wore the night Chelsea died.

Zac's phone buzzed. Bethenny, the office assistant. Odd. They were right down the hall. Why didn't she just come get him? "Let me take this." He pressed the button and stepped into the hallway. "Hi, Beth. What's up?"

"Sorry to disturb you. Did you have an appointment this morning?"

Zac stuck his bottom lip out, ticked through his mental calendar. Aside from court that afternoon, the Leeks interview was it. "I don't think so. Why?"

"There's a Stanley Vernon out here to see you." Zac snapped his head up. Stanley Vernon. The State's star witness. "He didn't specifically ask for you, but he wants to see the prosecutor working the Sinclair case."

A blood rush made Zac dizzy and he shook his head. *Stanley Vernon.* "I'll be right up. Lock him in my office if you have to, but don't let him leave."

He clicked off, then stuck his head in the office where Ray continued to observe the Leeks interview. "I gotta go." Ray raised his eyebrows in that what-the-hell look Zac had gotten used to. "I know it's my case, but I've suddenly got the State's key witness wanting to see me."

"He's here?"

"In reception."

Ray jerked his chin. "Go. Don't screw up."

Thanks for the vote of confidence. "That wouldn't be my favorite option."

For a change, Ray laughed. That was progress after the tension-filled couple of days they'd had. One thing Zac never wanted to be was the problem employee.

Forgoing the time it would take to detour to his office and grab his suit jacket, Zac hustled up the hall to the waiting area.

Beth spotted him coming around the corner and pointed to Stanley Vernon, a middle-aged man about six inches shorter than Zac. Thin with sloping shoulders, he wore a zipped-up windbreaker, jeans and the stooped look of someone carrying a heavy load.

He flipped a tan newsboy cap in his hands. Back and forth, up and down, the movement constant. Oh, yeah. This guy definitely had something on his mind.

Buzzing tension sizzled up Zac's arms. *Calm down here.* He extended his hand. "Mr. Vernon, I'm Zac Hennings. The new prosecutor on the Sinclair case."

"Hennings?"

"Yes, sir." Obviously, recognition dawned. "You met my sister the other day. She's the defense attorney on this case."

Vernon's eyes widened. "That's...different."

No kidding. "It sure is." Zac gestured down the corridor. "Let's talk in private."

Back in his office, Zac closed the door behind them while Mr. Vernon took in the files lining the office. "These all yours?"

"Yes, sir."

"Astonishing."

"We live in a crazy world." Zac settled into his squeaking desk chair and leaned back, all calm and cool. "What can I do for you?"

Vernon stared down at the newsboy cap, flipped it a few times. "I…uh." He looked up, stared right at Zac, his eyes heavy-lidded and desperate. Fierce hammering slammed in Zac's head. Whatever the man had to say was tearing him up.

"Mr. Vernon, talk to me. I can assure you, it won't be the worst thing I've heard." Hoping to ease the strain suddenly drowning the room, he cracked a smile. "Trust me there."

More cap flipping. "Your sister and the Sinclair girl."

"What about them?"

"They asked me questions. Got me thinking about that night."

Here it comes. "Go on."

"I was walking by the alley. It was noisy, though. The club door was open and people were in line waiting to get in. Between the talking and the music from inside I couldn't really hear anything."

"Okay."

"I saw someone, though, in the alley. A man. Definitely a man."

Zac would not help. Mr. Vernon had to come clean with no reminders or assistance. "I read that in your statement."

"Your sister. She asked me about the white shirt."

"Yes, sir. You testified that you saw a man in a white shirt. It's in the transcript."

He nodded. "I started thinking about that and, you know, when the detectives questioned me? I never said anything about the white shirt."

Zac drove his feet into the floor, forcing himself to remain still, not a flinch, not a nudge. "You didn't see a white shirt?"

Slowly, with what looked like great effort, Mr. Vernon

shifted his head side to side. "They told me someone else saw a white shirt."

Someone else? Who the hell was that now? Zac would have to go through Emma's files and find the other witness. After tracking down the transcripts, he'd seen that there were other witnesses called to the stand, but he didn't recall any of them mentioning a white shirt. Emma would know.

Forget keeping still. He had to move. Dispel some of the energy. He sat forward and casually leaned his elbows on the desk. "Do you remember a white shirt?"

More cap flipping. Once, twice, three times. "I don't think so."

As brutally hard as it was, Zac didn't move. He'd love to grab a notepad, but it might spook the guy. Besides, if he was about to recant—which it sounded as if he was— they'd have to write up his statement. "When you were questioned, did the detectives ask you if you remembered the white shirt?"

"Yes. They asked me and I said I wasn't sure. They said to think about it because they had another witness who said they saw someone in a white shirt. If I could agree with that, they could get the guy."

Right. Zac's guess? The other witness was bogus. Non-existent. Detectives had probably determined that Brian Sinclair had been wearing a white shirt. Hell, Brian probably told them that himself. When Brian became the primary suspect, the P.D. wanted someone to say they saw a guy in a white shirt in that alley. Stanley Vernon was their someone.

"You agreed?"

Mr. Vernon finally set his cap on the edge of Zac's desk and pressed both hands into it before pulling back. "They seemed pretty sure that Sinclair had done it. The way they put it to me was they were just tying up loose ends. I figured since they had someone else saying they saw a white shirt, it wouldn't be just me." He stared down at his empty hands—nothing to flip—and shook his head. "I wanted to help."

For a second, Zac pitied the guy. For two years he'd been thinking that he'd helped put a killer behind bars. Now he wasn't sure and the guilt landed on him like a tanker thrown in a tornado.

"Relax, Mr. Vernon. You're doing the right thing. I appreciate your coming forward. We need to clarify what you're saying here. Okay?"

"Okay."

Zac grabbed his notepad and pen. "Let's run through it. You don't recall seeing a man wearing a white shirt?"

"I saw a man coming from the alley, but I don't know what color shirt he was wearing."

AT IT SINCE 6:00 A.M., Emma had already spent four hours of her day at the dining room table studying constitutional law. The exam was only two days away and she had a nagging sense of panic that she'd flunk. She'd never flunked a test in her life.

Never.

Maybe Zac, the lover of all things constitutional law, could quiz her. Or maybe she was just looking for an excuse to see him.

And have sex with him—lots of steamy, sweaty sex that left her loose and purring.

She ducked her head and giggled. *Bad, Emma. Bad.* Her cell phone beeped and she snatched it off the table. Zac. Their pheromones must have beelined.

"Hey, handsome. I was just thinking about you."

"What do you know about another witness identifying the white shirt?"

And hello to you, too. Forget the purring. "In reference to the white shirt, there's no other witness. Mr. Vernon was it."

"You're sure?"

Pfft. Was he serious? "Of course. I can pull the witness files for you. I have them all sorted by time frame. If there was another witness who saw a man with a white shirt, it would be in the file with Mr. Vernon's."

"I need those files."

In the back of her brain, something snapped. A physical zap she'd never experienced against the back of her skull. "What's going on?"

"I can't say. Yet."

"You want me to turn over my files and you're not going to tell me why?"

Silence. "Do you trust me?"

Of course she did. "Completely."

"Then I need those files. You'll find out why soon."

Give him the files. She should talk to Penny first. *Give him the files.* "This is a good thing then?"

"I believe so, yes."

His answer came without hesitation. No pause, no moment to consider a response. Nothing. That had to mean something. If she truly trusted him, it meant turning over information without knowing why. Which she hadn't been inclined to do when it came to Brian.

But that snapping in the back of her head was new. Maybe a good sign. *Take a chance.*

"Give me an hour to copy the reports and get them to your office."

"Thank you."

It took Emma fifty-two minutes to call Penny, take a quick shower, copy the files and race them downtown.

Penny, being Penny, went to work on her contacts to figure out what the prosecution was up to.

While Emma drove, she speculated on the sudden need for these files. It had to be something regarding the Ben Leeks interview. At a red light, she tapped the steering wheel and mulled over the options. Maybe the interview had yielded a new witness and Zac wanted to know if Emma had a statement from said witness.

From the seat beside her, the phone beeped. Still waiting for the green light, she checked the ID and punched the speaker button. "Hi, Penny." The light changed and she made a left toward the parking garage.

"Are you there yet?"

"No. About to park."

"Park and call me. Do *not* go into that office until you talk to me."

Emma's stomach seized as she drove up to the ticket machine at the parking garage. "Is this bad?"

"No. I just don't want you driving when I tell you."

"Did we get a new trial?"

Penny huffed. "I'm not saying another word. Park and call me."

The lunatic hung up. What was that? She calls, gets Emma all wound up and then dumps her? Sheesh.

Still, her body hummed with an incessant energy, that same zapping current from before, that told her something big was about to happen. It took scouring five levels before she found an open parking space. Somehow, it seemed fitting. She'd waited all this time. Why not a few extra minutes?

She slammed the car into Park and dialed Penny. The phone beep-beeped. No signal.

"Gah! Stupid parking garage." Not a break to be had. She snatched the files and her purse and took off toward the elevator. She pressed the button. Waited and waited. The darn thing seemed to be on the second floor for a lifetime. Heck with this. She darted for the stairwell, checking her signal the whole way. Nothing.

The run down the stairs left Emma breathless, a not-so-gentle reminder that she hadn't exercised in months. Soon. With any luck, maybe soon she'd have time. Not that she'd ever had much luck, but a girl could dream.

Once on the street, three glorious bars appeared on her phone. *Thank you, signal gods.* She dialed Penny.

"What took so long?" her lawyer asked.

"Don't start. There was no signal in the garage and then the elevator was slow. I just ran down five flights. Please tell me what's going on."

She checked traffic coming both ways and stepped off the curb.

"Mr. Vernon just recanted."

Midstride, her right knee locked and buckled. Pain shot up her thigh and she stumbled, catching the files before they fell to the ground. A horn sounded, brakes squealed and a cabbie swerved. Near miss. She gasped and clutched her folders tight while the cabbie swung his fist. Another car horn blared and she jumped back onto the curb before being flattened. Wouldn't that be the kicker? Dying just as her brother got a new trial?

"Emma?"

Recanted. That's what Penny had said. *Please, God.* She drew a bumpy breath. Why did it feel as if someone had reached into her and ripped out part of a lung?

"I'm trying not to get squashed here." On the sidewalk, Emma straightened, drew a long, slow breath and adjusted the files in her arms. "Okay. I'm good."

"We're not supposed to know this yet, but Mr. Vernon just told Zac he never saw a man in a white shirt. He definitely saw a man. No white shirt. The detectives told him another witness saw a man in a white shirt and they asked him to confirm."

Now it made sense. "Zac is looking for the witness. That's why he needs my files."

"I just talked to my dad. We don't think there's another witness. We think the cops knew Brian wore a white shirt that night so they made up this other witness to convince Mr. Vernon they had the right guy."

Please, please, please. "So Mr. Vernon's testimony will get thrown out?"

"It's enough for us to file our post-conviction petition and probably get a hearing."

"Oh, Lord." Emma hurried across the street and sprinted up the steps leading to the building where Zac's office was housed.

"Don't get crazy on me, Emma. We are still months away from a hearing. These things take time, but this is all good. Great, in fact."

In the last ten years, the Sinclairs hadn't seen a whole lot of great. Suddenly, this Hennings bunch was offering an abundance of it. "I'm heading in. I'll call you when I'm done with Zac."

"Don't let on that you know. Play dumb. Make him squirm a little."

Emma scoffed. Everything was a competition between them. They literally thrived on it. "You two make me crazy."

"I love making him wonder what I'm up to."

The line for security stretched to the lobby door and Emma almost laughed. Hadn't the last two years of her life been filled with this hurry-up-and-wait mentality? Her phone beeped again. Popular today.

Zac. "I'm stuck at security."

"Okay," he said, then silence.

"Hello?"

No answer. She held the phone in front of her. "Really now? You hung up on me? Sheesh."

Craving peace, she turned the phone off—what the point of that was, she didn't know—but it felt good. *That'll teach them.*

STILL AT HIS DESK, Zac read Mr. Vernon's statement for the thirtieth time. The man had signed it and, with his guilt slightly assuaged, had gone on his way. Mr. Vernon's statement wouldn't be enough to free Brian Sinclair from prison, and who knew if he actually belonged there, but slowly, piece by piece, the case was starting to break open.

Alex Belson, the former public defender on Brian's case, swung into the office. Interesting timing. His rumpled suit jacket and hair that stuck up on the side indicated that Alex might be having a rough day.

Zac closed the folder containing Mr. Vernon's statement. "Hey, Alex. Visiting the dark side?"

He cracked a grin, but nothing about it appeared to come easy. "I figure it's a good reminder of why I belong elsewhere."

Zac sat back. "What's up?"

"I was in court and heard that a witness in the Sinclair case recanted."

News traveled in this building. Zac had always known that, but this was world-record speed. Being the defense attorney who took the case to trial, Alex probably wanted assurance that his butt would be covered. When it came to this convoluted mess, nobody was safe. "You heard right. Stanley Vernon."

Alex's head dropped an inch. "The guy from the alley?"

"Yeah. He came in this morning. Said the detectives

implied they had a solid case against Brian Sinclair. All they needed was corroboration."

"Oh, man." Alex winced. "I should have caught that."

Probably. But given that he was the fourth PD on Brian's case, anything could have happened. By the time Sinclair got to Alex Belson, the cops had him trussed up all nice and tidy.

"Your sister will be all over this."

"Any time now she'll have that post-conviction petition submitted."

Alex shook his head. "This case. Damn nightmare. The thing won't go away."

Not many things said in the company of trial attorneys shocked Zac anymore, but referring to the murder of a cop's daughter as *the thing* caught him short. Maybe he was wound too tight after the crazy week, but a young woman was dead, brutally murdered, and they may have incarcerated the wrong guy.

"There are issues, for sure."

Alex tapped his fingers against his leg. "Let me know if there's anything I can do."

As if Penny would let Alex Belson anywhere near this case. No. His sister would see this one to its conclusion.

Whatever that conclusion might be.

EMMA CHARGED OFF THE ELEVATOR, scooted by a few milling people and raced toward the receptionist's desk. Having seen her previously, the woman waved her through. "He's waiting for you."

"Thank you."

Emma made a left, angled around a guy who looked like a lawyer and her gaze zoomed in on the man striding toward her.

Alex Belson. The useless, waste of a public defender

who'd done nothing—*nothing*—for Brian. He'd barely lifted a pen. Even when Emma funneled him information from her research, he'd always come up with reasons to dismiss it.

Useless piece of garbage.

As they neared each other, his focus shifted to her, studying, remembering. He slowed his pace.

Yeah, you know me. Emma stopped in front of him, blocking his path. "I suppose you've heard the SA has assigned an investigator to my brother's case."

"I did. Good for you."

So smug. "Good for my brother. Finally."

Alex folded his arms and huffed an annoyed you-are-such-an-idiot breath. "You want to say something to me, say it."

Like a hard slap, his low, guttural tone knocked her sideways. Emma's jaw clamped tight. *Him, him, him.* Could it be? She squeezed the folders, gripped hard, her fingers nearly splitting from the pressure. *You want to die right here like Chelsea Moore?* Couldn't be. But all those times, all the evidence he'd refused to consider. She'd handed it to him. All he'd had to do was use it, which he'd never done.

Emma backed away, slowly moving around him.

"What?" he said. "You don't think I did a good job for your brother?"

"Emma?"

She turned, saw Zac striding toward her, his long legs eating up the space between them, and she wasn't sure she'd ever been so happy to see someone. The agony of her thoughts made her nauseous. What was happening? Sickness swirled and tumbled and slid and she backed up another step, needing distance. Needing *space*.

"Nice to see you again, Ms. Sinclair," Alex said from somewhere behind her.

Zac set his hand on her shoulder. Instantly, her pulse settled. His simple touch brought her mind back into focus.

"You look like hell. You okay?"

"It's him."

"Who?"

She turned back. No Alex. Gone. "Alex Belson. He's the one from the alley."

ZAC DRAGGED EMMA to his office to figure out what in hell she was talking about. Something had spooked her because all color had drained from her face. Nothing left but ashy white skin.

Could this day get any more bizarre?

He shut the door behind them, took the files from her and guided her to the chair. She mumbled something and he glanced at her.

"Did Alex say something to you?"

He sat on the edge of his desk directly in front of her, their legs almost touching. The tiny lines at the corners of her mouth pinched and she brought her gaze to his. Her dark eyes locked on his so hard it could have been a punch. Emma Sinclair was one pissed-off woman.

"He's the one who attacked me in the alley."

She'd totally lost it now, but Zac would slap on his neutral prosecutor face. "Emma—"

"It's him. I recognized his voice. The tone was the same. I recognized his voice."

Complete insanity. Zac rubbed both hands over his face then looked up at the ceiling, hoping any god in the general area would send him strength.

"You think I'm crazy," Emma shot.

"I think you're under pressure."

"I know what I heard."

"We all have Chicago accents."

"Not like him you don't. The tone he used was evil. I know what I heard."

Dug in. That's what she was. And in the short time he'd known her, getting her from this line of thinking would be no easy task. Having her walking around accusing a public defender of criminal acts wouldn't do her—or Brian—a damn bit of good, either. Zac tapped his foot, twisted his lips.

"Just say it, Zac."

He held his hands up. "I've known this guy four years. He's a civil servant and you think he's a murderer?"

"I didn't say that. I think he attacked me in the alley. Why he'd do that, I don't know, but I've given up trying to figure out the things that happen in my life." She scooted to the edge of her chair and touched his knee. "I'm sure it was him."

Any time now, he could use that strength from a nearby god. Couldn't he get a break? He shook his head then jammed his palms into his eyes and pressed until his eyeballs begged for mercy. He dropped his hands, stared at Emma and wondered just what the hell they were doing. "What do you want? I can't walk into my boss's office and tell him this. I need proof. You know that. After the Leeks kid, Ray already thinks I'm in over my head. I might as well resign right now because accusing a public defender of attacking the woman I'm sleeping with won't look good in my file."

Emma gawked. "So this is about what looks good?"

"No. I want to support you. I've done nothing but support you."

"That's not true."

A rumbling in his brain alerted him to his temper firing. *Check that.* He held his breath, let it out again and cocked his head. "I've chased down every lead I could find on this case."

"You chased down those leads hoping you'd find that Brian was guilty. You didn't count on him being innocent. That's okay because you're a prosecutor and I get that. What I don't get is how you say you've supported me. You've supported me because it made sense. Suddenly, something doesn't make sense and you're backing off. I guess I'm good enough to sleep with when conditions are favorable, but now I'm a liability." She stood, waved her arms. "When did you become such a coward?"

Oh, hell no. The muscles in his neck became twisted ropes squeezed so tight that any slack was gone. Labeled a coward, he turned apoplectic. "Are you *kidding* me? You think anyone else around here would take on this mess?"

The second—make that millisecond—the words left his mouth, he regretted them. *Damn temper.* Words like that could slice a woman in two.

"Now I'm a mess? My brother being falsely convicted is a mess? A *mess?*"

"That's not what I meant!"

She held her hands in a stop motion and jerked them at him. Hauling her shoulders back, she closed her eyes and curled her fingers. Within seconds, she opened her eyes again, her body not as stiff and outraged. "Forget it. This is getting us nowhere and it makes us both look bad. I know how that upsets you. But hey—" her voice was low, as if a thousand soldiers had pummeled it "—I guess it's time for you to learn that life isn't always fair. Believe me."

She swung away from him and cruised to the door. No drama, no stomping feet, no carrying on.

"Emma!"

She opened the door and held it so it wouldn't bump the wall.

Without glancing back, she said, "I think we're done here. Thanks so much for your time."

EMMA RACED FROM the elevator, blew by slower people standing in the lobby and focused on the exit, the one leading to fresh air. She'd been so stupid to think she could depend on anyone from the State's Attorney's Office to help them.

And she'd slept with him. Let him invade her not-so-iron heart. Heartbreak, at this point, was the last thing she needed. Not when life seemed to be on an upswing. Well, an upswing graded on the curve of Emma's crappy luck.

Now she had to deal with this attachment to Zac because as furious as she was with him right now, a slow-growing ache had formed in her chest—one she didn't want to feel. She knew what it was. This was how it started with her. She'd ignore the ache, work around it, justify it, whatever.

Then one morning she'd wake up paralyzed, unable to move or breathe or function and her world would be empty and suffocating and she'd want to pound on something until all that hurt and anger went away.

Broken hearts totally stank and something told her Zac Hennings had just made the first crack in hers.

Chapter Fourteen

Deciding he could stand some fresh air, Zac took an early lunch and called his father. At certain times in his life, regardless of his father's current status as the opposition, Zac gave in to the idea that he still needed his dad's counsel.

In a matter of days, he'd gone from the office pit bull to a guy his boss couldn't trust. All because of a woman he'd slept with.

Epic fail.

Zac stepped into the glass-walled lobby of his father's office building and waved to the guard. Hennings and Solomon didn't have the entire building. They had three floors, though, and the guards had seen Zac often enough to know him.

He signed in at the desk and made his way to the tenth floor. The receptionist juggled multiple ringing lines, but pointed him in the direction of his father's office, which worked for him, since he was in no mood for small talk. He'd even taken the long way to his father's office in a pansy attempt to avoid Penny.

When Zac stepped into the office, his father was holding the phone to his ear and rocking back and forth in his desk chair. He waved him in.

"My son is here. I'll call you back."

That fast, his father had rearranged his priorities, putting Zac at the top. No matter how old they got, his father always made time for his children. A good lesson to re-member. And suddenly Zac had a vision of Emma chasing after a bunch of kids. His kids.

Where's this going now? He shook it off. No time for those fantasies. Plus, she currently wasn't speaking to him, much less wanting to have his babies.

As usual, his father shook his hand then brought him in for a shug—the combo shoulder pat and hug.

"Nice seeing you, son."

"You, too, Dad."

His father stepped back, ran a hand down his custom-made shirt. "Have a seat."

"Mind if I close the door?"

"With a lunch-hour visit, I assumed this would be a closed-door session."

Just as Zac grabbed the door, Penny stormed by then skidded to a halt. Too slow for his sister, she set her hand on the door and squeezed into the office.

Her blue eyes drilled him. "What's this about?"

"I'm here for Dad."

Penny blew that off. "Emma told me about Alex Belson."

"I'm not discussing this with you."

"What about Alex Belson?" Dad wanted to know.

Penny kept her focus on Zac. "It's worth looking into. She said you wouldn't even consider it."

His sister was such a pain in the ass. "This might shock you, but I can't charge a PD without proof."

"What about Alex?" Dad asked again.

But Zac was rendered mute by Penny's accusing glare. She had something brewing in that crazy brain of hers and it couldn't be good. Not with the way she focused on him, her gaze sliding over his face pondering, considering.

"Hey," Dad said in that slow, controlled voice that let

them know his patience was wearing thin. "Someone answer me."

Zac faced him. At least until Penny lunged and landed a not-so-gentle punch on his right arm that sent a stab of pain clear to the bone. For a small woman, she had some fire. "Ow. What's that for?"

"You slept with our client! I can see it on your face, Zachary. Guilt. You *pig*."

"What the...?" Zac slid a desperate, sideways glance at their father. *Please help me.*

"Penny," Dad said. "Out. Now."

But Penny remained in her spot, her lips pinched and—if he knew his sister—holding back a whole lot of mean. "I knew you had a thing for her. I *can't* believe you."

Again, she whacked him on the arm. Now he'd had it. He didn't blame her for being mad, but he'd had enough of the drama-girl routine. "Hit me again and I'll move you out of here myself."

Dad stood. "Penny, *out*."

"Dad!"

Dad pointed to the door. "Out."

Suddenly, Penny was twelve again, throwing a fit because the boys got to play outside after dark.

Her perfect little nose wrinkled and she waved her fist at him. "Pig!"

Needing a minute, Zac jammed his palms into his eye sockets. This was so seriously messed up. He dropped his hands. "She's insane. I mean, is there any chance we're not from the same gene pool? Maybe I'm adopted and didn't know it?"

His father grinned. "Unless your mother is keeping a secret, I'm confident you're both mine." He gestured to the chair. "Tell me what's on your mind."

He dropped into the plush leather guest chair so unlike the crummy metal ones in his office. Everything about this office—the rich woods, the neat shelves stocked with law books, the orderly appearance of the desk—all of it screamed control and organization. "I think I screwed up."

"If you had sex with our client, I'd say you're right."

"Emma." *Ah, cripes.* Admitting this violation wouldn't be easy and Zac's stomach heaved. "I, uh…"

His father sat forward and folded his hands on the desk. "Your sister's assessment is correct?"

Thank you. "Yeah, but it's not ugly. Not like she made it sound. Emma is amazing and smart and dedicated. Who wouldn't want her?"

Dad held his hands up. "You're both unattached, responsible people. Things happen. But you're the prosecutor. An intimate relationship subjects your case to scrutiny. You know that."

"Exactly."

"You should have kept your hands off her until this case was over." He smacked a hand on the desk. "That didn't happen. So let's figure it out. You had a fight with Emma over Alex Belson?"

Right. Alex. "You know about Emma getting attacked in the alley."

"Yes."

"Alex came by my office this morning. He'd heard that Stanley Vernon recanted."

No reaction to this news. His father remained quiet. "Dad, I know you know. You've got spies everywhere."

Dad rolled his bottom lip out. "We'd heard something."

"Alex was curious about Vernon's statement. I didn't think much of it. I know I'd be curious if a witness on a case I'd worked recanted. Emma ran into him when he left my office. She looked upset and I asked her what happened." Zac threw his hands up. "She tells me she thinks *Alex* attacked her in the alley."

If trial lawyers got Oscars, Zac's father would have a

few—more than a few. When it came to an unruffled performance, he was a master. "You think she's imagining it?"

"No."

"Then what's the problem?"

"I'm not objective anymore. I froze. Part of me wanted to get nuts and protect her. She does everything herself. I hate that. But Ray is all over me on this. I was supposed to make it go away."

"And you didn't."

"I wanted to. I wanted Brian Sinclair to be guilty. I *wanted* to tell Chelsea Moore's family that we got it right the first time. Instead, I told my boss to assign an independent investigator because the case is seriously flawed."

His father sat back and took it all in. If a lecture was forthcoming, Zac knew he deserved it. His father's lectures were legendary. A person could turn to stone once Dad got rolling. Now, though, he was probably muted by his son's failures. Finally, he sat forward, leaning in, engaging. "What can I do?"

No lecture. *Got lucky.* Zac dragged his fingers through his hair, then tugged. Damn, his head hurt. How did he start feeling so old and exhausted? This case and the emotional warfare, that's how. "I don't know. I had to blow off steam."

"I see that." Dad let out the three-thousand-pound sigh. Zac hated that sigh. "You need to talk to Emma. Tell her you care. My guess is she doesn't know you're invested. She thinks you're willing to sacrifice her for your career."

Point there.

"Are you?"

Zac glanced up. Staring into his father's eyes, he knew the answer. Clear as day. "No."

"Kid, you're in a jackpot here."

"Thanks, Pop."

"What you need to do is make her understand that you

care, but back away. You have to. She knows as well as you do that this relationship is dangerous."

"I know."

"Then you put this Belson thing aside. I'll get one of my investigators on it. See if there's something there. This case has so many twists and turns, anything is possible." He drove his index finger into the desktop. "You stay away from Emma until this is over. You hear?"

"I know."

"But you did it anyway."

"Dad—"

"No excuses. Impropriety could destroy your career and keep this kid in prison when he doesn't belong there."

Guilt, hot and slick, shot up Zac's neck. His father was right. Distance from Emma was the smart move. He'd talk to her. Explain his position. Convince her it was the right thing for both of them. Then he'd walk away.

Temporarily.

He hoped.

After the you're-my-son-but-you-screwed-up talk, Zac detoured to Penny's office. He pushed the partially open door in. His sister sat behind her massive desk, doing something on her computer. She spotted him and shot him the death glare again.

She folded her arms. "Zachary."

"Where's Emma?"

"Dream on. You've done enough for one day." She sat forward and poked a finger at him. "You upset my client. For this, I will shred you in court. You'll *beg* me to stop."

His baby sister, warrior queen. "Spare me. I care about her." She opened her mouth, but he waved. "Forget it. Not discussing it. I have to talk to your client. Where was she when you spoke to her?"

Penny spun back to her computer and Zac stared up at the ceiling. *It'll be a miracle if I don't kill her.* He closed his eyes, took a few breaths and thought about an ice cold beer on a beach, in a hammock maybe. Breaking ocean waves… Sleep.

A minute later, after somehow finding the patience not to strangle his sister, he glanced back at her. "Great. Thanks for your help."

On his way out the door Penny said, "She's on her way home."

He turned back. "Thank you."

"You're killing me, Zachary."

"If it makes you feel any better, *I'm* killing me. This thing with Emma, it's not…" He stopped. He didn't know what it was. "I never expected to care."

Penny shifted front and dropped her hands on her desk, her gaze straight-on. "She's been through a lot. I've gotten to know her and she seems happy. As happy as someone in her position can be. She's coming out of the dark."

"I know."

"Then don't break her heart or I'll have to stab you."

She'd do it, too. He twisted his lips, made a show of rolling his eyes, but really, he wanted to hug her. She was a drama aficionado, but he loved her. "I'll fix it."

It took thirty-five minutes—long past Zac's lunch hour—to get through downtown traffic and reach Emma's Parkland neighborhood. On the way, he called Diane, his co-counsel on the murder case currently in jury selection, and asked her to handle the afternoon session. She had a better grasp of the case anyway and would be fine on her own.

He made the left leading to Emma's street and found it blocked by fire engines and patrol cars. Black, billowing smoke rose into the air from three doors down.

Sweat peppered his upper lip and he swiped at it. "What's this now?"

He parked at the curb and got out. A cop standing at the barricade held his hand up.

Zac flashed his credentials. The cop studied the gold-toned badge and glanced back at Zac who jerked his chin toward the emergency vehicles. "What's happening?"

"House fire."

His stomach pinched. *Couldn't be.* "You know the address?"

"225. White, two-story."

Bam—he might as well have been sucker punched. The hot dog he'd grabbed on the way over flipped like a gymnast in his gut. His vision swam for a minute. *Focus.*

"You okay?" the cop asked.

In his mind, he pictured Emma trapped in a burning home, overcome by smoke, falling over... *Stop.*

"Is anyone hurt? I was headed there. I'm a...friend of the family. How bad is it?"

"No one home. They're still knocking down the fire."

A car pulled up behind Zac, the rattle of its engine sounding all too familiar. For a moment, he couldn't move, the relief immobilizing. He massaged his forehead, his mind already moving to the next task.

He inched around. "This is the owner's daughter. She lives there."

"She can't go in."

"I know. I'll take care of it."

EMMA TURNED HER CAR OFF and stared at the thick, black smoke coming from the center of her block.

For a moment, she sat nestled in her seat belt, valiantly attempting to ignore her body's warning signals. The throbbing temples, the fierce pain shooting across her forehead and the flashes of white blinding her. She pushed the car door open and headed for the barricade where an officer stood with—Zac.

Why was he here?

She picked up her pace, her gaze cemented to the swirling red lights in the middle of the block. Zac's face—*oh no*—his face held the drawn look of a man about to be strapped into the electric chair.

She kept moving, though, staying focused on the middle of the block that, from the look of Zac, couldn't be anything she wanted to see.

Four feet from him, she pointed. "Is that my house?"

Surprisingly, the words came fast and direct. No shaking voice. No obvious panic. If they only knew.

"Emma—"

She pushed by him. "What's on fire?"

The officer slid in front of her. "Sorry, ma'am."

"Is that my house?" Zac grabbed her arm, but she jerked it free. "Tell me."

"Yes."

Blood roared. Just a screaming, pounding, eviscerating surge shredding her body. "Where's my mother?"

Zac eyed the cop.

"No one inside," he said.

For once, she gave in, let the momentum take her and she stepped back, forcing herself to stay upright. Her mother was safe. Zac grabbed her elbow. Slowly, her body in low gear, churning through the thick mud of information, she turned to him.

"Emma? Talk to me."

Her mother was safe. That should have been enough. As relieved as she was, Brian's ticket to freedom sat in boxes—*three high, six across*—in the basement. They'd barely put a dent in copying them. All her work, all her hopes, all her mother's dreams could be burning.

She had to get there. Had to see what was left. Couldn't stand here and wait. God, she was so tired of waiting. She sucked air through her nose, stared up at the thick black smoke and the overwhelming urge to tear the living hell out of something consumed her. Raw energy sliced down her arms into her fingers. She shook her hands, flexing and unflexing.

"Emma?"

The sound of Zac's voice. The man who'd lost faith in her and thought she was crazy only added to the agony and she backed up. Three steps. Then another for the extra room. That black smoke continued to torment her. *I need to see it.*

The cop's radio crackled and he unclipped it from his shoulder, spoke into it and turned his back to her.

Run.

She burst into a sprint, barreling around the edge of the barricade.

"Emma!" Zac hollered.

She heard the cop yell, but didn't dare slow down. She'd be there in seconds.

All at once, the house, the trucks, the firefighters, the billowing smoke came into view and she halted in the middle of the street. Ugly, flashing flames shot from the first-floor windows while firefighters yelled commands and directed thousands of gallons of pressurized water into the inferno. Fear spiked and she held her breath, willed herself to look at the basement window next to the porch.

Maybe it's not the basement.

Orange-tipped flames, almost beautiful in their slashes of color, flicked from the window and Emma knew.

An insane howling roared up her throat, clawing its way out and her legs wilted. Her head whirled and she held her arms wide looking for anything solid to cling to.

"Emma!" Zac yelled.

A chunk at a time, the emotional assault wrecked her

and her body gave out. She dropped to the ground in a wailing lump.

All the evidence gone. The files, the photos, the time lines—everything. Gone.

Her chest tore open, a good solid rip that left her exposed and vulnerable. And still she screamed. *Crack.* She glanced up as the porch overhang toppled.

Can't breathe.

Out of oxygen, she finally stopped screaming. She sucked in huge gulps of air. *Please, more air.* On all fours, she stared down at the grass and tears dropped from her cheeks to the backs of her hands.

Zac kneeled in front of her and she sat back. He cupped her cheeks in his hands. His mouth moved, but she heard nothing.

Chaos. Everywhere. *Make it stop.*

She jerked her head from his hands. The one who thought she was crazy.

Again, he grabbed her and held on. "Emma!"

Why is he here? The sound of his voice, commanding but gentle, broke through and she focused on steadying breaths. All surrounding movement drifted away. The roaring dulled and the agony in her chest eased. Sanity returning. "Zac?"

"You're okay, honey. You're okay." He let go, wrapped his arms around her and held tight. "I've got you."

He had her. He sure did. In a matter of hours he'd managed to devastate her then showed up to help. Would her life ever get uncomplicated?

"Why are you here? Did you know?"

He inched back. "No. I came to talk to you about this morning."

Oh, God. She wasn't ready for that. Not with this simmering anger, this *grief* over allowing herself to fall for a man she'd known would sacrifice her to get a win.

"All my files. They're gone."

"We don't know that yet."

A firefighter yelled and Emma averted her eyes, not wanting to see the charred remnants of their home. *Mom.* "I have to find my mother. I can't let her come home to this."

"Where is she?"

"I think she went shopping." She slapped her hands over her face then dragged them down. "This will kill her."

Zac stood, held his hand to Emma. "Start calling. I'll get with someone from the fire department, see what's what." He motioned to the house. "Maybe it'll only be the first floor."

And the basement. Where all the files relating to Brian's case, a recently very active case, were stored.

"I think someone torched my house. *Someone* wanted to destroy my files."

Someone who knew she had the only extensive evidence collection.

"Stop. Let me talk to the chief."

Emma snatched her phone from her jacket pocket. She had to find her mother. "That's fine, but this was no coincidence, Zac. And you know it."

ZAC'S THOUGHTS ZINGED like bullets at a firing range. As much as he wanted to believe that Emma's house going up in flames could be an accident, his mind wouldn't wrap around it. The house was old, at least seventy-five years old, so, yeah, it was possible something shorted and— zap—the house is flambé.

He grunted and dragged his hands over his head. Emma and her mom sat on the back step of the ambulance while Emma did what she could to console her mother. Not that it appeared to be working because Mrs. Sinclair wore the bombed-out look of a woman caving in.

Out of the corner of his eye, a flash of pink came into view. Popsicle Penny on a direct course to Emma and Mrs. Sinclair. Zac hustled over and intercepted his sister.

"Hey," she said. "How are they?"

He shrugged. "How should they be? We need to find them a place to stay."

"I did it already."

Probably a hotel. "Something better than a hotel. A condo or a rental house. Homey."

"Zac, I'm on it. One of our clients is out of the country for a year. His apartment is empty. Dad called him and he said they can stay there. It's seven thousand square feet and has a view of Navy Pier. I think they'll be comfortable."

I'll say.

"Penny?" Emma called.

Penny waved. "Let me talk to them, and you and I need to huddle. Something is seriously whacky here."

He stood off to the side, giving her privacy with her clients. When she reached them, Penny squatted to eye level and touched Mrs. Sinclair's knee. His sister was a lunatic, but she had a way of connecting with people on an emotional level. A gift she could turn on and off at will.

Another gene pool issue because Zac hadn't inherited that gift.

He slid his phone from his pocket, scrolled his contacts until he found Tom Carson, the investigator assigned to the Sinclair case.

"Carson," the man barked. He would never be congenial but he got his job done.

"Hey, Tom. Zac Hennings."

"What you got?"

"Do me a favor. See if you can find out where Ben Leeks was this afternoon."

"Junior or Senior and why?"

Zac glanced back at the smoldering house, then to Emma who still sat on the back of the ambulance talking to Penny. She didn't deserve this.

"Both. The Sinclairs' home had a fire."

"Torched?"

"Not sure. If it wasn't, it's an interesting coincidence. From the looks of the place, all of Emma's files are gone."

"Ah, that's rough. I'll get into it."

"Thanks. Where are we with Junior?"

"It looks like his alibi checks out. I talked to a bunch of his friends, plus some of Chelsea's. In a twisted way, I think he loved her. This kid's a numbskull, but murder? I'm not getting that."

Not exactly a surprise to Zac. "And the white shirt?"

"I can't find another witness who saw a guy in white. My take? The detectives knew Sinclair was wearing a white shirt and fed it to Stanley Vernon."

"To sum things up, Leeks is clean, the white shirt is out and Vernon has recanted."

Welcome to the afternoon showing of his case falling apart.

"You got it, hoss. Anything else?"

Alex. Zac rolled his lips in—*can't go there.* No proof. If he put an investigator on it, someone, somewhere in a position higher than Zac's would find out and his butt would be in trouble deep. Deeper than he already was.

"You there?"

A firefighter trudged by, dragging a giant iron tool. No idea what that was for, but the sight of it brought Zac to the injustice done here today. "One more thing: I'd appreciate your keeping it quiet, but see where Alex Belson was today. He's a Cook County public defender."

Tom let out a low whistle.

"Exactly. I'm way out on this. It's probably nothing."

"I'll look into it."

"Thanks. I need one more thing."

"What's that?"

"His address."

Chapter Fifteen

Emma watched Zac shove his phone back in his jacket pocket and glance at the remnants of her mother's home. Of *her* home.

The fire department's battalion chief had said the blaze went no higher than the first floor but water damage was extensive. The house would no doubt need to be gutted. All that remained in the basement was the charred wreckage of Penny's copy machine. Fascinating. Months and months of Emma's sweat gone and, with it, probably Brian's chance at freedom. She'd never give up, though.

Never.

She'd simply start again.

If they found that this was an act of arson, she'd hunt down the person responsible. She'd had enough resistance in her life to know how to fight back. Every day she'd work toward making her mother's life whole again, even if it meant giving up her own dreams.

"Okay," Penny said. "Let's call your insurance company. They'll get the house boarded up."

"I'll call," Mom said.

Before she could check herself, Emma swung her head sideways, her shock obvious to anyone within ten feet.

"Don't look so surprised," Mom snapped. "It's still my house."

Nice, Emma. Way to make your mother feel useless. "I know. I'm sorry. I just thought…I can do it."

"I know what you thought and I don't blame you. Makes me realize how much I've placed on your shoulders. I'll deal with the insurance company. If I need help, I'll ask."

Thank you. Emma wrapped her arm around her mother's shoulder and squeezed. "That's awesome, Mom. I love you. I promise we'll get this fixed. All of it."

Penny rose from her squatted position and surveyed the mess. "I'll talk to the chief and see if you'll be able to get in there. Until they're done investigating, I doubt it, but we'll see. Then I'll take you to your fancy new apartment. Sound good?"

"Yes," Mom said, her voice steady. Determined. "Sounds fine."

Maybe my mother is back.

Emma stood, wrapped Penny in a hug. "Thank you."

"You're welcome. I hate this for you."

Looking over Penny's shoulder, Emma spotted Zac talking with one of the firefighters. She still didn't truly understand why he was here, but at the moment, despite the emotional bloodbath unleashed on her, she should at least talk to him. "I need to speak to your brother."

Penny backed away and eyeballed her. "I could slap the two of you. I told you not to sleep with him."

A blast of horror snaked up Emma's throat. How embarrassing that Penny had figured out they'd, as Brian would say, done the nasty. Emma snorted. Even from prison, her brother made her laugh.

Exhaustion. It had to be exhaustion.

Penny jerked her head. "Talk to him. I don't want to hear about it. Not one thing."

"Yes, ma'am."

She wandered over to Zac, slowing as she got closer. Suddenly, she wasn't sure her presence would be welcome.

Not after her little psycho-meltdown in the street. His gaze shifted from the firefighter for a second and—*oh, what a guy*—he held his hand to her.

All she had to do was take it. Simple gesture. Sure they had issues to deal with, but if she chose to reject and embarrass him by not accepting the comfort he offered, they were as good as done. Like any man, Zac had his pride and she couldn't disrespect him. Not after all he'd done for them. Still, she was far from ready to pick up where they were before their fight.

If she couldn't trust him to support her, there was no point in allowing the relationship to continue. And he'd made it clear that his job was his priority.

The firefighter shifted to the side and nodded. Zac's hand still hung in midair. *Grab it*. No. *Don't embarrass him*.

She reached for his hand and held it. No squeeze, no caressing fingers, no indication of anything. Brutal compromise. The loose hold he had on her indicated his understanding.

Yeah, we've got some work to do.

"This is Emma Sinclair."

"Sorry about this," the firefighter said. "We'll be out of here soon."

The man left and Zac faced her, his fingers still linked with hers, barely hanging on.

"Penny told you about the apartment?"

Emma looked into his spectacular blue eyes, which always settled her. "Yes. She's amazing."

"I wouldn't go that far."

He smiled, though, and a piece of Emma's broken heart sheared off. Truth was she didn't know how to love the man prosecuting her brother's case. "I'm sorry we had a fight," she said.

"Me, too. I didn't like that. At all."

"I don't know how to do this, Zac."

"Me, neither."

"Penny was right. We have no business being in a personal relationship right now." She waved toward the house. "And after this…all my evidence…" Her voice hitched and she breathed in. *You can do this.* "I have no idea what will happen with Brian's case."

"There are some copies left."

"Not enough, Zac."

"I told Tom Carson to see where the Leeks kid was this afternoon. And Alex Belson."

After her house almost burned to the ground, he finally believed her. Still, he'd gotten there. Not that anything could change between them. "Thank you. I know that couldn't have been easy for you, but thank you."

"I want to support you, Emma. This thing is moving fast. I need a second to catch up. Form a plan. You're good at shifting on the fly. I need to process. Collect proof to back up my gut reactions."

"I shouldn't have hit you with the Alex thing and expected you to do something right then. I didn't think it through, but that's me. That's how I operate and I can't change that. If you weren't the prosecutor on our case, it wouldn't be an issue. I can't get around that. And, if Brian's petition is denied, he'll stay in prison. You'll be the one who kept him there. How would a relationship between us survive that?"

"Emma—"

She stepped back. "I know myself. At some point, I'll look at you and wonder if you could have done more. It wouldn't be fair, but I'd do it."

He nodded. Maybe he understood. God knew she didn't. "I'm sorry, Zac. It's over."

LONG AFTER PENNY installed Emma and her mother in their temporary digs, Zac stood on the sidewalk waiting for the arson investigator to come outside. Maybe he could give Zac the 411 on whether his findings were heading in the direction of arson.

Plus, Zac was in no hurry to be anywhere in particular. Not after Emma gave him the dropkick. All he'd wanted was for them to lie low until Brian's case got settled. Apparently, she had a different idea.

He propped an arm on a low tree branch and tapped his fingers against it. He couldn't think too hard about Emma. Wallowing in misery wasn't his style, but this feeling of each breath being trapped inside a crushed torso did nothing for his state of mind.

Better to focus on the Sinclair home and the implications it might have. In his gut, Zac had no doubt that someone had intentionally done this. No doubt whatsoever. Call it intuition or plain common sense, but he knew.

His phone rang. Ray. This would be a problem, considering that Zac was supposed to be in court and had asked his co-prosecutor on the trial to cover for him.

He clicked the answer button before it went to voice mail. "Hey, Ray."

"Where the hell are you?" his boss thundered.

"I'm at the Sinclair place. Someone torched it."

"Did you forget we're in the middle of jury selection?"

"I talked to Diane. It was a short day today. I figured she could handle it while I waited on the arson investigator."

"He'll send you a report."

"He's finishing up. Maybe he'll give me something."

"I don't know what you're doing. You're killing your career."

Ah, damn. *There's always the private sector.* He'd hate that, though. He thrived on being a trial lawyer and somehow he didn't see himself making the leap from prosecution to defense. Plenty of attorneys did, but he wasn't sure it was for him. Civil law might be an option. Another thing he couldn't think about now. "You told me to figure it out. Not my fault it isn't the direction you wanted."

"I'm about to pull you from this case."

Not a chance. But he'd stay calm. No yelling. "I'm making progress here. However this plays out, we can spin it so it works for Helen Jergins. If Sinclair is guilty, we'll prove it once and for all. If he's innocent, she's freed a wrongfully convicted man. Either way, it's good."

"You'd better hope it's good or you'll have bigger problems than just being pulled off this case."

A slam came from the other end. *Ooosh.*

Zac pulled the phone from his ear. Stared at it a minute. His boss had just threatened his job. Seriously? *Seriously?*

If doing the right thing got him this garbage, why bother? He'd never considered himself an idealist when it came to politics and he knew there were times political maneuvering dictated the outcome of a case, but he'd never been pushed face-first into it.

Emma had been fighting this wall of opposition for too long. Day after day of roadblocks. Of people telling her *no* and expecting her to accept it. Hell, he'd been one of them.

For him, it had been a week and he'd already hit overload. No wonder she'd flipped over his need for proof about Alex.

The arson investigator, Dick Jones, walked out of the house. Zac had introduced himself earlier and had told the man he'd be waiting.

"I can't give you anything official," the inspector said.

"I know. This is off the record, so to speak. Goes nowhere outside of this conversation."

Dick nodded. "Heavy charring in the basement and on the first floor. Also charring and smoke stain on the ceiling toward the back."

"Origin?"

"Looks like the basement floor. The stairs leading to

the first floor were burned through. Based on the condition of the floor and the pattern of the burn, I'd say it's arson."

Emma was right. "You'll be finished when?"

"Tomorrow. I'll write up my report as soon as we wrap up here."

Zac glanced up at the house. "Can anything be salvaged?"

"Maybe some clothes. Stuff from the second floor, but it all needs cleaning. A real mess."

This guy had no idea. "Thanks. I appreciate the info."

"No problem. Don't jump the gun on me."

Zac shook his head. "No. We're good." His phone rang and he checked it. Tom Carson. "I gotta take this. Thanks again."

He headed to his car at the end of the block. Almost four o'clock and he was still here. No wonder Ray was pissed.

"Hey, Tom."

"Leeks Senior was in court testifying this afternoon. The kid was at work today. Apparently he's a personal trainer and had clients until two."

Eh, there went that idea. Even if Junior didn't set the fire, he could still be involved. And his father couldn't be ruled out, either.

"Where this gets interesting," Tom said, "is Alex Belson."

Zac stopped walking and a car flew by him, the driver honking the horn and nearly giving Zac an explosive bowel movement. "Take it easy!"

People.

"You okay?" Tom asked.

"Yeah. Alex Belson?"

"He left court around eleven."

Which was right around the time he showed up at Zac's office. "He came to see me."

"Oh." Tom paused. Probably making a note. "How long was he with you?"

"Less than ten minutes. He walked out of my office then ran into Emma Sinclair. Couldn't have been more than fifteen minutes total he was in our office. Where did he go after that?"

"That's what's interesting. He called his office, probably when he left you and told them he was on lunch."

"Return time?"

"One-thirty."

Come again? Zac stood frozen. A two-and-a-half hour lunch.

"And before you ask, yes, I double-checked it. I have two people who confirmed it. Plus, he swiped his key card when he entered the office. The guard verified it."

He reached his car and leaned against the hood. "Any idea where he went to lunch?"

"None."

"Okay. How about his address?"

"I've got it."

Jumping into the car, Zac grabbed his notepad from the glove compartment. "Go."

"If I give this to you, are you gonna do anything stupid?"

"No."

"Zac?"

"Tom, I promise you. Nothing stupid. I'll have my sister put an investigator on him. See if he's up to anything. I don't want the SA's office behind it. That's all."

And I want to make sure he doesn't go near Emma. Zac didn't want to believe this guy was capable of attacking Emma or setting this fire, but he wouldn't take a chance. He shook his head, hoping some form of understanding over this screwed-up scenario would flash into his mind.

No luck. Tom rattled off the address.

"Do I want to ask what Brian Sinclair's former public defender might have to do with the fire at the Sinclairs'?"

Zac dropped the notepad and sat back in his seat. "I wish I knew, Tom. I wish I knew."

Chapter Sixteen

Emma walked out of the restaurant's kitchen, untied her apron and shoved it into her tote bag. Her feet did the normal protest and she eyed one of the barstools. If she sat down, though, she wouldn't get up. She'd crash right there and let the stress of the day seep from her body. She'd known plenty of exhaustion in her life, but this heaviness, which slowed her steps and made her dream of sleeping for a month, had kicked her to another level of tired.

Days didn't get any longer than the one she'd just had. Part of her had considered calling off work, but sitting around a strange apartment—no matter how stunning it was—thinking about her decimated home and her broken heart, courtesy of Zachary Hennings, wouldn't fix her problems. Plus, they'd need extra money for whatever deductibles the insurance company would hit them with.

The hostess locked the front door while they closed up. No Zac tonight. That's what happened when a relationship ended. All those comforting moments, like him showing up to see her home, went away and left that monstrous black sinkhole inside waiting for her to slide in and get smothered.

Not going to happen.

She'd long ago given up on happily ever after. The way her life went, if she found someone to share a happily-ever-after life with, they'd wind up getting run over by a bus. At least they'd die together. For some reason, she found that thought vaguely amusing and quietly laughed.

So morbid, Emma. And so unlike her. As much as people teased her about her willingness to persevere, she'd take it over this nonsense any day. What good would sitting here boo-hooing do? She needed rest and a good dose of Warrior Emma. At least that Emma knew how to move ahead.

"No guy tonight?" the hostess asked.

"No," Emma said, the word oozing from her mouth. "Emilio said he'd walk me to my car. He's finishing up in the kitchen."

Hoping to avoid further questions from the nosy hostess, Emma turned, faced the front window and—wham—her heart exploded, one giant blast of energy that made her arms tingle. On the other side of the glass, in the misty, freezing rain, Zac stood bundled in a coat and ski hat.

He's here. Emma leaped off the stool, buttoned her jacket and rushed to the door while the hostess flipped the lock.

"I thought you were waiting for Emilio."

"Um, no. Tell him thanks, though. Zac is here."

She scooted out before the litany of busybody questions came. Moist air smacked her cheeks and cars whooshed by, their tires kicking up water from the rainy evening. Emma pulled her hood up. "Hi."

"Hi back."

"You came."

A half smile quirked his lips. "Just because you dumped me doesn't mean I can't make sure you get home."

She dumped him. For good reason. At least she thought. *What am I doing?*

Something in her throat squeezed and her eyes throbbed. *No tears.* She swallowed once, warring with herself to keep it together. "I'm so confused and miserable. I don't know what to do."

He skimmed his finger over the curve of her cheek to her jaw and that light touch, so gentle and comforting, sent her into another battle with self-doubt. How could she let him go?

"Me, too," he said. "But it's been a lousy day and talking about it now won't help."

"You're always so logical."

"It's what I do." He jerked his chin toward the street. "Where are you parked?"

"Two blocks down. I got to work late and had to park in the garage."

"Let's get you there then. The roads are horrible. Freezing rain iced everything over. Drive slow tonight."

They walked in silence, the swish of tires against pavement providing a diversion to the destruction lying heavy between them. For once, they had nothing to say. How incredibly sad for both of them.

In the near distance, the parking garage loomed and Emma slowed. Pathetic? Yes. But she didn't want this time with him to end. If Brian didn't win a reversal, there'd be no future with Zac and it would be best if she just let him go now. Save herself the pain later. How sad that her life had become a study in saving herself pain.

At the corner, they waited for the walk sign to flash. A few cars idled at the red light, but all in all, a quiet night. The light changed and Zac stepped off the curb. On the cross street, a driver gunned the gas to make a left, spotted Zac in the street and slammed on his brakes. The car slid as if greased.

No.

Tires squealed from the opposite direction and Emma grabbed Zac's coat, hauling him backward as a speeding car barreled into the car making the left. An enormous crash of metal and shattering glass erupted and then, in seconds there was nothing but silence. Harsh, ugly silence.

Only feet in front of them was the wreckage of a destroyed vehicle, the windshield of the speeding car had blown out and a passenger lay draped across the dash into the open space where glass had been. No seat belt. Whether the person was male or female, Emma couldn't tell. Too much blood. Awful, soaking amounts of blood.

Zac tore into the fray and Emma dug in her purse for her cell phone. 9-1-1. Other drivers swarmed the scene, checking on victims while Emma was informed that an ambulance was en route.

She clicked off and felt a poke near her side.

"Say one word and this knife goes through you. I'll gut you right on this street."

Knife.

In front of her, neon red bounced off the building across the street and a police cruiser came to a stop just feet away. *Scream.* Emma opened her mouth.

"Not a word," the man repeated and his voice.

It's him.

"Move," Alex Belson said. "Toward the garage. After following you for days, I almost gave up when I saw Zac. I got a bonus with that accident."

He tugged the back of her coat and she drove her feet into the ground. The pressure of that knife on her back increased. "I got nothing to lose by killing you right here. And when I'm done with you, I visit your mother."

Emma started walking. At most, she had two minutes until they reached the garage. If they got there, she was dead. This she knew. *Never let them take you to a second location.* Wasn't that what all the safety experts always said?

No second location.

She'd have to run before they reached the garage, except he detoured away from the entrance.

She pointed. "The garage is—"

"Shut up."

Emma slowed, but Alex pressed her forward, nearly shoving her. She swung her gaze left and right, searching for a weapon. Lamppost. Garbage can bolted to the sidewalk. Fire hydrant.

Nothing useful.

Then she saw the sidewalk separate and her limbs turned cold, freezing, like icicles attached to her body. She halted and Alex laughed. Monster.

If he took her into that alley, she'd be dead. No question.

"Why...why are you doing this?"

"Because you won't go away. Subtle doesn't seem to work for you. What the hell is it with you women? I speak, but you don't listen."

What? She looked at him and he pressed the knife into her coat far enough that she felt the tip. Sharp. Deadly.

"Don't look at me," he said. "Eyes forward."

Across the street, two women came out of their car, hunched against the cold and strode in the opposite direction.

"Don't even try it," Alex said.

Emma's eyes went back to the mouth of the alley twenty yards ahead. *You're dead.*

"Please don't do this. I'll stop. I promise."

"Too late. I thought that idiot Leeks would do it, but you're just that damn fearless."

"You sent him?"

Again, he laughed, a guy simply enjoying a chat with his companion. "No. That's the beauty of it. He wanted your boyfriend to lay off his kid. Imbecile was helping me and didn't even know it."

So confused.

"The kid's a waste of space anyway. I loved her and he's an abusive psycho she couldn't stay away from. Stupid women. All of you."

"Chelsea?"

"And then I had to suck up to make sure I drew the damn case. Unbelievable. My life went to hell the minute I saw her. All I wanted was a damn report from her father and there she was, waiting for him to finish up. After that, it was over for me. Nothing but trouble."

They reached the alley. Emma stopped, threw all her weight into not moving. If she went into that alley, she'd never come out.

But Alex was bigger and stronger and he had that knife digging into her side. "Home sweet home, Emma."

Fight.

He shoved her hard enough to send her stumbling into the dark alley. Quickly, she bolted upright thinking fast. Weapon. Elbows, fists, legs. All she had. Water splashed—*he's coming*—and she whirled on him. Swung back into the general direction of his throat. Missed.

"Now she wants to play," he said in that voice, evil and menacing, that cut through her worse than any knife. "We can make this as hard as you want, Emma."

She ran into the alley, her feet slamming against the pavement. *Don't be a dead end.* Blackness surrounded her and her eyes slowly adjusted as she sloshed against the wet ground. *Oooff*—he tackled her. Her knees hit the ground first and she turned her head before doing a face plant. Her left cheek took the impact and pain exploded.

Hair tug. *Ow.* Straddling her from behind, he wrapped his hand tightly around her ponytail and yanked her head back, exposing her throat. Using his free hand, he looped something around her neck—*no, no, no.*

Emma kicked out, tried to get him off her. Too heavy.

The cord tightened, sliced into the minimal flesh at her throat and she gasped.

"Crazy bitch. I set your damn house on fire and you still won't give up."

He jerked the cord tighter and tighter still. *Get him off.* She flung her arm back. Nothing there. Except the pressure released. *Free.* Emma howled, her throat convulsing from the effort of her scream and the air blowing through it. The weight on her back disappeared. She flipped over, scrambled to her feet. Extra person. Too dark to see. Both on the ground.

"Son of a bitch." Zac's voice.

"He's got a knife!" Emma yelled.

Zac pounced before Alex got fully to his feet. He shoved him, forced him to the ground. Punches flew, Alex's head snapped back and Emma ran toward him. *Check his hands.* But Zac flew backward when Alex slammed him with a kick to his midsection.

Find the knife. Too dark. She'd never find it. Instead, she hurled herself at Alex giving Zac time to recover.

"Emma, back!"

And then Emma got the luck that had eluded her for so long. A shaft of moonlight broke through the clouds and illuminated part of the alley. Two feet from her, a glint of steel winked.

Knife.

She ran toward it, picked it up. "Got the knife."

And Zac went crazy. Punches flying, kicks connecting, elbows swinging. All of it, a reign of terror on Alex Belson so fierce she wondered if the man would survive it. Alex doubled over and Zac slammed his elbow into his back, sending him to the ground. In a split second, Zac pounced on him, digging his knee into the center of Alex's back.

"Hands out," he said. "Let me see them."

But Alex wouldn't surrender. He bucked and Zac

smacked him on the back of the head. Unable to wriggle free, Alex spread his arms flat.

Zac dropped his head, heaved a breath. "Dammit, Alex. What are you doing?"

ZAC LEANED ON THE COLD cement wall of the parking garage as officers loaded Alex Belson into a squad car. A truck rumbled by, that rotten egg smell of its exhaust hitting Zac, making his stomach seize. Nasty, that.

What had just happened?

A detective escorted Emma from the alley. They'd been questioned separately and would most likely be questioned again, but for now, they were done. He still didn't know what had happened to her. All he knew was that he'd looked up from the car accident and she was gone, walking away with some dude. He'd followed, keeping his mouth shut and his steps light, knowing he wouldn't allow Emma to get hurt.

Coming up next to him, Emma leaned against the building. "You okay?"

Always worried about everyone else. "Are *you* okay?"

She shrugged. "I don't know. I think he's the one. He didn't say it, but he said he loved Chelsea. Something about how she couldn't stay away from Leeks's son."

Zac nodded. "She and Leeks were on-again-off-again. Twisted relationship."

"I'm so confused. We trusted him. He let my brother go to prison. That filthy hunk of flesh wanted my brother to rot in a cell."

Zac dragged his hands over his face and suddenly her hand was on his back, rubbing in that way she did that made everything less intense. "I looked up and you were gone. If I hadn't looked up when I did, I'd have lost you, Emma. I wouldn't have known where you went. I've never been that scared."

She rested her head on his shoulder. "But you did look up. Thank you."

"I'm sorry I didn't believe you." He kissed the top of her head. "I could have lost you. How could I let that happen?"

Had there ever been a time when he'd been this uncertain? He'd always been the logical one in the family. Always making the right decision, and even when he didn't, it wasn't a big deal. No one got hurt or died. He'd simply learned from it and moved on. In his current state, if learning from his mistakes meant being without Emma, he didn't want to learn.

Her shoulder hitched against him and he looked down. Face collapsed, eyes squeezed shut. Crying.

Damn, he never wanted to see this strong, capable woman reduced to tears. Pushing himself off the wall, he wrapped her in his arms. "Sshhh, you're okay. I've got you. We'll figure it out. Somehow, we'll figure it out."

And they would. Because after this, job or no job, he wouldn't let her go.

Chapter Seventeen

The following morning Emma forced down dry toast, a relatively boring breakfast, while surrounded by the fancy marble and stainless steel of their temporary kitchen. If she broke something in this palace, it would take a year to pay for it. Her phone whistled and she punched the screen, scanning Penny's text summoning her to the criminal courthouse. In thirty minutes. Thirty minutes to shower, get dressed and face the end of rush-hour traffic.

Their lawyer truly was nuts.

At this point, with Alex Belson still being *interviewed,* the only thing Emma wanted from Penny was confirmation that Belson had killed Chelsea Moore and that Brian would come home. That's it. The terror of the previous night would be worth it if Brian came home.

Why? Emma texted back.

Just get there.

Emma sighed.

"What is it?" Mom asked.

Emma contemplated a response. Something must have been happening with Brian. But she didn't have the heart to tell her mother that. *What if it's not good?*

They were too far gone for that. No more sheltering

her mother. The load had gotten too heavy and this had to be—had to be—good news.

She met her mother's stare. "I'm not sure. She wants me down at the courthouse in half an hour."

"That's good, right?"

I hope so. "It could be nothing."

"I don't care. I'm going with you. It's time I started helping you."

Wow. How far they'd come in a week. All because of the Hennings family. Emma glanced down at the phone in her hand. Those crazy Hennings siblings. They'd drive her mad before this was done.

And yet she welcomed the madness.

Putting her thumbs to work, she texted Penny. See you soon. She dropped the phone, shoved her chair out. "Be ready in five minutes. I'm gonna take the fastest shower of my life and throw some clothes on."

"Put your hair back," Mom called as she charged down the long hallway behind Emma. "It's a mess."

Exactly twenty-six minutes later, Emma and her mother joined the back of the security line at the criminal courts building. On her tiptoes, Emma counted heads in front of her. Ten. Not as bad as usual, but they'd never make it in four minutes.

She texted Penny. A second later her phone rang. She didn't bother to look. She knew who it was. "Not my fault. I'm stuck at security."

"Here's the deal," Penny said, the words firing faster than usual. "My father, Zac and I are walking into Judge Alred's court. We've—the State's Attorney included—filed a joint emergency motion to vacate Brian's conviction and sentence."

Every word rolled into a massive ball in Emma's throat. She tried to speak, but only managed a high-pitched squeal. She spun to her mother and latched onto her arm.

Mom winced and Emma let up. "What?"

Finally, the massive ball trapping her words unfurled. "This is happening now?"

"Yes."

"Is the judge a good one?"

"He's perfection. A good guy and reasonable. Hang on… What?" A muffled sound came through the phone line. "He's ready for us. Hurry. Judge Alred's courtroom. 400."

"Wait."

Dead air. Emma jerked the phone from her ear and stared at it. *Don't get too excited.* The judge could deny it. Anything could happen.

Mom's face blanched.

Emma squeezed her mother's arm again. "It's good. They filed a motion to vacate Brian's conviction and sentence. In a little while we'll know if Brian is coming home."

"My God."

"Don't get your hopes up. You know our luck stinks."

Mom held her hands out, her eyes big and round and… well…happy. "But we've never gotten this far."

The gray-haired security guard Emma had seen several times before motioned her to the x-ray machine. "Step forward please, ma'am. Cell phone down."

She shoved her purse and phone on the belt. "Sorry."

He waved her through. "No problem."

Once through the machine, she grinned up at the guard. "My brother may come home today."

He offered a thumbs-up. "Good luck. Hopefully I won't see you here anymore."

Her mother stepped behind her, both of them grabbing their items off the belt. *This could be it.* Brian coming home.

Don't go there.

They got into the elevator, and Emma watched the numbers tick by until they reached their intended floor. Dragging her mother along, Emma dashed off the elevator, her low heels clickety-clacking against the tile floor. People cluttered the hallway, blocking her, forcing her to cut around them. *Just get there.* A door banged open and two men in suits stepped into her path. *Move.* Emma threw her arm out and angled around them. Her mother had better be keeping up. On her right, courtroom doors whizzed by. She checked numbers as she went. *Almost there.*

Courtroom 400.

She stopped and her mother plowed into Emma's back. Emma grabbed Mom's arm to keep her from falling over.

"Sorry. This is it."

She stared at the double doors, rocked onto the balls of her feet. "You ready?"

Mom breathed in. "I have to be."

"We've got this, Mom."

Emma swung one of the doors open, ushered her mother inside and eased the door shut. The soft click echoed and she winced. *Don't piss off the judge.*

She spun around, her gaze landing smack on the judge, a man appearing to be in his late forties. He sat behind the bench, two fingers pressed against his meaty cheek. His face gave away nothing. Not a scowl, not a smile, not a frown. He simply listened, and Emma imagined that she'd go mad wondering what the heck the man was thinking.

Zac spoke from his place at the prosecutor's table, his voice, as usual, assertive. Confident. Penny and her father sat behind the defendant's table, their postures tall but not stiff. Almost relaxed, but that couldn't be. Could it?

Judge Alred focused on Emma, then her mother, the only two spectators in the room. Not wanting to cause further disturbance, Emma slid onto the nearest bench.

So what if it was way in the back? She needed to sit before her legs gave way.

Her mother landed next to her and gripped her hand. This was it. Emma clung to her mother and directed her attention to the front of the room where the judge addressed Zac.

"Counselor, why is this a joint motion?"

"Your Honor, new evidence has come to light. After examining this new evidence, we determined that said new evidence changes the State's position."

Emma tapped her foot. *Yeah, yeah, we get it.* New evidence. Blah, blah, blah. Get on with it.

"Because of this new evidence," Zac continued, "the State joins in the motion to vacate and set aside."

Please, please, please. A loud whoosh filled her head, smothered the voices of Zac and the judge. She closed her eyes. Hot little stabs traveled up her arms and made her itch. *Please let him come home.* Never had she prayed so hard, but this warranted it. She wanted her brother back. Maybe she wanted a few other things, too, but Brian coming home was the priority. If that happened, they'd rebuild their lives as a family. And, if the world could be so generous, she'd be free to have her own life and maybe make Zac Hennings part of it.

That's what she wanted. Zac, her brother and her mother. With them, she almost believed anything could happen. With them, the impossible became possible.

An immense calm inched over her, slowly smothering the pinpricks her body had just endured. Her mind went quiet and a male voice sounded. The judge.

"Okay, counselors, motion granted. Defendant is ordered immediately released."

What? Emma snapped her head sideways. "What?"

Penny leapt to her feet. "Thank you, Your Honor."

Mom held her fingers to her lips before the judge yelled

at them. *Wait.* Emma turned to the front again, stared at Penny's back. Beside Penny stood Mr. Hennings and the two high-fived, their faces glowing. *It's happening.* On the other side of the aisle, Zac shoved a folder in his briefcase, all serious prosecutor but chances were he was dying to smile. He'd never give his sister the satisfaction. He'd make her beg for it.

The judge rose from the bench and rounded the corner, his long robe swaying behind him as he entered his chambers. Just like that, they were done.

Brian was free.

Penny whipped around, a mile-wide grin on her face. "*Now* you can talk."

But Emma shook her head. The words *immediately released* looped in her mind, over and over and over, and she breathed in. *Don't believe it.* Not yet. Not until they told her. Then she'd allow herself to believe that finally, after endless trudging through the justice system, they'd won.

Zac closed his briefcase, and turned to her. Their gazes held and he finally offered up a grin that sent blood racing into Emma's brain.

Penny stood in the aisle hugging Mom whose sad, wilting eyes were now gone. *My mother is back.*

Emma jumped up. Too fast. The rush made the room spin and she held on to the bench in front of her, taking it all in. The Hennings crew huddled together, father, son, daughter. Zac and his dad shook hands, slapped some backs and—they'd done it.

"Come here, girlfriend," Penny said. "Give me a hug. We won."

And Emma lost it. She held her arms in front of her as tears barreled out of her eyes. *We won.* Mouth gaping, happy sobs rocked her. Darn, she was tired. So tired.

The foursome gathered around her, their faces a mix of surprise, shock and—in Mr. Hennings's case—curiosity.

Mom had her own set of waterworks going and Emma had to look away. It was all too much. All the emotion that had been shoved deep inside, brutally packed away with the lid slammed down, came bursting free and she sobbed harder.

Zac eased her mother out of the way and stepped beside Emma. He slid his arms around her and squeezed. *He's so good.* She buried her face in his chest, bawling on his suit jacket and gripping the material at his back. *Just hold on.*

"You did it," he whispered, his lips pressed against her ear. "Why are you wasting time crying when you should be on your way to get your brother?"

Emma slammed her eyes closed. *He's coming home.*

Zac ran his hand over her head. "You're okay now. Sshhh. Emma, you did it. You put your family back together."

And then she laughed, a sort of pathetic snot-filled snort that at any other time would humiliate her, but for now, none of it mattered.

She backed away from him, grabbed the lapels of his suit jacket and tugged. "Thank you."

"Hey," Penny said. "What the hell?"

Emma rolled her eyes, but the feeling she had inside, that easy, settled hum of joy, made her attempt at irritation a lost cause. "You know I'll thank you, too. He makes me giddier than you do."

"Oh, please," Penny said. "Blah, blah, blah. We have paperwork to deal with and then you need to get on the road. Go get Brian and tonight we'll have a celebration dinner."

"But you're coming with us, right? To get him?" Emma turned to her mom. "Wait. I'm sorry. Do you want it to be just us?"

Mom dabbed a tissue over her face and grinned. "The more the merrier."

"Good." She went back to Penny. "Can you come with us?"

"If you want, I'll make it happen."

"I want." She turned to Zac. "And you, too. You should be there. We should all be there when he comes out."

He bent low and kissed her, a gentle brush of his lips, right in front of Mom and Penny and his dad and—*wow*—that's different.

Except he blew it by stopping. "A prosecutor welcoming a wrongly convicted man home. You're determined to get me fired."

She hadn't thought about that. She tugged on his jacket, only a little disappointed. Maybe more than a little. "Sorry."

"Don't be. It'll be worth it. Let's head north."

The courtroom door opened and they all turned. Detective Leeks stood in the doorway, his vile gaze slithering over them. *He shouldn't be here.* Not when he'd done so much to hurt them, to terrorize them and to steal Brian's life.

"Leeks," Zac said, but Emma threw her hand up and stepped toward him. Behind her, she sensed Zac following. "Why are you here?" he asked.

Leeks stood still, his arms now crossed over his chest. "Thought I'd take in the festivities. Guess I missed it."

Pulverizing anger blasted through Emma. Her body buzzed and the sudden urge to lash out consumed her. She halted in front of Leeks. His son hadn't even been guilty, yet he'd been willing to ruin another man's life to protect him.

She wiggled the fingers of her right hand as Leeks stood there, that disgustingly smug grin on his face, and Emma couldn't take it anymore.

Crack!

She smacked him. One solid blast and the man's head flew sideways. From somewhere behind her, Mom gasped.

"You go, girl," Penny said.

"Whoa." Zac shifted in front of Emma. "This is over,

detective. You're lucky I didn't have enough to charge you with having Brian Sinclair attacked in prison."

Leeks stared up at Zac, his eyes burning, but there was nothing to be done. Not unless he planned on taking on all five of them.

"We're celebrating," Emma said. "And you don't belong here."

HOURS LATER, Emma, her mother, Zac and Penny stood outside the prison gates waiting for Brian. Emma leaned against the gleaming black stretch limo Zac's father had provided and tilted her head to the sun. Spring, at least for today, had finally blessed them with its presence. All in all, a great day to welcome Brian home. Still, she had to admit, this was a scenario she'd never imagined.

Off to the right, Penny paced the edge of the parking area, talking on her phone. Mom stood by the gate, sometimes wandering back a few steps, but then returning, waiting for her baby to come to her.

Zac watched it all, occasionally checking his watch and sighing. For once, Emma didn't mind the wait. Not when anticipating the moment her brother would be free offered such excitement.

"There's one thing I'm wondering," Emma said.

Zac clucked his tongue. "Only one?"

"Hardy-har. A comedian now. Why did that nasty Detective Leeks threaten me? If his son was innocent, why did he care? I should have asked him that before I slugged him."

Zac gave her a thumbs-up. "That was a heck of a shot."

"He deserved it. I still wonder, though."

"I think he either wasn't sure his kid was innocent, or he knew the investigation had been screwed up and he didn't want their name dragged into it. Maybe both."

"I guess. It makes me sad for the Moore family. We all

trusted Alex Belson. They trusted him for very different reasons, but we were all traumatized. I hope that creep never gets out."

"He'll go away for a long time. Between the murder, obstruction of justice, what he did to you, arson, and the litany of other charges my office will come up with, he'll be an old man if he ever gets out."

A buzz sounded and Emma glanced up. Inside the fence, her brother stepped out of the building, flanked by two guards. Emma's pulse kicked. Brian wore baggy jeans and a wrinkled, button-down shirt—the clothes he'd been arrested in that were now a size too big. He held a bag in his hands, most likely his personal effects. From where she stood, Emma couldn't see if his bruises had healed. Who was she kidding? Even if they'd faded, eagle-eye Mom would probably notice and Emma would finally have to explain. Later. Much later.

He's coming home. Emma placed her hands over her mouth and looked up at Zac. "I can't believe it."

"Believe it." He put an arm around her and squeezed. "Emma Sinclair, I think you're the love of my life."

"You *think?* Charming, *Zachary.* Charming."

"I do what I can." He turned toward her, rested one arm on top of the limo. "I should thank you. At the beginning of this, I was bent on proving that your brother was a murderer. I had it all figured out. He did it and I was gonna be the guy to prove it. Except nothing was what I thought. I had to experience that. Plus, I got to meet you. Something tells me that will change my life in the best way possible. I don't want to freak you out, but now that this case is history, I'll be all over you. Just so you know."

"Is that supposed to scare me?"

"Nope. Keeping you updated."

She tugged on his jacket, went on tiptoes and kissed

him quick. "Excellent. And just so *you* know, I will be an eager participant as it relates to your affections."

"Glad we got that clarified."

Another buzz sounded and Emma faced front as the long steel gate slid open. Her brother stopped and looked at each guard, waiting for permission to leave. Apparently, he was stunned by the morning's activities. One of the guards set his hand on Brian's back, gave him a smile and shoved him through the gate.

The guards, like most people, were fond of Brian.

And then, for the first time in eighteen months, her brother stepped out of the prison gate. He stood there, on freedom's side of the entrance, staring at the pavement. Emma absorbed the simple joy of seeing her brother experiencing freedom. Let it heal her. No one moved. Not even their mother. Somehow, they understood that Brian needed a moment. Finally, he pushed his shoulders back and raised his head. His gaze locked on Emma's and held. Joy fused with the pain of lost time and unfurled in her chest. For months she'd imagined this moment, imagined the hoots and hollers and yet there was only quiet. The celebration would come later, but now, in the parking lot, the prison gate behind them, there was only Emma, Brian and their mother. Together.

Finally.

They'd done it.

Mom broke the spell and ran to Brian, throwing her arms around him. She sobbed, the sound of it loud and piercing and wonderful. Emma turned into Zac's side and buried her head in his shoulder.

Zac kissed the top of her head. "You did it."

Head still buried, she nodded. "He's coming home." She straightened, looked up into Zac's blue eyes and her smile, for a change, came easy. She'd smile more now. Life would be for living again. She grabbed Zac's hand and pulled him toward the gate. "We did it. He's got his life back."

"He's not the only one."

"Yep. And you, *Zachary,* will be part of it. Are you good with that? Because you have to help me with constitutional law."

"Honey, I'm great with that. We'll be a happy, twisted family."

Family. Emma's heart banged and she slapped her hand over it. For the first time since her father had passed, she pictured a complete unit. *Her* complete unit. Zac, Mom and Brian. If she threw Penny into the mix, she'd have the sister she'd always wanted. Even if Penny was crazy. Now, with Brian free, she'd grab hold of that unit and never let go. What more could a girl want? Finally, after years of losses, she'd won.

Her luck had definitely changed.

* * * * *

A sneaky peek at next month...

INTRIGUE...

BREATHTAKING ROMANTIC SUSPENSE

My wish list for next month's titles...

In stores from 21st March 2014:

❏ Josh – Delores Fossen

& The Bridge – Carol Ericson

❏ The Legend of Smuggler's Cave – Paula Graves

& Primal Instinct – Janie Crouch

❏ Diagnosis: Attraction – Rebecca York

& Relentless – HelenKay Dimon

Romantic Suspense

❏ Defending the Eyewitness – Rachel Lee

Available at WHSmith, Tesco, Asda, Eason, Amazon and Apple

Just can't wait?

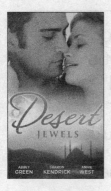
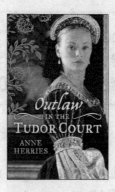

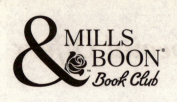 

Join the Mills & Boon Book Club

Subscribe to **Intrigue** today for 3, 6 or 12 months and you could **save over £40!**

We'll also treat you to these fabulous extras:

- 🌹 **FREE L'Occitane gift set worth £10**
- 🌹 **FREE home delivery**
- 🌹 **Rewards scheme, exclusive offers…and much more!**

Subscribe now and save over £40
www.millsandboon.co.uk/subscribeme

Discover more romance at

www.millsandboon.co.uk

- ❤ WIN great prizes in our exclusive competitions
- ❤ BUY new titles before they hit the shops
- ❤ BROWSE new books and REVIEW your favourites
- ❤ SAVE on new books with the Mills & Boon® Bookclub™
- ❤ DISCOVER new authors

PLUS, to chat about your favourite reads, get the latest news and find special offers:

- 📘 Find us on facebook.com/millsandboon
- 🐦 Follow us on twitter.com/millsandboonuk
- ❤ Sign up to our newsletter at millsandboon.co.uk